FATAL TIES

A Cassie Viera FBI Thriller

RICHARD BANNISTER

COPYRIGHT

Fatal Ties is a work of fiction. Names, characters, places, and incidents are either the product of the author's imagination or are used fictitiously. Any resemblance to actual persons, living or dead, events, or locales is entirely coincidental. No part of this book may be used, reproduced, or transmitted in any form or by any means, electronic or mechanical, including photocopying, recording, or by any information storage or retrieval system, without the written permission of the author, except where permitted by law, or in the case of brief quotations embodied in critical articles and reviews.

OTHER BOOKS BY RICHARD BANNISTER

MEGAN RILEY MYSTERY THRILLER SERIES

Devil's Pasture

The Lake Cabin

Magnolia Lake

Last Chance Road

Mosquito Ridge

AVAILABLE AT:

Amazon.com - Kindle and Paperback

BarnesandNoble.com - Nook

To my wife, Judi for her love, help, and understanding

AND

Nancy Petty for her helpful suggestions

Chapter One

TEN YEARS AGO

THERE IS NO TURNING back once she leaves here. Whatever she decides in the next five minutes will be utterly final.

She feels dizzy, and her stomach keeps heaving like she's about to throw up. For several long moments, her gaze flits around the back deck. There's a planter brimming with daisies and her favorite swinging seat. The privacy fence encloses a vegetable garden that she's lovingly tended.

Scattered on the deck are a blood-soaked sweater, a novel covered with her bloody fingerprints, and a knife whose crimson blade glistens in the sunlight.

"The cuts where the knife went through the sweater are a nice touch, don't you think?" the man suggests.

The woman remains silent. There is nothing nice about this. It's about as far from nice as it gets. She feels like she's stepping off the edge of a cliff, hoping her parachute will open, hoping she'll land somewhere better. Because all she has now is a living hell.

"You can never contact your friends again," the man says, fixing his gaze on her. "They might call the cops and turn you in or get word to your husband."

"He'll find me anyway," she replies, absently wiping a thin film of perspiration from her forehead. "He always does. This time, he won't hesitate to kill me." Her husband always seems to have a sixth sense about her. He knows the instant she lies to him about where she's been, what she's bought, or who she's seen. For the last couple of weeks, she's been in constant fear of her body language giving away her plans.

"He won't get the opportunity to hurt you once he's in jail," the man reminds her.

"Criminals get let off on technicalities all the time."

"I can make sure that doesn't happen. You know I have my ways."

"What about later?" she insists forcefully. "When he gets out."

"That won't be for a long while. Maybe someone in prison will shank him, so he bleeds out. I can set it up. Easy."

She turns to gaze into his eyes. "I don't want that. Promise me you won't."

"Fair enough." He waves his hand dismissively. "You can always change your mind."

"I won't. That's the one thing I'm certain of at this moment. As much as I hate him, I won't be responsible for his death."

The man pricks up his ears at the sound of sirens in the distance. "We must hurry. Cops are on their way. They'll arrest you once they see what you've done."

She ignores him. "You know, I never saw his cruel streak until it was too late. He was charming when we were courting. The slapping and punching didn't start until we were married."

She pauses, studying her fingernails. "But it isn't just the physical abuse. My husband is the king of gaslighting. I'm finally tired of being *that* woman. The woman who has to watch what she says or does. Always afraid of reprisals. The woman who has to submit to his desires whenever the mood takes him."

"It happens, but it ends today." The man's hand slips around her waist, and he draws her into him. Her slim body is stiff and unyielding. "Relax, everything will be fine. I'll come see you regularly. Heck, once you get a place, I can stay over at weekends."

This is the price for him helping her, but it's also one of the many things that makes her so afraid of the future.

"Okay, let's go." She finally steps off the deck into the driveway. When all is said and done, she can't face her husband anymore, and the man's 9-1-1 call has sealed her fate. The thought of jail terrifies her. "Which car should we take?"

"Mine. Your Honda will have to stay here. The surest way for anyone to find you is by tracking your car or your phone."

As they drive away, she looks back at the sweet cottage with its window boxes full of annuals. The curtains she picked out. The shutters she painted royal blue. She just hates to leave it all behind.

Tears roll down her cheeks. "Damn, this is the hardest thing I've ever done."

Chapter Two

PRESENT DAY

"MRS. BARLOW IS IN the kitchen, ma'am," the uniformed officer informs me as he lifts the yellow crime scene tape for me to pass. "Do you mind me asking why the FBI is involved in this case?"

"Just routine, officer." I duck under the tape, then turn to him. "We take an interest anytime the wife of a detective is found murdered."

"Detective Barlow is retired, you know," the officer presses, as if to tell me I'm wasting my time.

"Even so, we take an interest." I flash him a smile, knowing the feds are universally disliked by local law enforcement.

The house is an older split-level ranch-style home, nicely painted gray with white trim and green shutters. A freshly mown lawn blankets the front and side yards.

The hood of a green Volvo in the driveway is stone cold to my touch, suggesting it hasn't been driven in the last few hours. Upon climbing the front stoop, I find an open box of forensic shoe covers on a garden bench. I help myself to a pair and slip them on.

The front door is ajar. I push it open and step inside. My hand automatically finds the butt of my service weapon, even though I know officers have cleared the place.

It's been a while since I was here, but I remember the layout of the house. The fetid odor of death stings my nose as I move down a short hallway to a nicely appointed kitchen with top-of-the-line appliances. The blinds are drawn, and the only illumination comes from the under-cabinet lights. Wondering how officers got a good look at the body, I step to the bank of switches beside the door and stab them with the top of a ballpoint pen. The fluorescent ceiling panels flash on, casting the white cabinets, granite counters, and stainless-fronted appliances into sharp relief.

I move farther into the room and find Ava Barlow lying on her back behind the kitchen island. Her green eyes are dull and faded, staring sightlessly at the copper pans suspended from the ceiling. There's a smear of blood along the edge of the granite countertop where she grasped it for support. The streak continues down the front of a white cabinet to where the body rests.

Ava taught third grade for thirty years—longer than Pete was a detective. She retired the same month as he did. I know the couple planned to travel, and I hope they managed to get away to somewhere exotic . . . before this.

I move closer and squat beside Ava's body.

She's dressed in dark gray yoga pants and a blue shirt that's shredded and splashed with blood. Pink slipper socks cover both feet.

She was an attractive woman in her late fifties when I last saw her at her husband's retirement party a year ago. She used to be vivacious, and I remember her being embarrassingly drunk at the party and coming on to one of the younger detectives.

But as I look at her now, it's clear from her weight loss and her sallow cheeks that something other than age has taken its toll in the twelve months since I saw her. I make a mental note to check into her lifestyle.

I snap on a pair of forensic gloves from my pocket. Raising the elastic waistband of her pants, I peek inside but don't see any sign of interference with her clothing. Whatever the reason for the assault, it likely wasn't sexual.

The defensive wounds on her palms and the cuts across her chest say she didn't die quickly. I've seen these types of injuries before. Ava was trying to retreat from her assailant, holding up her hands for protection as he slashed his knife from side to side, trying to strike the poor woman anywhere he could.

I eye the deep jagged cuts in her neck. Once the knife tore into her throat, she would have collapsed to the floor. The blood pooled on the vinyl flooring under her long raven hair shows me her heart kept beating for a few moments after the attacker finally managed to sever her carotid arteries.

"Time for you to leave now. You've had your look-see," Police Detective Gary Reed says, coming into the kitchen. He's a greasy man with bushy eyebrows, a pencil mustache, and receding hair that is slicked back with way too much product. His brown suit and white shirt look like he slept in them.

He's been a constant source of irritation since I moved to Cedar Springs three years ago with my now ex-husband, Kenny. Reed never gives me any respect, and I ignore him, counting the number of knife wounds on Ava's hands, neck, and torso. I find twenty-three, including several that slash through her chest down to the bone. The medical examiner will give me a more accurate figure, but the actual number speaks to nothing more than the frenzy of the attack.

Detective Reed smirks as he moves closer. His gaze roves over my gray slacks and my white shirt, undressing me with his eyes. From crossing paths with him in the past, I know he finds me attractive, but he has a problem with me working in law enforcement because of my ethnicity. My parents emigrated from India to San Francisco when I was a baby. I am the first in my family to be given a western first name—Cassandra—and I go by Cassie. As proud as I am of my heritage, I'm eternally grateful for my American name.

The detective looks me in the eye. "Why are the feds interested in a straightforward homicide? The case against the husband is solid."

I get to my feet, snap a couple of pictures with my phone, then turn to him. "You think Detective Barlow did this to his wife?"

"Yeah. Anyone can see it was a frenzied attack. A crime of passion." He snickers at me for being so stupid not to realize that.

"True, but it might not be the husband." In my estimation, Barlow is cool and calculating. "If he intended to kill his wife, he could have done it in any number of ways that wouldn't have aroused our suspicion."

"Is that the best you can come up with?" Reed lifts his chin and purses his lips like he's a college professor addressing a roomful of students. "You FBI types always look for the most complicated explanation."

"It's early days, and we need to consider all possibilities. What would be Barlow's motive?" I ask.

"I don't know. What do old married couples argue about?" Reed hitches up his rumpled pants.

"Like I would know the answer to that," I scoff. It's common knowledge that my now ex-husband, Kenny, ran off with another woman two years ago—a week before my thirty-second birthday.

"Maybe Ava burned his dinner or wouldn't give him the kind of sex he wanted," Reed suggests, shrugging.

"Those sound more like your problems than Barlow's, detective."

"Don't go implying Hazel and I have problems because we don't. Wait! How did you guys even know about Mrs. Barlow's murder?"

"Intuition." I grin. A call from a forensic tech at the lab alerted me, but Reed doesn't need to know that.

"You're a bitch, Agent Viera. Now get off my crime scene." Reed is either a dinosaur or a sign of the times, depending on your point of view.

There's nothing more to be learned here until forensic techs process the scene and the ME autopsies Ava Barlow's body. "In case you hadn't noticed, we're both law enforcement. Don't come running to us when you screw up," I say as I breeze past Reed. I pause at the door and turn

9

to face him. "You do understand that the FBI is a federal organization. Federal authority almost always supersedes *local* authority." I emphasize local as if it were a bad word. "I can take this case over anytime I want. In fact, we feds will run an investigation in parallel with the police department's. We'll make sure you don't do any favors for your buddy Pete Barlow. Or anyone else at the police department."

"Fuck you, Agent Bollywood," Reed says, using his insulting nickname for me. He follows me down the hall, shouting a torrent of curse words.

I step out the front door into the glaring sunlight. It's only ten-thirty-five in the morning, but I can tell it's going to be another scorcher.

"Pretty sad what happened to Mrs. Barlow," the officer says as I duck under the yellow tape to leave.

"Were you here when they searched the rooms?" I ask, reading the name Officer Mason on his nametag. "Reed was too busy being a dick to tell me anything useful."

He stifles a chuckle at my comment. "Yeah. My partner and I were the first responders who found Mrs. Barlow. Detective Reed showed up just as we finished clearing the house."

"Any sign of a robbery—drawers pulled out, items strewn around?"

"No, nothing like that. Though we can't be sure that nothing is missing until Detective Barlow has checked."

"Where is Pete Barlow now?"

"Another patrol saw him at a gas station and scooped him up. They have him cooling his heels in an interview room."

"Any sign he was making a run for it?"

"Nah. Pete was two blocks from here. There's a gas station on both sides of the road. His vehicle was pointed this way as if he were heading home."

"How did you and your partner come to show up at the residence?"

"We answered a 9-1-1 call by a neighbor who heard Ava, uh Mrs. Barlow screaming. We were in the area and arrived in minutes. The front door was wide open, so we checked inside."

"What's the neighbor's name?"

Mason consults his notebook. "Mrs. Smythe with a 'Y.' She heard a vehicle drive off. Possibly a van, but she didn't see anything."

"Where does she live?"

A picket fence that's considerably taller than my five feet nine runs the length of the driveway, blocking any view from that side. But Mason indicates a two-story house on the other side. The upstairs windows peek over the evergreen shrubs at the property boundary. As I stare, a curtain moves as if someone is watching us. I plan to have an agent pay a visit to Mrs. Smythe.

"Anyone check for surveillance cameras?" It's an upper-class neighborhood, and I'd expect to find some.

"Not yet."

"Early days, I suppose," I say, adding cameras to my mental to-do list.

"Yeah." He snaps his shoulders back and straightens his spine as Detective Reed comes through the Barlows' front door, looking none too pleased.

"Thanks for your help, Officer Mason. I'd best be off," I say, as I see Reed bearing down on us.

"No problem. We're all law enforcement," he replies with a grin, reading my FBI creds hanging from a chain around my neck. "You take care, Senior Special Agent Viera."

I hurry through a sparse group of reporters and looky-loos gathered on the sidewalk in front of the residence. Ignoring the shouted questions, I slide behind the wheel of my Bureau car, half expecting Reed to rap on the window, but he doesn't. I'm not afraid of dealing with the man, but he's a complete waste of time and energy.

Checking my phone, I see a missed call from my ex-husband. The only reason he calls since the divorce is to mess with me. I think he wants to punish me for all the times I came home late from work, all the times he took second place to my job. Kenny is a cop himself and knew he was marrying one when he married me. We both worked long hours, but apparently, that was okay for him, but not me. Jerk. Now I wish he'd just go away and get on with his life and his new wife.

Instead of returning the call, I consider what might have befallen Ava Barlow. There was no evidence of a break-in at either the front or back doors and no sign that she'd just gotten home and been followed inside. The hood of the Volvo was cold, and you wouldn't step outside in the slipper socks she was wearing.

I feel sure that as a cop's wife for twenty-odd years, Ava wouldn't open the front door to just anyone. So, the crazy person who slashed at her twenty-something times had to look calm enough for her to not feel threatened when she answered the door.

Then there's motive.

Officers saw no sign of a robbery—the dead woman was still wearing an expensive-looking Rolex on her wrist. Nor do I think the perp was a crazy addict desperate for a fix.

But Ava's death was possibly the work of a lover, and I make a mental note to check into that.

She was targeted by someone who looked ordinary, possibly even charming, when she answered the door. But that same someone attacked her with a rage and fury you don't often come across, even in my line of work.

It's time to head back to the FBI office and brief my team. I have a feeling we are in for some long days.

Chapter Three

TWENTY MINUTES LATER, I pull into the parking lot at The Cedar Springs Resident Agency FBI Office. The satellite of the Sacramento Field Office is housed in a contemporary professional building with darkly tinted windows on Larkspur Lane. The other tenants include a title agency, an insurance agency, and a bank's head office.

I park my Bureau car next to an identical black sedan with US government plates. Stepping across the lot to a bullet-proof glass door bearing the FBI emblem, I swipe my key card and push inside. A central corridor takes me to another door, requiring another swipe of my card. My team's ground floor offices are nothing if not secure.

Special Agent Nick Stone is filling his coffee mug as I enter. He turns to me and quips, "The wanderer returns." He's six feet tall and built like a linebacker, with neatly trimmed dark hair and a ready smile.

I stand in front of the open-plan cubicles and raise my voice. "Okay, listen up. We've landed a new case. Conference room, now."

"That includes you, Todd," I add when he doesn't come

out from behind his bank of computer monitors. Todd is a civilian contractor and our tech analyst. He looks every bit the part—vintage horn-rimmed glasses, a beard that needs trimming, and shaggy hair. He only drinks craft beer and listens to his music on vinyl records. Today he's wearing khaki jeans and a red plaid flannel shirt, which is about as dressed up as he ever gets.

When he first started working here, Todd showed up in bib overalls. I was fine with whatever he wore, but Assistant Special Agent in Charge Preston Myles, my boss, spoke to him about appropriate attire.

Special Agent Stevie Wells is the junior member of our three-agent team. She stands, and the top of her blonde hair barely clears the five-foot-six modular dividers that ring each of our offices. "We heard you attended a murder," she says, stepping into the aisle and adjusting her rimless glasses. She's wearing a striped white shirt and navy pants. "The grapevine also said that Detective Reed was giving you a hard time."

"You're well connected as usual," I say over my shoulder as I move into the conference room and take the chair at the head of the rectangular, graphite-colored table. "Reed is a pig and a pain in the ass to deal with." I'd heard Stevie was dating someone in the police department, and now I know his name—Officer Mason. I resist the temptation to make a dig about the guy, but Stevie reads my thoughts.

"I guess that was a dead giveaway." Her face colors as she takes a seat. "We've been dating since Christmas."

"What did I miss?" Nick asks, following Todd into the room and easing himself into a chair beside him.

"Stevie's dating an officer, but we don't know his name." There's a mischievous look on Todd's face.

"Spill the beans, Stevie," Nick prods, setting his pen on the table exactly in line with his notebook.

"Okay, it's Officer Mason. Chuck Mason. We've been dating for months. It's not like it's some big secret."

"That's the first we've heard of it." Todd leans toward Stevie with an elbow on the table.

"Like my personal life is any of your business," she replies with mock indignation.

"Alright, settle down, kids," I tell them. "The deceased is Ava Barlow, wife of Retired Detective Pete Barlow. A neighbor heard her screaming this morning and dialed 9-1-1. Officers responded at nine-oh-five to her home on Juniper Way and found her on her kitchen floor, dead from a knife attack. Detectives have the husband in custody, but I'm not convinced he killed her."

"It's usually the husband," Stevie adds with a knowing look.

"The attack was furious. The killer waved the knife from side to side, slashing deep into Ava's palms and chest before finally cutting her throat." I pull up a picture on my phone and pass it around for the team to see. "I'm not saying the husband didn't kill her, but a detective like Pete Barlow would be able to think of any number of ways to kill his wife without attracting suspicion."

"Ugh," Stevie winces, swiping the screen to see all the ones I took. "Those are difficult to look at. Maybe the husband tried to make it look like a crazy person killed her."

"The other significant piece of information is that officers picked up Pete Barlow at a gas station driving *in the direction of* his residence."

"Did she let the killer in?" Nick asks, looking at the pictures, making a face at the level of violence.

"It's likely. There's no sign of anyone breaking into the house."

"So, it was someone she felt safe opening the door to."

"I'll bet dollars to donuts that officers will arrest the husband." Todd peers at the phone pictures, not showing the same level of disgust as his colleagues.

"I don't trust the police department to run an impartial investigation, especially with Reed as the lead detective," I say. "That's one of the reasons why we need to run a parallel investigation. We're going to divide up and learn all about the Barlows. Nick, I want you to find everything you can about Ava. Who were her friends, was she having an affair, and who did she come in contact with in the last two weeks? Todd, can you hack into surveillance video from residences on Juniper Way? Maybe we'll get lucky and find a picture of the perp driving away from the house." I know Todd takes a perverse pleasure in hacking into computers. The more difficult the hack, the bigger his rush. We just have to be careful not to use hacked evidence at trial.

He nods. "I can get the footage as long as the cameras are connected to the internet, and that's true of most surveillance systems these days. But you know folk don't usually point them at the street."

"They are sometimes misaligned. We'll take whatever we can get."

"I can look for ATM cameras. They often have a good view of the street."

"First, you need to ID a vehicle driving away from the residence," I caution him. "If we think an ATM camera can help us, we'll request the footage from the bank. Do *not* hack into any type of financial institution."

Everyone chuckles at that. "Yes, ma'am." Todd salutes me.

"Stevie, you're with me. We'll zoom over to the police station and crash Pete Barlow's interview."

A flash of disappointment crosses her face. I think it's because she didn't get her own assignment. She's only a year out of the academy and has a lot to learn.

"You drive, and let's take one of the sedans," I say to her as we get up from the table. "Lights and siren. We need to hurry in case they start without us."

She nods, then runs to pick up her bag from under her desk. I grab mine, and we hurry out the door together.

The black Dodge Charger I was driving earlier has heated up in the blazing sunshine, and Stevie starts it quickly, setting the AC to the maximum.

"Are they expecting us?" She looks over her shoulder and backs the sedan out of the parking slot.

"No, but let's see if I can change that." I pull out my phone and dial a number from my contacts.

"Chief Holder's office," a woman's voice announces.

"Margaret, this is SSA Cassie Viera. Is he available?"

"One moment, I'll check."

The voice that comes on the line is deep and gravelly. "This is Holder."

"SSA Viera here. I have you on speaker with Special Agent Wells. We believe you're holding Pete Barlow in custody. We're anxious to interview him in connection with the death of his wife, Ava."

"I was very sorry to hear of Ava's death," Holder says in a measured tone. "It's just tragic. Look, I worked with Pete for nigh on twenty years. I don't for one moment think he killed Ava, but we have to cover our bases. We can't show him any preferential treatment."

"My thoughts exactly, but he may have vital information about who might have killed her."

"I'm grateful you're looking into Ava's death, but a pissing match between the FBI and my detectives is the last thing I want. Pete and Ava were my friends back in the day."

"We promise to behave." *If your guys do*, I say silently to myself.

"How soon can you be here?"

"Ten minutes tops." I flash a look at Stevie, who nods and steps on the gas.

"Okay, but remember to keep it civil," Holder says.

When I end the call, Stevie chuckles to herself at my end-run around Detective Reed. "Nicely played, ma'am," she says.

I want to tell her not to be a brown-noser and not to call me ma'am, but that sounds a bit harsh. "If discussions with the detectives get contentious, leave the talking to me. You know how assertive you can get," I say with a big wink.

"Me?" Stevie takes a hand off the wheel and points an index finger at herself. "You're always telling me I need to be more assertive."

"Joking," I reply. "But keep in mind what I said to Chief Holder about keeping it civil."

We park in front of the police station, a run-down building that was once painted gray. As we climb out of the sedan, Officer Mason gets out of his cruiser and hitches up his duty belt. I greet him, but Stevie and Mason stutter at each other like a pair of high-schoolers.

"Your secret is out," I tell the officer with a grin as we hurry to the entrance.

"You're referring to Stevie, I mean Special Agent Wells?" he stammers.

"That's her, Mason," I chuckle as he holds the door open for us. Once inside, I spot Detectives Reed and Finch standing by the front counter and put on a more businesslike face.

Chapter Four

"WHAT IS SHE doing here?" Detective Reed asks as I step into the lobby of the police station. "And who's her little friend?" His gaze falls on Stevie. He's worked with her before, but just wants to belittle her youthful looks.

"If you get in my way, Reed, Pete Barlow will be in federal custody so fast it will make your head spin," I say.

Reed takes a step toward me, and Detective Finch tells him to knock it off.

"The witness is all yours, girls," Reed says. "Pete didn't kill his wife, and I have real criminals to catch." With that, he saunters off in the direction of the detectives' offices.

Finch shakes his head. He is tall with buzz-cut brown hair, a long straight nose, and warm caramel eyes set in a diamond-shaped face. I'd guess he's approaching forty. He's wearing khaki slacks and a light blue button-down shirt. I think his first name is Joey, but everybody calls him Finch.

"What a charmer," Stevie says.

"You know Special Agent Stevie Wells," I say to Finch.

"We've met before." He smiles and politely takes her outstretched hand. "Barlow's counsel just arrived. I don't know what kind of law he practices, but apparently, the guy is a family friend."

"Who's the lead detective on the case?"

"Technically, it's me, but Reed isn't above interfering. He's already spoken to Pete." Finch starts toward the interview room, but I stop him, saying, "Do you have Barlow's phone?"

"Yeah." He turns back to me. "Pete showed me how to unlock it. It uses one of those pictures where you connect the dots."

"Let's take a look at it before we talk to him."

"Hang tight." Finch strides off toward the offices.

"I've encountered Reed before," Stevie says to me. "Has he always been like this?"

"All the time I've been in Cedar Springs," I reply. "He's a worthless asshole. Hates anything federal. He'll warm up a bit once he accepts we're on the case. Still, I don't know why they keep him on."

"Why do you want to see the phone?"

"We might see something we want to ask Pete about."

Finch returns with a smartphone in a plastic evidence bag. He leads us into an empty interview room, sets the smartphone on the table, and dons gloves from his back pocket.

"You looked at it yet?" I pull a pair of gloves from my purse and snap them on.

"Yeah." He looks at Stevie and me and colors a little.

"What?" I turn the phone on. "Does he have porn on it?"

"Not exactly. Though there's a picture of a young lady the right age to be his daughter. She's naked on a bed." He swipes the lock-screen image.

I raise my eyebrows and thumb through the pictures in the gallery until I come to it. Stevie looks over my shoulder. The woman in the picture looks to be in her early twenties and is lying on an unmade bed. The pillows are awry, and the sheets are rucked up. She's naked, and her legs are parted.

Stevie nods. "That's porn, in case you didn't notice."

"It's not Ava Barlow," I quip. "Nice figure."

"If I had to guess, I'd say she's in a hotel room," Stevie says.

"Yeah. Anything else of interest for us to squint at, Finch?"

"Some steamy text messages with someone named Maura," he replies. "She could be the woman in the picture."

I tap my way to the texting app, and we read some of the exchanges. "Phew. I'm surprised he was okay with us looking at the phone."

"You think Ava knew about her husband's liaison with Maura?" Stevie shoots me a look. She probably thinks no one over forty has sex.

"I'm guessing not." Finch shakes his head slowly. "Keep in mind that Maura may not be her real name."

"Anything else besides the text messages and the crotch shot?" I ask.

"That's not enough for you?" He raises his brow.

"Well?"

"It deserves another look through, but all I saw were dog pictures and some political stuff."

"I didn't see a dog when I was at his house."

"Maybe it ran off because we haven't found it. Let's go talk to Barlow."

"Do he and Ava have kids?" I follow Finch into the corridor.

"No kids. You should lead the interview. I've worked with Pete in the past. How do you want to play it?"

"Head-on, like I would with any other person of interest. Even Holder doesn't want Pete given special treatment." As we reach the interview room door, I add, "Don't be afraid to leap in."

The lawyer and his client stand as we enter the pokey room stinking of body odor. Barlow is in his late fifties and slim, with a sagging chest and a paunch. His khaki pants and white button-down shirt are rumpled, but I don't see any blood on them. Ava's assailant would have at least a few splashes on their clothing.

"I'm Senior Special Agent Viera. This is Special Agent Wells, and I think you both know Detective Finch." When I set the evidence bag holding Pete's phone on the table, he eyes it warily.

The lawyer is more than a few pounds overweight and wearing a dark suit, a pinpoint stripe shirt, and a red tie. He introduces himself as Greg Hays and says he's known Pete for thirty years. "The death of Ava Barlow is a tragedy, but why is the FBI interested?"

We crowd around the table and take our seats on the hard chairs.

"I'd have thought her death was a local matter," Hays continues. "Pete and I were just discussing the possibility of someone high on drugs attacking his wife."

"What type of law do you practice, Mr. Hays?" I ask, loosening the buttons of my jacket.

"Uh, corporate law. Patent infringements and the like," Hays tells us, a puzzled look on his ruddy face.

"And you feel you can adequately represent Mr. Barlow?"

"Well, it's not as if you're going to charge him with anything, is it?" The brief chuckles for a few moments, then stops when he realizes no one else is laughing.

"We need to ask your client some questions. Let's dive in. Mr. Barlow, may I call you Peter or Pete? What do you prefer?"

"Pete is fine."

"Let me first say how sorry we are about the death of your wife. On behalf of the FBI and the Cedar Springs Police Department, I'd like to extend my heartfelt condolences."

"Thank you." A tear leaks from the corner of his eye, and he brushes it away with his hand.

"You and Ava have been married for some time, I believe."

"Thirty-two years."

"And you have no children?"

"Ava was never able to conceive."

"How about Ava's parents and yours?"

"Ava's parents died when she was in her teens. My father passed last year, my mother last January."

"We understand you've taken a retirement job," Stevie says.

"Financially, we're fine with my police pension, but I can't sit at home and do nothing. I work security at the hospital. Recently, I've been working the night shift." Pete's eyes flick back and forth nervously between Stevie and me.

"And Mrs. Barlow, was she employed?"

"No, she was not."

"And how did your wife fill her time?" I ask.

"She's very active in the community. She's on numerous committees, sewing circles. Like me, she wasn't one to sit at home."

"Can you make us a list of those committees when we're done here?"

"Sure."

"How has your wife's health been recently?"

"She hurt her ankle quite badly about six months ago. She finds it painful to get around, but she manages. Managed."

"Did she take any medications?"

"She took pills for her ankle pain and for her high blood pressure."

"Opioid medications like Hydrocodone?"

"Yeah."

"And she always took the prescribed amount?"

Hays almost jumps out of his seat. "Really, Agent, I must object strongly to this line of questioning. Let's not forget that Mrs. Barlow is the victim here."

I raised my hand to silence him. "I know this is difficult coming on the heels of Mrs. Barlow's death, but I'll ask any questions I think may relate to this murder investigation."

Pete's gaze lowers to the table. "She's been hitting the

painkillers hard since she hurt her ankle. The dose that the doctor prescribed didn't always control the pain."

"That's not uncommon. Where did your wife get the extra pills?"

"She knew someone who could get them for her." Pete's voice is a whisper.

"Do you have a name?"

"No. I didn't like to ask her."

Ava taking illegally obtained oxy, raises a big red flag. I shoot a glance at Stevie, then switch gears. "Did you work a shift at the hospital last night?"

"I did." Pete nodded.

"What time did your shift end?" Stevie asks.

"Seven-thirty this morning."

"A police patrol car picked you up at the Chevron station at nine twenty-six," I say.

"That's correct."

"That gas station is what, five miles from the hospital? What did you do in those two hours?"

"Again, I must strenuously object to your line of questioning." Hays puffs out his cheeks. "My client is a respected retired detective. Decorated, in fact."

"The quicker we can get questions like these out of the way, the faster we can move forward with the investigation," I respond. Hays' interruptions are becoming annoying.

"I took a shower in the changing room at the hospital," Pete says.

"Did anyone see you there or see you leave the hospital?"

"I don't believe so."

"How else did you fill that two-hour window?" Stevie frowns and leans toward Pete.

Pete shakes his head. "I'll have to think. My memory isn't working too good since I heard what happened to Ava."

I point to the evidence bag holding his phone. "Who is Maura?"

"I don't know that name."

"Perhaps I can jog your memory." I snap on gloves and pull out the phone, pausing to see if that is enough to get him talking.

Out of the corner of my eye, I see a pained look cross Detective Finch's face. "Tell her, Pete," he says. "They'll find out in time."

When Pete doesn't speak, I thumb up the hotel room picture and hold it up for him to see. "This is your phone, isn't it? Is her name Maura?"

"Oh my God," Hays exclaims at the sight of the pornographic picture. "Are there no depths to which you won't sink, Agent?"

Pete hesitates before saying, "That's Maura. We met in the bar at the Travelodge about two months ago. I've been . . . meeting her on and off ever since."

"I'll be speaking to your supervisor about this," Hays tells me, his face purple with rage.

I reach into my bag and pull out a pen and a business card. After writing Preston Myles' name and phone number on the back, I slide it across the table to Hays.

"Speaking to ASAC Myles won't have the effect you

imagine it will," I say. "He'll tell you we sometimes have to ask difficult questions, and in a murder investigation, they can't wait. Pete wasn't being forthright about Maura, and we need to check her out. A jealous husband could have killed Ava." I turn back to Pete:

"What is Maura's last name?"

"She never told me."

I regard him incredulously. "You met her on several occasions?"

"A half-dozen times, maybe. Always at the Travelodge."

"For sex?"

"And for her company," he insists.

Something is off about Maura. Pete Barlow is thirty-odd years her senior. If his house is anything to go by, he's not rich, and he's certainly not good-looking. "And you never asked Maura for her last name?"

"No."

"Do you pay her for sex?"

"I usually take care of the hotel bill, but she's not a hooker if that's what you're asking."

"Did Mrs. Barlow know about your liaison with Maura?" Stevie raises a puzzled eyebrow.

"She did. Our marriage hasn't been easy since I retired. Ava is seeing someone herself."

"She was in a romantic relationship?" I say. "You didn't think it important to tell us sooner?"

"I was ashamed."

"What is the name of the person she is seeing?"

"Ava never told me."

"Do you know if it was a man or a woman?"

"A man, of course," he scoffs.

"You know nothing at all about him? Age, skin color, anything?" Stevie's tone is skeptical.

"She didn't tell me, and I never saw him."

Hays is fidgeting around, his gaze flitting between Stevie and me. "My client has answered your sick questions. Can he go now?"

I look to Detective Finch, who says, "We'll have to detain him a little longer while we attempt to verify his alibi."

"This is preposterous," Hays splutters, stabbing the table with his forefinger. "I'll be speaking to Chief Holder and Agent Myles."

"It's Assistant Special Agent in Charge Preston Myles," I tell him. "We're done with your client for the moment."

We all stand, and Finch summons a uniformed officer. Pete Barlow screams blue murder when Finch tells the officer to take him to a holding cell. As we move into the corridor, Hays turns his back on us and makes a beeline for the chief's office.

"He won't get anywhere with Chief Holder," Finch says. "Since Pete is a retired detective, it's even more important than usual to investigate his wife's murder by the book. We can't be seen affording him any special treatment."

"What do you make of his alibi?" Stevie asks.

"Hinky." Finch shakes his head. "There's something he's not telling us."

"There's no point in duplicating our efforts," I say, shouldering my bag. "What are you going to do next?"

"Figure out if Pete had time to kill Ava between the end

of his shift and when he was picked up at the gas station."

"Has he changed his clothes since you picked him up? I didn't see any blood on them," Stevie points out.

"He had time to take a shower and change," Finch says grimly.

"What time is the autopsy?" I ask.

"I'll find out and let you know. I knew Ava, so I may give her autopsy a miss. What a mess."

"We're going to focus our efforts on the mystery boyfriend." I look at Stevie, who nods in agreement.

Chapter Five

WHEN STEVIE AND I step through the inner door to our office, the room is silent but for the rattle of keyboards.

Nick jumps up in his cubicle, his six-foot frame easily clearing the top of the dividers. "How did Pete's interview go?" His steel-blue eyes are sparkling, and he flashes us a smile.

"The Barlows are a weird pair," Stevie says as we gravitate to the conference room. I set my bag on the floor and hook my jacket on the back of a chair before taking a seat at the table. Nick joins us, folding his tall frame onto a chair.

"Pete and his wife both have lovers," I tell him,

"*Had* a lover in Ava's case." Stevie corrects me. "How common is that for a couple that has been married for thirty-odd years?"

"Unusual, I'd say. From what I've heard, most couples who've made it that far in a marriage are committed to one another." My mind flashes to my failed marriage with Kenny. He ran off with his gym instructor after only four years. It's not a secret, but I choose not to remind everyone of that tidbit.

I turn to Nick. "Before we get into Pete's interview, tell us what you've been up to." Sensing my messy bun is falling apart, I remove the claw clip, fish a hair tie from my bag, and pull my jet-black hair into a ponytail.

"Like you asked, I've been getting background on Ava Barlow," Nick responds, "and it may answer your questions about what happened to the Barlow's marriage. Ava was on a ton of committees. There's the Economic Development Board, the County Audit Committee, the Veteran's Memorial Hall Board, the board of Big Brothers Big Sisters, to name just a few. I called some of the other members. No one liked the woman. She was grouchy, arrived late for meetings, or didn't show up at all. An all-around nasty piece of work. But the petty grievances don't seem like they rise to the level of a vicious knife attack like the one we're investigating."

"People murder each other for the stupidest reasons, but it doesn't sound like the best use of our resources at this point."

"How did Pete put up with her all those years?" Stevie asks.

"A couple of the people I spoke to said Ava wasn't always like that," Nick continues. "I also paid a visit to the neighbor who heard Ava's screams and dialed 9-1-1. She says she often saw a man coming and going from the house when Pete was away. I think her upstairs windows overlook the Barlow house, but she must be keeping a close eye on them to make a statement like that."

"The visiting male meshes with what we heard at the

interview," I say. "Ava was in an extra-marital relationship, but Pete didn't even know the guy's name. Pete himself is in a relationship with a woman named Maura. Says he doesn't know her last name. They meet at the Travelodge in town. She's half his age and a looker, so something strange is going on there."

"That does sound odd," Nick agrees. "The neighbor couldn't provide much of a description of Ava's mystery caller, but it's worth having her work with a sketch artist."

"Can you run with that?" I ask.

"Sure thing, boss." Nick nods.

"If the Barlows were leading separate lives, I can understand Pete not knowing the name of Ava's lover. But having sex on multiple occasions with a woman he only knows as Maura does seem strange."

"You sure Maura isn't a hooker?" Nick asks, raising an eyebrow.

"Pete said he doesn't pay her, but it's safe to say she's after something of his."

"Maybe Pete is secretly a multi-millionaire," Stevie suggests.

"If he's rich, why is he living in a very ordinary house with a wife he doesn't speak to?" I reply.

"We may not have the answer, but it gives us two possible suspects," Stevie adds. "Maura's partner, if she has one, and Ava's mystery boyfriend that the neighbor saw."

I nod. "Finding their identities is our number one priority. From the injuries Ava received, she was likely slain by a man, but Maura could be connected to the killer."

"I forgot to mention that one of the board members told

me Ava was frequently high," Nick adds.

"Pete said Ava injured her ankle six months ago, and she's been abusing opioids for the pain." Stevie uses air quotes around the word pain. "She gets the drugs from a mystery supplier—another possible suspect to add into the mix."

"The neighbor mentioned Ava was often aggressive. She'd argue about the slightest thing. That was one of the problems people had with her. Opioids have a depressive effect, so I'm thinking she was on something else as well. Uppers like speed, crack, or meth," Nick suggests.

"The medical examiner should be able to tell us," I remind him, "but it will take a while for the tox screen to come back." I step over to the whiteboard and uncap a blue felt marker. "The suspects we have so far are Maura's partner, Ava's boyfriend, and Ava's drug supplier." I write that on the board. "Our current task is to find these people."

"When you're all finished, I have some video to show you," Todd says from behind me.

I didn't notice him join us, and his voice startles me. "Let's take a look at that next."

We follow Todd to his office. He sits in front of his giant computer monitors while the rest of us stand behind him, waiting for the show to begin.

He slurps his coffee. "I haven't been able to find a camera that covers the front of the Barlow residence, but I've hacked into the next best thing—cameras mounted on houses on either side. Vehicles that appear on one camera then the other a short interval later are obviously cruising past the murder house without stopping. Cars that only pass through one camera are arriving at the house or leaving."

Todd takes a slug of coffee before continuing:

"I've limited my search to video captured between eight o'clock and nine-fifteen this morning. In that period, only one vehicle passes through one camera but not the other, meaning it stops outside the Barlow residence or very close by. I only have a narrow view of the street, so I don't have a make or model, but I can tell you it's a dark blue passenger minivan. It arrives at eight-forty-seven and leaves at three minutes after nine—about six minutes after the 9-1-1 call. Watch the monitors as I play the videos." He pounds his keyboard and works the mouse.

As Todd said, both cameras are aimed at the front yards and capture only a sliver of the street. Sure enough, at eight-forty-seven, we see the side of a dark blue minivan slowly cross the edge of the video on the left screen. Nothing appears on the right-hand screen because the vehicle has stopped near the Barlow residence. Next, Todd fast-forwards the videos to nine-oh-three. This time, we see the minivan on the right-hand screen as it drives away from the murder scene.

"That's brilliant," I say. "Is there any way to see the license plate?"

I hear my desk phone ring, and Stevie says, "I've got it," as she steps into my office to answer the call.

Todd says, "The long scrape in the paintwork on the driver's side makes the vehicle distinctive, so I'm searching for it on cameras that are farther afield. If I can find a dark blue minivan with a better view of the license plate, that scrape will tell me if I'm looking at the same vehicle."

"Keep at it. But remember, no hacking into banks," I tell him with a wink.

Todd gives me a scornful look.

Stevie appears beside me. "That was the head of the police forensic department, Jason Clark, who just called. His people have finished processing the Barlow house, and he said we'll want to hear what they found."

"Why didn't he tell you the results?"

"I don't know. I think Jason only wants to deal with you."

"No, no, no. That's not how it works at all." My phone chirps with a text, and I pause to read it. "The message is from Detective Finch saying the ME has started Ava's autopsy. You want to come with me, Nick?"

"Sure," he says, grabbing his jacket.

"Stevie, go see Jason, and don't leave until he gives you a complete debrief of what the forensic team found."

"Yes, ma'am."

"And don't call me ma'am. Ever. I answer to Agent Viera or Cassie."

"What if Jason will only speak to you?" she asks.

"You're a Special Agent with the FBI, Stevie. Grow a pair. You don't take shit like that from anyone."

***

HIDDEN AWAY BEHIND the county administration building is a squat brick rectangle that houses the medical examiner's office. It reminds us where we might end up, and no one wants something like that in a prominent place.

After punching in the key code, Nick and I push through the glass doors and follow the corridor to the changing room. Without uttering a word, we quickly don protective gear—gowns, gloves, hats, and safety glasses.

Another door takes us into the examination room, its walls and floor tiled in pale green. The air is an awful mix of disinfectant and decay. Strains of The New World Symphony by Dvořák come from a battered CD player in the corner.

Two people hover over something that looks more like a piece of meat from the butcher's than anything that was once human.

Yolanda Jensen, the medical examiner, is a five-foot-six firecracker with tawny skin and auburn hair done in a pixie cut. She's a vivacious fifty-something who seems to bounce as she moves around the gaping chasm that once was Ava Barlow's body. "What time do you call this?" she chirps. She's wearing light blue scrubs and a fitted skull cap covering the top of her head.

"Or maybe you intended to show up when we're almost done?" she adds after a pause, taking an oddly shaped scalpel from Terrell, the morgue assistant. He's a lanky black man with a wispy beard.

"We didn't have all day to watch you take the poor lady apart," I reply, not moving too close to the victim.

"All day? You know I'm speedy, not like some of the old fart medical examiners I won't name who work in nearby counties."

"How does Mrs. Barlow look?"

"Oh, she's quite dead, sweetie," Yolanda chuckles as she makes an incision.

"I appreciate your keen powers of observation. How did she get that way?"

"Even a layperson could tell you. Someone took several whacks at her throat with a knife. Severed the blood vessels feeding her brain."

"Is whacks a new technical term?" Nick quips.

"Sure thing, baby, along with bops on the head and slugs to the gut."

"Got a time of death for me?" I ask.

"After eight and before nine oh-five this morning, when officers arrived at the scene. Come closer. You won't see anything from over there."

I move to stand beside the area where Yolanda is working. Nick hangs back. He's behind Stevie in the up-chuck sweepstakes. He only threw up at his first autopsy, whereas Stevie has to run to the bathroom almost every time. I need to bring her more often, so she gets used to the blood and gore, but bodies are not that common in a place like Cedar Springs.

But the sight of Ava's dissected face makes bile rise for a moment, even in *my* throat. Then I have it under control again.

"See here." Yolanda uses her scalpel to point at Ava's flayed nose. "Her septum is eroded, and there's a white powder in her turbinates."

"Turbinates?"

"Nasal passages. The victim had a serious coke habit. That's not all. Take a look here." Yolanda fights the rigor mortis setting into Ava's body to lift her left arm and rotate it to show the inside. Deep knife wounds cut across the hand and wrist from the victim's futile attempt at defending herself. But the medical examiner is using her scalpel to indicate an area of the inside arm that is nearer to the elbow.

"Needle marks?" asks Nick, who's plucked up the courage to move closer.

"Yeah." She forces the arm higher. "Look at the veins. They're all shriveled from what she's been injecting into herself. Could be meth, coke, even heroin. We'll know for sure when we get the tox screen back. She'd have been loopy much of the time." Yolanda waves her scalpel for emphasis.

"Yeah, I got that from talking to the people who knew her, but they probably wouldn't have guessed it was from a drug habit," Nick says.

"A trained eye would have spotted it in an instant," Yolanda tells him.

"Can you tell how serious a habit she had?"

"It's been going on for a good few months—nine or ten, I'd guess. If someone hadn't killed her, she would have been dead within two years."

"Her husband is a retired detective. He pulled the pin a year ago." I'm referring to his retirement date.

"Well, he wasn't doing much detecting around his wife. Either that or he didn't care."

"I'm guessing the latter. Anything sexual?"

I cringe when Yolanda parts the woman's organs with a scalpel. "Oh right. She has the clap, and almost certainly, whoever was boning her does too. I'm guessing it wasn't the husband."

"She was having an affair. We need to find the guy, but we don't know much about him. Except we're looking for someone with the clap. That should help, right?" I joke.

Yolanda guffaws loudly.

"Anything else?"

"Just the message," she whispers, like she's telling me a secret.

"The killer left a message? You've been holding out on us." I give her a mock stern look.

"It won't tell you much. It was on her upper belly, but it's lost now we cut her open. Terrell will show you."

"The killer must have lifted her top because I didn't see any writing at the scene," I mutter.

Yolanda nods, and Terrell motions for us to follow him to a workstation with a camera attached. He types with two fingers and clicks the mouse. Ava's lily-white torso fills the screen. The slashes to her breasts are brutal, but the words carved below them with the tip of a knife capture our attention:

YOU ARE NEXT.

Chapter Six

"WHO DO WE think the message carved into Ava's belly was intended for?" Stevie asks, taking a seat with Nick and me at the conference room table.

"Pete Barlow, I guess." Nick shrugs one shoulder.

"It changes the dynamics a bit." I lean back in my chair and interlace my hands behind my head. "Ava's killing could be all about Pete. Possibly revenge for something he did while he was a detective."

"He was a cop for twenty-five years," Stevie states. "That's an awful lot of cases to search through. He's bound to have pissed off dozens of people in that time."

"He should be inclined to help us if he believes there's a threat to his life. Let's see if he'll talk to us tomorrow," I suggest.

Todd comes to the open door. I think he feels left out when we three agents meet, and I make a mental note to invite him to the next informal gathering. "Pull up a chair," I tell him. I turn back to Stevie. "Did you manage to talk to Jason about the forensic sweep at the Barlow's home?"

"Eventually. I'm sorry, but he's kinda odd. I had to

assert my authority to get him to tell me anything."

"He's prejudiced against women."

"Now, you tell me," she teases.

"I can talk to him next time," Nick volunteers.

"Hell no!" I exclaim. "Guys like Jason are all about controlling and punishing women who challenge male dominance. The police department may be a hotbed of misogyny, but we can't let stupid beliefs get in the way of doing our job."

Stevie shakes her head. "Officer Mason isn't at all like that." She takes a small notebook from her pocket. "Jason didn't tell me much that we don't already know. The techs found a bag of coke hidden at the back of a cupboard. About five hundred dollars' worth. More than you'd usually find for personal use. Ava's cell has a lot of calls to a burner phone. The texts to that number are pretty racy, so I imagine he's the boyfriend. Sometimes they sexted with one another."

I frown. "Let me guess. We have a picture of the boyfriend's dick."

"Exactly. All it tells us is he's white, a hairy dude, and uh, a big boy." Stevie's face colors.

We all burst out laughing. I see Nick's mind working overtime. "Depends on who you're comparing it with," he says.

"None of your freaking business," she tells him, but it brings out more chuckles.

"How about tracing the burner phone?" Todd asks when everyone quietens down.

"The forensic guys tried that," Stevie says, "but it didn't

work out."

"Didn't work out?" Todd repeats skeptically. "Get me the number, and I'll give it a go."

Stevie writes in her notebook, then tears the page off and slides it across the table to Todd. "Knock yourself out, wonder boy."

"You won't be smirking if it leads us to the killer, and we sew up the case."

"Did Jason mention anything else?" I ask her.

"A couple of things. The Barlows slept in separate bedrooms and used separate bathrooms, so there was little love lost between them. Secondly, the team found some, ah, DNA deposits on the sheets. Results should be back in a few days."

"That right there could give us the boyfriend's identity," Nick suggests.

"Unless it's Pete Barlow's semen," I remind him.

Stevie shakes her head. "Not something I want to spend any time thinking about."

"Maybe Pete killed Ava, and he invented the boyfriend to throw us off." Todd is guaranteed to come up with outlandish suggestions.

"Why would Pete brand his wife with that message?" Stevie asks him.

"Again, to throw us off."

I push my chair back and stand. "Pete isn't high on the list of suspects. I bet he knows a half dozen ways to make someone disappear without a trace. Let's quit before this meeting deteriorates any further." As the room empties out, I check my phone and see another missed call from Kenny, my ex-husband. "What the hell does he want?" I say a bit too loudly.

"Someone bothering you?" Stevie asks, coming back into the conference room.

"Just my ex, Sergeant Kenny Gayle," I say in a low voice. "I've missed three calls from him today. I can't think what he wants. Interacting with him is usually a painful experience and something I avoid like the plague."

Stevie closes the door, so we're out of Nick and Todd's earshot. "You divorced a while ago, didn't you?" She tilts her head to one side, and a look of concern crosses her face.

"Yeah. The year before last."

"Maybe it's time to hit the dating scene. You're an attractive woman."

"It's usually criminals that ask me out on a date," I snicker. "On the few occasions that it's a stand-up guy, I always decline. Even after two years of separation from Kenny, things are still too raw for me to consider starting a new relationship."

"Wow. Kenny really did a number on you."

"I guess." His walking out on me shattered my confidence. Not wanting to get into that with Stevie, I put my phone away and open the conference room door. "Check social media. I'd like to know what people are saying about Ava's death."

"Probably 'Ding dong, the witch is dead,' but I'll look," she says as we step out of the room.

"Keep an open mind. It's not unknown for killers to brag about their crimes online."

***

MY PHONE BEEPS as I climb into my Bureau car to drive home. Two more missed calls from Kenny. Something is up, but I decide to wait until I have a glass of wine in my hand before calling him. I need to dull my mind before the inevitable argument.

My four years of marriage to Kenny were rocky, but I never saw his affair coming. Shame on him and shame on me. He ran off with his gym instructor. Shaylin is a pretty young thing and thirteen years his junior. On the couple of occasions when I've needed to speak to her, she behaved like a complete bitch.

Kenny's parents were wealthy, so he's a trust fund kid, but I never saw a penny of that money when we divorced two years ago. We sold the house, and the settlement left me with enough money for a deposit on a more modest place—a nicely converted miner's cabin. I don't know that even one wall of the original house is left, but people renovate rather than build from scratch to get around regulations.

It's not late, but the outside lights on the garage come on as I pull into my driveway. There are a few things I don't especially like about the place. The front door opening into the living room, for example. Or the fact that it only has two bedrooms. But the house is gingerbread-cute, and it was all I could afford.

I dump my bag on the kitchen counter and retrieve a wine glass from the cupboard and a bottle of chardonnay from the fridge. Pouring myself a full glass, I gulp down half

46

of the soothing liquid before picking up my phone and selecting Kenny's number from my contacts. I don't know why I still hang on to his information because there is no reason for us to interact outside of work.

So what does he want?

Kenny picks up on the second ring. "Where the hell have you been? I've been calling you all day."

"Spare me the lecture, Kenny, and get to what you have to say," I snap. "Did somebody die?"

"It's Jasmin. She was picked up last night for being drunk and disorderly outside a bar in town."

Jasmin is my sister. She's three years younger than me and has been a ball of trouble since the day she was born. My parents couldn't control her. She became pregnant twice, had two terminations, and was arrested for shoplifting all before she was twenty. Doubtless, I have hundreds of relatives in India, but Jasmin is my only family in the US except for my uncle Ajay Viera. And he doesn't count. Ajay and I rarely see one another, and that is fine by me. The last time we met was at my father's funeral. He told me that my chosen profession reflects poorly on the family name. Like I was going to thank him for that pearl of wisdom.

"Where is Jasmin now?" I ask Kenny.

"We released her mid-morning."

"Did *you* pick her up?" He is vindictive enough to arrest my sister just for the sport of it.

"Not guilty. Jasmin was so high on coke and booze she could barely stand. The arresting officer said she was trying to pick a fight with passers-by."

"Damn. I'll try and find her."

"You're welcome, Cass." He says curtly and ends the call.

Whenever I see Jasmin—which thankfully isn't often—she's always two weeks clean and sober. Always just started going regularly to AA and Nar-Anon meetings. She's only ever been to rehab once. I doubt I'd believe her if she told me she was going again.

She's never given me the name of her dealer. If I ever find who it is, I'll hunt him down and bust him. He doesn't sound like a drug lord, just some petty lowlife. I'll turn him over to the locals—Detective Finch, not a moron like Reed.

Whenever I meet her at the door to her apartment, she is either manic, telling me about the most insignificant parts of her life, or she's sullen and withdrawn, giving me nothing but yes-no answers and icy stares.

Often, she is excited that she's found Jesus. *For the umpteenth time.* Of course, I don't have anything against that, but her faith is as deep as an application of lotion. It's gone after a couple of showers.

Somehow, she manages to hold down a job. She's a nurse at one of those plastic surgery places. They advertise that they can fix you up in no time with a boob job, tummy tuck, or butt lift. If drive-through liposuction were a thing, they'd do it.

The head doc is a slimy grease ball who I wouldn't trust to file my nails. He must either tolerate Jasmin's moods and hangovers, or she puts out the most amazing sex. I'm guessing the former because she's never been able to hang onto a boyfriend for more than a week or two.

I call Jasmin's cell phone, but a recording says, "You know what to do."

"I heard you were picked up. Call me."

I pace the living room for a half-hour until she finally calls.

"What do you want?" are the first words I hear.

"Where are you, Jaz?" I ask, figuring I need to know that before I piss my sister off, and she hangs up.

"At a friend's house."

"A guy?"

"Well yeah. I'm not gay, am I?" Jasmin's voice is dripping with sarcasm.

"Tell me where and I'll come pick you up."

"You're always so predictable, Cass. Always trying to rescue me from the big bad world."

"You know you need rescuing sometimes."

"Not today, and I'm working tomorrow, so you can fuck off." Jasmin hangs up, and I'm left staring at my iPhone, wondering what to do about my baby sister.

I flop onto the couch. She doesn't know that I can track her phone, so I summon up the app. She's about two miles from here in a low-rent district.

Realistically, I've not eaten much all day, and the wine has made me lightheaded. I need to fix myself something to eat before I do anything.

I'm not an expert cook, one of the many things Kenny complained about. But I know enough basic recipes to get by. I take boneless chicken thighs, zucchini, red bell peppers, onions, and mushrooms from the fridge and chop them.

I don't know what I'd do without the electric skillet. It's still sitting on the counter from this morning when I used it to make breakfast. I sauté the diced chicken, then toss in the vegetables.

Sitting on a stool at the breakfast bar, I gobble the stir-fry too quickly and give myself indigestion. I need a roommate to talk to, someone to at least slow me down at mealtimes. A couple of tablets from a jumbo bottle of antacid, and I'm feeling ready to confront Jasmin.

Five minutes later, I'm out the front door and climb in the black sedan. Jasmin's location on Santa Fe Avenue is unchanged from when I first looked. It's ten-fifteen p.m., and I'm guessing she's planning to spend the night with whoever she's picked up.

It's a short two miles, and I pull up in front of a white stucco house. Thirty years ago, the homes in this street would have been nicely maintained. But now, the front yard is full of thigh-high grass and weeds, the stucco is cracked, and tiles are missing off the roof. There might as well be a sign in the front yard saying nobody living here gives a rat's ass.

The drapes are not drawn, and the lights are on. I move to the sidewalk. Adjusting my position, I see Jasmin reclining on the couch. It looks like she tried to dye her hair brown, but it's too light a color and looks odd with her Indian skin tone. Sitting beside her is a scrawny-looking white guy with long greasy hair wearing a tee shirt and jeans.

She has her hand inside his fly while his arm is up her skirt. Empty beer cans litter the floor around them. This isn't the doctor she works for by any stretch of the imagination. I shake my head, wondering if she met this guy today after getting out of the lockup. Don't get me wrong, we've all had one-night stands, but this is a pattern of behavior with her. She bounces from guy to guy, looking for her soul mate or just crazy-good sex. I'm not sure she ever finds either.

I feel like a voyeur, and I'd rather not see what is about to happen next, especially since she's my sister. Stepping away from the window, I play in my mind how the discussion will go if I hammer on the front door and confront Jasmin. Not that I begrudge her sex just because I'm not getting any.

Sex isn't the issue. Jasmin's arrest for being drunk and disorderly tells me her life is spiraling out of control. I've seen it many times before. It's sad because she rents her own place and has a decent job, whatever I might think of the guy she works for.

In the end, I head back to the car and drive home, a bitter taste in my mouth. I feel I'm supposed to protect her. Our mother asked me as much right before she died. But Jasmin has never let me do anything other than a lousy job of being her big sister.

Chapter Seven

THE NEXT MORNING, Stevie and I leave work and head to the police station to interview Pete Barlow. But not before ensuring Nick and Todd are focused on locating the owner of the blue minivan.

"I want to swing by the Barlow residence on the way," I tell Stevie after we climb into the black sedan. "It's one thing for Jason to tell us Pete and Ava led separate lives, but I want to see it for myself. Can you navigate?"

"Sure thing, boss." Stevie is unusually quiet, and I wonder what she's brooding about.

"You can confide in me if you want," I tell her softly.

"It's nothing."

So now I know it is something, but I'm not about to press her for details.

"Left at the next intersection," Stevie says after consulting her phone.

"Ah, I remember now."

"It's Chuck—you know him as Officer Mason. I thought we were exclusive, but my roommate says she saw him talking to a long-term girlfriend he says he's broken up with. Apparently, they were acting pretty chummy with one another."

"Kissing and cuddling?"

"An embrace, and he looked very pleased to see her."

"You might be overreacting. Ask him about it. Some people stay friends after breaking up. But if he doesn't give you an honest answer, you need to find someone else."

"Thanks."

"I know from experience that being lied to is the worst thing. But I'm the last person to ask for dating advice. I told you things didn't work out with Kenny."

"Not to beat a dead horse, but you're beautiful. I'm sure lots of men find your black hair, chocolate-brown eyes, and dark skin attractive. Detective Finch, for starters.

"And you know this how?"

"Chuck thinks you're hot. And you only have to see the way men look at you when you're not watching. Detective Finch is always checking out your butt."

"Good to know. But after being on the shelf for so long, dating seems like a big step." A couple of beats later, I continue. "That was a smooth move, Agent Wells, to get me talking about my love life."

We giggle loudly, then lapse into silence until I say, "Did you find any chatter about Ava's death on social media?"

"Oh, wow. While I didn't see a 'ding, dong the witch is dead,' most people are saying good riddance. Then there are all sorts of rumors. Things like she was a member of a satanic cult, or her death was a twisted sex crime. A lot of cruel remarks."

"People are saying these things because she was a

woman?"

"I don't think the comments would be quite so salacious if she were a man. The fact that the killer wrote something on Ava's body has leaked, but not everyone knows what it said. People are speculating it was an occult symbol like the sigil of Lucifer or the numbers 666."

"Sigil of Lucifer? You sound well informed about satanic signs."

"It's also called the seal of Satan. It came up in a case we studied at the academy. Also, I once knew a guy who was into satanic tattoos. I ditched him when I learned he went to, uh, meetings."

"You never can tell about folk." I shake my head while I negotiate the traffic and turn onto Juniper Way.

"The tats should have been a clue, but I was barely eighteen at the time and rebelling against my parents." She hesitates, "Oh damn, Chuck is here."

I pull up in front of the Barlow house and see a very bored-looking Officer Mason guarding the scene. "Act natural," I tell her. "Don't say anything about your suspicions. Wait until you know more."

"Good morning ladies, I mean agents," Mason says, lifting the crime scene tape for us to duck underneath. "You're my first visitors of the day." He prints our names on a clipboard.

"You drew the short straw again?" I say.

"No, I'm the most junior officer."

"How much longer are they going to have you standing here?"

"They're releasing the scene at the end of the day. Say,

Stevie, my sister came to town yesterday for a quick visit. I'd like you to meet her this evening if you have the time."

"Your sister?" She looks surprised, then catches herself. "That would be lovely."

"Seven at my place? She's staying with me for a couple of days. I'm giving her my bed while I sleep on the couch. I thought we could all go out for a bite and drinks."

"Sure."

Stevie gives me a look as we climb the front stoop.

At thirty-four, I'm ten years older than she, and I reflect on the ups and downs of young love as we step inside the split-level home.

"*His sister?*" She says after closing the door. "I don't usually have trust issues with men. I'm going to kill my roommate."

"It was probably an honest mistake on her part."

Stevie shakes her head.

The metallic odor of blood hangs in the air. Doorknobs and frames are covered with black fingerprint dust. Through the open kitchen door, I can see numbered evidence markers still dotted around the counters and floor.

To my left, there's a living room. I want to skip it for now—I'm more interested in the sleeping arrangements. "Let's look up there." I indicate a half flight of stairs that may lead to the bedrooms. "I want to see just how much Pete and Ava ran into one another."

"To know whether he's telling the truth about not seeing her boyfriend?" Stevie asks.

"Yeah. Also, the ME pointed out that Pete should have spotted Ava was high. Heck, we run into enough junkies in our line of work to know what it looks like."

"Perhaps they'd both moved on to other people, and he just didn't care."

"Wouldn't he care on just a human level if the woman he's been married to for decades starts to self-destruct?"

A frown creases Stevie's forehead. "What about the boyfriend? It doesn't sound like he was looking out for her either."

"Good point." I try a door at the back of the house, and we step into an addition containing a separate living space. The kind you might build for an aging parent.

I'm guessing the room was untidy even before the search. There are two recliners, a television, and a coffee maker atop an otherwise bare desk. I see a charger cable and assume forensics took the laptop. A microwave stands on a small fridge. I tug open the door and see it's filled with instant meals and cans of Michelob Ultra.

"You could live here and never need to go into the rest of the house," Stevie observes.

"This isn't new construction. We should ask Pete if it was built for a parent."

"When the marriage fell apart, one of them moved in here."

A door opens into a bedroom with masculine furnishings and an unmade bed. Strewn on the floor with the covers is a pair of pajamas my father might have worn. Holes in the bottom sheet show where techs have taken sections for DNA testing. A variety of condom packets are scattered atop a nightstand.

"Looks like Pete lived here," Stevie says, eyeing the male

shaving products in the tiny bathroom.

"There's even a separate way out." I cross the living room to an outside door and twist the deadbolt, stepping onto a small deck. It overlooks an overgrown fenced yard that ends in woodland. Stairs lead down from the deck to a path that snakes around the side of the house toward the street. "Assuming Ava got the rest of the house, they could have gone weeks without ever seeing each other."

We make our way back to the original part of the house and come across the master bedroom. The closet and the dresser drawers reveal only Ava's clothing, and the bathroom is filled with feminine products.

"I got my question answered," I tell her. "Why doesn't Jason's report mention that Pete was occupying the separate living space at the back? That's a detail he should have told you. It's also a conflict of interest for the police forensic lab, considering they think Pete is a suspect."

"What can you do?"

"Nothing much at this point, but if we find another scene connected to this case, I'll think about calling in an FBI forensic team from the Sacramento Field Office."

***

ARRIVING AT THE police station and having Detective Finch take us to the interview room where Pete Barlow is seated with his attorney-friend feels like déjà-vu. The one pleasant difference is not meeting Detective Reed.

Pete and Greg Hays stand when we enter the room, but there are no friendly handshake greetings this time.

Instead, Hays asks me, "Why is my client still in custody? You haven't produced a shred of evidence showing he had anything to do with his wife's death."

"Your client's release is not up to the FBI. But until we know more, he remains a person of interest," I reply as we settle at the table.

"Unless someone changed the constitution, you can't detain a person without charges," Hays bellows, waving his finger at us.

"Perhaps Detective Finch can give you some answers."

Finch shoots me a stern look. "As Agent Viera rightly says, your client is a person of interest, and California law allows us to hold him in custody for forty-eight hours." Finch glances at his watch. "He's been here for twenty-six hours, so I ask both of you to be patient a little longer. I am going to Mirandize him today. Peter Barlow, you have the right to remain silent. Anything you say can and will be used against you in a court of law. You have the right to an attorney. If you cannot afford an attorney—"

"Yeah, yada, yada," Pete says, "I know how this works. Ask your questions so I can get out of here and take a shower; put on fresh clothes."

Once again, I'm the lead interrogator. "At your wife's autopsy, the ME found evidence of serious drug use."

"I told you yesterday that she started hitting the oxys hard after she injured her ankle." Pete crosses his arms over his chest and leans back in his seat.

"There's evidence that she snorted coke and used IV drugs like crystal meth."

"That's not possible," Pete spits.

"Are you saying you weren't aware of this?" I fix my eyes on Pete.

"I'm saying I don't believe you."

I open a folder and pull out a glossy of Ava's left inside arm, sliding it across the table. Pete gawks at it with genuine surprise.

"See the needle marks." I use a pen as a pointer to circle the red spots. "Her veins are withered from IV drug use."

Pete shakes his head. "I knew about the coke but not the crystal meth."

"Then maybe you can explain this." I slide him another photo of a partly opened bag of white powder. "It's been identified as coke. About half a grand's worth."

"I have never seen that. Where did you find it?"

"At the back of a cupboard in the kitchen." I slide him a photo showing the package in place before it was removed.

"I never go in that part of the house."

"Where do you live?" I know the answer, but I have to hear it from him.

"Ava and I separated eighteen months ago. Not physically, but emotionally. With the downturn in the housing market, we couldn't afford to sell the house and get separate places. So, I agreed to move into the addition at the back of the house. It has its own outside door, so we never needed to see one another. I paid the utility bills and gave Ava what amounted to a monthly spousal maintenance payment."

"I didn't notice you weren't together at your retirement party last year."

"We were good at putting on an act when the need

arose." His face clouds with sadness.

"When was the addition built?"

"Five years ago. Ava's mother got to the point where she couldn't take care of herself. Alzheimer's. After she passed, it stayed empty for a year until Ava and I decided to use it to get away from each other."

"If you never saw her, how did you know she was abusing pain pills?"

He thinks for a moment. "Holder's wife told me. She used to meet Ava for coffee once a week."

"One of the big questions is where your wife got the drugs from."

"I have no idea. As a retired detective, I couldn't be involved in any of that, so I left her to her own devices."

"You must have known something about her drug habit. Didn't you care at all about your wife's health? You were married for almost thirty years."

"Agent Viera, I must object," Hays snaps. "You're badgering my witness."

"It is telling that you called him your witness, not your client. We're not in a courtroom now, Mr. Hays. I can badger him all I want." I turn to Pete. "Are you sure you don't want better representation, Mr. Barlow?"

Hays goes into a huff but doesn't speak, while his client says, "Greg stays. I have done nothing wrong, and I have every confidence in him."

"I'll ask you again, Mr. Barlow," I insist. "You knew your wife was taking at least pain pills and coke, and you know what drugs can do to a person. Weren't you concerned enough to get her some help?"

Pete slams his hand hard on the table, his gaze turning icy. "No, I was not concerned. Ava turned into a bitch these last few years. I secretly hoped the drugs would kill her."

I let his words hang in the air for a moment before saying, "We spoke to some of the board members she worked with. They said she was . . . disagreeable. Why do you think that was?"

"Ava took her mother's Alzheimer's diagnosis and death hard. It changed her, and it got to the point where I couldn't put up with her any longer."

"You heard about the message the killer left on your wife's body—'YOU ARE NEXT'. We think it was intended for you. In fact, we believe Ava's murder could be some kind of revenge against you."

"If that's the case, the killer failed miserably because I'm glad she's gone—if I didn't make that clear enough earlier."

"Aren't you concerned that the killer might come after you next?"

"Well, I'm safe here in the lockup."

"You've put a lot of people in prison over the years. You must be able to make a list of people who wish you harm."

"Write down the names of everyone I've put away. There's your list of people who want to harm me."

I catch an odd look in his eyes. "You know who might have done this, don't you?"

He hesitates for a long moment before saying, "I'm through answering questions. Take me back to my cell. By the clock on the wall, you have twenty-one hours to charge me, or you have to release me."

He laughs haughtily as if he has the upper hand.

Chapter Eight

I BARREL THROUGH the door to our offices and pull up short, surprised by the presence of a visitor. "Uh, hello, Preston," I stammer.

Assistant Special Agent in Charge Preston Myles Junior, my boss and the top agent at the site, is just leaving. In some ways, the guy is totally cool, calling agents by their first name. He's also a bully whose only real interest is playing politics and climbing the FBI ladder. Fortunately for us, he mostly harasses other departments. I sometimes think he resents managing a remote outpost like ours, with only eleven agents divided into three teams. It's probably the equivalent of being banished to Siberia for someone who aspires to be upwardly mobile.

Myles is trim and obviously takes care of himself. He wears rimless glasses, and his naturally curly hair is plastered down with product. Put a white coat on him, and he'd pass for a hospital doctor. But, as usual, he's wearing a dark suit, white shirt, and college tie—the official uniform of the FBI.

Stevie doesn't stop as quickly as I do, and she elbows me

hard in the back. I try not to react. Falling over each other isn't a good look.

"I've just been talking to Nick and Todd. The work they're doing is excellent. I hear you've just come from speaking with Pete Barlow." Myles pauses, waiting for a briefing.

"We're about to rule him out as a suspect, but there's still a question whether he knew about the coke found at his house. The attack on his wife was savage and done by someone with a lot of pent-up rage. The perpetrator could be angry at Ava, but we think she was more likely killed as a warning to Pete."

"Someone from one of his past cases with a score to settle?" Myles raises his eyebrows.

"More than likely. We'd hoped Pete would be able to give us a shortlist, but he wasn't forthcoming."

"Why do you think that is? If you're right about the motive, the killer has to be after him next."

"He's holding something back. Possibly an occasion where he skirted the law."

"Sounds like you're making progress. Keep up the good work, Cassie." With that, Myles disappears out the door.

"Phew," Stevie says as we step into Todd's office, "I thought we were in for a tongue lashing."

Nick and Todd are seated with their eyes glued to the three computer monitors.

"Looks like you two impressed the boss, so we won't have to see him for a couple of days." I give Nick a long look. "Have you solved the case? Cured cancer?"

"No, but we've found the owner of the blue minivan."

Nick is trying to appear nonchalant.

"Who is it?" Stevie asks.

"Pull up chairs. You need to hear the whole story." Nick shuffles his chair deeper into the office to make room, but it would be too crowded with all of us seated. Stevie and I opt to stand behind Todd's chair and look over his shoulders.

"Over to you, wonder boy." Stevie cranes her neck, eyeballing the nearest screen, which is filled with the picture of a fast-food eatery.

"As you already know, I've been searching for camera footage in the immediate area of the murder. I was looking for anything that shows a dark blue minivan with a long scratch down one side. This is the only video I've found so far, but it's killer. Uh, no pun intended. Eight minutes after we saw the minivan leave the Barlow residence, an identical vehicle pulls into a McDonald's drive-through three blocks away."

Todd's hands glide across the keyboard, and a different image appears on the screen. I lean in for a closer look.

"You can see the same long gash on one side." Todd's words are coming rapidly. He's in full geek mode. "Overgrown bushes block part of the license plate, and all we see of the driver is his arm as he picks up his order—"

"We can get their credit card receipts from the eatery," I interrupt excitedly.

"Let him finish," Nick snaps. "What he's found is brilliant."

"Despite the bushes, the camera gives us the last three digits from the plate—four, two, nine." Todd plays the video to get the best image. "We also get a view of the hood, and that's enough to tell us it's a Chrysler Voyager."

"The problem is that we don't know the model year," Nick says. "I ran a DMV search, and forty-seven vehicles across the state match the model and the partial plate. It's a popular minivan as it can hold seven people.

"It was speeding past the cameras at Barlow's neighbors, so we all missed something on the side of the vehicle." Todd's words come at a mile a minute as he works the keyboard, selecting a different view from the camera.

"There's writing on the side," I say breathlessly. "But it's been mostly scraped off by the damage."

"I have image processing software that can recover the words. Would you like to know what it says?" Todd rubs his hands together like a magician about to pull the proverbial rabbit out of the hat

"The suspense is killing me," Stevie says.

"Sunshine Assisted Living, Cedar Springs."

Nick takes over the narrative: "I ran a new DMV search, and they own a vehicle that matches the model and the partial plate." A look of triumph crosses his face.

"I bet it's stolen. I don't see an assisted living resident pulling off a vicious knife attack," Stevie suggests. She's probably right, but I flash her a frown. At times, she can be a little negative without realizing it.

"There you go again, Stevie, dashing all my hopes and dreams," Todd quips.

"Let's go talk to them now," I say. "Nick and Stevie, you're with me."

They both check their weapons and shove spare clips into their pants pockets, but I'm not seeing a gun battle with anyone at the assisted living facility. Still, it's best to always be prepared.

As we hurry out the door, Todd looks like the kid that no one wants on their team.

***

THE DRIVE INTO Sunshine Assisted Living Village takes us past a sign showing they also provide independent housing and care for individuals living with Alzheimer's and dementia. Once we're through the wide-open gates, the road is lined on both sides with compact houses rubbing shoulders on tiny lots. They are all nicely painted in pale blue or sand yellow with white trim.

"Could you see yourself living here when you retire?" Nick asks, pushing his aviator sunglasses higher on his nose. He always wants to drive. He's not particularly sexist, but I can't help thinking he has a problem being driven around by a woman.

"When I'm old and gray, I suppose," says Stevie. "But it's not a phase of my life I'm especially looking forward to."

"I'd like to retire early and travel while I'm still active," Nick says, slowing the car for a speed bump. "Sitting on my porch and watching the sun go down doesn't appeal."

"You're in the wrong job if you want to make enough money to do some serious traveling," I tell him. "Hotels and airfares are expensive. Even if you choose RVing, it's not cheap."

"Maybe I'll find a rich widow to marry." After a pause, Nick continues, "There's the main building and a sign pointing to the office."

The place is two-story and as big as a motel. I suspect this is where they house the residents who need round-the-clock care. "Let's keep driving. It looks like the road loops around the back. Maybe they park their vehicles there."

"Look at Pete Barlow," Stevie says. "He makes it to retirement, and his wife turns into a bitch he can't stand. Then someone kills her."

I turn to her in the back. "It can happen, so choose your spouse wisely."

"How's Officer Mason?" Nick asks, sighting Stevie in the rearview.

"He's not about to move in with me. Why is my love life always such a hot topic?"

"We're not getting any, and we can live vicariously through you." I know Nick broke up with his girlfriend a month ago.

"Like I'm going to give you details," she huffs. "I didn't know I was having sex for all of you. That's majorly creepy."

Nick slows the car to a crawl as we reach the back of the main building and pass a dark blue passenger van parked in the lot.

"You see our guy's license plate?" I ask him.

"Negative. This is a full-size van. But the color and the lettering on the side match the minivan we saw in the video."

"They must run a shuttle service into town for the residents," Stevie adds.

"Have they reported it stolen?" I ask Nick.

"Not that I could find. But there's a CCTV camera

mounted on the back of the building. Maybe it snapped a picture of the killer."

"Let's go back to the office and ask them."

After making a U-turn, Nick drives to where we saw the sign for the office and pulls into a parking slot. "You think three agents will overwhelm them?"

"Well, I'm not sitting in the car," Stevie snaps.

"I was going to volunteer to stay here," Nick turns and tells her. "But you are the most junior agent."

"Enough! We're all going in," I snap.

The automatic entrance doors open with a whoosh of air. There's a whiff of disinfectant masking some nasty odors. The signs for the office take us down a corridor and into a spacious room decorated in pastels.

A middle-aged woman looks up from behind a desk. "How may I help you?"

I step forward. "I'm Agent Cassie Viera with the FBI, and these people are Agents Stone and Wells. We'd like to ask you about a vehicle that may be missing from here."

"I'm Mary." She comes around her desk and greets us individually. "Three FBI agents for a missing vehicle. Isn't that a bit excessive?"

"It was used by an individual to commit a serious crime."

"Oh, my." Mary's hands fly to her cheeks.

"It's a dark blue Chrysler Voyager minivan." I hand her a slip of paper bearing the license number. "Can you see if you can locate it for us?"

Mary sits behind the desk and reaches to a cabinet full of ring binders. She selects one and opens it on her desk.

"Let's see. Yes, that's one of ours. It should be in the lot." She points to the back of the building.

"It isn't. Do you know where else it might be?"

"Well, I don't know." Mary strokes her neck, thinking. "It goes between here and town. Nowhere else."

"Where do you keep the keys?" Stevie asks.

"The driver is supposed to place them on top of one of the rear tires."

"So, anyone could have driven it?" Nick exclaims, his tone incredulous.

"No one uses it unless they are authorized," Mary insists.

"Someone has driven it and used it to commit a murder," I say.

"Oh, my. Let me get a hold of the driver for you. Sam will know where it is."

"You'd better pray he doesn't," Stevie whispers.

Ten minutes later, we're in a room I'm guessing they use for talking to prospective residents. A man in his late fifties named Sam sits across the table from the three of us, looking suitably intimidated. His salt and pepper hair is thin on top and at his temples. My phone is taping the interview, and Stevie has a notepad out.

"What's your last name, Sam?" I ask.

"It's Jackson. Samuel Jackson, like the actor. Do I need a lawyer?"

"Have you committed a crime?" Nick asks.

"I don't think so. But you never know with you feds. I think you make stuff up sometimes."

"Were investigating a murder committed yesterday," I

tell him. "And I can assure you we're not making that up. Are you the perpetrator?"

"Of course not." Sam wrinkles his nose.

"Then you don't need a lawyer. But please tell us where you were between the hours of eight a.m. and nine a.m. yesterday."

"Goodness. Uh, I got in to work at eight o'clock and talked to Mary, then at eight-thirty, I ran a group of residents into town."

"Where in town?"

"I drop them where they ask me."

"And yesterday?"

"Let's see, Safeway and the Western Bank."

"Do you know the residents' names?"

"Only the first names of some of them. Mary will have their full details."

"Do you recognize this license number?" I slide a sheet of paper across the table to him.

He pulls reading glasses from his pocket. "Yeah, that's Bertha. But I took Ada yesterday."

"You give the vans girl's names?" Stevie asks in surprise.

"Yeah." He looks embarrassed for a moment. "We have a full-size van and a minivan—Ada and Bertha. We take Bertha when we only have one or two passengers."

"And you always leave the keys on the back wheel?"

"Sure, it's handy. You sure Bertha isn't there?"

"Positive," Nick says. "You didn't notice, uh, Bertha missing yesterday?"

"I saw she wasn't in her usual spot. But I had complained to maintenance that the fuel gauge wasn't working. I thought they'd taken her in to fix it. They do that sometimes without telling me."

"Did Bertha used to have a long scrape down the driver's side?"

"Yeah, that was me. There's this wall—"

"When was the last time you saw Bertha for sure?" I interrupt.

"The day before yesterday. In the morning. I gassed up Bertha and Ada."

"That's all the questions we have for you," I say, looking at Stevie and Nick for confirmation. "Thank you, Sam. You've been a big help."

Sam's complexion improves, now the interview is over. "It's the darndest thing, someone taking poor Bertha."

Back in Mary's office, we have her dump the last two weeks of surveillance video onto a memory stick. We'll give it to Todd for him to work his magic.

"I hope you get Bertha back for us. She has sentimental value," Mary says.

"If we find her, she will be held as evidence," I say, thinking my words sound strange. I set a business card on the desk in front of her. "You should contact your insurance company and tell them it's a total loss. They can talk to me if they have questions about you not being able to recover it."

"What do you think about giving vehicles girl's names," Stevie asks as we reach our black sedan. A blast of stifling air hits us as we climb inside.

"I think I'd go with names like Rocket or Beast," Nick says, starting the engine and pulling on his seatbelt.

"That speaks volumes about you," Stevie quips.

"What do you mean by that?"

"You're a masculine kind of guy. It's a compliment. How about you, boss?"

"I'm at the other end of the spectrum. I called my first car Primrose. But no one gets to analyze me."

Chapter Nine

"THE MINIVAN WAS stolen," Todd says, aghast. "Damn. After all that work."

I'm standing in the aisle outside his office. "It's not lost. The police have an APB out for it. We'll catch the guy, thanks to you."

"How did he know the van would be at the assisted living facility, with the keys on the wheel?" Nick sips on a mug of coffee.

"Maybe he has a friend or relative there, and he's visited them in the past, though I'm not sure that helps us." I hand Todd a memory stick. "That's surveillance video from the facility. I'm hoping it will answer the question of how he got there. The place isn't walking distance from anywhere."

"On it," Todd says, giving me finger pistols.

"Listen up." Stevie is moving toward me and staring at her phone, her forehead creased with surprise. "I just got a text from my contact at the police department. They've charged Pete Barlow with his wife's murder."

"What?" Nick and I say in unison.

"On what grounds?" I ask. "Is there fresh evidence we

don't know about?"

"My, uh, contact doesn't say."

"Well, ask him," Nick says, waving his coffee mug at Stevie.

"Hold up," I say. "Better to do it through the proper channels. I'll call Detective Finch."

I dial, and he answers on the second ring. I put the phone on speaker. "I just heard—"

"I know what you're going to say," Finch replies. "It wasn't my decision."

"Then whose decision was it? I thought you were the lead detective on the case."

"I thought so too. Apparently, it came out of a meeting Reed had with Chief Holder."

"What about the blue minivan? It's not a coincidence that it arrived at the murder scene around the time Ava was killed."

"Beats me. I'll see what I can find out and call you back."

He hangs up.

I turn to Stevie and Nick, shrugging. "While we wait for Todd to process the video from the assisted living place, I'd like to go over the motives for killing Ava and make sure we're not overlooking anything. I also feel the need to use the whiteboard, so let's move to the conference room."

"You're discounting Pete killing her?" Nick asks.

"If we believe she was killed by the driver of the blue minivan, the timeline doesn't work for the husband. The minivan leaves the Barlow residence at nine-oh-three and then goes to McDonald's. Pete is detained at the gas station

74

at nine-thirty-six, driving in the direction of his house in his own car and wearing clothes without a trace of blood on them. Extremely unlikely he's the killer, but not impossible."

When we're settled around the table with mugs of coffee, I stand at the whiteboard and say, "Let's go through the reasons Ava might have been killed. Nick, give me one."

"It's random. A crazy tweaker feels compelled to kill someone for a reason that only makes sense to him."

"Great. I'm going to jot all the motives on the board, and then we'll discuss them."

I finish writing and say, "Stevie, another one, please."

"Ava's death was an act of revenge against Pete Barlow by someone who thinks he was wrongly convicted."

"Right. They may actually have been wrongly convicted or feel it was unjust," I say as I print it on the board. "Another one, Nick?"

"She didn't pay her drug dealer on time or at all. Or the dealer found out she'd revealed his name."

"Good. Especially if he's a member of a gang. The bar isn't very high for gang members to feel disrespected. Any more, Stevie?"

"Ava's man-friend became jealous. Maybe he caught her sleeping with someone else.

"Or he just found evidence that she had?" I jot it down. "Any more?

Stevie shakes her head.

Nick says, "The husband hired someone to kill his wife. We know he hated her."

"Right. Let's review them and figure out the next

actions. Let's start with a crazy tweaker. This guy will be the hardest to catch. How should we go about it?"

"Go through recent knife attacks looking for anything similar," Nick says.

"Yes. That's yours, Nick, though we'll prioritize the order we work on them at the end."

"That's what I get for opening my big mouth," he says with a rueful grin.

"Was the knife ever recovered from the scene?" Stevie nurses her coffee mug.

"No, it was not, so the perp took it with him. Nor were there any knives missing from the knife block, so it doesn't seem impulsive. That scenario is even less likely when you consider the planning required to steal the minivan. Stevie, how should we follow up if Ava was killed by someone Pete sent to prison?"

She hesitates a moment. "Go through Pete's old cases. It's not like he was forthcoming when we asked him for a list."

I note it on the board. "Okay, that's yours, Stevie, but you'll need help because of the sheer volume of cases. Give priority to people who were recently released from jail."

She nods.

"Next, Ava's death at the hands of her drug dealer is pending for the moment. Jason-the tech-guy sent a sample of the coke found at the residence to the FBI lab in Sacramento. They may be able to match it to a single dealer. Next, a jealous man friend. The worst kind. Anyone?"

"Did Todd trace the phone Ava was calling?" Stevie asks. "That would be the best way to identify the fancy man."

"Not yet. I know he's working on it, and he sounded confident about tracing it." The marker squeaks as I make a note on the board. "There's one possibility we haven't mentioned. The man-friend and the drug supplier could be one and the same person."

"If Ava Barlow dated a drug dealer, that's risky behavior," Stevie gasps.

"The drug dealer might be a low-level guy with just a handful of customers. It doesn't alter how we investigate the murder, but it's something to keep in mind. Yes, Todd?" He's just come into the room, and his expression says he has something.

"I've got video of the minivan theft."

"Great. Any progress tracing the burner phone Ava was calling?"

"I've been kinda tied up with surveillance video. It's been turned off every time I've tried to ping it."

"Keep at it. In the meantime, Nick, you're looking for similar knife attacks, and Stevie, you're looking through Pete's last cases for someone particularly aggrieved. But first, let's check out what Todd has found."

My phone chimes as we step out of the room. I answer, "Yes, detective, I'm putting you on speaker."

"There's no new evidence against Pete," Finch says, "but they believe he hired a hitman. Reed thinks the hot chick Pete was boning helped him set it up."

"They have any kind of proof to support the hitman theory or the connection to Maura?" I ask.

"Just that Pete hated his wife."

"Are Reed and Holder just pulling ideas out of their asses?"

"Holder has me looking into the Maura-hitman angle. It may be a ploy to keep Pete in custody past the forty-eight-hour deadline."

"Unless you have strong evidence, any decent attorney will get the charges dropped and Pete released."

"Then it's a good job he's sticking with the lame-brain friend."

"You really think Pete had something to do with Ava's death?"

"Yeah, but I don't know what. Her death is too convenient for him. We also think he's connected to the bag of coke."

"Um." I'm lost for words.

"Sorry, but I've got to go," he says hastily.

After I end the call, Nick says, "You know Finch will do a decent job of investigating the hitman angle. Eliminating it if necessary."

"True. On the plus side, it's one less thing for us to look at," Stevie says.

"Let me show you what I've found." Todd takes a seat at his computer and works the keyboard while we stand behind him.

"The time of interest starts at twelve-oh-seven a.m., the night before the murder. It's a real grainy nighttime video, but I've managed to identify the motorcycle. It's a Yamaha TW200. One of those funny things with the small wheels. Like a clown drives at the circus."

"What motorcycle are you talking about?" Stevie asks

him.

"Just watch the video." Todd palms the mouse, and the footage starts to play.

To begin with, all we see is an inky parking lot. The Voyager minibus and the Transit passenger van are the only vehicles visible. Glowing white areas show where the infrared lights from the cameras illuminate the scene. The rest of the lot is a sea of gray and black tones.

A man riding a motorcycle comes in from the right. He stops between the camera and the back of the Voyager and uses his foot to lower the kickstand. He makes a motion like he's switching off the engine, then turns to face the camera, but it's impossible to make out his features. Apart from the bandanna covering his nose and mouth, I can't make out anything, not even if he is black or white.

We watch in silence as he strides to the side of the van, and his hand reaches above the rear tire.

"He knows exactly where to find the key," Stevie murmurs.

After unlocking the minivan's rear doors, he climbs inside the back.

"Now, what's he doing?" Stevie asks.

"Folding the seats down," Todd tells her.

"He's putting the bike inside," Nick exclaims. "He's a big dude. Look at the width of his shoulders."

The man disengages the kickstand and picks up the motorcycle effortlessly, rolling it into the back of the minivan.

"He's strong," I say. "How much does one of those weigh?"

"Two hundred and thirty pounds," Todd replies. "I looked it up just now. He's also a giant. The minivan is five feet ten inches high. I can't tell his height exactly because I don't know the angle of the camera, but the guy is several inches taller than the van."

"Can you get an exact figure if you study the video more?"

"Not within a couple of inches. There might be a tech in Sacramento who can."

"See that the lab gets a copy with a request for height and weight."

The perp closes the rear doors, hurries to the front, and climbs behind the wheel. Moments later, the minivan drives out of range of the camera.

"Does he appear on any other cameras?" I ask.

"None that are useful. This one gives the best view."

"Why did he steal this particular vehicle?" Nick rubs his eyes.

"So he could put his bike in the back. Or because he knew the van wouldn't be missed. Or both?" I suggest.

"But why didn't he just ride his bike to the house the morning he killed Ava?" Nick palms his chin.

"Maybe there's something conspicuous about him or the motorcycle that people would recognize," Stevie suggests. "Something we aren't able to see on the grainy nighttime video.

"It's possible," I say, interlacing my fingers and stretching my arms over my head. "These look like the actions of a hitman to you?" I ask. "I mean, a professional hitman, or woman, doesn't ride around on a clown motorcycle stealing vans in the middle of the night."

"Perhaps he's just starting out in the profession," Todd quips, grinning. "Or is killing people for money considered a trade?"

"Be serious for a moment," Nick tells him. "The boss is right. Despite the speed with which he steals the van, this is very amateur hour."

"And a pro wouldn't slash a woman to death," Stevie says. "A pro would have killed Ava Barlow with one quick silenced shot to the heart and one to the head. Reed and Holder's idea stinks."

Chapter Ten

JASMIN LIVES IN a run-down building on Pioneer Drive. I figure she won't tumble to the fact that I'm tracking her phone if I visit her at her apartment. I'm only two miles from my house, but the feel of the neighborhood is markedly different.

It's a soulless part of town. Gang symbols are spray-painted on walls and road signs. Weeds clog the front yards and cracks in the sidewalk.

I double-check the Bureau car is locked, then climb to the second floor. The walkway is open to the air, and the odor of rotting garbage slaps me in the face.

When I rap on her door, a scurrying sound comes from inside. Like Jasmin knows it's me, and she's hiding things she doesn't want me to see. After a long minute, the door cracks open on the chain, and I see a sliver of her tawny face and skinny frame.

"What the fuck do you want?" she snaps.

"Are you going to invite me in, sis?" I ask in as pleasant a voice as I can summon.

She curses again and releases the chain. I follow her

into a room furnished with estate-sale furniture. She's wearing extra-tight denim shorts that barely hide her butt cheeks and a torn white T-shirt. Distressed, I think they call it, though it looks like she may have ripped it herself.

The air is heavy with cigarette smoke, and I open a window to be able to breathe.

"Why did you do that?" she hisses.

I didn't come here to criticize her, but I can't help myself. "You're a nurse, Jasmin, for heaven's sake. You know what cancer sticks do to you."

"You get more like mom every time I see you." She settles into a worn recliner and studies her nails.

I prop my backside on the edge of the couch, wary of the stains I might sit on if I sink too far into the cushions. I want to tell Jasmin that she desperately needs a mother even though she's thirty-one, but I bite back the words. "How are things?" I ask, suddenly at a loss for words.

"How are things? You came all the way across town to ask me that? Look around and use your powers of deduction. Isn't that what the government pays you for?"

Her words surprise me. Jasmin is usually oblivious to the crappiness of her one-bedroom apartment and her ten-year-old car. I notice a pair of boxers on the floor. "Is someone else here?"

She follows my eyes. "Those are mine."

"Since when did you start wearing men's underwear? I step to the closed bedroom door and open it cautiously. The bed is unmade, but the closet-size room is empty,

"Why don't you ever believe me?" she pouts.

"Because you lie, Jasmin," I say, perching back on the

edge of the couch. "You lied to mom and dad all the time. You lie to me."

She glares at me in icy silence.

I check myself. The conversation isn't going the way I intended. "Sorry, Jaz. I just wanted to see you. I do worry that you're okay."

Her frosty look softens a bit. "Mom and dad gave you a nice life. I was left with nothing."

Jasmin blames her situation on everyone but herself. While I spent my teenage years focused on studying and a future career in law enforcement, she spent her time in high school chasing guys, partying, and smoking pot.

She was almost expelled when a teacher discovered her giving oral sex to Charley Winters in a stall in the boy's bathroom.

Fortunately, my dad knew the principal and convinced him that Jasmin was coerced into the act. She was only suspended for a week, but Charley's parents didn't have the same pull, and he was expelled.

At eighteen, Jasmin went to the local community college but dropped out in the middle of the first semester. She was pregnant and had a termination. A year later brought another pregnancy and another termination. Remembering that period of her life always feels like a gust of icy wind.

When she was twenty-three, she enrolled in a nursing course and somehow managed to graduate.

Since then, she's worked at more urgent cares, hospitals, and doctor's offices than I can count. Surprisingly, she's stuck with the job at the plastic surgeon's office for over two years now.

I know that nothing I say will change the course of her life. "It's been exactly a year since dad died," I say, "so I was thinking of walking to the cemetery and putting some flowers on his grave. If you want to come."

"Walk? Who walks anywhere anymore? You were dad's golden girl who could do no wrong. He was always riding me about something."

That's because she was such a screw-up. I swear her behavior sent mom and dad to an early grave. "Granted, their ideas of how young Indian women should behave were from another time and another culture, but they loved us both equally."

"If you think that, you must have slept through your childhood."

"I haven't eaten dinner yet. You want to grab some takeout?"

"No one delivers to this area, Cass. Anyway, I've got a half a sandwich in the fridge left over from lunch at the Peppermill."

"Someone took you out to lunch?" I know that's the only way she ever eats in a restaurant.

"Yeah. One of the patients wanted to thank me for the way I looked after her."

A spark of hope for her blooms in my chest. Then a magazine slithers off an end table to the floor. My gaze falls on a piece of a mirror and a single-edged razor blade that she must have covered up before she answered the door. I want to kill her, but I manage to swallow the thought. "Are you using again?"

She follows my gaze. "That's Derek's."

"You're saying you're not doing coke?"

"We all need something to take the edge off." Jasmin shakes her head at my ignorance for not knowing that.

"You remember the last time you were taking the edge off. It landed you in rehab." That time it was pills, lots of them. No one was quite sure whether she'd tried to kill herself.

"That was eight years ago before I went to nursing school. I'm a different person now. Wise up, Cass. Most people use recreational drugs now and then. The only reason you don't is because of your fancy job."

"Coming here was a mistake," I say, rising to my feet. "I thought we could have a little chat. Shoot the breeze like two sisters."

"The only thing you ever want to talk about is why I'm not like you. We're different people. With your job and your fancy qualifications, I thought you were brainy enough to figure that out."

"I know we're different, Jaz, but it's about right and wrong."

"What, you're going to bust me now? You're a self-righteous bitch. You should go."

"I hate parting like this," I beseech her.

"Yeah, well, you should try being a bit more civil instead of coming here and trying to lay down the law. Seems like you can't switch off your job."

I start to shake as I slip out her door, wondering why speaking to Jasmin always goes so horribly wrong.

Chapter Eleven

"AS YOU REQUESTED, I've been looking into knife assaults in case we're dealing with a serial killer," Nick tells me. "But after I discounted bar-fights—the ones where one idiot pulls a knife on another—I was left with nothing. I went back five years and searched up to a distance of seventy-five miles from here. NCIC shows no unsolved cases like the attack on Ava Barlow," he says, referring to the National Crime Information Center database.

"That's a shocker," I say, propping my butt on the edge of his desk. "It's been two days since she was killed, and we have nothing. I don't know what I'll tell Myles if he stops by for another progress report."

"Speak for yourself," Stevie cries over the top of the office walls. "I've been making progress."

"So, spill the beans," Nick whoops.

Stevie joins us, "I've been looking at folk arrested by Pete Barlow, who have recently been released from prison. Give me five more minutes to check out one of the names, and I'll show you what I've found."

"Let's have a meeting when you're ready," I tell her.

My phone rings. A glance at the caller ID shows it's Detective Finch. I step toward my office as I answer, "This had better be good."

"I have some forensic results for you. I'm standing outside your front entrance, but my code doesn't work."

"Myles changed all the codes yesterday," I say, stepping into the corridor. "The geeks picked up chatter about a threat to FBI offices."

"And we police schmucks weren't deemed worthy of a notification of the change?"

"I guess we forgot about you." I flash him a conciliatory grin.

Finch pockets his phone as I swing open the glass front door.

"I'm wondering what's so important that you couldn't have called."

"I thought you might be missing me." He gazes at me with a raised brow.

"Can't say that I was." I wink before leading the way inside.

"Let's say the air is fresher on this side of town." He follows me into our offices, carrying a battered leather briefcase.

"We have donuts today, thanks to Stevie. Help yourself." I indicate a pink box beside the coffee machine.

"You feds get all the perks, but I'm good." He pats his belly. "Got to watch my weight."

I grab an old-fashioned donut for myself and top up my coffee. I'll have to pay for the calories at the gym this evening.

Nick and Stevie appear, and we settle around the table. Finch pulls a brown folder from the briefcase he's deposited on the floor beside his chair.

"What's going on over at the police department?" I ask, thinking we usually hang out in his office.

"It's become politically incorrect to follow any line of inquiry not pointing to Pete Barlow's guilt. Holder had the nerve to suggest I'm not a team player."

Nick's brow creases. "Why does the chief have it in for the guy?"

"I don't know the details, but there's bad blood between them going back years. Holder's a straight shooter while Barlow's a cowboy. Let's say he wasn't above manipulating evidence if the need arose."

"Some of the people he arrested could be innocent?" Stevie exclaims. "That's a powerful motive for murder."

"Maybe it is a case of revenge," I say. "The perp went to the Barlow house looking for Pete and took his vengeance out on Ava instead."

"I've been compiling a list of people who Barlow arrested and who have been released in the last six months," Stevie says, consulting her notebook. "Out of the five names I've found, three have been making a lot of noise about Pete setting them up."

"Criminals always claim they were framed." Finch shrugs.

"The noise these three are making in the press is over the top. There are newspaper articles implying something was wrong with their trials. None of the articles blame Barlow. Yet."

"We have to be a bit careful what we say about Pete," Finch advises us. "I observed him being fast and loose with the truth. I don't know for a fact that he ever planted evidence."

"You're saying he lied on the stand?" Stevie persisted.

"Do not say anything outside of these four walls. Any suggestion that Pete lied under oath or planted evidence would create a lawsuit nightmare. Twenty-five years of cases would be opened back up."

I fix my eyes on Finch. "Knowing your friend Pete was corrupt changes where we put our resources. As Stevie says, a wrongful conviction is a powerful motive for murder. Was this what you came here to tell us? The best time to deliver this little gem was two days ago." I take a bite out of my donut and munch it angrily.

"That's not what I came to see you about, and you may be blowing my words out of proportion. Holder placed a rush on the DNA from the Barlow residence and got a thirty-six-hour turnaround. Fingerprints and DNA from Ava's bed match a small-time drug dealer, named Leo Kessler—"

"Wait a damn minute. Never mind the DNA, you would have had the fingerprint match yesterday," I snap, remembering the black forensic dust on the headboards in Pete and Ava's bedrooms. "Why were we not informed straight away?"

"I didn't know about the match to Kessler until this morning and came straight over here to tell you. Jason gave the results to Detective Reed, who failed to share them with me. He's trying to shut me out of the investigation."

"Why would he do that?" It makes me wonder what else the police department is holding back. I could kick myself for not bringing in an FBI forensic team. But it isn't too late to have them review the evidence.

"At my office, it's become sacrilege to believe that anyone other than Pete or his hitman may have killed Ava," Finch insists. "I can't look into it, but you can." His eyes flash to Stevie and Nick.

"What do you know about Kessler?" It irks me to see petty politics at the police department disrupt an investigation.

"Barlow arrested him for drug dealing seven years ago. Kessler's been out of jail for about a year and a half."

"He's on my list of five people to check out," Stevie adds, consulting her notebook. "Kessler is claiming that Pete shafted him."

"Pete wasn't completely crooked. He just massaged things a bit." Finch looks like he is regretting letting the genie out of the bottle.

"Do we think that Ava's man-friend and her drug dealer were the same individual?" I wonder aloud.

Finch nods. "It seems so. Ava was having sex with a guy who her husband arrested. Could be coincidence, I suppose."

I cannot stop myself from laughing out loud. "That's no coincidence. Kessler had some ulterior motive for supplying drugs to Ava and screwing her. If I had to guess, I'd say he was getting back at Pete. But we know Pete didn't care who his wife was having sex with."

"Ava must have told Kessler that for him to be ballsy

enough to screw her in the master bedroom," Nick suggests. "Otherwise, he'd have feared Pete coming after him with a shotgun."

"It was mighty convenient for Kessler that Pete never saw him," I say. "Had they met, Pete would have known something was up."

"Remember the neighbor mentioning that a man came around when Pete was out," Stevie says.

"I bet Kessler had a copy of Pete's work schedule at the hospital," I say, shaking my head. "I've come across swinging couples in the course of my work, but the situation in the Barlow household was crazy."

"I have more forensic news for you," Finch admits. "DNA from Pete's bed matches a young woman named Maura Haskins. She's twenty-three years of age."

"Pete's phone was chock-full of messages to someone named Maura. I'm surprised she gave him her real first name," Nick says.

"When we interviewed him, he claimed he only ever met her at the hotel," Stevie adds. "Her DNA in his bed proves otherwise."

"I guess he lied," Finch mutters, like it's expected.

"Why was Maura's DNA on file?" I ask him.

"Maura dropped out of high school and drifted from one job to another. One of those money-making ventures was prostitution. Placer County Officers picked her up in a sting four years ago."

"Was she jailed?"

"She got probation and community service."

"Just the one offense?" I ask.

"She's either seen the error of her ways, or she's become more careful."

"You think Pete knew she was a hooker?" Stevie asks.

"Tough to say. Pete's rather rough," Finch reminds us, "so it might not have bothered him. He could even have found it a turn on."

Stevie grimaces. "Just when I think I understand men and sex, I find out I don't."

Nick turns to her. "For heaven's sake, don't tar all men with the same brush as Pete Barlow."

Finch opens the brown folder. "I brought Maura Haskins and Leo Kessler's booking photos." He slides two eight by tens across the table.

The seven-year-old picture of Kessler shows an unattractive man with a slim face and receding hair. He's scowling at the camera, and it's difficult to know what Ava saw in him. Maura is a different story. She has curly black hair framing a cheerleader-pretty face with high cheekbones and a nice smile. I turn to Finch, waving her picture. "Have you compared this with the naked woman we saw on Pete's phone?"

"There's no doubt that it's her."

"Any indication Kessler and Maura knew one another?" Nick asks, picking up Kessler's picture.

Finch shakes his head. "None at all. I'm guessing they most likely didn't."

"That's where you're wrong. Let me summarize the case," I say. "A while ago, Ava and Pete's marriage fell apart, but they couldn't afford separate houses. Pete moved into the addition. We don't know how much later he started meeting up with a gorgeous woman for sex. He's nothing special in the looks department, and Maura is thirty years his junior. I have a hard time believing she's not after something from him. Money is always a possibility. Meanwhile, Ava hooked up with Kessler, a known drug dealer that her husband put in prison seven years ago. Kessler supplied Ava with drugs, and her mental health started to go downhill. He's also after something. Whatever that something is, we need to consider the idea that Leo Kessler and Maura Haskins were up to their tits in this together. It surprises me that neither Pete nor Ava suspected it."

"It's a line of inquiry," Finch concedes.

It also surprises me that no one in the police department has thought of this possibility. But past experience tells me Finch is the best we have to work with, so beating him about the head will not help our cause. "I don't suppose you have an address for either of them?" I ask him.

"Sorry, no. I thought you could try tracing the numbers that Pete and Ava's phones called," Finch says, getting to his feet and lifting his briefcase onto the table. He pulls out an evidence bag with a black smartphone inside and lays it in front of me. A yellow note is stuck to the bag. "Pete's phone. There's a diagram showing how to unlock it. In the current climate, I can't ask Jason to track Maura's number."

"We'll give it a go, but we'll also try other ways of locating them. Todd hasn't had any luck tracking the burner phone Ava was calling. He thinks it's switched off with the battery removed.

Finch hefts his briefcase.

"Are you leaving?" I ask.

"Yeah, I should get back."

"We need a copy of Leo Kessler's file. We can get Maura Haskins' file from Placer County."

"I'll sneak you a copy."

"Sneak me a copy? Is there something in the water at the police department?"

"Holder will be okay about it. He just won't agree with me helping you look for them. He has a poor view of anything connected to the federal government."

"That includes the FBI?" I decide it's pointless to make an issue out of it with Finch. "You've got to do what you've got to do," I tell him and walk him to the main entrance.

"Let's keep the lines of communication open," I add, pulling open the glass door.

He nods.

As Finch hurries across the lot to an unmarked sedan, I reflect that he's an attractive man. He's not wearing a wedding band, and I wonder about his situation. After being out of the game for so long, the thought startles me.

Chapter Twelve

AT LUNCHTIME, I take the team to In-N-Out Burger. We're all apt to skip meals when the pace on a case becomes intense. Everyone needs to loosen up, and times like this are a good stress-reducer. The four of us have only been together a few months, and we're still feeling one another out.

At mealtimes, I usually try to steer the conversation away from work topics, especially on days like this when the place is packed with bikers who could overhear us. Stevie, Nick, and I look out of place in our white button-up shirts and gray slacks, but Todd blends right in. He's wearing a red plaid shirt and jeans. Thank goodness the bib overalls never made a comeback after Myles warned him.

Our tech guru is the wry comedian of the group. Occasionally, he can overstep the line, but he responds well when we verbally slap him around. Calling him by his full name of Theodore usually works.

Todd is my height of five-nine, but stocky. He plays bass guitar in a group and says they have a gig this Saturday at a local bar. I'd go and listen, but I would stand out like a sore thumb. The dance floor is usually crowded with kids in their early twenties, and I'm positively ancient at thirty-four.

Our number comes up, and I fetch our meals. I transfer the items to the table, and hands reach out like a pack of locusts to grab the sodas, burgers, and fries. All the ketchup packets are gone when I return from bussing the tray to the stack.

"Don't push it," I tell Todd, and he grudgingly shares some from his stash.

Two flabby bikers with long straggly hair and wearing rough leather jackets are taking up more than their fair share of room at the next table. One of them spots me and shifts his chair in an inch, saying, "That's all the room I've got, darling."

"I've got it," I reply and manage to squeeze my comparatively slim frame into a chair.

Stevie tells us about a whitewater rafting trip she's taking with Mason. They are camping at the far end before returning. I've never clocked her as the outdoorsy type. She's quite short and slim for an agent, and I sometimes fear what will happen if she ever gets into a fistfight with a bad guy.

Stevie spent her first six months as a full agent in the Cyber Crime Unit—basically a desk job—before transferring to my team. So, she's still very green when it comes to field work, but she thinks she's a seasoned agent. I worry her inexperience will lead her to misread a situation and get her beaten up, or worse. But I tell myself she wouldn't have graduated from the academy a year ago if she couldn't look after herself.

"You and Mason sound pretty serious." I feel envious and consider that a good sign I'm moving on from Kenny.

It surprises me when she tells us she and Mason are getting engaged.

"Uh, that's great," Todd says, sweeping his fingers through his hair.

For a moment, I think I see Nick's chest clench at the news.

"Congratulations. How long have you two been dating?" he asks, flashing her a half-hearted smile. It seems an odd comment. Stevie might be moving a bit quickly, but I hope he's not about to suggest she's rushing into things. I've caught him checking her out on several occasions, but I figured it was just a guy thing. Now I realize he has feelings for her. But I'm glad she's with Mason and not Nick, as agents in a relationship can't work together, and I like my team the way it is.

"We started going out seven months ago when I moved to Cedar Springs," she replies, looking puzzled and maybe a bit put out by Nick's question. "I didn't tell you guys about our relationship until recently."

I've known Nick since the academy. After our training, we went our separate ways. A couple of high-profile cases boosted me to Senior Special Agent, so I ended up as his boss when we came together again. If he resents me for that, he doesn't let it show.

We get back to the office, looking like we've overeaten.

It's mid-afternoon when Stevie calls over the cubicle dividers for me to come and see something. I find Nick in her office looking over her shoulder as her fingers strike the keyboard like machine-gun fire.

"You're going to love this," she says, pulling up a website.

The heading says, "FREE LINDA," but the text below is too tiny for me to read. There's the booking picture of a forty-something woman. Her curly blonde hair is up in a messy bun, and she holds up a sign displaying her name and a date that was almost four years ago.

"That's Linda Haskins," Nick exclaims.

It takes me a moment to twig what he's telling me. "How is she related to Pete Barlow's girlfriend, Maura Haskins?" I ask, though I suspect what the answer will be.

"Her mother," he replies. "Guess who arrested her?"

"Pete Barlow?"

"Bingo."

I shake my head. "No wonder Pete said Maura never shared her last name with him. He arrested her mother. This case gets weirder and weirder."

"Linda Haskins was a local high school teacher who was convicted of embezzling from her school. She was released eleven weeks ago after serving three years. A GoFundMe page and a blog claim that the principal was the true embezzler, and he framed her."

"Another hinky Pete Barlow arrest?" I exclaim. "His cases are like a house of cards waiting to collapse. It makes me wonder who else knows that. Maybe Chief Holder, and it's the reason he wants Pete locked away."

"Linda is currently living in a halfway house on South Street." Stevie says, "I've spoken to the warden, and she is expected back from her job at the Home Center at four-fifteen. She might know how to find her daughter, Maura."

I usually reward the agent who brought me information by taking them to the interview. Besides, Linda may respond better to a woman, and Stevie needs the experience, so I pick her. I check my watch. "Let's head over there in half an hour," I tell her. "And notify the warden that we're coming."

"Sure thing, boss."

I sense Todd standing beside me and turn to him. His excited expression tells me something is afoot. "What have you found?"

"The tech department got back to me on the video of the perp stealing the minivan. Comparing the thief with the vehicle's height and taking the placement of the camera into consideration, they put the guy at six feet two inches tall. That's the same height as Leo Kessler."

***

A HALFWAY HOUSE is a structured environment where inmates who've served their time are forced to live while they are reintegrating into the community. The usual term is four to six months.

Jensen House is named for a local council dignitary. To call the place a dump would be an insult to dumps. I'm guessing the building was a boarding house back in the day. But that must have been eons ago, and no one has updated the furnishings or painted the walls since.

The warden is a stocky woman with the physique of an

Olympic weightlifter. Her tweed jacket and skirt are the same color as her gray hair, which is clipped short in no discernible style. She marches across the day room's threadbare carpet like she's on a hike. I expect her to have a name like Helga, but she turns out to be a Julia. When we identify ourselves, she tells us that Linda Haskins has lived there for two and a half months.

Julia has us wait while she fetches Linda from her room.

We've stowed our weapons in a lockbox in the car, as neither Stevie nor I know the protocol for visiting a halfway house.

We gaze out the front window at the traffic on South Street until Julia reappears with Linda Haskins in tow. Not surprisingly, she has lost weight since her booking photo, and her face is gaunt.

We introduce ourselves, and Linda replies with a disinterested shrug. I turn to Julia. "Is there somewhere private where we can talk?"

"You can use my office," she says and unlocks the door to a room with file cabinets and a desk.

After locking all the drawers, she promises to return with a third chair. I tell Stevie and Linda to take the seats while I wait for Julia to reappear. She comes into the office carrying a folding wooden contraption that looks like a death trap, but I think it will support my one-thirty-five pounds and lower my backside onto the slats.

When Julia is gone, I give Linda our names again as she's staring vacantly around the room.

"The warden says you work at the Home Center," I say.

"Yeah," she replies without making eye contact.

"What do you do for them?" I'm thinking job prospects can't be great when you've served time for embezzlement.

"I started out sweeping the floor and emptying trash cans. They have me stocking shelves now." Linda seems to notice us for the first time. "Why are you asking me these questions?"

"We saw the internet postings saying you were wrongly accused." It's not primarily why we're there, but it isn't a total lie. If our investigation into Pete Barlow goes the way I expect, her conviction could possibly be overturned. "Can you tell us in your own words what happened?"

Linda's eyes light up, and she looks like the schoolteacher I imagine she once was. "I used to teach fifth grade English. The entire school started a campaign to raise money for local firefighters. It was called 'Save the Dimes,' and we asked parents to set aside change from their pockets and purses and donate it to the fund." She croaks the last few words and apologizes for her throat.

"Can you get Linda something to drink?" I ask Stevie. We pause till she returns with a bottle of water. Linda gulps it hungrily, then continues:

"The response to the 'Save the Dimes' campaign was excellent, and soon we were seeing kids bring in not just coins but five and ten-dollar bills. Each classroom had a large glass jar, and we put the takings in there as they came in. Then a kid named Tyler brought in a suitcase full of bills. It didn't look like anything you'd have legally. I thanked Tyler but saved counting it until after class. There were almost fifteen thousand dollars in the case. I took it straight to the principal's office."

Linda pauses to sip more water.

"You thought this was from an illicit dealing like drug distribution or prostitution," Stevie says.

"Exactly. But Tom, he was the principal, persuaded me not to call the police, saying we should just add it to the fund. The firefighters desperately needed the money for fresh supplies. Then police arrested the boy's father on blackmail charges and came to the school looking for the money. All they found was the empty suitcase bearing my fingerprints in a closet in my classroom and a fund that wasn't big enough to support the fifteen grand ever being added. I found out later that Tom told detectives that he'd given the suitcase full of money back to me and begged me to turn it in."

Tears leak from Linda's eyes. I see a box of tissues on the desk and hand it to her.

She composes herself, saying, "I'm sorry it upsets me so."

"It's quite understandable," I tell her.

"The detective was a man named Pete Barlow. He behaved like a sexist prick, pardon my language. He didn't believe a word I said and totally accepted Tom's version of events. My daughter, Maura, hired a private investigator who found that Tom had used the money to pay off a loan shark. They took the evidence to this Detective Barlow, but he just sat on it, and I went to jail for something I did not, could not do."

"That's awful," I say, shaking my head.

Stevie dabs a tear from the corner of an eye, no doubt

finding Linda's account as credible as I do. I plan to seek out that missing evidence, but not before I've arrested Ava Barlow's killer. Still, I feel deceitful and unclean for what I say next:

"I'd like to speak to your daughter. It sounds like she has all the facts of your case. Do you know where I can find her?"

"She's as angry at Detective Barlow as I am for what happened. Maybe more so. She's working with a friend named Leo something to set my case right. I'm secretly hoping for a big payout from the city."

"Leo Kessler?" I prompt, trying not to appear shocked.

"That's it. Maura told me not to tell anyone where she is until they've worked a few things out."

"She sounds busy. Do you ever get to see her?" Stevie asks.

"Once a week after work on Tuesdays. That timing works out best for both of us."

"Jensen House is near the downtown area. Lots of coffee shops to meet Maura at, and there's always the park if you both feel like a stroll," Stevie says softly.

"It's too hot to stroll. We always meet at the Chocolate Bunny Espresso. It's just two blocks from here," Linda replies, smiling.

I shoot a look of approval at Stevie. I'll make a decent agent out of her yet.

Chapter Thirteen

THE JUNE HEAT is unrelenting, and perspiration prickles my back by the time Stevie and I reach the Chocolate Bunny Espresso. The coffee shop belies its cute name. Looking through the window, I can see it's a Starbucks knock-off. A waitress is hurrying to wipe the tables and straighten the chairs as if the place is about to close.

Todd calls before we can push open the door.

"I found Maura's address. 250 Russell Street. She lives in unit six," he announces.

"Isn't that the ritzy apartment complex overlooking the river?" I ask, remembering it from a previous case.

"Yeah—The Country Club Apartments. Want to guess how I found it?"

"The phone book?"

"Nah, she's unlisted. I got it from a friend at the elections office."

"Smooth."

"You good with that?" he asks.

"Get me a warrant, and I'll be living the high life," I tell him. "Any time in the next thirty minutes will do."

"I don't know—"

"Get Nick to help. Call me when you have something." I hang up before he can object.

Stevie smiles—she's been listening to the conversation.

When we step inside the café, the waitress turns our way. "I'm sorry, ladies, but we're closed."

"Federal agents, ma'am. I'm Agent Viera, and this is Agent Wells. We'd like a few minutes of your time." We brush our jackets aside to display the badges clipped to our belts.

The woman freezes, and her eyes almost pop out of her head. Her mouth moves like she's trying to speak, but no words come out.

"This doesn't concern you personally, ma'am," Stevie says. "We're looking for information on a patron. If you have the time."

The waitress is on the wrong side of forty, with a blonde ponytail and ruby red lips. She looks relieved as she straightens and sets the rag on the table. "Of course."

"Can we get your name?" I ask.

"It's Norma Hodges."

"Is anyone else here?" We always ask that question for our own protection.

"No, just me."

"Can you tell me if you've seen this woman before?" I pull up a picture of Linda on my phone and hold it out for Norma.

She removes a pair of glasses from a pocket and squints at the picture. "Yeah. She comes in here pretty regularly. Tuesday afternoons, if I remember right. Has she just got out of jail?"

"What makes you ask that, ma'am?"

"The Jensen House is just up the street. Women from there come in for a coffee or a glass of water. They all have that same expression."

"We're interested in who she might have met here," Stevie says.

"Pretty young woman. Early twenties. I'd guess it's her daughter."

"This her?" I thumb up Maura's booking picture.

Norma hesitates. "The young woman who comes in is a blonde, but the face matches. I suppose she could have dyed her hair since that picture was taken."

I flash Stevie a look and gaze around the wood-paneled walls. "Does that camera record?" I point a finger at the only one in the room. It's on the far wall and aimed at the cash register, but it might be a dummy.

Norma nods. "Yes, we record it."

"You know how to work the system?" Stevie asks.

"You betcha."

We follow Norma into a back room with a desk and a computer. She settles into a chair and taps the keyboard. A picture of the empty café fills the screen. "That's what it sees right now," she tells us. "You want to look at last Tuesday afternoon?"

"After four, we think," Stevie says.

Norma's hands glide across the keyboard and work the mouse with surprising dexterity.

"You've done this before," I observe.

"Only a couple of times. I'm a computer science major,

but I took time off to have kids. So now, this is the only job I can find."

Norma finds the spot on the video and cues it up for us to watch.

The picture is grainy, but we see Linda Haskins come through the door and find an empty table. A couple of minutes later, a blonde woman in her early twenties enters the café and looks around. She spots Linda, and the two women embrace. The quality isn't great, and they're all the way across the café from the camera. We get a much better view of the women when they come to the counter to order.

"Freeze it, please." I've seen enough of these systems to be able to run them as well as anyone. But Norma doesn't need my help.

She complies, and I hold up the photo of Maura on my phone to compare it to the woman in the video.

"It's Maura Haskins with blonde hair," Stevie says. "I don't think it's a wig."

Norma nods. "It was her own hair. I can always tell."

Ten minutes later, we step out of the Chocolate Bunny Espresso with the video copied to a memory stick.

"It's too bad that a woman with a degree has to work here," Stevie says.

"I wish I could find her a job in her chosen field. But in many professions, you fall behind if you're away from them too long."

"It's a problem that especially affects women."

"Something to think about if you and Mason want kids."

Stevie shrugs. "The jury's out on that one."

My phone chimes.

Todd says, "Nick is on his way to Maura's apartment with the warrant. He's meeting a representative of the landlord at five-thirty."

***

THE COUNTRY CLUB apartment building on Russell Street is a stylish three-story structure with a gabled roof and a brick façade. Rico Amaro, the landlord's representative, takes Stevie, Nick, and me to the leasing office, where he dons glasses to study the warrant.

"What is this regarding?" he asks.

"I'm not at liberty to say," I reply, a little irritated by his manner.

"We don't let just anyone in here," he says, eyeing Stevie.

"We're the FBI, Mr. Amaro, and we have a valid search warrant." *You prick,* I want to say. "I'll arrest anyone who gets in the way of our executing it."

"Judges will sign anything cops give them."

"We can also remove any documents and equipment pertaining to Ms. Haskins from this office. Are you going to tell us where to find such documents, or do we have to empty all the drawers onto the floor?" I indicate a gray four-drawer file cabinet in the corner.

"The leasing documents are in the top drawer," Amaro sighs. "You'll need to make copies as we need the originals."

"We're taking the originals, sir."

"You can't—"

I brush past him and slide open the top drawer. The

documents are arranged alphabetically, so I pull out Maura's paperwork and set it on the desk. "Her application says here she's a Pilates instructor. Is that correct?" I gaze at Amaro.

"If that's what it says."

My eyes scan the application. "It also says here that Ms. Haskins has an income of ten thousand, nine hundred dollars a month. Does that sound right to you for a gym instructor, Mr. Amaro, because I think it stinks?"

"Many of our residents have supplemental income," he says in a self-righteous tone.

"We'll see. Please show us to Ms. Haskins' apartment." I turn to Nick. "Agent Stone, please stay here and see what you can find."

"How about the computer?" Nick nods at the black laptop on the desk.

"Impound it." It's not absolutely essential, but I'm feeling less than charitable.

Stevie and I take the elevator with Amaro, who won't stop whining about the laptop. My stomach lurches as we rapidly ascend to the third floor.

I'm trying to let the stream of words flow over me, but he's still complaining as he unlocks the door to unit six and steps inside.

"Thank you, Mr. Amaro, but you're going to have to wait outside."

He looks about to object until I give him a stern expression and reach for my handcuffs.

When he's gone, Stevie says, "I wonder what he's trying to hide?"

I step to the window and admire the view of the river. "Amaro's up to something, that's for sure."

My gaze sweeps the living room. The dining set is high-end chrome and glass. The biggest flat-screen TV I've ever seen is mounted on a wall opposite a chocolate-brown couch with beige throw cushions. We step into the kitchen. The appliances are all top-shelf.

"She's not a Pilates instructor, is she?" Stevie asks.

"Nope."

We move into the bedroom. A leopard-skin comforter covers the bed, but it's the giant mirror on the ceiling that gets our attention.

I glove up and go for the nightstand drawers. One of them sports a condom selection, and the other an address book. I fan the pages but don't recognize any of the men's names or most of their sexual preferences. I hand the book to Stevie, who checks it out for herself.

"Maura's a hooker." Stevie snaps on gloves and opens the closet doors, gazing at the skimpy outfits.

"Keen powers of observation there, agent."

The bathroom is messy, like Maura took a shower and left in a hurry. Stevie picks up a bottle from the vanity. "Honey blonde hair dye."

"I'm guessing she got out of Dodge City after Ava was killed and Pete arrested. Can you take the living room while I finish in here?" I answer a knock at the door and let Nick in.

He looks around. "Nice place."

"Maura is a working girl," I say.

"Figures. I found an unlicensed Saturday-night special

in the leasing office desk drawer. Amaro is cooling his heels in the back of my car."

"Find anything linking him to Maura or our investigation?"

"No, but he had to know that her johns were coming into the building."

"True, but I doubt we'll get anything to stick to Amaro on the prostitution angle. Can you drive him to the police station and have them book him on the firearms violation? Then you're done for the day. Stevie and I have got this, and there's no point in all three of us working late."

I spend twenty minutes tossing the mattress and searching the bedroom before Stevie joins me and asks what I've found.

"A handgun from under the mattress, a roll of cash, and a couple of baggies of coke. You?"

"You need to come listen to the answering machine messages."

"I didn't realize anyone still used them," I say, following her to a six-drawer chest in the dining area. The top drawer is pulled out, revealing a pink answering machine inside.

"Probably didn't want to give out her cell phone number. The first few messages are from men wanting appointments. You don't want to hear the types of sex they're into, but you need to listen to the last message." Stevie stabs a finger on the play button. She taps another button repeatedly to skip forward to the last message.

A gruff voice says, "*It's Leo. If you run into Ricky, don't say anything to him. I just found out he's a snitch. Let me deal with him . . . End of messages. To replay—*"

Stevie shuts off the machine. "I wonder who Ricky is?"

"I don't know, but it doesn't sound good for him. The call validates Linda's claim that Kessler and Maura knew one another."

"Could it be another Leo?"

"I don't believe in coincidences. Bag up the machine. You find anything else?"

"Old photographs of Maura when she was little. But nothing that will help find her. You think we need to call in a forensic team?"

I shake my head. "The techs won't tell us any more than we already know. Can you pull the apartment phone records? Tomorrow is fine."

Chapter Fourteen

"HOW GOES THE Barlow case?" I ask Detective Finch, plowing my fork into the Pad Thai noodles. He's using chopsticks, but I can't be bothered with them. It's the day following our search of Maura's apartment. The two of us are eating lunch on the patio at Fat Luca's, a middle-of-the-road Thai place, where people mostly come for the view.

Beyond the iron railing at the edge of the deck, the ground falls away sharply, giving patrons a panorama of the rolling hills of Northern California. They're prettiest in the spring when they are still green before the summer sun scorches them brown.

"You'll have to ask Detective Reed. I'm off the case," Finch mutters.

"That's a shame. Have you been put on something more pressing?" I ask, though I can't think of anything higher profile than the murder of a retired detective's wife.

Finch's lips tighten into a thin line, and he shakes his head. "I caught a shoplifting case."

"For real? Detectives investigate shoplifters?"

"It's my penance for pushing Reed too hard on Pete

being innocent."

"That's bullshit. Holder and Reed still think he hired Kessler to kill Ava?"

He shrugs. "I don't know what they think anymore."

"Chief Holder always seemed a straight shooter."

"It's not the first time this kind of thing has happened. I've come to think that Reed has some dirt on the chief."

I blow out my cheeks. "You ever hear of a confidential informant named Ricky?"

"Sure. He was Pete Barlow's CI. He gave me information for a case last year, but we ended up not using it, so I can't speak for the quality of his leads. How did his name come up?"

I tell him about the answering machine message we found at Maura's apartment.

"So, Maura and Kessler know Ricky?"

"Seems so."

"You want to arrange a meeting with Ricky?"

"He may know Kessler's whereabouts."

"You gonna warn him that Kessler's coming after him?"

"I can use it as leverage to get him to give Kessler up. How do I get hold of him?"

"Ricky works at Olympic Tires in town." Finch refers to his phone and gives me a number. "Leave a message saying you need tires for a 2005 Monarch tractor. When he calls back, insist that you have a diesel tractor of that vintage."

"I'm guessing there's no such thing."

"Right on. The tractor company only started four years ago." Finch stretches his arm across the table, holding his phone to show me a picture of Ricky. He's a black guy, in his thirties, near as I can tell, with a droopy mustache, scrappy beard, and dreads.

"I'll give him a call."

"Find anything else at Maura's apartment?"

"We confirmed that she's a hooker," I tell him. "We have her client list, but I haven't looked at it in any detail. We located a café where she meets her mother every Tuesday."

"You going to stake the café out next week and nab her there?"

"In four days' time? I can't wait that long. No, I'm pinning my hopes on Ricky leading us to her and Kessler. I may have someone put a tracker on his car while I speak to him."

We lapse into silence for a few moments.

"Did you see Jackie Ricci's latest piece on Channel Five *Eye in the Sky News*?" Finch asks.

"Nah, I never watch it. She always has an agenda. What is it this week?"

"Police brutality." Finch raises a brow.

"That resonates with a lot of people these days."

"Remember the sex trafficker we stopped this last spring?"

"The one who knifed the teenage girl in Sierra County?"

"That's him. A loser by the name of Cody Devlin."

"Didn't he beat you up pretty badly?"

"Yeah. Reed and I pulled his car over, but Devlin wouldn't get out. We ended up having to drag him from the car. As soon as his feet touched the pavement, he started swinging at Reed and me. Devlin's a big guy. He landed a couple of punches on my jaw before laying into Reed. It took all our strength to get the guy on the ground. I was holding him down, waiting for Reed to snap on the cuffs, but instead, he started kicking Devlin in the ribs."

"That was stupid. Someone saw what happened?"

"A kid recorded it on his phone."

"Crap."

"Jackie Ricci has her own segment on the news, and they keep playing the tape over and over. She cut out the part where Devlin attacked us. Reed lives with another reporter at Channel Five, Hazel DeRosa, so I was shocked that they aired the video." Finch seems to have lost his appetite and pushes his plate to one side, his meal only half-finished. "The edited video plays like we dragged some poor citizen from his car, threw him to the ground, and I sat on him so Reed could kick him."

"But you didn't kick him?"

"Can't say I didn't want to after he punched me, but no, I didn't. I managed to stop Reed by grabbing his foot while keeping Devlin restrained. But that part was cut out too. I'm always getting tarred with the same brush as Reed."

"Has Holder said anything to you?" I ask, pushing my plate away.

"The kid who shot the video posted the entire thing on his social media page a few weeks ago. He doesn't have a big following, so the video didn't go anywhere until Jackie Ricci got hold of it. When Holder saw the unedited original, he went easy on Reed. It would have been a different story if I'd been the one doing the kicking."

"What a messed up department you work for. Maybe don't tell Reed I'm looking for Ricky or about the café where Maura meets her mom."

"That will be easy. We're barely speaking." Finch gives a hollow chortle.

"You ever thought about working somewhere else?"

"Like the Bureau?" he asks as the waitress stops by with the check.

"Why not? Or in a city with a more functional police force."

"If I left Cedar Springs, I'd never see you." He gives me a half-hearted smile, and his brown eyes twinkle.

I flash him a grin. I can't deny there's a spark between Finch and me. Despite my two-year celibacy after Kenny left me, I wonder if I should pursue him. I mean, what is there to lose?

"Holder and Reed treat you like crap," I tell him. "It sounds almost abusive."

"Maybe Reed's misdeeds will catch up with him."

"There's more about assaulting suspects?"

"Pretty sure there is, but like I told you yesterday, I can't give you anything specific."

I'm glad about that. If I heard of specific problems with Reed, I'd be obliged to pass them on. And if the FBI were to open an investigation into the Cedar Springs Police Department, any chance of a relationship with Finch would go out the window.

As we drop cash onto the check, I admit to myself that I want to date him. That feeling has been a long time in coming with anyone.

Chapter Fifteen

IT'S LATE IN the day and dropping dark when I park in front of a strip mall that includes Hobby Lobby, CVS, and Target. After saying goodbye to Finch, I left Ricky a voice mail with the magic phrase. The snitch seems to be on first-name terms with Maura and Kessler, so I'm hoping he can give me some background information on the pair and tell me where to find them.

Ricky called me back within the hour and sounded stoic when I warned him his cover was blown. As much as I wanted to hear what he had to say, I decided to wait to ask my questions about Maura and Kessler.

Ricky agreed to meet me at eight p.m. behind the strip mall, which is where I am now.

I climb out of the Bureau sedan as Nick and Stevie's car pulls in beside me. I've brought them along to monitor the encounter from a distance in case Ricky or one of his mates pulls anything.

We check our radios and weapons, then head for the loading dock behind the Target store—Ricky's chosen meeting place. We've all ditched our charcoal gray pants and blue FBI windbreakers in favor of the dressed-down hiking gear we keep in our lockers. For Ricky's sake, we don't want to telegraph what's happening to anyone watching.

"What do you make of Chief Holder pulling Finch off the case?" Nick asks me as we try to look as if we're out for a casual stroll, not three FBI agents on a mission.

"I've long thought there's something rotten in the police department." I turn to Stevie. "You need to watch your pillow talk with Officer Mason lest anything gets back to Chief Holder or Detective Reed. We might end up investigating the pair."

"My fiancé and I have an unspoken rule never to discuss cases," she assures me.

"Oh, it's official now, is it?" Nick asks.

Stevie holds up a finger displaying a not-so-modest engagement ring. "When we talk, Kenny's name comes up now and then," she adds, referring to my ex, who is a police sergeant. "He has some kind of beef with Mason."

"Mason shouldn't feel special. Kenny has a beef with everyone," I say.

"I feel like I'm in a spy movie," Stevie says as we round the back of the building housing Lumber Liquidators.

"Just stay sharp," I tell her, fingering the butt of the Glock holstered at my hip. Lights mounted high above each store's loading dock are just coming on. We pass a mobile generator trailer ready to power the store in the event of a rolling blackout. Cutting the power on days when the fire danger is high has become a thing here in California.

"Stay here," I tell them as we reach a green dumpster

with a view of the back of the Target store. "I don't want to spook him."

My watch reads five to eight. There's no sign of Ricky as I cover the last hundred feet to the loading dock. I move into the shadows and wait, wondering if I'll get more of a reaction to his blown cover than I did on the phone. Will he even know Kessler's whereabouts?

I start to think something is wrong when it gets to eight-fifteen, and Ricky hasn't shown. Has he stood me up, or did I misunderstand the meeting location or time? I click on my flashlight and check around the line of green dumpsters in the off-chance he's hiding there.

A stand of trees and a chain-link fence separate the delivery truck access road from the highway beyond. I sweep the light around the base of the maples and spot something that doesn't look right—a dark mound on the parched earth.

I jog closer, a queasy feeling forming in the pit of my stomach. The man lying there is black with a droopy mustache, scrappy beard, and dreads. Ricky is a big man, but whoever slit open one side of his neck had to be even more powerful. The defensive wounds on his hands and arms are not unlike those I saw on Ava Barlow.

I feel for a pulse on his remaining carotid artery, but there's enough blood soaking into the ground to tell me he's dead, and he was killed here. I use my radio to summon Stevie and Nick, then I call Dispatch.

Stevie glances at the body, then shies away. There's a lot of blood on Ricky's white T-shirt, and she doesn't throw up. That has to count for something.

Nick clicks on a flashlight and crouches next to the body for a closer look. "The wounds appear similar to those on Ava Barlow," he states. "You think it's the same perp?"

"Yeah." I nod. "Kessler got to Ricky before he could talk to us."

"Maybe we'll find some physical evidence this time."

"Let's hope so." But I'm not optimistic after Ava's body was a forensic bust.

"Here's what puzzles me," Nick says. "After you warned him, Ricky wouldn't have told Kessler that he was meeting you, nor anyone else he's ratted on."

"He had to have told someone. How else would anyone have known the timing and location of the meeting?"

"And that person told Kessler?" Nick asks.

"Or the person he told killed him."

"I don't get why he was killed here?"

"Someone has sent us a message not to fuck with them."

A police patrol car is the first vehicle to show up. The officer who steps out the passenger door looks only vaguely interested in my badge, but he's plainly surprised to see three federal agents. We hardly ever beat them to crime scenes. The other officer is more openly hostile, but complies when I tell them to secure the area. Few men in uniform like a woman telling them what to do.

Ten minutes later, an unmarked SUV parks just beyond the newly strung yellow tape. We're losing the light, but I recognize Detective Reed's slicked-back hair and rumpled clothing.

He strides toward me, an arrogant sneer on his face.

"What the hell are you people doing here, Bollywood?"

"We're agents to you, detective," I snap.

He saunters over to the body, and I follow. Reed doesn't appear to have a flashlight, so I aim mine at Ricky's face and the defensive wounds on his hands.

"Did you do this?" he asks, getting in my personal space.

"Don't act stupid, Reed. Is the ME on the way? I'm interested in the time of death. I was due to meet Ricky here at eight, and I can't imagine he arrived more than a few minutes early. He must have been killed right before I got here."

"That right there makes you a witness." Reed is only three feet away, but he's shouting. "You need to give me a statement, then stay away from the investigation."

"Keep fucking with me like this, Reed, and I'll have you for interfering with a federal investigation." I stab my finger at him for emphasis. "Ricky's injuries are similar enough to Ava Barlow's for me to take over the investigation."

Reed just glares at me.

"If that's all right with you," I add sarcastically.

"You don't know Ricky like I do," he insists. "The guys he hangs with."

"Sounds like you'll be an invaluable part of the investigation," I say, trying to sound sincere, but I can tell Reed doesn't buy it. He's old school, and I can tell he still thinks women should stay home, cook meals, and look after the kids.

His gaze stays fixed on mine for the longest moment until Yolanda Jensen, the medical examiner, shows up, ending the standoff. "Break it up, guys. Back in your own corners," she says, muscling her way between Reed and me.

"Who found the body?"

"That would be me." I give her the circumstances of my meeting with Ricky and why he was likely killed no earlier than seven-forty-five. Reed continues to give me the stink-eye.

"You're probably right on the timing," she says, "but let me get a temperature reading."

I duck out of Reed's gaze and move to where Nick and Stevie are standing. "Pull surveillance video from Target and the CVS next door. I also saw cameras in the parking lot. They likely belong to the city. Get me that footage too. I don't care if people have already left for the day. Get them back into work. If you find anyone standing around at the front of the stores, ask them if they saw a dark blue Chrysler Voyager minivan."

Chapter Sixteen

"IF I HADN'T arranged to meet Ricky, he'd still be alive," I half-whisper into the phone. "That's the simple truth of what happened to him. We both know that, and I'm not surprised Reed is bellyaching about it."

"You can't think that way, Cassie," Finch insists. "It's more than possible Kessler would have killed Ricky anyway for being a snitch regardless of you arranging to meet him. It's not healthy to take responsibility for something you had no control over."

He's not wrong, but I say, "Todd has been working on surveillance footage from the strip mall, and he's hovering outside my office like he has something to show. I enjoyed lunch yesterday. Let's do it again soon."

"You have a nice day, Cassie," he says. "And try not to let a prick like Reed get under your skin."

After we end the call, I reflect that Finch is good for me. He's perceptive and level-headed when I'm not. I vaguely recall yelling at him for not telling me promptly when Maura and Kessler were identified from their fingerprints. But now I realize he was balancing my need with politics at the police department. I resolve not to get so aggravated at him the next time we disagree.

I turn to Todd, hovering at the entrance to my office. "You got something?"

"Cameras caught the blue minivan arriving and leaving the strip mall, but it won't help us identify the driver."

"Let's take a look." I follow Todd to his desk. Nick is there working the mouse and pointing at the screen while Stevie watches. Todd is extremely particular about his computer, so I expect him to explode.

"Find something distinctive about the guy?" Todd asks Nick, seemingly unperturbed by the invasion of his workspace.

"Maybe," Nick says without taking his eyes off the screen. "Hold that thought for a moment."

Todd turns to me. "The perp has his back to every camera we've looked at. He either knows where they all are, or he's the luckiest SOB on the planet."

"Can you do anything with that?" Nick indicates a monitor displaying a paused video. It shows the back of a man I assume to be the perp.

"What in particular?" Todd asks, stepping toward him.

"There's a distinctive tattoo on the back of the guy's neck. If you keep playing the video, it looks like a snake."

"I think it looks more like a gang symbol," Stevie says.

I lean in while Nick plays the video, but I see nothing more than a fuzz ball. "It's like an inkblot test. What you see is more related to you than the subject."

There's a lull in the conversation while Todd watches the video like a connoisseur holding a glass of fine wine up to the light. He replays the clip several times before offering an opinion. "Right now, it's as much like a gang sign as a snake. But I might be able to do something with it. I've never tried this, but I think if I overlay many frames on top of one another and run a process on them, it should make his tattoo recognizable. But it will take me a while—possibly days." He strokes his straggly beard thoughtfully.

"Can't you just zoom in and get a bigger picture?" Stevie asks.

Todd laughs. "Like in those TV cop shows where they zoom into a terrible picture, and suddenly you can read the entire license plate?"

Stevie stays silent, probably guessing her idea is about to be kicked to the curb.

"It's pure fiction," Todd continues. "Imagine you're listening to an old AM radio, but you can't hear the station for the hissing and pops coming over the airwaves. If you turn up the volume, the station gets louder, but so does the interference. It doesn't help you hear what's going on any better."

We stare at Todd like he's just explained the meaning of the universe.

"But you can do something better?" I ask excitedly. "Something that might reveal the tattoo on his neck."

"I think so. I just don't know whether the result will be enough to ID the guy."

"So, what are you waiting for?" Nick asks, faux impatience in his voice.

"Okay. Out, out. I've got work to do." Todd shoos everyone from his office, flicking his fingers like he's herding cats.

We back into the aisle, and I turn to Stevie. "I'd like you to find what prison Leo Kessler was in and get them to send us pictures of his tattoos."

"Do you remember when he was sentenced?"

"I believe Pete Barlow arrested him seven years ago, and he served five."

"On it, boss."

I turn to Nick. "Let's go talk to Ricky's coworkers."

We step into the parking lot and see ASAC Preston Myles bearing down on us, his lips pressed into a thin line.

He stops and holds up his phone. "What the hell is this, SSA Viera?" I notice he's not greeting me as Cassie, his usual form of address.

The headline on the Channel Five website reads, 'POLICE INFORMANT KILLED BY COP'S WIFE'S KILLER.' A subheading says, 'FBI seeks drug dealer and his girlfriend for the double slaying.' I see the article was penned by Hazel DeRosa—Detective Reed's live-in woman-friend. Could the guy be any more obvious?

He yanks the phone away before I can read any more, but I'm pretty sure I saw Kessler's name in the text. "How the hell do they know all that? How can the death of some lowlife informant turn into this?" Myles snaps.

"Damn," I reply. "That could only have come from the police department, sir. Detective Reed is their lead on this and Ava Barlow's murder, and he's openly hostile to the Bureau's interest in the case."

"Your involvement is absolutely appropriate given Retired Detective Barlow's connection to the police department."

"The article was penned by Reed's live-in woman-friend, Hazel DeRosa, and he's leaked to her in the past."

"Detective Reed lives with a reporter at Channel Five News?" Myles asks in obvious outrage.

"Apparently so." I'm hoping the assistant special agent in charge will quash any future leaks to the media. I have no desire for my investigation to become a headline-grabber, but it may be too late for that.

He stifles back a comment, his face flushed. But his tone is carefully controlled when he asks, "How is the informant's death connected to Barlow's wife?"

"It's just a theory based on the similarity of the knife wounds, but we can't say with complete certainty that the murders are connected. I'm hoping forensics or the medical examiner will turn up a link."

After the briefest hesitation, he sounds resolute. "Okay, here's what's going to happen. The FBI will take the lead on both cases under your command, SSA Viera. You're to use FBI resources for forensics and only share information with the police department when absolutely essential. I'll speak to Chief Holder. Understood?"

"Yes, sir."

"And make sure your people stay away from the media?"

"Of course, sir." I want to add that I can't control Reed, but ASAC Preston Myles is already strutting off.

Nick says, "That won't sit well with anyone at the police department."

We open the doors to our sedan and slide inside. "Like

turds in the punch bowl if I had to guess," I say. "But Reed and Holder's feelings aren't our concern." However, I care about Detective Finch's feelings, and I don't know how he will react.

"Myles is forcing us to snatch the case from under their noses. That's exactly why officers resent us."

"We have our marching orders," I remind him.

Olympic Tire and Auto Service is housed in a single-story concrete building. I feel more than one pair of eyes watching us as we park at the side of an open roller door.

We're barely out of the car when a squirrelly looking young man with a mop of greasy black hair trundles a hefty floor jack our way. "Problem with the car or looking for new tires?"

"Federal agents." We badge him, but he doesn't appear at all surprised to see us.

"You here about Ricky?"

"We are. What's your name?" Nick asks.

"Arlo Banks."

"You see Ricky working here yesterday?"

"Yeah."

"Was he any different from usual?"

Arlo hesitates for a long while.

I say, "We're looking for the person who killed him. You should answer the question if you have any information."

"Late afternoon, a guy stopped by. Ricky was rattled after speaking to him and left early."

"What can you tell us about the guy he spoke to?"

"He didn't get out of the car. Ricky talked to him through the window.

A balding man in a grease-stained sports jacket strides toward us, saying, "I'll take care of this, Arlo. Ben needs help with a tire."

"Hold it right there, sir," I say, raising my hand. "What's your name?"

The man stops short, eyeing our sedan's US Government plates. "Carson Smiley. I'm the manager. What is this about?"

"We're investigating the death of Ricky Kelly, and we need to question your employees."

"Do you have a warrant?"

"We don't need a warrant to speak to them, sir," I tell him politely but firmly.

"Arlo has said all he needs to."

We come across people like Carson Smiley all the time. You could ask them if the sun is shining, and they'd ask for an attorney or refuse to answer. Maybe they get a sense of power from not answering our questions, but they don't understand that their lack of candor makes us think they have something to hide.

Nick and I move closer to Carson, and I get in his face. "We believe the suspect in a double homicide was here yesterday and spoke to Ricky. If you impede our investigation, I'll think you had something to do with Ricky's death, and I'll take you in for questioning, keep you there overnight. I'm tempted to do that anyway."

When he doesn't answer right away, I half turn to Nick, "What should we do, Agent Stone?"

"He's mixed up in the murders somehow," Nick says.

"Okay, hands behind your back, sir." I pull out a pair of

handcuffs.

Carson's tough-guy act crumbles, "Okay, okay. What do you need to know?"

"Arlo here was just telling us that Ricky spoke to someone in a car in the late afternoon. Someone that upset him. Did you see that?"

"We speak to people in their vehicles all the time here."

"Have you forgotten what I said about arresting you?" I pull my handcuffs back out for effect. "We'll also need to take your employees in for questioning."

"Okay, yeah. Ricky got into an altercation with someone in a minivan."

"Color, make, and model?" Nick snaps.

"A Chrysler," Carson replies. Turning to Arlo, he asks, "Do you remember any more about it? We need to get these agents out of our hair."

"It was a dark blue Chrysler Voyager," Arlo admits.

"Do you have surveillance cameras?" My eyes scan the front of the building, but I don't see any.

Carson guffaws loudly. "Nah. Can't afford anything fancy like that."

"And you say you didn't see the driver, Arlo."

"Sorry."

"Was the driver a man or a woman? Black, white, big or small?" Nick asks.

"It was a big white guy."

"See any tattoos?"

"His arm was leaning on the window, and it was well inked. A full sleeve."

"You remember anything about the tattooing?"

"Just a lot of blue ink, sir."

"You've been most helpful, Arlo," I tell him. "Thank you. You have a good rest of your day."

We climb inside the car, and I fire up the engine.

Nick turns to me. "So Ricky spoke to Kessler in the late afternoon. Presumably, that's when he mentioned the meeting behind the Target store."

"You know, I'm eighty percent convinced Kessler is the killer, but I'm not all the way there. We still go full speed after him and Maura, but the perp could be someone we don't even know about."

Chapter Seventeen

I'M HALF EXPECTING to find Ricky's apartment ransacked as the building super slides a master key into the lock.

"Terrible what happened to him," the super says, holding the door open for Nick and me. He's a short, barrel-chested man with gray hair and a ruddy complexion. Despite his somber expression, the creases around his eyes tell me he's usually jovial with a ready smile. Put a white beard on him, and he'd make the perfect Santa.

The apartment is a stark contrast to Maura's pad. The furniture doesn't all match, and the window affords a view of the air-handlers on the roof of the adjacent building. But the place is neat and orderly—not at all what I was expecting. There's the usual clutter you see in a well-lived-in home, but everything is in its place, and there's a place for everything. There are no empty beer cans on the end table, no chip wrappers on the floor. The throw cushions on the couch and chairs are fluffed and nicely arranged. A dishcloth is neatly folded on the kitchenette counter beside a sink empty of dirty dishes.

"I'll leave you to it," the super says, turning to the door.

"Why don't you stick around if you have the time. I can see we're going to have questions."

"I don't have anything on today, so my time is yours. It's Joe, by the way."

"Cassie and Nick. Who else lives here?" I ask. "Everything is too tidy for this to be a bachelor pad."

"A young lady by the name of Tessa. I don't know her last name, but I may have it on the rental agreement."

"What can you tell us about her?" Nick asks.

"Nice woman. I'd guess she's in her mid-thirties, about fifteen years younger than Ricky. They just got back from vacation. She works at The Paper Superstore—it's like a Staples."

"Where did they go on vacation?"

"I think it was Jamaica."

Memories of my honeymoon there with Kenny flood my mind. He picked a fight with one of the locals and came off second best. We ended up hightailing it back to Miami to get him proper medical attention for his broken teeth and dislocated jaw. I should have taken it as an omen of things to come.

"Have you seen visitors come here?"

"I've seen Tessa with girlfriends, but I always pegged Ricky as a loner."

I eye the Virgin Mary on the mantel above the gas fireplace. It seems incongruous in the apartment of a guy who was around drug dealers. We move into the bedroom. Two almost empty drawers are partly pulled out, and a bra hangs off the side of one of them. A dress is strewn on the floor.

"Oh my," Joe says. "What happened here?"

"Did someone toss the place?" Nick asks.

I step to the open closet doors. "No, Tessa left in a hurry," I say, pointing to the empty coat hangers and the impression on the carpet beside an overnight case.

"We need to speak to Tessa," I tell Joe. "Can you see if you have her details?"

"I'll be right back."

"You think he knows too much about the couple?" Nick asks when we're alone.

"Nah. He's naturally chatty." My phone rings, and I see it's Jasmin. I usually reject her calls during work hours, but I see an earlier text from her with the message: 9-1-1.

"What's up?" I ask her.

"I need money fast. My landlord just came over, and he's threatening to throw me out unless I pay the back rent."

I feel exasperated that Jasmin is always getting herself into financial difficulties despite her having a decent job. If I had to guess, the rent money went on booze and drugs. "How much do you owe?"

There are several beats of silence before she answers. "About three months."

I figure her *about three months* is closer to four or five. "I can't deal with this right now, Jaz. I'm working."

"I can come to wherever you are, sis. It won't take you a moment to write me a check."

All her life, Jasmin has had the notion that my money and my things are communal property. Because I've carved

136

out a better life for myself, she thinks it only fair that I share my wealth with her. It's maddening. "Even if I wanted to give you that big a check, I don't even have enough money in my bank account to cover three months of your rent."

"Write me a check for two months. He'll probably take it and let me stay."

"I can't do this right now." I hang up and see Nick standing in the doorway, looking concerned. "My sister," I explain. "She thinks what's mine is hers, but what's hers is her own."

"I have a brother like that," he says, nodding.

Joe comes back in the room, cutting short a conversation I didn't particularly want to have with Nick.

"It's Tessa Geddings," Joe says, handing me a sticky note. "She gave me the address of her sister as a reference. She also gave me the name of her supervisor at The Paper Superstore. It's all on the note."

We thank Joe graciously and head downstairs.

"Where first?" Nick asks when we reach the car. "Her work or the sister?"

"I'm guessing we'll find her at her sister's, but it won't take five minutes to check her work."

The Paper Superstore is in a strip mall, and it's exactly like a Staples store. We push through the glass doors, and the only human we see is the girl behind the cash register at the checkout. She looks about fifteen, but she has to be older to work there.

She appears startled when we badge her. "FBI? Wow." Her name tag reads Taylor. She pulls out her phone to record our interaction, but I tell her to put it away and ask where I can find Tessa Geddings. When Taylor tells us she hasn't seen Tessa today, I ask for the supervisor by name.

Taylor leans into a stalk microphone and blasts a thousand-watt message for Mrs. Osier to come to the front as the FBI is here.

She appears from the back of the store, buttoning up a lilac smock that seems to be the uniform they all wear.

We badge her, and I say, "We're looking for Tessa Geddings."

"She hasn't been in today," Mrs. Osier replies. "Her man was killed yesterday. What is wrong with you people? Don't you watch television? It was on Channel Five News yesterday evening and this morning."

"Thank you for your help," Nick says politely before I can reply with something more caustic.

"You saved me there," I say as we step out of the glass doors. "I don't know why people have to be so fucking rude and treat us like we're lower on the food chain than vermin."

Nick smiles. "You're not wrong, but I can't give you a reason why they do that."

On the way to Tessa's sister's house, Nick makes me swing through the In-N-Out Burger. He goes for a double-double burger and fries while I choose a grilled cheese sandwich that I can munch on while driving.

We park at the curb outside Alisa Geddings' home on Third Street, an older ranch-style home painted a dull brown color. I help myself to some of Nick's fries, telling him it's to speed things up. He flashes me a wry grin and hands me a paper towel to wipe my fingers.

The woman who answers the door is attractive and in her mid to late thirties with golden skin. Her long dark hair is pulled into a loose ponytail. I'm a step below her on the front stoop, and I meet her milk-chocolate-colored eyes rimmed with red. She dabs at them with a tissue.

"Alisa Geddings?" I ask softly.

She nods, and I continue, "I'm SSA Viera with the FBI, and this is Special Agent Stone. We'd like to speak to your sister, Tessa, if she's here."

"This isn't a good time. My sister has just lost her partner of ten years."

"We know, and we're trying to catch the person responsible."

I can see Alisa is wavering. Then a voice comes from within. "Who is it, Ali?"

"Cops."

A woman, the spitting image of Alisa, comes to her sister's side. She looks us over and says, "They can come in."

The two women show us to a couch in a cozy living room. Oversize seascape paintings cover the walls.

"You're Tessa?" I ask. "Are you twins?"

"Yes," she says, taking a seat in a recliner and rocking gently. Alisa stands at the fireplace, her arm on the low mantel, looking none too happy about our presence.

"We're sorry for your loss, Tessa. We're federal agents. You can call me Cassie, and this is Nick."

She gives a barely perceptible nod.

"I'll try to keep my questions brief. Do you have any

idea who might have done this thing?"

"Leo fucking Kessler, that's who."

"Was Ricky in contact with him recently?" I ask.

"I can't say for sure. But Ricky said Kessler was always threatening him over something."

"Ricky worked for him?"

"I guess it doesn't matter now what Ricky did. He sometimes ran errands for Kessler. Ricky's job at Olympic Tire didn't give him much free time."

"And these errands included drug deliveries?" Nick asks.

"Yeah, mostly."

"Did Ricky tell you he was a confidential informant for the police?"

"He told me he was a snitch, yeah. We didn't have any secrets."

"And there's a good chance that got him killed," Alisa snaps.

"He was found behind Target, wasn't he?" Tessa asks. "Do you know what he was doing there?"

I could tell her it's under investigation, but I cannot say anything but the truth. "Ricky went there to meet me," I say softly.

"I didn't catch who the hell you are," she says, getting to her feet, anger bursting through her eyes.

"I'm a federal agent with the FBI."

The corner of Tessa's box of tissues catches me on the forehead.

"You got him killed!" she screams. "I lost my lover and my best friend because of you."

Nick and I leap to our feet and start backing toward the door. Tessa takes a swing at me, but Alisa puts her arms around her twin sister's waist, pulling her back. This is just as well, because I'm sure Nick doesn't want to have to restrain her.

We hurry outside and down the front stoop. We're almost to the car when we hear Tessa. She's standing in the front doorway screaming, "Killers," at the top of her voice, over and over.

Chapter Eighteen

"YOU'RE IN TROUBLE," Stevie says as a greeting when I get into the office the following morning and drop my purse onto my desk.

"Nothing new there. What specific brand of trouble am I in this time?" I reply.

"ASAC Myles came looking for you. I told him you'd popped out for a quickie with a certain police detective," she teases. I'm noticing a new air of self-confidence in her since she got engaged. I'm also astounded that my newfound attraction to Detective Finch is that obvious.

Todd's in his cubicle, but I hear him chuckle as if Stevie made the best joke ever.

"Any idea what Myles wants?" It's never a good sign to be called upstairs.

"Not sure, but he didn't look happy and used the words 'as soon as.' By the way, you have a mark on your forehead."

"Ricky's girl, Tessa, threw a box of tissues at me." I lick my finger and rub the spot where the corner of the box struck me. "Feels sore."

"That looks much worse," she says. "My foundation is

the wrong shade for your skin tone."

"Look in my bag."

She opens my purse and pulls out a compact. "Got to have you looking flawless for your execution." She dabs the sponge on my forehead and blends it in. "Much better. You're ready for whatever ASAC Preston Myles has in store for you."

As I climb the stairs to the second floor, I rack my brains for any transgression I might have committed in the few hours since I saw him in the parking lot. Have Tessa and Alisa lodged a complaint already? Has Reed somehow set me up?

Myles has a proper office with a door and an assistant named Beryl, who is old enough to be my mother. She looks over the top of her reading glasses then uses the phone to tell Myles that I'm here, even though he's only ten feet away in his fishbowl of an office. I figure she must have worked for a big corporation, or this is another of Myles' quirks.

Beryl sets her phone on its cradle. "You can go through now."

I step into Myles' office and shut the door.

"Ah, Senior Special Agent Viera. Cassie, have a seat."

I see he's back to using my first name again and take it as a good sign. He points to the chair facing his desk as if I wouldn't know where to place my butt without his help.

"I spoke with Chief Holder about him dropping the investigation into Ava Barlow and Ricky Kelly's deaths, but he refused," Myles tells me like it's a big surprise.

As if that wasn't predictable.

He continues, "The man is a dinosaur who should have

retired years ago. I could employ other measures like having Sacramento speak to him or the mayor, but in the end, it might be best if you try to work with his people. I'm sorry."

He's speaking as if it was my idea to cut the police out of the investigation, and I hope he hasn't given Holder that impression.

"Of course, sir. It won't be a problem."

"Holder promised me that Detective Reed will suffer the consequences of his actions in leaking information about your case to the press."

I nod.

"You'll be liaising with Detective Finch. He's their new lead on the case."

There is a god. I nod again.

"Any new progress to report, Cassie?"

There's no point in cluttering his mind with too much information that may only come back to bite me in the ass. I say, "We have a promising lead from surveillance cameras at the strip mall. I'll let you know if it pans out."

"Good. Good. Sacramento can help you clean up the images."

If you don't mind waiting two weeks or more.

"I'll keep that in mind, sir."

Myles coughs and goes back to reading a document on his desk to let me know the meeting is over.

As I descend the stairs from the rarefied atmosphere of the second floor, Detective Finch comes in through the main entrance to the building, his travel coffee mug in his hand.

"Ha. Speak of the devil," I say.

"My ears were burning." He flashes me a smile.

"What brings you to this side of town? Come to gloat about your promotion?" I swipe my key card at the door to our offices and follow him in.

"You just came from speaking to Myles?"

"Yeah."

"Do we need to find somewhere quiet?" He furrows his brow.

"Nah. Come to my office. The peasants need to hear what we have to say."

"Who are you calling peasants?" Todd pipes up.

"Yeah, who?" Stevie adds her voice.

"Sounds like your peasants are revolting." There's a twinkle in Finch's eye as we settle into chairs in my office.

"They're revolting all right," I say, lobbing back his softball comment. "Why don't you go first?"

"As you probably heard, Reed is off the case, and I'm in charge—"

"Excellent news," I butt in.

"But you've no idea of the damage that Myles did in suggesting to Holder that we drop the case. Was that your idea?"

"Hell no. Is that what people think? Myles read Hazel DeRosa's article online and went ballistic."

"I can't say what Holder thinks, but Reed believes it all came from you making a power play, as he calls it."

"Crap."

"You need to watch your back with Reed. The guy is tightly wound and filled with rage at the best of times. He has a special kind of hate for you. I fear it's turning into a vendetta."

"I'm going to have to keep my head on a constant swivel?"

"Yeah. Relations between the FBI and the police have never been that great, but you've no idea of the harm Myles just did. Things are at a low ebb."

"You mean the officers won't support us?"

"Officer Mason will for sure," he chuckles, lifting himself out of his seat and trying to look over the divider to where Stevie sits.

"You know I can hear you speaking about my fiancé," she says.

"The officers will show up when needed," he continues. "They'll just bitch more than they used to."

"It's not humanly possible for them to bitch more." I shake my head.

"Is Officer Mason going to get caught between the two departments?" Stevie asks.

I turn and see her standing just outside my office.

"He'll be fine," Finch tells her. "He has a lot of buddies, and they are happy he's engaged."

"What's in your hand?" I ask Stevie.

"Photographs of Kessler from the prison."

"Come show us."

Nick is leaning over my office divider as Stevie spreads four glossy photos on my desk, tapping the one showing the back of Kessler's neck. "See the lightning bolt tattoo. It's much smaller than the one we saw on the surveillance video."

"You heard we spotted a tat on the neck of the guy who killed Ricky?" I ask Finch. "Todd is trying to enhance it."

"Yeah, but I'm not sure what these pictures prove. Kessler could easily have gotten it changed since he was released."

"Sure, but it's food for thought. I agree it's too soon to rule anyone out."

Lines crease Finch's brow. "Holder is still convinced Kessler killed Ava, and Pete paid him. I'm inclined to agree with the chief."

"We'll just have to catch Kessler and see what he has to say for himself."

Finch gets to his feet. "I'd best get back. Who knows what Reed is doing while I'm gone?" He turns to me when we reach the door. "Want to go out for a drink this evening?"

A bolt of adrenaline shoots through me. "Are you asking me out on a date?"

He grins. "If you want to call it that."

My mind won't work properly, but I hear myself say, "What time?"

"The Dusty Rose at seven. Does that work?"

"Sure." I watch him exit through the glass to the parking lot, wondering what is wrong with me. I don't have any problem meeting a strange guy behind Target, attending autopsies, or using my pistol when needed. But I get butterflies when Finch asks me out for a drink. Go figure.

When I get back into our office area, Stevie says, "This latest development has me worried about my relationship with Officer Mason."

"What do you think might happen?"

"The other officers might resent him, or the people here may think that I'm consorting with the enemy."

"Never going to happen," Nick exclaims.

"Nope, never," Todd adds.

"Not from me either, and you heard what Finch said about the other officers' attitude toward Mason."

"I guess," Stevie frowns.

"It's me who's going to have the harder job navigating the politics."

"And watching your back for Reed," Nick adds, joining us. "What do you think he might do?"

"The guy is bad news. I wouldn't put it past him to sabotage the investigation if it makes me look bad. Or give me a beating if he thought he'd get away with it."

"Here," Todd says, placing a rectangle of black plastic in my hand

"A stun gun," I exclaim. "Where did you get it?"

"The place where everything illegal comes from."

"Take it," Nick says. "Reed won't do anything while we're around. You need to worry about the times when you're alone."

"I'll think about it," I say, slipping it into my pocket.

"I've got something to show you all," Todd says. We follow him to his cubicle and crowd around his monitors. The picture of the back of the man who killed Ricky is still grainy, but the tattoo is almost discernible.

Nick leans in, squinting at the image. "Still looks like a snake to me."

"Nah. It's a five-pointed crown," Stevie says.

"I guess we'll have to wait a little longer," I tell them, "but it leads me to the next item of business—expanding the list of suspects. I've been remiss in allowing us to become so narrowly focused on one person." I turn to Stevie. "How many people are on your list of convicts who Barlow sent to prison and who have been released recently? We said released in the last six months, didn't we?"

"We did," she says. "I'm up to six individuals."

"Let's get their names on the whiteboard."

"Right, boss."

"Since you had so much success getting Kessler's picture, Stevie, can you pull prison photos of the other six?"

"On it."

"Your assignment, Nick, is to talk to their parole officers. Are they all employed? Have any of them gone AWOL?"

"Got it."

"Todd, if any of the agents need you to help them with researching these individuals, that task has priority over cleaning up the picture of the tattoo."

Todd groans.

"I'm not saying it's not important because it is. But we desperately need to expand our list of suspects."

"But recognizing the tattoo will slim down the list of suspects, so we don't waste time on the wrong ones," Todd insists.

"If we find someone with a matching tattoo on their prison photo, it will send them to the top of our list. I was hoping that would be the case with Kessler. But the converse isn't true. We can't eliminate anyone who doesn't have a neck tattoo on their prison photo, as they could have had it inked since. Everyone good with our direction?"

All three team members express their agreement.

Chapter Nineteen

"I JUST RECEIVED Ricky's autopsy report from the medical examiner," I tell the team. We're seated at the conference room table. "Not surprisingly, he died from bleeding out. There's only one item of note. Like Ava, Ricky was branded by his killer. The word 'RAT' was carved into his chest."

"Perhaps Ricky-the-snitch was killed by someone else he grassed on to the cops," Nick suggests.

"We can't rule that out, but it's not something I want to devote any time to at this juncture. Ricky and Ava's deaths were so similar—the knife cuts to the throats and a message carved into their bodies. We also have the blue minivan at both locations. We have to assume Ricky and Ava were killed by the same person."

"Fair enough, boss."

"So we think that Kessler, the guy who was dating Ava Barlow, killed her then Ricky," Stevie says. "And Ricky was killed because he knew where to find Kessler?"

"That's one scenario," I say. "Another possibility is that Ava was killed by someone wanting to exact vengeance on

Pete Barlow."

"You think Ricky somehow knew what the killer had done?" Stevie questions.

"Maybe. Ricky was killed because of what he knew. Anything else to talk about before we dive into Stevie's list of people who could have had a grudge against Pete?" I ask.

"I've been following up on the first scenario and running a comprehensive background check on Leo Kessler," Todd says. "A few months before Kessler was arrested on drug charges, he was suspected of being involved in a robbery at a private residence. Gold bars valued at two hundred grand were stolen. Pete brought him in for questioning, but there was insufficient evidence to hold him. For some reason, this isn't in Kessler's police file."

"Was the gold ever recovered?" I ask.

"Negative," Todd says. "The gold was in the form of three bars, but it could have since been melted down."

"Anyone ever charged in the theft?" Stevie asks.

"Also negative, but the so-called homeowner was later done for money-laundering."

"That's sweet," she laughs. "I'm surprised the theft was reported."

"Another story in the stupid criminals series," Todd says, snickering.

When the chuckles die down, I turn to Stevie, "Let's wade into your list of individuals who were arrested by Barlow and recently released from prison. We're talking about people who could have killed Ava because they harbored a grudge against Pete."

"First up is one Dirk McCloskey," she says, stepping to the whiteboard and printing his name. "He was convicted ten years ago of murdering his wife, Zoe. Her body was never found, just a large quantity of blood, her bloody sweatshirt, and a knife with his prints on it. He's always maintained his innocence, saying Barlow set him up—"

"Don't they all say that?" Nick interrupts.

"Wait until you hear the kicker," Stevie continues. "When Barlow took a SWAT team to McCloskey's house to arrest him for killing his wife, he found Kessler there. The police grabbed Kessler for suspected drug use, but there wasn't enough evidence, and he wasn't charged. McCloskey went to prison for ten years. Got out a few months ago."

"And Zoe's body was never found?" I ask.

"No, as surprising as that seems," she says. "At McCloskey's trial, the prosecution suggested he buried her somewhere, but the defense claimed Barlow set him up."

"Did they put forth a reason why Barlow would do that?" I frowned.

"McCloskey was a serial wife-beater, and Barlow investigated many of the 9-1-1 calls, but Zoe always said she fell and hurt herself. You know the drill, boss."

I shake my head. "Sadly, I've heard it too many times."

"Didn't Kessler eventually go to jail for drug charges?" Nick asks.

"That was three years after Zoe's death, and it was for distribution," Stevie says.

At the sound of someone coming into our offices, I lean back to gaze through the open door. I'm shocked when I see who Detective Finch has with him. "Let's pick this up later,"

I tell the team, getting to my feet to greet the visitors.

Alisa Geddings looks worn out. She's wearing a navy tunic top with a paisley design over white pants, and her long dark hair is up in a messy bun.

"Alisa would like to make a statement," Finch tells me, "but she wants to speak to the two agents who came to her house."

"Of course. Thank you for coming in." I summon a smile for her, then turn to Nick, who is heading back to his office. "Can you come and join us?"

"Sure, boss."

"May I get either of you something to drink? Tea, coffee, soda, water?" I ask our guests. Finch declines, but Alisa goes for water, and I fetch her a bottle from the fridge.

"How can we help?" I ask Alisa when we're seated around the table.

She takes a few sips of water, and I can see something akin to embarrassment in her eyes. "I am so sorry for the way my sister and I treated you both yesterday." Her gaze flashes between Nick and me. "Ricky's death is so horrible, but I'm sorry we directed our anger at you. You're only trying to do your job and catch the person responsible."

"No problem," I say. "It was like water off a duck's back. I'm sorry for your loss. I can't imagine what it must be like for you and your sister."

She sips at the water bottle, leaving a trail of amber lipstick around the rim. "Tessa and I are both convinced that Leo Kessler killed Ricky." She pauses again, and I hope that's not all she's come in to say. I appreciate her apology, but it doesn't ease the guilt I'm feeling for her brother-in-law's death.

Alisa seems to be searching for the right words. They come out in halting sentences, punctuated by sips from the water bottle. "A year ago, I dated Leo Kessler a few times . . . It was stupid of me . . . I didn't know what he was like . . . The last time we met, he drugged me and raped me."

"I'm so sorry to hear that," I say softly.

"We'd been to a club, and I had more to drink than I should have."

"Girl, don't ever blame yourself for what happened," I insist.

"After we left the club, he drove me to a house in the hills . . . that's where it happened. Tessa and I think you might catch him there."

"Were you examined at the hospital? Did they collect physical evidence?"

"No, nothing like that. I'd rather forget about what he did to me. We want you to arrest him for Ricky's murder."

"Do you recall the address where Kessler took you?"

"I will never forget." She slips the torn-off corner of a newspaper across the table. The date shows it's from almost a year ago, and there's an address hand-written in the margin. I figure Alisa scribbled it down after she was raped.

"Nick will make a copy for you," I say, turning to him.

He reaches for the slip of paper, but Alisa stops him. "Keep it. I'm done hanging on to the past. It will be enough for me that Kessler is in jail for Ricky's death."

I thank Alisa profusely as she leaves with Finch. He promises to return after dropping her at her car.

"What do we do next, boss?" Nick asks after I've filled in

Stevie and Todd.

"Check the ownership of the house." I perch at my computer and type in the address. "It's owned by a company called Acorn Holdings." I key that name into another database. "It's a blind shell company."

"Now what?" Stevie asks.

"Hold tight a moment." I punch the number for a department at the Sacramento Field office into my desk phone. A voice comes on the line:

"Vice, Agent Nicholson." When I ask him to check for any connection between Acorn Holdings and Leo Kessler, he says, "One moment SSA Viera."

I regard Nick and Stevie expectantly while I wait with the phone on speaker.

Nicholson comes back on the line. "The shell corporation is Kessler's. I should warn you he's part of an ongoing drug investigation, and you're not to approach him."

"This is a homicide investigation. Kessler's killed two people."

"Nevertheless, I must caution you to stay away from him."

"Thank you for the information, Agent Nicholson." I end the call and see that Detective Finch has joined Nick and Stevie.

"Problem?" Finch asks.

"Vice just told me Kessler's part of an ongoing investigation."

"Well, I haven't heard that. I can pick him up."

"Whenever we ask vice about a drug dealer, they are

always part of an ongoing FBI investigation," I tell him. "The agents in vice are arrogant pricks who think they run the Bureau. I won't pay attention to their silly games. We first need to stake out the place to make sure Maura and Kessler are there. We don't want to go in half-cocked and find they're out."

"I'll alert our SWAT team and put them on standby," Finch says, pulling out his phone.

"Stevie, I'll take you with me on the first shift," I say to her. "I don't believe you've been on a stakeout before."

"Not since we did a mock one at the academy."

I turn to Nick and Finch. "You two guys take the second shift. You may be late home, though I'm hoping we'll get a bead on the targets before then. As soon as we confirm they are there, we'll have SWAT breach the house, and the four of us will follow them in. Nick, can you get a warrant started?"

"Sure."

"I think we should have both stakeout teams near the house and ready to move in," Finch suggests. "We don't want to miss Maura and Kessler."

I pause for a moment, considering the idea. "Fair enough. Stevie and I will move out shortly. We'll take a plain-wrap Bureau car. You two follow on as soon as the warrant is submitted." As I'm speaking, I pull up an aerial map of the property, and the others crowd around to watch. We're gazing at an isolated house with a circular driveway surrounded by woodland.

"I'll take my personal car," Finch says. "You can recognize our unmarked cars a mile away."

"If you're okay with that?"

"It's been through stakeouts before."

"Looks like we may have to park there and hike into the undergrowth." I use a finger to indicate a side road about a hundred yards from the target house. "Otherwise, they'll see the cars. Time to get dressed-down," I tell Stevie. "See you there, guys," I holler as we head to the women's locker room.

I'm pulling on a pair of jeans when my phone buzzes. It takes a moment to retrieve it from my gray pants, and I answer without checking the caller ID.

"Well," Jasmin says, "are you going to lend me the money to pay my back rent? I'm dying here."

"No, I'm not." I've lent Jasmin money before, and it never gets paid back. "Where did all the money you earned go?"

"I've had a lot of expenses. First, my boyfriend's TV crapped out, and I had to buy him a new one. Then I needed new clothes for work. My old ones looked awful."

"You wear scrubs at work, or did you quit working for the plastic surgeon?"

"People see my street clothes when I arrive and leave."

"And what are you doing buying expensive things like a television for your boyfriend when you don't have money for the rent?"

"God, you're just like mom and dad. Are you going to help me or not?"

"I'm not giving you another cent. As a nurse, you earn nearly as much as I do."

"That's because you're a loser working in a loser job."

She hangs up before I can reply.

Stevie is giving me a funny look, so I say, "My crazy sister is behind on her rent. If I give her anything, she'll spend it on booze and drugs or give it to some lowlife who is sponging off her."

She gives me a pitying look.

"I'm not expecting a firefight, but make sure you take plenty of ammo," I tell her.

"Copy that." She pats her jeans pocket. "Kevlar vests are in the car?" Like me, she's dressed in a sweatshirt, jeans, and tennis shoes.

"Affirmative," I say. "And bring a jacket. We don't know how late we'll be there."

Chapter Twenty

"ANY SIGN OF them?" Stevie asks. "Should we move to the rear of the house?"

We're at the residence where Alisa was sexually assaulted by Kessler. We also hope to snag Maura here. Stevie and I are lying side by side on an old blanket behind a small berm. It's a warm day, and our sleeves are rolled up. Our position gives us a decent view through the front windows. The county assessor's listing on my phone says the house is 2350 square feet, but it looks larger. The clapboard exterior needs a fresh coat of paint. Anything other than lime green next time. The gutters are clogged with pine needles, I'm guessing from last winter, but maybe the winter before.

If Leo Kessler is living here, I can't imagine that home maintenance is high on his list of priorities.

It's the oak slats in the blinds that make the house look like something from another time. Fortunately for us, they are mostly raised, though we haven't yet spotted Maura or Kessler.

"Maybe they're upstairs," I tell her. A pair of dormer

windows facing our way reveals that the house has a second story built into the sloping roof.

"We've been here for twenty minutes and not seen any sign of life," she insists.

"Stakeouts are a game of patience. We could be here for hours. The hood of the Beemer parked in the driveway was warm when I felt it."

"You do realize that they could have two cars."

"It's not likely that they drove here in the Beemer a short while ago and left in another car. The simplest explanation is that they're somewhere inside the house."

"One of us should stay here while the other checks the back," she suggests.

"It's too exposed behind the house. I don't want to risk spooking them before the others get here."

The side door opens, and a man I assume is Kessler struggles out with a pair of suitcases. He's wearing stained jeans and a beater T-shirt. I track him with the binoculars to the car, catching sight of his back. There's a tattoo on his neck, but it looks like a lightning bolt and seems smaller than the one we saw on the man who murdered Ricky. I get a sinking feeling that Kessler might not be the person we're looking for.

He sets the cases down behind the trunk while he takes a breather. He's tall, but not as broad-shouldered as I imagined.

"He either has something really weighty inside those cases, or he's not our man," I tell her.

"How so?"

"The perp who stole the minivan lifted a two hundred

and fifty-pound bike into the back without breaking a sweat."

"Maybe he's been up all night boning Maura," she quips.

"Not useful."

I don't hear Nick and Finch until they slide onto the blanket alongside me.

"Anything?" Finch asks.

"Just Kessler, and it looks like he's leaving soon," I say, handing Finch the binoculars. I see Kessler pop the trunk and load the two cases. He leaves the lid up and heads back inside the house.

"No sign of the blue minivan." Nick's voice is a shouted whisper.

"They probably know we're looking for it," Finch suggests. "It's either in the garage, or they ditched it somewhere."

Maura comes out of the house looking cool in sunglasses, a tank top, and white jeans. She opens a car door and throws a jacket onto the backseat, followed by her purse.

"How far out is SWAT?" I ask Finch in a low whisper. "Our targets are close to leaving."

He speaks into his radio. I don't hear what he is saying until he curses and turns to me. "SWAT is twenty-five minutes out."

"That's no fucking good. What happened? Kessler and his woman will be long gone by then."

"They have this armored vehicle that's ex-military. It's bomb proof, but one of the tires was flat. You can't go to

162

Walmart and have them slap on a replacement."

"Surely they have other vehicles?" I snap. "Hell, I'll go fetch them in my car."

"The armored vehicle is their first choice for situations like this."

"So you really don't know when they'll be here." I lock eyes with him.

"Pretty much," Finch confesses. "I'm guessing we have Reed to thank for the delay."

"I knew I should have brought in an FBI SWAT team." I pause to think. "Okay, we're going to have to take Kessler and his girlfriend ourselves. We need to catch them in the open before they get inside the vehicle and lock the doors. Finch and Nick will apprehend Kessler, Stevie and I will take Maura. We need to work our way along the side of the driveway under the cover of the brush. If they see us, we'll move in from wherever we are. Got that, everyone?"

I look both ways and catch three nods.

"No more talking. I'll give the order to go." I set off crab-walking through the undergrowth, keeping my head down. The rest of the team follows. It's a killer on the thighs.

As we move toward our intended position, I keep an eye on what's happening through gaps in the undergrowth. Maura comes out of the house with a pair of store bags and sets them down. Kessler has his back to us, and I can't hear what he's saying, but I can tell he's not happy about all the stuff Maura is bringing.

She is facing our way, and we've almost reached our destination when she cranes her neck. Kessler spins around as she points a finger directly at us.

"Go. Go. Go," I scream, and we race to cover the twenty-five feet to our targets. "Federal agents. Get down on the ground."

Maura freezes, her mouth agape in surprise. Stevie and I tackle her, and she lands hard on her butt with the two of us on top of her. She wriggles from under us and gets to her feet, but I manage to grab her leg.

Stevie screams as Maura snatches a handful of her hair and yanks it. But I strike Maura's forearm with a Karate chop, and she lets go.

From the corner of my eye, I see Kessler bolting to the side door like a racehorse.

"You bastard, Maura yells through clenched teeth.

She takes a swing at my chin, white-hot rage streaming from her eyes.

I dodge the blow and land one in the pit of her stomach. She gasps and exhales sharply, groaning.

Maura tries to claw me—her teeth go for my fingers, and her nails bite into my forearm. But when my other fist connects with her chin, she collapses back to the ground, stunned.

Stevie and I roll her on her front. She's spitting every swear word I've ever heard and a few I haven't as we slip on the cuffs.

I see Finch and Nick on Kessler's heels, but he manages to enter the house and slam the side door shut. Finch grabs the doorknob too late, and we hear the sound of a bolt engaging.

Nick doubles back, and I hear him smash a front window and knock out the remaining glass so he can climb in.

Finally, Finch kicks his way through the side door with a resounding crash, and he moves inside. But no one guesses what Kessler is up to until we hear the ATV fire up.

"Crap. He's cutting and running." With Maura subdued and cuffed, I leave Stevie to guard her while I take off toward the sound of the revving engine.

I pump my legs, my feet slipping on the loose gravel. I round the corner of the house and fly into a dense cloud of blue exhaust fumes.

Through the haze, I see Kessler speeding away from me on the ATV. I sprint after him, but it's an exercise in futility. I stop and sight down my pistol at the back tires, but my heart is racing, and my shots go wide.

Kessler returns fire over his shoulder as his tiny vehicle picks up speed and reaches a narrow path cutting through the woodland. His aim is not even close. Seeing I'm not going to catch him, I bend over with my hands on my knees and gulp air.

"We blew that," Finch says, appearing beside me, his expression dark. The sound of the ATV's engine is fading into the distance.

"That's an understatement," I snap. "Put out an all-points bulletin for Kessler. If it weren't for bad luck, I'd have no luck at all."

"On it. Will you call your people?"

"Pointless." I shake my head as Nick joins us. "The powers that be already have three agents on the case, so they won't commit more resources to a bottom-feeder like Kessler. I could kick myself for not checking around back when Stevie suggested it. I could have easily disabled the ATV."

"Don't beat yourself up," Finch says, placing a warm hand between my shoulder blades. "How far can he get on that thing?"

"Far enough," I reply.

Nick is checking his phone. "The warrant for the house is approved."

"I'm calling in an FBI forensics team," I say, punching a number into my phone. "Except for you, Finch, I'm done with relying on anything from the police department."

After ending the call, I retrace my steps to the driveway. Maura is sitting on the ground with her back against the side of the house.

"Go fetch the car," I tell Stevie, and she trots off.

"Think you're pretty smart, do you bitch?" the prisoner asks, giving me a smile that's as warm as an ice cube.

"I guess so because I'm not the one in handcuffs facing two homicide charges."

"Ha, you're funny." She spits at me, but I dodge the loogie. "I've never killed anyone."

"Maybe not, but your boyfriend Kessler has, and that makes you an accomplice."

"You'll never catch him."

"That's where you're wrong."

"Who is he supposed to have killed?"

"Ava Barlow, for one."

"Leo never laid a finger on her."

"We know he was fucking her, so that's not true."

When she doesn't reply, I continue, "Nothing to say?

We'll talk to you downtown."

Chapter Twenty-One

I'M SITTING IN an interrogation room at the police station, waiting for Maura to be brought in. We have a couple of interview rooms and a similar number of cells at our local FBI offices. They're more for emergency use, as we don't have a whole staff to keep an eye on the prisoners. I could request personnel from the Sacramento Field Office, but even ASAC Preston Myles would ask me why I'm not using the police's custody facilities. And he's always mistrusted them as much as I have.

I mean, what use is a law enforcement department who can't rustle up a SWAT team and have it show up on time? Or ever? I stayed at the house until the FBI forensics team arrived, and SWAT still hadn't put in an appearance.

My money is on Reed screwing with us. If I ever find proof, I'll have his badge. The rest of the police will thank me if they have any guts.

The door opens, and a heavy-set female officer brings Maura in and shoves her down into a seat across the table from Finch and me.

No one has attempted to clean the prisoner or had her

change into an orange jumpsuit. Her face and clothing are smudged with dirt from the driveway. After grappling with her on the ground, I'm in a similar condition, but I have washed my face and straightened my hair.

Finch gives Maura her Miranda warning. When he asks if she understands her rights, she gives a slight nod.

"Out loud for the tape, please," I say.

"Yes."

Even with that single word, I can tell her voice has lost the combative edge it had back at the house.

"Am I correct that you're declining to have a lawyer present?" I don't want an attorney getting her testimony tossed out by saying Maura didn't fully understand her rights. It's happened.

Another feeble "Yes" comes from her lips.

"You know you're facing charges that could include murder?"

"Leo Kessler hasn't killed anyone, and neither have I."

"I just got a call from the head of the forensic team going over the house where you were staying," I continue. "They've found a substantial quantity of drugs in your luggage and in the shopping bags you were carrying. Charges against you will almost certainly include drug possession with intent to distribute. That's a five-year stretch right there."

"Five years?" She sounds horrified. "The drugs belonged to Leo. I had nothing to do with them."

"You were carrying them out to the car."

"No. No. I didn't know that the packages contained drugs."

"Do we look gullible to you, Maura?" I ask. "We found coke at your apartment."

"Leo must have left it there. I swear it was his thing, not mine."

"Why did you resist arrest if you did nothing wrong?"

"I didn't know you were real cops."

"Okay, that's it. We've heard enough stupid lies." I get to my feet, and Finch follows suit.

"What should we charge her with?" he asks.

"Two counts of murder and drug possession with intent to distribute," I say. "Let's go."

"No, no, you can't go," Maura screams. "I didn't do the things you're accusing me of."

I stop at the door and look back at her. "If you don't cooperate, we have to charge you."

"No choice in the matter," Finch adds.

"All right, I'll talk, I'll talk. Come back. What do you want to know?"

We saunter back to the table. I take a seat, but Finch stands, saying, "She's wasting our time. I've got witnesses who are willing to cooperate."

"You're right—" I start.

"On my father's grave, I swear I will tell you anything you want."

Finch takes a seat, appearing reluctant.

"Let's start at the top," I say. "What were you doing with Pete Barlow?"

"We had a relationship."

"We're way beyond that point, Maura. Pete's in his fifties and not remotely good-looking. You, on the other

170

hand, are twenty-three and hot. Oh, wait, you're a hooker. Was Pete paying you?"

"No way. I only take high-level clients."

"So, what was your motive for having sex with him? I know it was something you and Leo Kessler were into. I just can't think what."

Maura hesitates, and I start to get to my feet again.

"Stop, stop, I'll tell you," she says, the words coming out in a rush.

"If it's not the truth, all bets are off."

"A few years back, Pete Barlow, Detective Barlow as he was then, arrested Leo for distributing drugs. This was way before Leo and I got together. At the time of the police raid, Leo had some gold bars."

"Kessler was suspected of stealing them from a private residence, but he was never charged," I tell Finch. "I haven't had time to catch you up on that discovery. Go on, Maura. I think I see where this is headed."

"Leo believes Detective Barlow took the gold for himself."

"And Leo thought that if he cozied up to Ava Barlow to keep her distracted while you seduced Pete with booze and sex, he might tell you where he stashed the loot. Am I right?"

"Pretty much."

"And did Pete tell you?"

"He more or less admitted he had it stashed away somewhere. But I never learned where he kept it."

"Something is puzzling me," Finch says. "Pete arrested Kessler, and now you're saying Pete stole his gold. So why didn't Pete recognize Kessler when he got together with Ava." Sometimes we already know the answer to the questions we ask.

"You must have seen Pete and Ava's house," Maura replies. "They led completely separate lives. Leo was very careful never to bump into Pete, and he warned Ava never to mention his name."

"You sure you never found out where Pete hid the gold?" I ask.

"It took a long time to earn Pete's trust. He used to be a cop. Pete was so close to telling me where to find the loot when someone went and killed Ava."

"How do you know Leo didn't kill her?" Finch asks. "After all, everyone says she was an unpleasant woman."

"Because her death ruined everything. Cops were everywhere. There was no way Leo and I could go forward with the plan. We thought about lying low until the heat died down, but we were afraid that someone investigating Ava's death would come across the gold."

"How did you and Kessler get together?" I ask.

"We met in a bar a year ago. It turned out we both hated Pete Barlow. Leo hated him for stealing his gold. I hated Pete because he got my mother jailed for a crime she didn't commit."

I turn to Finch. "I'm done here for now. How about you?"

He nods, and we get to our feet.

"So, what are you charging me with?" Maura asks, her eyes wide.

"Nothing for now," I reply. "But you'll have to stay in

the lockup until we catch Kessler. We'll see where we are after he corroborates your story."

Finch makes a phone call, and the heavy-set female officer comes into the room. Maura screams, angrily protesting her innocence as she's led away.

"What do you reckon about her testimony?" Finch asks, taking a seat across the table from me.

"I found her believable. She answered the nagging question of why she and Kessler seduced Pete and his wife."

"Nothing Maura said lessens my suspicion that Kessler killed Ava and Ricky," Finch adds.

"What do you imagine was Kessler's motive?"

"My money's on him attacking Ava in a drug-fueled rage. Look at the injuries she suffered."

It sounds possible, but it feels like trying to squeeze myself into pants that are a size too small. I believe Ava was killed by an as yet unknown person, but it's not worth arguing hypotheticals until we have more evidence. Instead, I say, "I have no difficulty imagining Pete not checking gold bars into evidence."

"I can't get my head around a decorated detective like Pete doing such a thing." Finch shakes his head. "Nor can I agree with Chief Holder's idea that Pete paid Kessler to kill his wife."

"You're letting your personal relationship with Pete color your judgment. Why don't we ask him about it? You still have him in custody, right?"

"How about we go for that drink at the Dusty Rose and talk to Pete in the morning?"

"I've hardly eaten since breakfast. One glass of wine on

my empty stomach, and I'll be out for the count. I wouldn't say no to a meal, provided we don't discuss the case."

"Sounds good. Any preferences?"

"Nowhere exotic. My clothes are filthy. I'm stinky and need a shower. But if I go home and take one, I'll collapse on the bed and fall asleep. So, you'll have to put up with the smell and tiredness if you want to dine with me."

A smile plays on his lips. "I think I can manage that. Let's go. I'll drive, and we can decide where to eat on the way."

Chapter Twenty-Two

THE TACO HOUSE is a gem of a place. The menu isn't vast, but everything they serve is fresh and delicious. I'm finding it's also perfect when you're feeling self-conscious about the state of your clothing after rolling around in the dirt with a suspect. Patrons come straight here after a day at the river, so my soiled jeans and shirt blend right in.

Finch and I are seated outside on a deck illuminated by light globes strung between the trees. We're halfway through a dish of nachos, and the waitress has just set a plate of fish tacos before me and served Finch a chicken super burrito.

I've relented on the alcohol, and we're both enjoying bottles of Dos Equis.

"You know all about my crazy sister who thinks I should subsidize her rent and her drug habit," I say, "and my ex-husband who ran off with his gym instructor. Time to fill me in on your life. How come there's no Mrs. Finch?"

"It's a long story," he hedges, unrolling the foil from the end of his burrito and taking a bite.

I nibble the corner of a taco. "The night is young. We've

got as much time as you need."

"It's not something I share with anyone."

"You invite me out to dinner, and now I'm anyone?" I say in a faux haughty voice.

"I seem to remember it was you who suggested getting a meal," he counters.

"But it was you who invited me out on a date at the Dusty Rose."

"Now we're on a date?" he teases.

"Okay, How about your childhood? Is that any less controversial than your love life?"

"I grew up in Antioch. I have a younger sister who followed in my father's footsteps and became a doctor."

"So how come you didn't go along with what sounds like the family tradition?"

"I was always a disappointment to my father in school. My grades were decent, mostly A's and the occasional B, but never quite good enough for him. An A grade should be an A-plus. You know how that goes."

"Indian fathers are the worst for pushing their kids through school, let me tell you. Usually just the male offspring, but my firsthand experience proves that's not always the case."

"How was he with the guys you dated?"

"Very picky. He probably would have come after you with a shotgun," I chuckle.

"Anyway, after disappointing my father in school," he continues, "I thought I'd choose a profession that would frustrate him more."

"Seriously? That's your reason for working as a

176

detective in the police department?"

"Rebellion—sure. The job has grown on me since. Especially when I get to work with sexy FBI agents."

"Stop it, you're making me blush," I say, fanning my hands at my cheeks. "Remember what I said. I'm not used to attention from men. I've been out of the dating scene for a long while."

"Nah, it's the jalapeños that are making you warm."

We chat about this and that until the waitress clears our table.

"Cassie," he says, taking my hand. "I need to tell you something about me."

"Oh, God. What, you're an alcoholic? You're gay? You're married? Which is it?"

"I was married for five years. My wife died in tragic circumstances."

"I am so sorry to hear that. I shouldn't have made fun of you earlier. What happened?"

He's gripping my hand tighter, massaging my palm with his thumb. Tears leak from the corner of an eye, and he brushes it away with the back of his free hand.

"I used to have a sports car. One stupid, horrible night seven years ago, Brylee and I were coming home from a movie. The night was dark, and it had just stopped raining, so the pavement was wet. But we were laughing and joking like we always did."

"You don't have to go on," I say softly.

"I want to. A truck coming toward us took a bend too fast and jackknifed. Brylee swerved to try and avoid it, but her side of the car ended up going sideways into the front wheel of the truck."

"She was killed instantly?"

"No. Brylee was semi-conscious after the accident. I only had a couple of scrapes. She tried to speak to me but couldn't. I held her hand until the paramedics arrived, but it was too late for them to help her. An autopsy later revealed that her aorta had ruptured. The doctor told me there was nothing anyone could have done for her, but I still think there must have been something. Something I could have done to prevent her from dying."

"That is simply the most tragic thing I've ever heard."

"Afterward, there are a thousand what-ifs. What if we hadn't gone to that movie? What if we had gone out for a meal instead? A thousand different ways to blame myself for what happened."

"Listen to me," I say, locking eyes with him. "In no way was Brylee's death your fault."

"A part of me knows that, but another part will never forgive myself."

"I'm glad you felt able to tell me."

"I don't tell many people about Brylee or the accident because it puts a damper on any relationship. Usually, after people see how much her death hurt me, they start to treat me as if I'm fragile or heap sympathy on me. Or else they take on the sorrow themselves, but it quickly becomes a burden for them, and they have to distance themselves from me. I don't want to become a tragic figure to you."

"I promise not to treat you any differently."

"People have promised that in the past, but it's not as easy as it sounds. Many times, I've wanted to be able to untell someone. To take it back."

"I promise to do my best. That's all I can do, isn't it?"

"You're right."

"I don't know how dating would go for us, but I feel sure that we'll always be friends."

After the meal, he drives me to the FBI offices to pick up my car. As the downtown buildings flash past my window in a blur, I reflect that we never picked up the playful banter from earlier in the meal. "I'm determined not to let your wife's death torpedo our relationship before it's started," I tell him. "Let's go for that drink at the Dusty Rose in the next day or two."

"Sounds good to me." He flashes me a grin.

When we pull to a stop next to my car, I lean over the center console to kiss his cheek, but he turns, and my lips land on his.

We're too tentative for a full-on kiss, but I say, "That was nice," and hop out of the car, feeling happier than I have in a long while.

Chapter Twenty-Three

"MEETING IN TEN minutes," I shout, setting my coffee and bag on my desk. I flop into the chair, hoping my day will be less demanding than yesterday.

"Come see us when you're settled," Nick shouts over the top of the dividers. "We're in Todd's office."

"No rest for the wicked," I reply. I find Nick and Stevie staring over Todd's shoulders at his workstation. They move aside to allow me to squint at the screen. The tattoo from the suspect's neck at the strip mall is definitely clearer than the last time I checked.

"We still can't make out what it represents," I say. "But now Todd's cleaned it up, I can see it something round. Maybe a coiled snake."

Stevie hands me Kessler's prison photograph, and I compare the two.

"The one I glimpsed on Kessler's neck yesterday was smaller and spiky like the lightning bolt we see in this picture from the prison. Different enough from the surveillance video for me to have serious doubts whether he killed Ricky."

"I'm hoping we catch the guy soon, and we can compare Todd's work with the real thing," Nick says. "I mean, how far can he go on an ATV?"

"Excellent work, Todd," I say, though I know a jury could look at the two pictures and reach a different conclusion. "I think you've taken this as far as we need for now. As Nick says, let's see what Kessler's tattoo looks like when we capture him."

Todd looks a bit pained but points his fingers like pistols. "Sure thing, boss."

I wish he wouldn't do that, but I think he'd be deeply offended if I tell him I don't like it after all this time. "Let's head to the conference room."

When we're all seated, I update them on Maura's interview.

"She really folded on Kessler," Stevie says.

"So Maura and Kessler dating the Barlows was all about recovering the gold bars that Pete Barlow took," Nick observes. "Who would've guessed?"

"We geniuses didn't." My phone sounds, and I answer, "You're right on cue, Finch. I'm putting you on speaker," I emphasize in case he says anything cute about dinner yesterday. "What do you have for us?"

"I first checked on the claims made about the theft by the money launderer."

"The guy had to be the biggest dip-shit ever to go to the police after he got robbed," Stevie interrupts. "Isn't that Money Laundering 101? Never call the cops."

"Thank you for pointing that out, Agent Wells," Finch says. "The guy claimed that three gold bars valued at sixty-five grand apiece were taken."

"And he'd already gone to the trouble of laundering the money that purchased the gold," Todd chuckles.

"The peanut gallery is lively this morning," Finch says. "Next, I searched through items that were checked into evidence when Kessler was arrested. No gold bars. I even checked around that date in case it had been misfiled in the evidence book. Nada, nothing."

"It supports Maura's testimony," I say.

"Unless someone else took the gold from Kessler, and he's trying to smear Pete."

"Long shot, Finch. A very long shot. And then you have to come up with another reason for a looker like Maura dating an old fart like Pete. Not to mention a drug dealer dating a bitch like Ava."

"I guess."

After the call ends, I say, "Anything else to share?"

"Yeah," Stevie says. "I've been going through my list of recently released convicts with a grudge against Pete Barlow, looking for anything suspicious. Two of them have missed meetings with their parole officer. It's not common as it means an automatic return to prison. Dirk McCloskey, who I mentioned before, has missed two meetings. He's the guy who stabbed his wife to death. He's believed to have buried her, but her body was never found. Paul Henderson also murdered his wife, and he's missed one meeting. It might mean something. Might not."

"Keep following up with the parole officers, and let's find out all we can about the two men. Do you know of a connection between them?"

"They both did their time in Folsom prison, if that helps."

"Delve deeper. Did they share a cell or hang out together? Anything else?"

My phone sounds again. "Yes, Finch," I answer. "I'm still with the team. Business or personal?"

"Very much business. Officers spotted Kessler at a 7-Eleven on Bear Park Drive, but he fled."

"Damn. Is he riding the ATV?"

"Negative, he's on foot. Bring your team; we stand a decent chance of capturing him."

Chapter Twenty-Four

"WHERE IS EVERYONE?" I ask Officer Mason, who is waiting for us outside the 7-Eleven where Kessler was sighted.

"So far, it's just Officers Wilson, Taggart, and me. The sales assistant recognized Kessler from the news and called it in. We were the nearest patrol units. Wilson and Taggart tried to grab the fugitive in the store, but he bolted toward the industrial park behind. A little bird told me you were on the way, so I hung back to wait for you."

An unmarked patrol car pulls into the forecourt, and Detective Finch jumps out.

"Are more officers on the way? Stevie asks Mason.

"I hope so, ma'am, but there's a big-rig accident on the interstate, and we're stretched thin."

I chuckle to myself at Mason calling his fiancée *ma'am*. "Any sign of the ATV he was riding?"

Mason points a hand down the road. "It's about a quarter-mile that way. Looks like he ran out of gas and hiked to the store."

"It's a relief that we don't have to chase an ATV," Nick

says. "But I don't fancy our chances of capturing him in the industrial park, considering the size of our crew. Most of the buildings are abandoned, giving him plenty of places to hide."

"Let's get going," I say, leading the way down the side of the 7-Eleven building. I turn to Mason. "You know if he was armed?"

"Can't say for sure, ma'am, but he didn't pull a gun on Wilson and Taggart."

Then how the hell did he get away?

The thump of helicopter blades makes us all look up.

"Channel Five *Eye In The Sky News*," Mason says. "They listen to our radios. Detective Reed's friend works there as a reporter."

"I don't see any other news crews." I strongly suspect they were tipped off.

"It's a safe bet that Reed alerted them," Finch says.

We check the dumpster behind the 7-Eleven. There's nowhere else for Kessler to hide here, so we cross the road to the industrial park.

"Taggart, what's your position?" Mason barks into his radio.

"Near the furniture store. We lost sight of the perp. Wilson thinks he slipped inside the abandoned warehouse behind."

"Terrific," I say. "Rats, puke, and garbage."

"Be aware the FBI is on the scene," Mason tells Taggart.

"SSA Viera here. Stay put, Taggart," I say into my radio. "We're heading to your position."

We skirt the back of a strip mall and find the two

officers staring at the furniture store.

"What the hell happened?" Finch asks them, his mood dark. "How the hell did Kessler give you both the slip?"

Taggart sneaks a glance at Wilson and says, "Kessler's fast. Ran like a rabbit."

"He's for sure in that warehouse," his partner adds. "The locks are busted on most of these abandoned buildings. They've become a hangout for kids and vagrants."

As Taggart leads the way to the warehouse, I gaze at the news helicopter hovering over a building off to my right.

"Think they know something we don't?" Finch asks.

"I'm wondering the same."

As we reach the door, my phone rings, and I answer, "Viera."

"Special Agent Viera?" A voice asks.

"Affirmative. Who is this?"

"Jackie Ricci, Channel Five *Eye in the Sky News*. Look up to your right. We're waving."

I see the pilot wag the tail of the chopper.

"We have information for you. But first, I'd like an interview on the guy you're chasing, Leo Kessler."

"I'm kind of busy right now, Jackie. What do you have for me?" I stay more polite than I feel toward her—she could be broadcasting this conversation.

"Only if you promise to give me an interview when you capture Kessler."

"I'll give you one if you have actionable information."

"Live, on-air?"

"I suppose. What do you have?"

"You're looking for your fugitive in the wrong place. Ten minutes ago, he went into the building we're hovering over. He hasn't come out."

"Thank you. We'll check it out." I give everyone a 'follow me' gesture and set off at a trot toward the chopper's location.

"I should warn you that we have cameras focused on the building," Jackie says.

"I'll be sure to behave myself."

"And I'll hold you to that interview. Call me back at this number."

"Will do." I end the call and turn to Finch, who is jogging alongside me. "Score one for the news crew."

"Was that Jackie or Hazel?"

"Jackie. I owe her an interview, but it's a small price to pay."

"Remember, she's the bitch who aired the edited video purporting to show me holding down a suspect while Reed kicked him."

"Duly noted, but I'm not about to turn away help."

The building in question is a two-story wooden structure. If I recall, it once housed a bookstore and a coffee shop. A dress store and a hair salon were on the upper level. Now the place is boarded up. The city took the landlord to court for failing to pay taxes, and the whole thing folded.

The wash from the chopper is beating down on everyone's head, and the noise is almost deafening as I order the officers around the other side. "And try not to let him give you the slip this time," I tell them. The lock on the door in front of me is busted, and who knows how many other ways there are out of the building.

"I'll take the lead," Finch says, moving toward the door. "We can split up once we're inside."

"The officers don't think he as a gun," I tell everyone, "but assume he still has the revolver we saw at the house. Stay alert and stay safe."

Finch flattens himself against the siding while I stand behind the door and wrench it open. We swing into the doorway together, flashlights aimed into the darkness alongside our pistols. There's a powerful odor of pot and human waste as we step inside.

Sweeping my flashlight around, I can tell from the shelving that this area used to be the bookstore. Plasterboard has been ripped from the walls, and several shelf units toppled. I never understand why some people get such pleasure in destroying things. Syringes, fast food wrappers, and used condoms litter the vinyl flooring.

I send Nick and Stevie to check out the back room while Finch and I step through a hole in the wall. We arrive at what must have been the coffee shop. The tables, chairs, and counter are all gone, but menu boards on the walls still announce the delights you could once enjoy here.

"Break room and bathrooms are clear," Nick shouts. "He must be upstairs. How do you get up there?"

"Looks like there was a separate way in from the street, but someone's left us a convenient access hole in the wall." I shine my flashlight's beam at the kicked-in plasterboard.

"Fall in behind me," Finch says, and he leads the way into a room that must have served as a foyer for the upstairs stores.

"Why the hell did Kessler pick a stinky place like this to go to ground?" Nick complains.

"You think Jackie was having you on?" Stevie asks me as we climb the stairs.

"She must believe Kessler is here because we can still hear the drone of the chopper overhead. I imagine Jackie's waiting to catch us perp-walking him out," I tell Stevie.

On the second level, there's far less trash on the floor. A wide corridor runs past both shopfronts. They are inside the building, so no one bothered to board them up.

The window glass is gone. "Watch yourselves, folks," I say. "Glass underfoot."

We quickly clear both store spaces without finding Kessler.

"I hate to break it to you, but the television reporter was playing you," Stevie says.

I bring a finger to my lips for everyone to stay silent and play my flashlight on an access hatch in the ceiling with a table underneath.

Even in the dim light, I see them all nod. Finch gives me a disgusted look. I know he's not relishing crawling through the pink fiberglass insulation in the attic. I'm not either—it makes me itch and cough for a week.

"I'll do it," I whisper to Finch. "You'll have to boost me up, but watch where you put your hands."

"I can't lift you without—" he starts to protests.

I cut him off. "Joke. Let's go."

We climb onto the table. Finch lifts me slowly, allowing me to raise the hatch lid a bit and shine my flashlight around without presenting much of a target. The beam catches a figure in the far corner. He doesn't appear armed, so I say to Finch, "Heave my ass higher."

When Kessler doesn't move, I shout, "Don't make me come up there and get you. You're not getting away from here, and I'm starting to itch just looking at the pink insulation."

He raises his hands and steps across the joists toward me. I pull myself into the attic space and pat him down, taking a knife from his belt, but there's no revolver.

"I'm Senior Special Agent Viera, and you're under arrest for drug distribution."

Leo Kessler mutters a barely audible curse.

"You jump down first." I indicate the access hole. "Agents and a detective are waiting for you below."

After reading Kessler his rights, we lead him down the stairs and out of the building. Finch and I flank the prisoner with the two agents behind, giving Jackie's camera a proper perp walk. I send Officer Mason to fetch his car, and Finch dismisses the other officers.

The chopper's powerful spotlight tracks our progress all the way to the road. There, Mason helps load Kessler into the back of his cruiser.

Ten minutes later, I climb into my car and call Jackie Ricci. She gives her audience a lead-in, saying, "I'm joined now on the phone by Special Agent Viera of the FBI. Agent, we just saw your dramatic arrest of Leo Kessler. What can you tell me about the charges?

"We just arrested Leo Kessler on drug distribution charges."

"He's facing federal charges?"

"That's correct, Jackie."

"And they carry a stiffer penalty than state charges?"

"I can't speak specifically about this case. But federal charges are decided by an AUSA, and terms are usually longer."

"That's Assistant United States Attorney?"

"Correct."

"Isn't this your second attempt at arresting Leo Kessler?"

"Yesterday, we attempted to arrest him at a house he owns, but he fled the scene."

"Do you blame yourself for his escape?"

"Not at all, Jackie," I say, keeping my cool, "it was a fluid situation, and three agents were moving fast to arrest him and his partner before SWAT could get there."

"Will Kessler also be charged with the murders of Ex-Detective Barlow's wife, Ava, and Ricky Kelly?"

"Both those murders are part of an ongoing investigation, so I can't comment on them."

"But Kessler was in a love triangle with Detective Barlow and his wife, wasn't he?"

"I'm sorry, I can't comment, but I would like to thank you for the assistance that you and Channel Five's helicopter gave us in the arrest of Leo Kessler."

"We're always happy to help law-enforcement, Agent. Well, there you have it, folks, straight from the mouth of the FBI agent in charge of the—"

With my part over, I end the call and head to the police station. I'm looking forward to hearing what Kessler has to say.

Chapter Twenty-Five

"WHAT DID HOLDER want? I ask Finch as he joins me in the interview room."

He shrugs. "Nothing much."

"Nothing much? You were in there for fifteen minutes."

"Holder has a hard-on for charging Kessler with Ava and Ricky's murders," he says, settling into the chair beside me. "Apparently, Reed agrees with the chief, though I don't know why his opinion on the subject matters."

"Isn't that putting the cart before the horse? Did you mention Reed's leak to the TV news crew?"

"I could hardly complain since we wouldn't have captured Kessler without the help of Channel Five's helicopter."

"That's scarcely the point. Reed bends the rules to suit himself. He needs to be held accountable."

Finch flicks his eyes at the one-way mirror, and I guess that Chief Holder is watching the interview.

An officer brings Kessler into the room and shoves him down into a chair across the table from us. His receding brown hair is mussed, and he looks defeated in the orange jumpsuit. Seeing him again makes me feel itchy from my brief trip into the attic at the industrial park.

Finch reads Kessler his rights, and I feel a relief when he doesn't lawyer up.

"You are being charged with drug distribution," I tell him. "The murders of Ava Barlow and Ricky Kelly are on the table."

"I didn't kill either of them," he spits.

I'm starting to believe him. "Where were you on the evening of the fourteenth through the following morning?"

"With a guy."

"You didn't have to think too hard to know when that was," Finch observes.

"The fifteenth was the morning Ava was killed. I watch the news just like anyone else, and I knew you'd try and pin her murder on me."

"So, help yourself," I tell him. "Who were you with when she was killed?"

"Guy called Big Mac. I don't know his actual name."

"From the evening of the fourteenth through the morning of the fifteenth?"

"Yeah. I stayed at his place. Ask him."

"Big Mac, the local crime boss?"

Kessler nods.

"You sleeping with the guy?" Finch asks scornfully.

"Hell no." Kessler brings his handcuffed fists down onto the metal table with a resounding crash, making Finch and me recoil. "I'd had a few too many to drive home, so I stayed at his place. Ask him."

"You know his word isn't worth shit?" Finch says.

"If I'd known I needed an alibi, I'd have been with someone more reliable. But that's where I was. I was sorry to hear that someone whacked Ava."

"You also knew that Ricky Kelly was a police informant," I say. "You left a message on Maura's answering machine saying you were going to deal with him. A few days later, he turns up dead. What are we supposed to believe?"

"I was only going to rattle him. Tell him to get out of town. Other people knew he was a snitch. People who would kill him without a second thought."

"Oh right. You were trying to protect Ricky," Finch says scornfully. "Quite the gentleman, aren't you?"

"You cops lie so much you think everyone else does," Kessler snarls, white-hot hate flashing through his eyes.

"He was killed the evening of Friday the eighteenth. Where were you between seven and eight in the evening?"

"With Maura."

"Right," Finch says with heavy sarcasm.

"We had dinner at Ramone's. I bet they have cameras. So get off your asses and check it out."

"Oh, we will," Finch says. "Don't you worry about that."

"Good!"

"Maura told us you were seeing Ava to try to locate the gold that Pete Barlow took from you," I say, trying to get the interview back on track.

"Yeah, well, Maura talks too much."

"She also told us where it came from."

"I'm not getting into that, but your Detective Barlow stole it from me."

"The guy is a decorated detective."

"Decorated detective, my ass. You all think he's some kind of saint, but the guy's as dirty as hell."

"We'll ask him about it," Finch says.

"You need to tear his house apart. It's there somewhere, but Maura and I couldn't find it."

"We might just do that," I say, thinking his testimony about Pete stealing the gold sounds credible. "You know a guy by the name of Dirk McCloskey?"

"Yeah. He was in Folsom with me. We shared a cell for a while until I grew tired of him telling me all the time how he didn't kill his wife. How Barlow set him up for her murder. I believed the guy, but you can only hear that so many times. So I faked an injury and said McCloskey had done it. Got myself transferred to another cell. Why are you asking about him?"

"He skipped parole, and we're looking for him. How about a Paul Henderson?"

"I shared a cell with Henderson after McCloskey. What is this?"

I find it interesting how our suspects are connected. "How recently did anyone tattoo the back of your neck?"

"What?"

"Just answer the question," Finch says.

"Maybe it is time for me to ask for a lawyer."

"That would be a mistake," I tell him. "We have a picture of the back of the person who killed Ricky. If you didn't kill him, it's in your interest to answer these questions. When did you last get a tattoo on the back of your neck?"

"I last had it worked on six months ago, give or take."

"This was since you were last inside?" I ask.

"Yeah. The gal kept the same design as I've had for years."

"I need a picture of it," I say, getting to my feet.

"Don't you need a warrant for that?"

"Not if you want to help yourself by proving you didn't kill Ricky Kelly or Ava Barlow."

"This is weird, but go ahead."

"Pull down the collar of your jumpsuit for me," I demand, moving behind him. I snap a picture of his neck. The tattoo doesn't appear to match the one from the surveillance camera, but I'll have to study them side by side to confirm.

Chief Holder steps into the room, looking none too pleased, and addresses Finch, "A word with you outside, detective."

It doesn't sound like I'm invited, but I join them in the corridor anyway, closing the interview room door behind me.

"You think he killed Ava and Ricky?" Holder asks, directing his gaze at Finch.

"He might not have. We should check his alibis to be sure."

"An alibi with Big Mac is worthless. The guy will lie to protect Kessler."

"I've had dealings with Big Mac in the past. I can check it out," I say.

Holder ignores me, staying focused on Finch. "You're to charge him with both murders, detective."

"We have Ava's killer on video, lifting a two-hundred-and-fifty-pound bike into the back of the blue minivan. Kessler doesn't look capable. Shouldn't we at least wait until we've checked the surveillance cameras and spoken to Big Mac?" I insist.

Holder turns to me, fixing his eyes on mine. "This is my department, and I'll run it as I see fit, agent." His eyes swing back to Finch. "Just get it done, detective. Kessler's story about the gold is complete fiction. I know Pete, and he wouldn't have stolen evidence."

He turns to leave, then stops.

"And release Pete Barlow. I'm convinced he had Kessler kill his wife. But as Pete's attorney says, we can't hold him indefinitely without any evidence."

***

PETE BARLOW STEPS out through the glass door of the police station and cups his hand into a shade against the brilliant June sunshine. His eyes flit nervously around the parking lot. Truth be told, with the vermin who killed Ava still on the loose, he would be happier staying in the holding cell. Pete doesn't for one moment think she died at the hands of Leo Kessler. Whoever carved the message into her body threatening him is still out there.

Greg Hays, his attorney, looks around to make sure they are out of earshot. "I hear from my source that they think you frequently fabricated evidence. I can't represent you unless you tell me everything."

"When you're a detective, you sometimes know an

individual is guilty beyond a shadow of a doubt. But you may lack the evidence to put them behind bars. At times like that, I had to be expedient and cull the herd for the greater good. One of the miscreants coming after me later was always a possibility. But I never expected them to kill poor Ava." Not that she was much of a loss for him. "Maybe I'm next."

"Stop worrying, Pete," Hays says. "Ava's killer is in custody, and you're in the clear. We're in the blue Volvo over there."

The sun has turned the inside of the vehicle into a blast furnace. Greg throws his briefcase on the back seat, then climbs inside, hurrying to turn the AC to its maximum setting.

Pete's gaze takes one more sweep of the parking lot before settling into the scorching seat. He takes no notice of the dark blue minivan parked nearby. No one has warned him to watch for one.

"We could sue the police for wrongful imprisonment," Greg suggests, pulling onto the main road.

But Pete only grunts. His eyes are drawn to the SUV's rear window, checking for a tail.

"Pete, for God's sake, relax. I spoke to Detective Reed, and he's certain Kessler is the guy who killed Ava. They wouldn't have charged him if there were any doubt."

"I'm not so sure. Holder is impulsive."

"It stands to reason it was Kessler. He was having sex with Ava and supplying her with drugs. I've seen the photographs. Only a dopehead could have done that to her."

Pete had to give Kessler props for hooking up with Ava right under his nose—without him knowing. She kept his last name a secret, and Pete never saw them together.

When he doesn't hear a reply, Greg says, "Sorry, man, I didn't mean to sound insensitive."

Pete shakes his head. "No worries. It's been over between Ava and me for years. She used to be fun, but she turned into an angry bitch."

"You want me to drop you at your car or the Travelodge?"

"The hotel for now." He doubts Kessler has blabbed as it would incriminate him too. Just to be sure, though, he should go to the house soon and move a few things around. That Indian FBI agent is acting like a dog with a bone.

"There's a suitcase of clothes in the trunk that I picked up from your house. I don't imagine you want to go near the place."

"Thanks, Greg. I need to write you a check."

"No worries, man. It's on me."

"You're a terrific friend, Greg." Pete has always regarded Greg as a good old boy, but the guy has come through for him.

"Sure. Let's have a round of golf soon. Take your mind off things."

The men stay silent until the Volvo pulls into the hotel's forecourt. Pete jumps out first, scanning for trouble.

The blue minivan slowing to a stop behind looks like a family vehicle. Not something a killer would drive.

Chapter Twenty-Six

THE SHAMROCK IS an Irish pub in a depressed neighborhood on the city's south side. It's an area where patrol cars are seldom seen. I'm guessing the police would rather let criminals settle their own beefs. Officers swoop in after the shooting stops, haul the bodies to the morgue, and arrest anyone stupid enough to be standing around. Call me a cynic if you want.

"What's the point of coming here if Chief Holder won't accept Big Mac's word?" Stevie asks.

"Checking Kessler's alibi will validate our feeling that we should be looking elsewhere for Ava and Ricky's killer. If Holder stays hung up on Kessler, it's his loss." When we reach the entrance, I say, "Leave the talking to me and try not to shoot anyone if they get in our faces."

We push through the swing doors, and we're almost bowled over by the sweet aroma of hops liberally mixed with the stench of body odor and cigarette smoke. The walls are completely covered with guitars, trombones, and photos of the owners Patrick and Big Mac with a host of minor celebrities. The bar is similarly adorned with vintage bottles of every stripe. It's like the place entered the most decorated bar competition—fifteen years ago. Now it all looks rather tawdry.

The line of patrons at the bar are old-timers with dusty clothes and overgrown facial hair. They turn and watch us like a pride of hungry lions that have just spotted a pair of tasty gazelles.

As we move toward an inconspicuous door at the back, the nearest yokel squawks, "Well, looky what we have here. It must be my birthday. Wanna have some fun, girls?" He pats his lap like we're a couple of schoolgirls, and it makes me think that Stevie and I are much too old for his taste.

"Knock it off, Amos," the bartender says. He's a rotund man with lamb chop sideburns and thinning gray hair pulled into a comb-over. He gives me a broad grin. "How's it going, Agent Viera?"

We pause by the bar. "Can't complain. Looking good yourself, Patrick," I tell him. The patrons settle down and go back to their drinks after hearing we're FBI and, more importantly, I'm a friend of the establishment.

"Brought a mate with you this time?"

"Patrick, meet Agent Wells. Patrick used to be a cop, but we don't hold that against him," I tell Stevie.

She gives Patrick a nod and a friendly smile.

"I often worked with the Bureau back in the day." Patrick turns his gaze back to a beer he's pulling.

"Is he in?"

"Big Mac is upstairs, or he was last time I saw him. Don't piss off the new bouncer. He broke a few bones before we got him trained."

"Good to know." We push through a door at the back of the bar and trudge up a flight of well-worn wooden steps, our footfalls echoing around the stairwell. The landing at the top doubles back and brings us face to face with a man the size of a refrigerator. His black sleeveless top does little to hide the corded muscles of his broad shoulders and neck. He's clearly someone who takes weight training to a whole other level. There's a revolver on one hip and a fifteen-inch machete on the other.

I can see why Big Mac chose him—the guy is as intimidating as hell. But size is not always an asset. I could draw my pistol and pump two bullets into his chest before he could lay a hand on either of his weapons. Big Mac would understand if we said the bouncer was about to attack us.

"You cops lost?" muscle man growls.

"It's actually agents," I say as we badge him.

"FBI? That's worse," the big man chuckles to himself as if he's cracked the best joke ever.

"We're here to see Big Mac."

The smile fades. "He don't want to see no feebs. Get out of here, girls."

"You're new here, aren't you?"

"What's it to you?"

"Want me to call Big Mac and tell him you won't let us in. Or maybe I'll fetch Patrick."

The hulk falters for a moment, thinking about my words.

The door behind him opens, and Big Mac steps into the corridor. He's a few inches shorter than my five-nine and slim in an athletic kind of way. His nickname must have started as a joke, or perhaps it refers to his vast criminal enterprise. He has a tawny complexion and intelligent blue eyes that seem to shine into your soul.

"What's going—?" He stops in his tracks, and his face lights up. "Agent Viera. How the hell are you?" He grasps my hand. Big Mac is not your typical mindless gangster, by any stretch of the imagination.

"Good. And you?" I ask.

"Can't complain, but I probably will." He flicks his fingers at the hulk, who disappears through the door.

"And who's your lovely friend?" Big Mac asks, turning to Stevie and grasping her hand.

"Special Agent Stevie Wells," she says.

"Don't mind me," he tells her. "I'm a sucker for a pretty face."

"Don't get too taken with her," I say. "She's engaged to be married."

Big Mac grins. "Her fiancé is one lucky guy. Come on back, and tell me why you're here."

He leads us through another drinking area, this one just for punters. The gambling rooms are in a rabbit's warren, farther in the building. He stops at the door to a mid-sized office and holds his hand out like a traffic cop for us to enter. Unlike the rest of the joint, the desk and chairs here are thoroughly modern.

"Please, have a seat," he says, indicating a pair of comfortable-looking office chairs. He slides into a chair behind the desk and rests his elbows on the leather top. "Now, what can I do for you today, Cassie?"

"I don't know if you remember Detective Pete Barlow. He's retired now, but his wife Ava was killed a few days ago."

"I heard. Terrible business."

"We arrested a guy by the name of Leo Kessler for distributing drugs."

He nods. "I heard."

"Kessler was in a relationship with Ava Barlow, and the police, in their wisdom, have charged him with her murder."

"I didn't know that."

"It will be in tomorrow's paper, but I don't believe he killed her. He's given us your name as his alibi witness, and I wonder if I can run a few dates by you." I fish out my phone to check them.

"Of course. I've seen Leo a few times in the last week."

"It may take a while for your friend's situation to improve, as Chief Holder has a hard-on for charging him. But it will allow me to focus on the real killer."

"Fire away."

"Kessler says he was with you on the evening of June fourteenth through the morning of the fifteenth. Some of your friends were there, though he doesn't recall much about them."

He scans his phone. "Leo is correct. We had aperitifs here at five, then went to Rosalind's for dinner. Leo would do well not to remember the names of the friends we were with. I trust you won't be troubling them?"

"Of course not. Your word is always good with me."

"After dinner, we came here for a few games of cards,

you understand."

I nod to indicate that I won't mention that they were gambling.

"We played cards until the small hours. My friends left at maybe two o'clock, but Leo was in no condition to drive home. We were the last people here, and there aren't any taxis at that time in this podunk town, so I took Leo home with me and tucked him up in the spare room."

"You saw him the following morning, June fifteenth?"

"I did. I awoke at seven-thirty, and Leo was still snoring loudly. I finally had to rouse him at nine-thirty because I had to come into the office, and his car was parked here."

Stevie looks about to speak, so I kick her foot and shoot her a look.

"Thank you," I say. "That's all I need. Your statement exonerates Leo Kessler for Ava Barlow's murder. As I said earlier, the police may not be quick to accept your statement, but finding the real person who committed the murder is the best thing I can do for Leo. Other charges will probably stem from the substantial quantity of drugs Leo was caught with."

Big Mac cocks his head, and a frown clouds his face as he becomes aware of the howl of police sirens. We listen to them draw closer. As they wail to a stop on the street outside, he jumps to his feet. "Is this anything to do with you?" he snaps at me.

"Of course not. How could you think such a thing?"

"I have to leave."

Stevie and I stand as Big Mac hurries from his office. It takes only moments for the upstairs drinking area to empty out down a back stairway.

"What the hell is going on?" Stevie exclaims.

"I can only guess that it's something to do with the police department." We wander into the empty bar area as feet thunder up the stairs and burst into the space where we are.

"Cedar Springs SWAT. Get down on the ground," the lead officer orders us. Behind him are three more SWAT officers. All four are outfitted in black uniforms, body armor, high-top boots, and face masks. All four are pointing MP5 submachine guns at Stevie and me.

"FBI Agents. Stand down." I brush back my jacket to reveal my badge. From the corner of my eye, I see Stevie following my lead. "Don't touch your weapon," I tell her.

"Toss your weapons on the ground, girls," the lead SWAT officer snaps.

"Federal Agents. Stand down. Are you deaf?"

"Toss your weapons down and lay on the floor." He advances on Stevie and me.

"Don't be a fool, Brandon," one of the other officers shouts.

"They're fucking FBI, Brandon," another yells. "We're not here for them."

I see Stevie has her phone out, filming the confrontation.

"Listen to your mates, Brandon. Don't do anything stupid," I say, struggling to keep my voice even. But Brandon is on a power trip and advances on Stevie.

"Down, you stupid bitch." He still has his weapon aimed at her center of mass, while the other three officers now have their stances relaxed. Clearly, they don't want to be part of the drama. I'm deathly afraid that someone is going to get shot.

Stevie is backing up, but Brandon shoves her to the ground. She lands on her backside but doesn't appear hurt. She holds up her phone and carries on filming.

I've had enough and grab Brandon from behind. In one swift movement, I trip him onto his back and draw my pistol, aiming at a gap in his body armor. I'm relieved when none of the other officers point their weapons at me.

"You're under arrest for assaulting an FBI agent."

I see Detective Reed at the back of the room, smirking. "Stand down, fellas," he yells. "You've done enough."

"Done enough, you prick?" I thunder at him. "I'll have your badge for this. You're done as a detective."

Then I look in horror as I see that Brandon isn't done. He's on his back with his submachine gun pointed at the front of the room where Reed and the other officers stand. In the tussle with me, his helmet has slipped and partly covers his eyes. Despite the pistol I have aimed at him, he fires a burst of his weapon, screaming, "Die bitches."

Two officers go down, and I see Reed dive for cover.

Before I can react, Brandon fires another burst, taking out a section of the ceiling.

My rage at Reed and whoever put a weapon in the hands of this kid makes my blood boil. I don't want to kill him if there's another way to end this. I fire two shots at his bulletproof vest, hoping to stun him, bring him to his senses.

My shots only serve to make him aware of me. He starts

to swing his weapon my way, squeezing the trigger, firing in an arc that cuts through the ceiling like a knife through butter. An arc of fire that's coming for my head as he screams, "Bitch," over and over.

His visor is up, revealing enough of his head for a kill shot. But I choose not to take it. Instead, I fire a bullet into his arm, and Brandon's finger comes off the trigger in the nick of time. He begins to rise, so another of my rounds goes into his thigh. Even if his actions today don't doom him from serving as an officer, his injuries will.

Brandon is screaming blue murder, but I step over, unhook the now hot submachine gun from his uniform, and toss it aside.

Ignoring his screams. I roll him onto his front and handcuff his hands behind his back.

I check on Stevie, who is still on the ground, covered in plaster dust from the ruined ceiling.

She looks okay and is still filming.

At the other end of the room, two of the three SWAT officers are down on the floor, groaning. I hope that Brandon's shots struck their body armor, and their injuries are limited to bruises. I search out Detective Reed. He's sitting on the floor, with his back against a wall. His face is ashen and covered with flecks of blood.

I hope his injuries aren't anything trivial.

Chapter Twenty-Seven

STEVIE CALLS THE next morning while I'm standing at the mirror over the dresser, pinning my hair up in a bun. I snatch my phone up hurriedly, hoping she isn't having a delayed reaction to getting shoved to the floor.

"My backside is a bit sore, but I'm okay otherwise," she tells me. "You heard anything more about Brandon's injuries?"

I take a deep breath. "Nothing life-threatening is all I heard. That's all I want to hear. I don't want to press anyone for details about shattered bones and torn ligaments."

"I doubt he'll play the violin again," she quips.

"It's not funny," I chide. "Though a bit of gallows humor is probably in order. We barely made it out of there with our lives."

"Exactly. It's the only way I stay sane. I never heard what happened to the SWAT members who got shot."

"Their body armor protected them from serious injuries," I tell her, "but both officers have cracked ribs and bruising. Detective Reed's vest stopped one bullet, but another grazed his shoulder."

"They were amazingly lucky. You saw we have another meeting with Myles at nine. Chief Holder will be there. You think we'll get an apology?"

"I'm not holding my breath, and I'm certainly not looking forward to a rehash of what happened. I thought that yesterday's meeting with Myles was the end of it. Did you see who else will be at today's meeting?"

"Just you, me, and the bigwigs, but I wouldn't be surprised to see someone from legal. Anyway, the reason I'm calling so early, boss, is that my car barely made it home yesterday. Can you give me a ride into work?"

"Sure thing. I just need to grab coffee and a slice of toast, and I'll be there. Hang on, that was my doorbell."

"You expecting anyone?" she asks.

"Negative. Who comes around this early? Gotta dash. I'll see you in forty-five."

Grabbing my pistol from the nightstand, I hurry across the living room to the doorbell camera. Seeing the identity of the mystery caller, I fling the door open. "What the hell, Jasmin?"

"I need coffee." She hurries past me, making a beeline for the kitchen.

"What are you doing here at this hour?" I snap, though the suitcase she's carrying is a bit of a giveaway.

"What do you think, sis? Use that detective's mind of yours." She taps the side of her head. "My landlord threw me out for not paying the rent." She opens a cupboard and grabs a mug, filling it from the pot I put on earlier.

"I told you I don't have the money to pay your back

rent."

"Three thousand would have done it." She lets out a breath, turning to face me and leaning her backside against the cabinets. Her hair is mussed like she just rolled out of bed, and she stinks of booze.

"When did this happen?" I snap, grabbing a mug and filling it to the brim with the life-saving amber liquid.

"He was waiting for me yesterday afternoon when I got home from work. Last night I stayed with a friend, but we were thinking I could move in with you."

"Your boyfriend has it all worked out?"

"He helps me out, which is more than anyone else ever does."

"I can't do this right now. I have to get to work. Aside from the booze, are you clean?"

"I've been clean for weeks. Well, maybe a little pot now and then. I told you the coke was Derek's."

I look her in the eye, but I can't read her.

"Do you have any money?" she asks, taking my shopping list from under the magnet on the fridge door. "I can run to the store for us. I'm not working today."

I find my purse and drop a C-Note onto the counter. "Take a shower and clean yourself up, Jaz. You stink something awful."

"You should try having a drink sometime, Cass. It might make you less of an uptight bitch."

"I have to leave for work." I can't help myself and slam the door as I leave.

Twenty minutes later, I stop in front of the single-story ranch-style house that Stevie shares with a female officer, and I see her hurrying toward the passenger door.

"Morning." She flops into the seat beside me, tugging on her seatbelt.

"Sorry, I'm late. We'd better go straight to the station," I say, checking my watch and pulling away from the curb.

"Who was at the door?"

"My sister Jasmin. The one who wanted me to pay her back rent. I refused, and her landlord kicked her out."

"So, she's living with you now?" Stevie sounds more than a little surprised.

"Not if I can help it. We'd fight all the time. Drive each other crazy. It worries me enough, leaving her alone in my house for the day."

"What's her problem?"

"Men, booze, and drugs, in that order. I'd like to think it's an opportunity to straighten her out, but I've tried that before, and it hasn't worked."

"Damn."

"I don't want to talk about her right now." I glance at my watch. "I'd better step on it."

"You think the meeting could be about something else?" she asks. "Like the case?"

"I'm pretty sure it's the SWAT attack part two. Did you tell Officer Mason what happened?"

"He was completely shocked and came straight over. But he wasn't surprised to hear it was Brandon Farley. Mason says the guy has problems with authority and women. He hangs out with an extremist faction."

"What's shocking to me is that they hire men like that to work as officers."

"Mason could see I was upset, so we had consolation sex. What did Finch have to say?"

"He was totally shocked too. And very kind and understanding. He insisted on taking me out for dinner at Ramone's."

"Anything big happen?"

"We kissed in the parking lot, and he invited me back to his place for a nightcap. But I told him I was too tired."

"That's a lame excuse. The guy is a hunk."

"I need to ease into whatever comes next in the relationship. I haven't had sex in two years."

"That's quite a dry spell. You couldn't pick a nicer guy to get back into the game with."

"I'm hoping our disagreements about the case don't kibosh our relationship before it starts. We agreed not to talk about the case, but it sneaks its way into the conversation."

I park the Bureau sedan next to Myles' Mercedes, and we hurry inside the police station. Holder's office is at the far end, and we find my boss waiting for us outside the closed door. It would be an understatement to say he looks fit to be tied.

I think he prides himself on being a snappy dresser, but today his sense of style seems to have deserted him. Certainly, for a senior FBI agent about to confront a police chief. A navy blue shirt and pink tie peek out from between the lapels of a gray suit that is much too light for my taste.

"You both recovered from the attack?" There's a smoldering fire in his eyes as he speaks.

We tell him we're good, and he pushes inside the office

without knocking. Holder rises from behind his desk, looking like he'd rather be anyplace else. He's a short, stocky man with a lined face that says he's been around the block a few times. His salt-and-pepper hair is thin on the top of his head, receding at the temples.

He opens his mouth to speak, but Myles cuts him off, saying we need to watch the video first.

Holder lets out a frustrated breath, then aims a remote at a wall-mounted flat-screen, lighting it up. "I've seen this more times than I want to," he grumbles.

Myles turns to Stevie and me. "Have you seen it yet?"

We shake our heads. Given a choice, I'd rather not relive the events.

"Then we all need to get calibrated on what we're talking about," Myles insists.

Holder already has the video cued and reluctantly presses play on the remote.

The volume is up, so we hear what people are saying. It almost makes me physically ill to watch it unfold. The video jerks around as Brandon shoves Stevie to the floor. When the camera finds him again, his visor is halfway up, and his face is more twisted in rage than I remember. I see myself throwing Brandon to the floor and saying he's under arrest for assaulting an FBI agent.

Holder pauses the video. "See there," he snaps. "Agent Viera escalated the situation." He points an outstretched finger at me.

Myles pivots slowly to the chief, his face contorting. "SSA Viera acted entirely by the book. She clearly warned your SWAT team right at the start that they were FBI

Agents and showed her ID. But your officers kept advancing on my agents. Now play the damn video."

When we get to where Reed tells the SWAT officers that they've done enough, Myles raises his hand, and Holder pauses the video again. "This raid was a blatant attempt by Detective Reed to embarrass and intimidate my agents. It's criminal and simply inexcusable, Holder. If you don't fire Reed's ass, I'll have my agents arrest him and make sure there's a photographer from one of the nationals to document the event."

Myles nods to the chief, and the video restarts. The volume is still cranked up, and when Brandon starts shooting wildly, it sounds like the speakers may pop off the wall.

It's only when I see the replay that I realize just how lucky Stevie and I were. It's a miracle we didn't suffer injuries or worse.

Something inside me recoils when I see myself shoot Brandon. First, the warning shots into his body armor, then the ones into his forearm and thigh.

When the video finally ends, Myles' voice is calmer, "When your officer says, 'Die bitches,' that's clear intent to kill my agents. I'll be pursuing federal attempted murder charges against him as soon as he gets out of the hospital."

"She shouldn't have shot him so many times," Holder crows, nodding his head toward me.

Myles steps to the chief and gets in his face, jabbing a forefinger at his chest. At six feet two, the assistant special agent in charge has the height advantage. "Your kid is lucky that SSA Viera was there. I'd have shot him in the head."

Holder looks humiliated, and I question my boss's decision to dress him down in front of Stevie and me. I suppose he wants to show us that he sticks up for his people, but it's pandering to my baser instincts and becoming cringe-worthy.

"Next steps," Myles continues. "A team is coming from Sacramento to review all your personnel records and weed out any other Brandon Farleys you've hired. You are to extend them every courtesy, or I'll go after your job. Understood?"

After the meeting has broken up, Stevie and I drive back to the FBI offices.

"That was wonderful to behold," she says, "but watching the video again made me feel ill. I dread to think what Brandon would have done if you hadn't shot him."

"My sentiments completely."

"Can we swing by Starbucks and pick up a coffee, boss?"

"Sure thing. I'd understand if you want to take a day off to recuperate."

"I'm not giving Brandon Farley or Reed the pleasure of sidelining me," she insists. "A latte will fix me up just fine."

There's a line of cars at the drive-through, so we park and go inside to order at the counter.

My phone chimes while we're waiting for our drinks to be made. It's Finch, and I step to a quiet corner to answer.

"You doing okay this morning?" he asks, not sounding his usual self.

"Sure. We just got out of a meeting. Myles ripped Holder a new one," I say, maybe a bit too gleefully.

Finch's tone turns grim. "Something has come up. I'm

at the Travelodge in town. Pete Barlow has been stabbed."

Chapter Twenty-Eight

THE CEDAR SPRINGS Travelodge is a six-story concrete structure on Mission Street. When Stevie and I step out of the car, reporters and looky-loos are crowding the sidewalk near the entrance. We nod to Jackie Ricci and her cameraman, then badge the two officers controlling access to the hotel. My feet sink into the plush burgundy carpet as we cross the lobby to where Detective Finch is standing with chief crime scene tech Jason Clark.

"What the hell happened?" I ask as they turn to me, their faces reflecting the gravity of the situation.

"All we know at this juncture is that Pete was released from the lockup yesterday afternoon. According to his attorney, he drove straight here and checked in." A grim-faced Finch eyes his watch. "Approximately an hour ago, a maid came across a man stabbing Pete in the doorway to his room. The attacker saw her and ran off."

"What about Pete's injuries?"

"Paramedics were just loading him into an ambulance when I got here. Unconscious and in need of surgery was all I could get from them."

"Was the maid able to give you a description of the attacker?"

"A big, tall white guy is all she's told us so far."

"As little as that is, it's consistent with our description of the guy who killed Ava and Ricky.

"There's a lot of blood on the carpet, so it's not looking good for Pete," Jason adds.

"Crap. I sent Nick to the hospital, so I should get a report from him soon," I say. "Anyone see Pete yesterday evening or this morning?"

"He had room service for dinner yesterday," Finch says. "The waitress who took breakfast to his room this morning said Pete was fine when she saw him at eight-thirty, and she didn't notice anything out of the ordinary. Greg Hays, his attorney, spoke to Pete on the phone at nine-fifteen. Same story as the waitress."

"Who even knew Pete was staying here?" Stevie asks.

Finch shakes his head. "Hays, of course. Pete may have mentioned it to someone at the police department. Outside of that, I have no idea."

"Pete's assailant could have followed him here when he was released yesterday," Stevie suggests. "Paid a visit to his room this morning."

"But who knew about his release?" I ask.

"Only a few people," Finch says. "But I'm leaning toward someone notifying the killer."

"Are you suggesting someone at the police department tipped the perp off?" Stevie asks.

Finch fixes his eyes on her. "It's not impossible, but don't go jumping to conclusions."

"Have you interviewed anyone on the front desk?" My gaze turns to a twenty-something blonde standing behind the counter. Her expression is vacant, her face deathly white.

"Like you, I just got here." Finch follows my line of sight to the young woman.

"I'll speak to her." I motion for Stevie to follow me.

Badging the receptionist, I say, "I'm Agent Viera of the FBI, and this is Agent Wells. Is there somewhere quiet where we can talk?"

"I'm not supposed to leave my post under any circumstances." She's a slender young woman wearing a navy blazer, white shirt, and black skirt. Her blonde hair is pulled into a sleek braided bun.

"Is it all right if I call you Christie?" I ask, eyeing her nametag.

"Okay. I spoke with Mr. Barlow when he checked in yesterday. Is he dead?" A tear leaks from the corner of one eye, and she blots it with the back of her hand.

"We don't know his condition, ma'am," Stevie replies. "You'd be better off taking a seat. Officers are stopping anyone from entering the hotel, so no one will be checking in."

Christie reluctantly nods and lifts a gate for us to step behind the counter. We follow her to a break room with computers and fax machines.

The receptionist mechanically clears a sandwich wrapper and a half-empty glass from a table. We settle into black leather chairs. Christie delicately folds her legs and regards Stevie and me expectantly.

"Can you give us your last name, ma'am?" Stevie has a notebook out and a pen in her hand.

"It's Graves. Christie Graves."

"And you say you checked in Mr. Barlow when he arrived yesterday?" I prompt.

"Yeah."

"Did you see anyone with him?"

"There were a couple of people in the lobby at the time, but I didn't pay them much attention."

"Did a porter help Mr. Barlow with his luggage?"

"He only had one suitcase and said he could manage it on his own. This is all so horrible." She wipes a tear from her eye.

"We need to look at your surveillance video, ma'am." Stevie leans forward with her forearms on her thighs.

"I'll have to get permission from my manager." Christie pulls a cellphone from her jacket pocket and calls a Mr. Tompkins.

"Are there other ways into the hotel?" I ask while we wait for the guy to show up.

"Guests are only supposed to enter through the main entrance, but maids and porters sometimes prop a fire door open while they take a smoke break."

Moments later, a short man appears, tugging on a dark suit jacket over his white shirt and blue tie. From his mussed hair and bleary eyes, he looks like he has just woken up. "What's going on, Christie? Who are these people? I've spoken to you before about bringing guests back here."

Stevie and I get to our feet. "We're with the FBI, sir," I

say. "Agents Wells and Viera. And you are?"

The man stops dead in his tracks. "Adrian Tompkins. Will someone tell me what is going on?"

"There's been a stabbing, sir," I tell him. "One of the guests. Please take a seat."

"What? Where?" Tompkins appears confused.

"Just sit down and answer our questions, or you'll need to come with us," Stevie says. I'm proud of her forceful tone and menacing look.

Tompkins finds a chair and sits. He seems irked, and I doubt he's used to being told what to do.

"What's your job here, Mr. Tompkins?" I ask.

"I'm the assistant manager."

"Can you account for your movements in the last hour?"

"I've been taking a nap."

"Can anyone provide you with an alibi?"

"Alibi? I don't need an alibi." Tompkins looks put out at the idea.

"Yes, you do, sir," Stevie insists.

"I was alone."

"And you're allowed to nap during office hours?" I ask, aiming to put him on the defensive. From the corner of my eye, I catch Christie stifling a snicker.

"Not exactly, but I had a late night, a family emergency."

"For now, you need to show us your surveillance video. You'll need to answer more questions later." I give him my best steely-eyed glare.

"I'm not sure I can do that without a warrant."

"Then you need to get your manager here pronto. Perhaps he can also vouch for your tendency to take naps at work," I snap.

"I can show you the video," Tompkins states, having a change of heart. He steps to a desk and sits in front of a computer. "We have ten cameras; where would you like to start?"

Twenty-five minutes later, and after much back and forth with Tompkins, we have something. Video from this morning shows our suspect getting out of a blue minivan and crossing the lobby to the elevators. Unfortunately, the man is a ghost. He keeps his head down, giving us images of his back and a very oblique side view. We never see him leave and surmise he left by one of the open exit doors that Christie spoke about.

From the blue minivan and the guy's build, it's not a stretch to believe it's the same guy who attacked Ava Barlow. And that fact reinforces my belief that she was killed as a surrogate for Pete. I get Tompkins to copy the video to a stick, hoping Todd can do something with it and confirm my suspicion.

My phone rings, and it's Nick. "Pete Barlow is in surgery. A shallow knife wound to the chest and a deep one to the abdomen."

"They think he'll make it?" I ask.

"The quantity of blood he lost is a major concern. It might have injured his brain. There's not much for me to do here at the hospital. The doctors say he'll be in surgery for hours."

"Come join us at the Travelodge. No actionable evidence yet, but I'll fill you in when you get here."

"See you shortly, boss."

The call ends, and I tell Tompkins not to leave town. Stevie and I step through a door into the corridor and almost collide with Jackie Ricci and a cameraman. She's wearing jeans and a black T-shirt bearing the words, '*I'm a reporter. Anything you say or do can end up on the news.*'

The cameraman shrinks back, but Jackie stands her ground.

"How the hell did you two get in here?" I ask.

"Nice to see you too, Agents Viera and Wells." She nods to Stevie. "I thought you would know how easy it is to get into places when you know the right people."

"This is a crime scene. I have to escort you both out of here."

"You're going to want to hear my information. It might open up some leads for your case."

"You saw the assailant?"

"Not exactly, but I have information that could help you find him." She raises her brow and purses her lips.

When I hesitate, she continues, "Remember how helpful I was when you were searching for Leo Kessler."

"What's the price?" With Jackie, there's always a price.

"An on-air interview. Not today, because we have this story in the bag. But maybe when there's a significant development."

"I'll bite, but it had better not be something I can learn from Google."

"There's no way anyone else would tell you this," she scoffs. "You'll see in a moment."

We find the break room empty and pull chairs up to the table. The guy with the camera stays standing and swings it

224

my way like he's about to tape me.

I place my palm over the lens. "Okay, you're leaving, pal. Agent Wells, please show our friend here to the front entrance."

The cameraman looks at Jackie, who says, "I'll meet you out front, Malcolm."

When they've left the room, I fix my gaze on the reporter. "This had better be good."

"Oh, it is. I think Agent Wells would like to hear it too." She steps to a Keurig on a refreshment table and pops in a pod. "Would you like one?"

"Nah, I'm all coffeed out."

Stevie comes back into the room, and Jackie offers her a cup, but she declines.

"We're on a tight schedule, Jackie," I remind her. But she takes her time adding sugar and creamer to the Styrofoam cup before taking a seat across the table from us.

Jackie is in her early thirties with warm beige skin and dark wavy hair. Her black eye makeup is overdone, and she's wearing mauve lipstick on her wide lips. A skinny white button-up tank barely contains her ample, tanned breasts.

"I'm working on a story about a local extremist group who call themselves the Priesthood," she tells us. "They harbor various views, but they all share a fear that a secret Marxist government is about to seize power in the US. Apparently, this takeover will happen with the help of federal agencies like the FBI and key people in the military. According to the beliefs of this group, the communist regime will get rid of the presidency, tear up the constitution, and abolish elections. No one will be allowed to own weapons of any kind, not even handguns or rifles."

"How on earth do these nut-jobs have any bearing on my case?" I let out a deep breath.

"Patience, Agent Viera. Hear me out. Officer Brandon Farley is a member of the Priesthood."

"How does that work? I thought you just implied they were anti-law enforcement."

"I didn't say they all are. Their anger is mostly directed against federal agencies like the FBI and the ATF. But even the most ardent anti-law enforcement types are willing to use sympathizers in the police force to meet their goals. The attack on you by the SWAT team was no accident. One or more members of the Priesthood want you dead. I assume it's because your investigation is threatening one of their members or maybe a sympathizer."

"You're telling me the SWAT attack was a setup to kill me? I find that hard to believe."

"I've been provided with the video of what happened in the upstairs at Big Mac's place."

"How the hell did you get it?"

"You know I'll never reveal my sources. Brandon was supposed to stage some kind of 'accident' with his assault rifle and shoot you." Jackie nods at me. "Possibly both of you." She glances at Stevie. "But his feelings about women got the better of him, and he went crazy.

"He was supposed to murder us?" Stevie exclaims, her eyes wide.

"Murdering you would have triggered too wide an investigation. I believe he was supposed to injure you,"

Jackie says. "Something that would take you out of the game for a while."

"It was Detective Reed who ordered the SWAT raid," I exclaim. "Are you saying he's also involved with this group of people?"

"I haven't seen anything specific about him on their message board, but it seems like a safe conclusion. I heard ASAC Myles wants him fired, but Chief Holder is dragging his feet."

"How the hell do you know all this, Jackie? You must have listening devices in the chief's office."

"How I got the information isn't your concern," Jackie chuckles. "I'm not about to publish what I've just told you. What's important to you is that a member of the Priesthood, or someone they sympathize with, likely killed Ava Barlow, Ricky Kelly, and now stabbed Pete Barlow."

"I'm going to need your login code to the Priesthood's message board."

"Sorry, no can do," Jackie shakes her head. "If you start tramping around their board, you'll raise their suspicions, and I'll lose access to it. I need to finish my article."

"If I tell Myles, he'll want to subpoena you."

"You must have read how well that's gone for law enforcement in the past. You can't tell him."

I lean back in the chair, thinking. "You have a list of the members of this group?"

"Sorry, I don't. They all use pseudonyms on the board. That's why I don't know what Detective Reed might have said about you."

"Then how did you know about Brandon?"

"Right after the SWAT incident, there was a burst of activity on the board. A lot of messages about a loyal freedom fighter—that's how they refer to members of the Priesthood—who'd just been shot by an FBI bitch."

"They could be coming for us," Stevie exclaims.

"Ordinarily, I'd thank you for the tip," I tell Jackie, "but I suddenly feel very unsafe."

"It's better that you know you have to watch your backs." Jackie gets to her feet and hitches up her pants by the belt loops. "I'd best get going."

"If you see a threat to my life or one of my agent's—"

"I'll alert you immediately. But understand that I didn't know about the SWAT attack until after it happened."

Stevie verbalizes my thoughts. "So we may not see the next attack coming for us until it's too late."

Chapter Twenty-Nine

STEVIE'S ASHEN FACE says it all as we head out to the hotel lobby, but I tell her to keep Jackie's words between the two of us for now. We don't know who we can trust.

My phone dings, and I check a text from Todd.

Finch breaks away from Officers Mason and Taggart to speak to us. "Found anything?"

I slowly shake my head. "Surveillance cameras caught the perp getting out of a blue minivan and entering through the foyer, but there's no clear shot of his face. I'll see if Todd can clean up the video, but I'm not holding my breath."

"If Pete pulls through, he'll owe his life to the maid who witnessed the attack. After all, the perp ran off when he saw her. I'm hoping we'll have more luck with his description when she sits down with a sketch artist," Finch tells us.

"I wouldn't count on it, based on the luck we've had so far. Did the attacker leave any trace evidence behind?" I ask.

"Jason doubts the perp entered the room—Pete was knifed right when he answered the door. There are too many stray fibers in a hotel corridor to find anything useful."

"I just received a text from Todd. He got the video from Ramone's, and he's confirmed Kessler's alibi that he was eating there the night Ricky was killed. We're literally back to square one."

"Kessler's innocence for Ava and Ricky's murders will be a tough sell to Chief Holder."

"Who does the chief think knifed Pete Barlow? Kessler's in jail, so it sure wasn't him."

"I need to speak to him to see where his head is."

"I don't honestly care what Holder believes, and with today's knife attack to investigate, he won't reassign you."

Finch shrugs. "Let's hope not."

"There's nothing more to be learned here, so Stevie and I are heading back to the office."

As we cross the lobby, Stevie says, "Now that we've proved Kessler didn't kill Ava and Ricky, we're a week into the case, and we have no leads."

"Hmm," I grunt, not wanting to sink into negativity. "We believe the killer is connected to this Priesthood group."

"Assuming what Jackie told us is real. We only have her word that the Priesthood exists. Even if it's true, I don't know how that's going to help us."

We reach the main entrance just as Nick comes through the revolving door.

"You leaving?" he asks.

"There's nothing useful here," I tell him. "I'm sorry you've had a wasted journey. Have you had lunch?"

"Not yet."

"I saw a diner on the corner of the block as we drove in. I need to bring you up to date on something Stevie and I just heard."

The Early Bite Coffee Shop is your typical basic diner. The place is too busy for our kind of shop-talk, but it turns out to have seating in a courtyard behind. I push through a swing door and find all the outside tables empty—perfect for our sensitive discussions.

A smiling waitress appears with menus and fills our cups with coffee. "In town for the convention, are we?" she asks, mistaking us for business folk because of our formal attire.

"We are," Nick says, flashing her a smile.

After the waitress leaves, Stevie asks him, "Do you even know what convention she thinks we're here for?"

"Evidently something that requires a suit, so it can't be too bad."

"Okay, listen up." I quickly lay out for Nick what Jackie Ricci told us.

"Damn. Was she suggesting that Ava and Ricky's killer is a member of this Priesthood group?" he asks.

"That's the implication. The group wants us injured and off the case."

"Like the FBI doesn't have any other agents to put on the investigation," Stevie scoffs. "Criminals are so stupid."

"Helps us catch them," I quip.

"Why wouldn't Jackie tell us how to access the Priesthood's message board?" Nick asks.

The waitress arrives and takes our orders, which turn out to be bacon, fried eggs, and hash browns all around. As if any of us would come to a diner and order a salad.

She hesitates a moment before asking, "You're all morticians?"

"In a manner of speaking," Nick replies cryptically. "We frequently deal with dead bodies."

A puzzled look crosses the waitress's face as she collects the menus.

After she disappears back inside, we all burst out laughing.

"Jackie wouldn't give us access to the message board because the group would spot us flat-footed cops and cut off her access, too," Stevie says with heavy sarcasm. "Then she wouldn't be able to finish her stupid article."

"There's a lot more than her damn article at stake if we don't catch the murderer and he kills another person," Nick snaps. "Maybe even one of us."

"We can't let these people intimidate us. They believe in this Marxist government takeover crap. Believing stuff like that must make them feel smarter than everyone else," I suggest.

"We can't subpoena Jackie?"

"Subpoenas never work with the press," I say. "The reporters go to jail and become a rallying cry for other reporters."

"How credible is Jackie Ricci?" Nick asks. "I don't watch the local television news."

"She was pretty convincing when she spoke to Stevie and me," I say.

"I don't doubt that the Priesthood exists, but could she be mistaken about their ties to the SWAT raid? Reed could have ordered the raid to get a rise out of you, not suspecting that Brandon Farley would shoot the place up. Brandon could just be another misogynistic asshole whose tiny brain short-circuited when he encountered a pair of women who wouldn't obey him."

"It's possible," I tell him. "But we should err on the side of caution until we know more. Regardless of whether Reed is a member of the Priesthood, he's seriously messing with our operations. First, he canceled SWAT at Kessler's house, allowing him to escape. Then, he authorized the raid at Big Mac's, knowing Stevie and I would be there checking Pete Barlow's alibi. I don't know that Big Mac is ever going to believe I had nothing to do with the SWAT team showing up."

"The raid headlined on the Channel Five morning news," Stevie says. "Reed's woman-friend, Hazel DeRosa, was speculating what happened to Brandon. She interviewed one of his high school girlfriends, who was surprised he became an officer. She claims he tried to strangle her. She complained to the cops, but Brandon was never charged. Another girl claimed he slashed her tires when she wouldn't go to the senior prom with him. No charges, again."

"Some law-enforcement guys always tend to believe a man's explanation over a woman's, present company excepted." I take in a deep breath.

"So, what's the plan, boss?" Nick asks.

"Top priority is to make sure none of us falls victim to this group. We have to be observant. Keep our heads on a swivel. Check new environments carefully, drawing weapons if we're at all unsure. But offense is the best defense. I want you to dig deeper into Stevie's list of Barlow arrestees who were recently released. Check their social media accounts for threats against law enforcement. Also, check out anyone communicating with them. Let's interview their relatives. I don't care how you two divvy up the work or how much of Todd's time you use."

"The two Barlow arrestees who've skipped out on their parole officer—Dirk McCloskey and Paul Henderson—are at the top of my list," Stevie says. "They both claim to live at Paul's father's ranch. When they missed a parole meeting, US Marshals checked there, but the father alleged he hadn't seen Paul in a while, and said he'd never heard of McCloskey. Paul's sister supposedly lives at the ranch. I've also been looking into McCloskey's prison visitors. According to the authorities, a woman claiming to be his sister visited him a few times. I'll try to locate her."

"Based on the men skipping parole and giving a false address, you're right to give the pair priority," I say. "Let's pay a visit to the father, shake the tree, and see what falls out. How about the guys lower down the list?"

"We'll look deeper into them and visit the ranch," Nick says, and Stevie nods.

The waitress arrives and serves our meals. "Can I get you anything else?" she asks, resting her hands on her hips.

We shake our heads, and I say, "No thanks," standing to take off my jacket and hook it over the back of my chair.

She eyes the shield on my belt. "Oh, you're cops?"

"FBI agents," I tell her. When she's gone, I continue, "We need to check everyone for neck tattoos. That means visiting them in person. We might be able to get some help from the police department. That is if I haven't worn out my credit there."

"Can we eliminate the ex-cons who don't have a tat on the back of their necks?" Stevie asks.

"If we've checked them in person. One more angle is to contact Sacramento and get a list of anyone in our area who they've flagged as a potential domestic terrorist."

"And research them too?" Nick asks.

"At least see if they have ties to Pete Barlow." I massage my temples. We have no solid leads, and we're casting blindly around for suspects. "Chasing Kessler has thrown us way off track. Now we've eliminated him, we need to research these people yesterday and regain forward momentum." Patience isn't one of my strong suits.

"Will you speak to Myles about the threats from the Priesthood?" Stevie has regained some of the color she lost when we talked to Jackie. At least she has Mason for support, I reflect. I have Finch, but Nick has no one, as far as I know.

"I'll catch Myles tomorrow. He's visiting the Sacramento Field Office today."

"We have our work cut out," Nick observes, and I nod grimly.

After lunch, we head to the office, but the afternoon seems to pass in no time. We find an address for McCloskey's sister, but our progress on checking the other suspects isn't nearly enough.

Chapter Thirty

ONE HUNDRED MILES from Cedar Springs, an elderly lady is paying for her purchase. "This is the best hardware store in Placerville," she says. "The people who work here are always so helpful."

"Well, there's only Daisy and me, so thank you," Zoe replies, smiling and tendering the woman's change. "Let's hope the new fill valve takes care of your running toilet. You sure you have someone to fit that for you?"

"No worries, my dear." She lays a hand on Zoe's thin arm. "My neighbor is a retired plumber. And tell Daisy to get better soon."

"I will."

"Bye now."

The doorbell dings as the woman exits the little hardware store, leaving Zoe alone with her thoughts. She's petite, with dark hair pulled into a ponytail.

She checks her watch. Almost closing time. Then she'll go home and see if Daisy wants bread and soup again for dinner or if she feels ready for something more substantial.

It has been four days since Zoe rushed her friend to

Marshall Hospital ER with severe stomach pain. Doctors quickly figured it was appendicitis and performed surgery to remove the inflamed organ.

Zoe brought Daisy home two days ago, but the older woman went straight to bed saying she felt exhausted and weak. Not at all what the discharge nurse recommended and most unlike Daisy.

Zoe feels too exposed working at the counter. Even though she is over one hundred miles from Cedar Springs and anyone who knew her all those years ago. Her usual position is in the backroom, totaling invoices and receipts or ordering products. But with Daisy only two days out of the hospital, she has no choice but to step up to the plate.

Daisy has been more than generous over the years, refusing to take any money from Zoe for the spare bedroom she rents and very little for utilities.

"I enjoy having you around," Daisy says whenever Zoe broaches the subject of rent or helping more with the semi-annual property taxes. "Besides, I couldn't run the hardware store on my own anymore. I'm getting old."

"You're only sixteen years older than me, and I'm only thirty-four," Zoe reminds her whenever the subject of age comes up. "Fifty is the new forty."

Daisy usually shrugs her shoulders and says she doesn't feel forty anymore.

Zoe breaks out of her reverie and regards the case of assorted light bulbs and the shelves that need stocking. Leave them until tomorrow, or hurry and get it done today? It's not like Daisy will be back anytime soon. Better to get it out of the way.

She uses a knife to slit the tape securing the top of the box and carries it to the LED lighting display. Squatting on the floor, she takes the bulbs out one by one, inspects the wattage, then slots them onto a shelf. It's tedious work, and she checks her watch again. Only fifteen minutes to closing time. After that, anyone who can't wait until tomorrow will have to go to the Home Store farther up the road.

That's what Daisy would say.

The door to the store opens with a ding, and footsteps shuffle to the other side of the shelves where Zoe is working. She hears someone rummage through the wrenches but doesn't bother to get up. She's nearly done emptying the box, and there's a bell on the counter for patrons to summon her when they're ready to pay.

Footsteps draw closer, and a man rounds the end cap display stacked with snacks and candy.

"Do you have any larger wrenches—?" he begins, then falters as his mouth falls open. He's in his thirties with a stubble face and a shaved head. His thick neck, muscular arms, and broad shoulders scream bodybuilder. He's wearing a beater T-shirt and grimy jeans.

Zoe locks eyes with the newcomer. Ice water flows in her veins as they stare at one another in silence for several long moments.

"Zoe? Zoe Kelly? What the hell?" he exclaims.

"My name is Zoe Pegney. I'm afraid you have the wrong person," she says forcefully.

"Don't bullshit me, woman."

Zoe gets to her feet as Paul Henderson takes a step toward her, towering over her and weighing the wrench in his palm.

"What the fuck is going on, Zoe? We all thought you were dead."

Waves of panic flood over her as she backs away from the man.

He sticks the wrench in his jeans pocket, pulls out his phone, and snaps a photo of her. "People won't believe this picture when I show them."

She makes a split-second decision and races around the far end of the display into the center of the store. It's time to set her plan into motion.

Grabbing her purse from under the counter, Zoe dashes through the stock room and out the back door. She's glad to be wearing sneakers as she sprints down the sidewalk. Maybe Paul won't be able to catch her in his work boots.

Her heart beats with a frenzied rhythm as she races to the corner. At the sound of the store's back door crashing open, she dares to look over her shoulder. The street is empty except for Paul. He's fifty feet behind but gaining on her, and the silver wrench is in his hand.

Zoe has thought about this moment so many times over the past years. Now that it's finally happening, the scene feels more like a movie playing in her head. For a moment, she wonders if it's real.

Then she forces her mind to focus on her plan. The preparations she made in case her husband or one of his friends should come looking for her.

As her feet pound the blacktop, her breath comes in spurts, and she thinks about dialing 9-1-1.

No, that would lead to questions. Her past would be laid

bare.

She might even go to jail—her, the battered wife.

The press would have a field day.

The injustice of it all crushes her chest almost as much as her breaths.

It is just her luck that the street is empty. But then anyone would be reluctant to tackle a man Paul's size. Instead, they'd most likely film him as he beats her senseless with the wrench. Such are the depths to which society has fallen, she reflects.

She pauses at a house. If she knocks on the door, will anyone let her in with Paul in pursuit?

No!

Stick to the plan, she tells herself.

She doesn't dare look back as she darts down a narrow alley between two houses.

Stick to the plan.

Roof tiles lie among the tall weeds surrounding the empty Victorian on the corner. It was once boarded up, but kids and vagrants have ripped the plywood off a ground-floor window at the back.

Zoe knows where she's going to hide, though the idea makes her body vibrate with stark terror. She climbs on the wooden packing crate planted below the open window. Slipping inside the house doesn't go as well as it has in the past, and she lands in a crumpled heap on the musty carpet.

The boarded-up windows make the house almost pitch black inside. Her eyes haven't had time to adjust, and she's blind. Feeling in her purse, her fingers close on a flashlight. She clicks it, and the beam shines on peeling wallpaper and a sea of garbage on the floor.

Fast food wrappers crunch under her feet as she races into the hall, trying not to think about rodents, syringes, or condoms. Scrambling up the rickety stairs, she ignores the smell of human waste then pauses at the top, listening for any sign that Paul is following her into the house. But the pounding pulse in her ears and her thundering heart blot out all other sounds.

Four open doorways lead off the upstairs hallway to bedrooms. The door to the bathroom, the source of the stench, is missing. There's still a four-poster bed in the largest bedroom, and it's clear people have been using it for sex. Dashing to the far side of the bed, she peels back the rug and lifts the hinged top of a hidey-hole. It took her a week to hollow out the coffin-like space using tools and supplies from the hardware store.

Her legs feel like gelatin as she climbs inside and lays down. There's just enough room for her to pull the rug back into place as she closes the lid. There were cracks of light around the window-boards in the bedroom, but the space she's lying in is darker than pitch.

All she can do is wait and hope Paul didn't see her enter the house. It gives her a moment to reflect that her life as she knew it is over. Living in the cottage with Daisy and helping her with the store is gone. Zoe has to skip town as soon as it's safe for her to leave the hideaway.

But where will she go? Her plan doesn't go beyond hiding under the bedroom floor.

She hears a crash downstairs, followed by the sound of heavy footsteps crunching through the garbage in the hall.

Crap. Paul is in the house.

A sing-song voice says, "Come out, come out wherever you are. I'm taking you back to Cedar Springs. But I can't say Dirk is going to be pleased to see you. Not after he spent ten years in prison for killing you."

She hears Paul moving from room to room and cursing as he runs into walls in the darkness.

Her heart feels like it might leap out of her chest as footsteps pound the stairs. She squeezes her eyes tighter and bites her knuckles to stop herself from screaming.

The sing-song voice returns as footsteps enter the room. "Come out, come out wherever you are. It's time to come out and play, Zoe. No one will care when Dirk kills you. Everyone thinks you're already dead."

Chapter Thirty-One

IT'S LATE, AND the traffic is light as I drive home.

The nearer I get to my house, the less I'm looking forward to seeing Jasmin and the mess she will have made of the place. I don't know how long I'll be able to endure her living with me. She's hard on everything she touches, appliances, utensils, pots, and pans. So, I'm prepared for breakages.

I fully expect to see a chaotic scene. I'm particular about putting things back in their places, but Jasmin is the untidiest person I know. In the past, it's been a recipe for discord between us, and I see more of the same ahead.

As I pull to a stop outside my house, I see Jasmin's red pickup parked askew in the driveway, blocking both slots, but that's typical too. At least she's been out and hopefully picked up groceries. My fridge isn't stocked to feed two adults.

I pull into the curb and switch off the engine. It's dusk, but all the front windows are dark. My phone rings as I step onto the sidewalk. "Hi, gorgeous," says Finch.

"I'm guessing this is a social call," I chuckle. The

motion-sensing outside lights come on as I start up the driveway.

"Not entirely. I want to let you know that Holder has dropped the murder charges against Kessler."

"And I'm supposed to thank him for that?" The crickets and cicadas sound extra loud this evening.

"Bad day, Cassie?"

"I've let my team become too focused on one person, and now we're back to square one. On top of that, I'm about to find out what my sister has done to my house." I'm not ready to tell him about the Priesthood.

"How much damage can one person do in one day?"

"You'd be amazed," I hoot. As I climb the front stoop to the darkened house, I wonder if Jasmin is taking a nap.

I push open the front door and turn on the lights, feeling a prickle of unease. "There's half a bag of chips scattered over the couch. She's opened a fresh bottle of red wine and nearly drunk it all."

"Oh, my," I exclaim into the phone as the fluorescent light panel in the kitchen blinks on. "This is a disaster zone. Looks like she started to bake a cake or something. There's a mixing bowl overturned on the hardwood floor, and the ingredients are everywhere. I think the white powder is flour." I dip a finger in and taste it. "Yep, it's flour." I feel the heat from the wall-mounted oven and turn it off. "Where are you, Jasmin?" I move from room to room, needing to turn on the lights to see what I'm doing. A feeling of dread that's taken root in the pit of my stomach begins to grow. Something is terribly wrong.

"Is she napping?" Finch asks.

"Not in either bedroom."

The bathroom door is locked. I listen but don't hear anything. "Open the damn door, Jasmin," I shout, slapping my palm on the painted wood surface.

Nothing.

Thankfully, it's one of those doors you can unlock from the outside with the aid of a special pin. I slip my phone into the pocket of my pants, ignoring Finch's demands to know whether everything is all right.

It most definitely is not all right.

I stand on tip-toes, and my fingertips find the pin where I left it on the molding above the door.

The skinny end of the pin slips through a hole in the center of the handle, and the lock clicks open.

I hurry inside, flicking on the light,

My feet stop short, and I let out a scream.

Jasmin is lying on the floor on her belly, her head inclined to one side. There's a pool of puke on the carpet near her mouth, and it appears she's wet herself.

Finch's voice is yelling from the phone in my pocket, but I first have to know if Jasmin is still alive.

Stepping alongside her body, I crouch on my haunches to place two fingers on her neck. Her skin is cold and clammy, but there's a faint pulse. Her breathing must be shallow, because her chest is barely moving. I doubt she's taking in enough life-giving air.

Snatching the phone from my pocket, I shout to Finch, "Jasmin has overdosed. I have to get her to the ER."

Chapter Thirty-Two

I QUICKLY ARRANGE to meet Finch at the ER and end the call. I think I can pick Jasmin up in a fireman's lift and get her to the ER faster than waiting for an ambulance. But a siren grows louder, then stops in the street outside. Heavy footsteps on the front stoop draw me into the living room. Two paramedics in green scrubs, a man and a woman, burst through the front door carrying a stretcher.

"Ambulance?" the man asks questioningly.

"What address were you called out to?" I'm wondering if someone phoned them about Jasmin and ran. But I want to be sure they're not looking for another medical emergency.

"Two eighty-nine Willow Drive. Female, thirty, OD."

"You're at the right place. She's in the bathroom." They follow me down the hall. "I just found her. She has a history of drug use, but I don't know who the hell called you."

The man sets down a large bag, and they go to work on Jasmin.

"Dispatch said it was a male who made the call. He wouldn't give his name, sounded intoxicated," the female medic offers.

"Who are you, and what's your relationship to her?" the man asks me.

"Agent Cassie Viera. The patient is Jasmin Viera. She's my sister."

"FBI?"

"Yeah. Did the caller say what she's taken?"

"Negative."

I scan the bathroom and check the cabinet over the sink. There's nothing but my stuff. Hurrying into the living room, I spot a fine white powder on the coffee table and taste a small sample. "Got some coke," I shout. Jasmin's purse is on the floor beside the couch. Inside, I find a small plastic bag holding pills I recognize. "And some Molly." A second bag holds more white powder. I dip a finger inside and taste a couple of granules. "Crap. I've found a bag of heroin, but I don't see a syringe."

"She really hit the jackpot!" the woman shouts back. "Your sister is as good for transport as she's going to get. You riding with us in the back?"

"I'll follow. I've got a government car with lights and a siren."

Three cereal box-shaped buildings comprise Cedar Springs Hospital. I pull into the ambulance bay next to the rig transporting Jasmin. The back doors swing open, the woman jumps out, and together the paramedics push my sister's stretcher into the ER.

I've seen a lot of dead people in the course of my job, and Jasmin looks just like them. Her usual tawny complexion has a grayish tinge, and her features are drawn. I hope to hell they can resuscitate her.

I badge the security guard and follow the paramedics into the ER. I shouldn't be using my position in a situation like this, but I don't care.

My senses are hit by the twin odors of disinfectant and antiseptic. I stand to one side as medical personnel surround Jasmin and roll her onto a gurney. I'm wearing my professional face, mostly because I don't fully comprehend that it's my sister who's surrounded by tubes and beeping instruments. I'm used to seeing people treated in the ER, but they are always a perp or a victim. Never anybody close to me.

"Sats are dropping . . . eighty-five . . . eighty. She's bradying down," a female voice exclaims.

"Anyone know what she's taken?" an older doctor in blue scrubs asks of anyone who's listening.

I list off the drugs I found in her possession. "I didn't see a syringe, so she may not have taken heroin."

"We see a lot of cases of Coke laced with Fentanyl," he shouts over his shoulder. "Okay, let's intubate her."

I watch the doctors and nurses work on Jasmin as they lose her heartbeat. Her back arches as the paddles are applied to her bare chest. After two rounds of shocks, her heart rhythm returns.

"How does she look?" a familiar voice asks.

I turn and see Finch standing beside me. "Not good," I tell him. "They've lost her pulse once, and I see on the monitor it's about to happen again."

"Giving her two of epi," someone shouts.

"Charging to two-hundred. Clear."

Jasmin's back arches again from the jolt of electricity.

Nothing.

My heart is in my mouth. This is it. She's dying.

"Charging to three-fifty. Clear."

On the second blast, someone calls out, "Sinus rhythm."

I bury my face in Finch's chest. "I don't know how long I can watch this."

A nurse who's not involved in the resuscitation steps over. "Do you know this woman, agent?"

I wonder how she knows I'm FBI. Then I glance down and see my ID is clipped to my waistband. "She's my sister."

"You shouldn't be watching this."

The nurse shows Finch and me to a waiting room, and we sit on blue plastic chairs with a tubular chrome frame. They are so hard they make the ones at the DMV seem comfortable.

"She seemed fine this morning," I tell Finch. "I gave her money for groceries, but she must have blown it all on drugs."

"Any ideas where Jasmin got them?"

"None. She must have had a guy over at my house. When she OD'ed, he dialed 9-1-1 then split."

"What an upstanding citizen."

"I think I know where he lives. I might pay him a visit. Oh, Finch, I can't believe this is happening." I let go, and tears stream down my face.

He slips his arm around my shoulders and draws me closer. A clean, folded handkerchief appears, and he proceeds to dab my eyes and cheeks.

"We'll just have to wait and see what happens."

I like that he doesn't offer me any platitudes. This could

well end badly for Jasmin. Badly for me too.

After we've been there for forty-five minutes, the older doctor in blue scrubs comes into the waiting room. I stand and meet his piercing blue eyes. They must have seen everything humans can do to themselves and one another.

"Agent Viera, is it?" He shakes my limp, damp hand, and I wonder how many thousands of times he's had to deliver bad news.

"Cassie, please." My eyes feel raw from the tears I've shed.

"Cassie, I'm Doctor Kent. We've managed to stabilize your sister, and she's on her way to the ICU."

"What's her prognosis?" I feel Finch slip his arm around my waist.

"I wish I knew. Unfortunately, she has some brain swelling, so we've placed her in a medically induced coma. We'll keep her that way for a few days. We don't know what will happen when we try to wake her up. She may be relatively normal, or she might have mental or physical impairments. Or she might never wake up. I'm sorry, but we'll have to wait and see."

"Can I see her?"

"Of course, but after that, I suggest you go home and rest. It's extremely unlikely there will be any change in her condition until we try to wake her. I'm sorry I don't have better news."

After he's left, Finch and I cross the ER en route to the ICU. Who should come through the main doors but Detective Reed pushing a handcuffed man ahead of him. His gaze alights on me, and he stands with his captive, blocking my path.

"I heard about Jasmin over the radio. Bad luck having a druggie for a sister," Reed smirks.

"Fuck you, Reed," I spit. "How come you still have a job?"

"Guess you could say I'm bulletproof."

I'd like to slap the stupid grin off his face. But that would only play into his hand.

"Crawl back under the rock you came from," Finch snaps.

"You should hang out with better company," Reed tells him. "Her kind," he jabs a thumb my way, "shouldn't even be in the country, let alone working for law enforcement. It shows how far the feebs have sunk."

Finch takes a step forward, but I hold out an arm to block him. I can fight my own battles.

"Do as your girl says," Reed tells him.

"Screw you, Reed," I say. "I'd only have to tell ASAC Myles you're still working, and he'll arrest you."

"Don't expect Brandon Farley's buddies to ever back you up. They are none too happy with you for shooting him." Reed's grin widens. "Oh, well, I've no time for idle chat. Got to get this one processed." He pushes his prisoner toward the triage nurse.

As we board an empty elevator car, I ask Finch, "Any idea what Reed has on Holder?"

"Evidently something." He shakes his head and jabs a button. The doors rumble closed, and the car lurches upward. "Watch your back. Reed and Holder aren't fans of anything federal."

"They're against the federal government?"

"They think it should stay out of the state's business."

As we exit the elevator on the third level, we almost collide with Officer Mason.

"You've had a wasted journey," he tells us. "Pete's still unconscious."

I realize he's guarding Pete Barlow and thinks we're there to question him. "My sister is here," I say.

"Sorry to hear that. Orderlies just brought a woman up from the ER."

"Thanks," I say and hurry on, not wanting to engage him on the subject.

We find Jasmin in one of the cubicles. Her color looks better than when I saw her in the ER, but she's been intubated, and a machine is breathing for her. Her petite body is dwarfed by the medical instruments surrounding her bed. I've no idea what they are telling me, but the gentle beep of her heart rate monitor is rhythmic.

Jasmin doesn't flinch when I lean in and kiss her cheek. Her skin is cool and clammy. I straighten and turn to Finch. "Now, what do I do?"

"The doctor said she's going to be in a coma for a few days. Go home and get some sleep."

"It seems wrong to leave her when she's like this," I insist. "I'm feeling angry and sad and hurt all at the same time."

Finch shakes his head. "There's nothing more either of us can do here. You look as drained as I feel."

"Can you sleep at my place tonight, just for company? I don't want to be alone." Right now, there's no one I trust

252

more than Finch.

"Sure," he says, "I was thinking the same thing."

He follows my car to the house. The lights are still on from earlier, and the front door is unlocked.

He eyes the mess on the kitchen floor and picks up the overturned mixing bowl.

"Just leave it," I say. "I'll clean it up in the morning. Jasmin must have decided to make a cake when she was high. I'm guessing she fell and knocked over the bowl. Her guy friend must have helped her to the bathroom where she passed out."

"Some friend who leaves her lying unconscious on the floor."

"Jasmin sure can pick them. Would you like a hot drink?"

"I'm good, thanks. You should try to get some rest."

I show him to the spare room and get a pair of guy pajamas from the top drawer. "Don't ask. It's a long story."

We hug goodnight, and I don't want to let go of him. Finally, I step back and thank him for being a friend.

With no appetite for taking a shower or cleaning up the mess on the bathroom floor, I change into a T-shirt and shorts and climb into bed.

But my mind isn't ready to surrender to sleep. I keep asking myself why Jasmin turned out the way she did. I'm four years older. Maybe there was a time when she was eleven or twelve when I could have influenced her. Though by then, I'd pretty much given up on her. Jasmin used to steal my things. The few times when she returned them, they were broken. She'd lie and cheat to get what she wanted.

I let out a sob for the sister I might have had and another for the sister lying unconscious in the hospital across town. Then a torrent comes for how screwed up the world is.

After tossing and turning for a half-hour, with rushes of adrenaline washing through me, I climb out of bed. Crossing the hall, I tap gently on the spare room door, doing my best to get control of myself.

"Come," Finch shouts.

"Did I wake you?" I ask, pushing into the room.

"Nah. I can't sleep either."

"I feel so guilty about the times I could have helped Jasmin," I say, sitting on the foot of the bed and wiping my tears with the palms of my hands. "She was a tearaway right from when she was a toddler. I was the complete opposite. Quiet, respectful of my parents. A kid who did as she was told. I can't help but think she'd never have been so reckless or gotten into drugs if only I'd used my influence. Instead, I gave up on her."

"I've said it before, and I'll say it again—this is not your fault. The life choices Jasmin made brought her to this point. I can sense you've always had a lot of guilt about her. You need to find a way to let go of that."

I hesitate, considering his words. "You're right, but that's easier said than done. I've been feeling guilty about her for so long."

"I know she's difficult."

"It's like she's missing the impulse control part of her brain."

"And you think you could have fixed that how?"

I hesitate, gazing into his eyes. "Would you, uh . . . ? Would you hold me?"

He gives me a rueful smile, as he draws the covers aside. I climb onto the bed next to him and roll onto my side. He spoons me, wrapping his arm tenderly around my waist.

"That feels good, Finch. Can I stay here all night?"

"Sure."

"I don't want sex. Someday when the moment is right, but not tonight."

"Of course," he chuckles, pulling the covers over us. "But I have been known to snore."

"Me too."

"Great. We can have a competition."

"I love you, Finch. Even if you are rather stubborn at times."

"I love you too, Cassie, despite your backhanded compliments." He nuzzles his face into my hair, and a deep, dreamless sleep pulls me under.

Chapter Thirty-Three

WHEN I AWAKE the next morning, Finch and I are still lying in the same position. The previous evening comes flooding back to me. Jasmin, the drugs, the hospital. Finch's breaths are purring from him, and his chest is rising and falling, brushing against my back.

I gently lift his long muscular arm aside and climb out of bed. Gazing at his face, I wonder for a moment if we did anything I don't remember. My T-shirt and shorts are still in place, and I wouldn't have put them back on after sex. It's not that I don't trust Finch. It's myself I don't trust.

I race into my bedroom, grab my phone, and call the hospital. After a brief delay, I'm connected to the ICU charge nurse. She tells me there was no change in Jasmin Viera's condition overnight. Yay! Good for the time being, but the future is still uncertain.

When I get back to the spare room, Finch is just coming round, his eyes barely able to open. I finger comb the hair out of his eyes, then plant a kiss on his lips.

"How is Jasmin?" he asks, guessing that I've already called the hospital. When I tell him, he says, "No change is good, right?"

"My thoughts exactly. The nurse also said the doctor was encouraged by Jasmin's progress, but she cautioned me that the critical time will be in three days when they try to wake her."

After showering, separately, I might add, we head to the Lamplighter for breakfast. It's a retro-diner that oozes chintz. Clusters of globe pendant lamps hang over the counter, and the secluded booths are upholstered in orange.

We both need something more substantial than coffee after the stress of the previous night, and the place is perfect for both canoodling and private discussions.

Finch looks the way I feel—bleary-eyed and barely functioning. I'm sure the waitress thinks we've had a night of wild sex as she brings us coffee and menus.

She's blonde and wearing a retro red and white striped dress and a vintage paper hat. "I'll be back to take your orders when you've had time to look at the menus." She flashes Finch a smile and moves on to the next booth.

"She's perky," I say, my eyes moving to the specials.

Finch just grunts.

I reach across the table and place my hand on his. "Thanks for being there for me last night. It means a lot."

"How are you feeling?"

"Weary but resigned about what might happen to Jasmin."

"If she makes it, this should be a heck of a wake-up call for her."

"She's not a quick study when it comes to wake-up calls. She's had several in her life."

Finch grunts. "If nearly dying doesn't do it, I don't know what will."

"On a work-related topic, can you keep something to yourself for now?"

He looks over the top of his menu. "Of course."

"I spoke to Jackie Ricci at the Travelodge yesterday. She's been looking into an extremist group called the Priesthood. She says the person who killed Ava and Ricky is a member, as is Brandon Farley, the officer who went crazy at the SWAT raid."

"How does she know all this?" He folds the menu and sets it down.

"She's able to monitor their message board."

"Did she give you a link?"

"I'm still working on that. The kicker to the story is that she's seen messages discussing how Brandon was supposed to 'accidentally' shoot Stevie and me in the raid."

Finch gazes into my eyes, his brow furrowed. "That's a stretch. It would mean Reed was also involved with this group since he ordered the raid."

"I don't have any trouble believing he's into conspiracy theories."

"What would be the group's motive for shooting two federal agents?"

"Maybe we're getting too close to the killer."

The waitress appears with coffee and takes our orders, Huevos Rancheros for Finch, a Spanish omelet for me. She flashes us a smile, then gathers up the menus and hurries back to the kitchen.

"Did Jackie happen to have Ava and Ricky's killer's

name?" Finch's face is tinged with disbelief.

"She did not," I reply, ignoring the obvious sarcasm.

"Look, Cassie, I can accept that Jackie is investigating this group, but having a SWAT team shoot Stevie and you to protect one of their own sounds like pure fiction to me. The full force of the FBI would descend on them."

"Not if Brandon had done a better job of making it look like an accident. Or if Stevie hadn't recorded it. He could have claimed we were going for our weapons."

Finch rubs his chin, gazing into the distance, before bringing his focus back to me. "I still don't see it. Reed is an asshole, but I can't see him being involved in an attack on two federal agents."

"It's not impossible."

Finch shakes his head, and I don't feel like arguing with him. We lapse into silence for a few moments.

"Look, about last night at the hospital," I say. "I don't need you to fight my battles with morons like Reed. I can take care of myself."

"Duly noted." Finch sips his coffee.

"Regardless of whether we believe Jackie, I can't ignore what she told me. Having been appraised of a threat against the Bureau, I have no alternative but to take it seriously. Myles is back in the office today, and I'll be talking to him later."

"As much as I think Jackie is blowing smoke up your ass, you have no choice but to take it to your boss."

The waitress appears with plates of food. After setting them down, she asks if she can get us anything else.

"I'm, good, thanks," Finch replies.

"Me too." I catch Finch staring at the waitress' backside as she heads to another booth. "Please don't mention the Priesthood to anyone at the station."

He focuses back on me, a touch of embarrassment in his eyes. "I would never share your confidences. I believe Jackie when she says she's looking into the group, and I have no doubt there are members in the police department. It's the conspiracy to commit murder that I have a problem with."

***

WHEN I GET to the office, I find the three members of my team sitting around the conference room table.

"So sorry to hear about your sister," Stevie says. "We weren't expecting you in today."

"How is she doing?" Nick asks. "We heard she was taken to the ER in an ambulance."

I set my bag on the table and flop into a chair, feeling suddenly weary. "Yesterday evening, I arrived home to find Jasmin lying on the bathroom floor, unconscious from a drug overdose. She coded twice in the ER, but doctors managed to stabilize her. She's in the ICU in a medically induced coma."

"That's terrible," Todd says. "Is she going to be okay?"

"We won't know until doctors try to wake her on Saturday or Sunday." For now, my feelings about Jasmin have to be set aside. I have a job to do. "You all seem very busy. What's new?"

"Stevie told me about your meeting with Jackie Ricci at

the hotel," Todd says. "You think the killer we're hunting is a member of the Priesthood?"

"I do. But that is beside the point. Having been alerted to a credible threat to our lives, we need to investigate this extremist group. All the better if that leads us to whoever knifed Pete Barlow and to Ricky and Ava's killer."

"We were discussing ways to access the Priesthood's message board," Todd continues. "It's frustrating that Jackie wouldn't tell you where it's hosted."

"She claimed that we'd attract the group's attention and get her shut out along with us. Was that a valid concern?"

"The board must have crappy security for members not to have noticed Jackie logging on. I doubt one more fake account would make a difference, especially if we're just watching and not posting messages."

"So, how do we find it?" I'm feeling the effects of my late night and would like nothing better than to crawl into bed.

"They could have set it up in any number of ways," Todd tells us. "There are message board hosting services. Some charge a fee, while others will host your board for free. It requires zero expertise. They could call their board something innocent, like *car repair*. That would work well for them, provided that members watch their language and don't attract the NSA by discussing hijackings and bombings. Explicitly talking about killing FBI agents is also a no-no."

"Ways to trace that?" Stevie asks.

"Check bank accounts for regular monthly payments to a service, or break into the house of one of the members and check out their computer."

"If we do something illegal to locate the message board," I say, "anything we find on it could get thrown out at trial."

"Legal won't work," Todd exclaims. "Once we find the board, we'll need to hack into it to read the messages. That's against the law the last time I checked."

"Once you locate it, I'll speak to an assistant US attorney, and we'll get a search warrant that will also cover hacking. You said there are other ways of setting up a board."

"If they have a member with some technical expertise, they could have installed the software on a computer in someone's home. It's not that difficult, and if they put it on the dark web, we're screwed."

"Needle in a haystack time?" Nick asks.

"Pretty much. Unless we gain access to one of the member's computers or phones."

"Damn. This looked so promising when Jackie told us about it," I say.

"Don't give up just yet. Let me look at the social media accounts of members and see if they provide any clue," Todd offers.

"Here are a couple of names," Nick says. "Detective Gary Reed and Officer Brandon Farley. That should get you started."

"The threat of violence from this group has made us all a little spooked," Stevie tells me. "Is it real? Should we be worried?"

"Detective Finch was skeptical when I told him about the threat. He believes the group is real, but not the part about them actively trying to kill us. He could well be right, but we shouldn't take any risks. Keep your heads on a swivel at all times and keep your weapons within easy reach. And don't tell anyone we're investigating the Priesthood. We suspect Reed is a member, but we don't know who else in the police department might be one."

Stevie's face colors. "I already told Officer Mason, but I'm positive he's not a member."

"Nothing we can do about that now," I say. "Give Mason a call when we're done here and tell him to keep his mouth shut. What else?"

"An agent at the Sacramento Field Office got back to me," Nick says. "No one we're currently looking at is on the extremist watch list, but the father of one of our suspects is on it. Russell Henderson was suspected of a bombing that killed three people at a women's clinic fifteen years ago. But there wasn't enough evidence to arrest him. Remember, Russell is the owner of the ranch where his son Paul Henderson and Dirk McCloskey claimed to be living. But Russell told US Marshals he hadn't seen Paul in a while, and he'd never heard of McCloskey.

"We talked yesterday about you and Stevie paying a visit to the ranch to ask about our two prime suspects who claim to be living there," I remind them. "Now you can check Russell out as well. Use the pretext of his son skipping meetings with his parole officer. Todd, search social media for Russell's views on this government takeover nonsense. If it's one of his beliefs, mark him down as another potential member of the Priesthood."

"You got it, boss," he says, giving me the pistol fingers.

263

It's as corny as hell, and I wish he wouldn't, but I imagine it's baked into his psyche.

"You have your assignments. Let's get to it and shut these idiots down. It should also lead us to the murderer we're chasing. I'm going upstairs to see what Myles thinks about the threat to our safety."

I find Myles' assistant Beryl at her desk outside his fishbowl office. I know she can see me, but she continues typing for a couple of minutes, her eyes flashing between a document and her screen. As if she's writing the great American novel and doesn't want to lose her train of thought. It's a dance she does with everyone who comes to see the top agent. I imagine she's really emailing one of her girlfriends about lunch or exchanging the latest juicy piece of gossip.

Finally, she looks up. "Can I help you, Agent Viera?"

"I need to speak to Myles." I can see he's alone in his office and not on the phone. It's a mystery what value Beryl adds.

"May I tell him what it's regarding?" she asks.

"Someone is threatening to kill FBI agents."

"Oh, my." She gets on the intercom to Myles, who says, "Send her in."

I step into the office, and the boss waves me to a seat. It's a relief when he doesn't mention Jasmin. He steeples his fingers as I lay out the information Jackie gave us about the Priesthood.

His brow creases when I mention the intended murder of Stevie and me by the group. When I'm done, he stays silent for a long moment.

"An extremist group plotting to kill federal agents? Using police resources to enact their plans? I would need to send this type of allegation up the chain of command to the director forthwith. But I can't do that in good conscience if the only evidence we have is the word of this television reporter."

"Yes, sir."

"Cassie, I have no doubts that the Priesthood exists, but I find their motive for killing federal agents a stretch. I can't completely discount it, and nor should you. The safety of your team is paramount. You did the right thing bringing this information to my attention. But I need you to verify the threat through another source before I act. I want you to talk to this reporter again and threaten her with a subpoena if she doesn't give you access to the group's message board. Understood?"

"Yes, sir."

"Keep up the excellent work, Cassie." Myles clears his throat and turns his attention back to the document he was reading when I came in. It's my cue to leave.

Chapter Thirty-Four

"NOW WHAT?" STEVIE asks as Nick noses the black sedan up to the barrier across the driveway. Overhead, a sign hanging from an arch announces, *'Smoke Tree Ranch.'* On the other side of a low rise, the green metal roofs of several buildings are visible.

"Let's see if Russell is home." Nick rolls down the driver's window and operates a push-to-speak button on an intercom. "FBI Agents Stone and Wells to see Mr. Russell Henderson."

"Do you have an appointment?" the female voice asks.

"No, ma'am, we do not. We were hoping to have a quick word with him."

"Let me see if I can find him. He may be out at the stables."

Nick raps his fingers on the steering wheel while they wait.

"This is exciting," Stevie cracks after several long moments have passed. "You think she's forgotten about us?"

Before Nick can reply, the barrier slowly rises, and the

female voice comes back on the intercom. "Mr. Henderson has a few minutes to speak to you. Follow the driveway and park in front of the main building. Someone will meet you and show you where to go."

When the barrier is fully raised, Nick eases the car forward until they come to an intersection. "Where do we go?"

"See that sign that's fallen over?" Stevie says, squinting through the windshield. "Stables left, barn right, and I can see it says the main building is straight ahead."

"They need to seriously improve their signage."

"You think the boss is getting off track having us interview this guy?"

"Paul Henderson and Dirk McCloskey, the two suspects at the top of your list for killing Ava Barlow and Ricky Kelly, list this place as their home address. Moreover, Russell Henderson is on an extremist watch list. In my view, she's right on track," Nick says as he pulls the car into a parking space in front of an enormous ranch-style house. Sprinkler jets arc over a pristine lawn surrounded by shrubs and flower beds. It looks like an oasis in the parched California landscape.

"I could live here, no problem," Stevie says. As the two agents climb out of the sedan, a woman in her late twenties approaches. Her silky blond hair is cut to a stylish mid-length.

"Welcome to Smoke Tree Ranch, agents." She looks like the consummate businesswoman dressed in a dark blue pantsuit and cream blouse. Black leather boots with three-inch heels make her tower over Stevie's five-foot-five height. "I'm Delia Henderson. Russell is my father. We spoke on the intercom moments ago."

Nick and Stevie shake her hand and show their IDs, which Delia peers at intently before saying, "Right this way, agents. Excuse my caution, but the horse industry is a cutthroat business. You wouldn't believe the lengths criminals will go to collect a semen sample from a prize-winning racehorse."

"Who knew?" Stevie mutters to herself as Delia leads them through a pair of oak doors that look like they'd repel a battering ram.

They pass through a hallway into a wood-paneled room with a huge glass display cabinet filled with medals and awards.

"Father will be out shortly. In the meantime, please have a seat." She indicates a pair of high-backed leather chairs. "Can I get you some refreshments while you wait?"

When Nick and Stevie decline, she adds, "Nice meeting you both," before leaving through an oak door.

When they're seated, Stevie leans over and whispers, "The place reeks of money. Not at all what I was expecting."

"Paul Henderson must be the black sheep of the family," Nick replies, his voice low, "considering he was recently released from prison after serving a seven-year sentence for murdering his wife."

"Murder sentences never seem long enough to me," Stevie murmurs, interlacing her hands on her lap.

"You think petty thieves should be locked up for years," he counters.

"Quite right." Stevie nods. "Thieves are the scourge of

the earth."

"Don't look now, but there's a camera with a winking red light on the far wall. It's a reasonable assumption that there are also listening devices in the room."

"Duly noted."

After a few minutes, a tall man with a full head of graying hair swept back from his rosy face bustles into the room. A long aquiline nose gives him an aristocratic bearing. He's wearing a red checked shirt, jeans, and knee-high boots. "So sorry to keep you waiting, agents. I'm Russell Henderson. He extends his hand to Stevie and then Nick before pulling up a chair and sitting facing them.

Russell waves their IDs away with a sweep of his hand. "I have no doubt you're who you say you are. Now, what can I do for you?"

"Your son, Paul Henderson's name has come up in the course of our inquiries," Nick says. "But we're having difficulty locating him."

"What inquiries would those be, son?" Russell leans forward with his forearms on his knees.

"I'm sorry, but I'm not at liberty to say. But Paul has nothing to be concerned about. He's just a witness."

Russell's eyes narrow. "To be honest, I've only spoken to him once since he was, ah, released."

"Do you know where he's living? Apparently, he gave this address to the parole authorities."

"I'm sorry, I don't. Paul is a bit of a hothead and marches to the beat of his own drum. I've tried to get him interested in the ranch, but he never took to it." Russell raises his brow expectantly, waiting for another question.

Hotheaded? That's what you call a guy who murdered his wife? Stevie wonders. What kind of person are you? She half expects Russell to say boys will be boys, but he doesn't.

"We're also looking for an individual named Dirk McCloskey. He also gave your ranch as his home address."

Russell shakes his head slowly. "Several of the ranch hands live on the property, but I've never heard that name before. I can ask Delia if you'd like."

"Would you mind?"

Russell leaves the room, returning moments later with Delia in tow. "My daughter has reminded me that Paul used to know a Dirk McCloskey."

"When they were in their teens," Delia adds. "That was twenty years or more ago."

"Have you seen your brother recently?" Nick asks her.

"Sorry. I've only seen him once since he was released."

"Do you know why Paul might have skipped out on his parole meetings? The penalty is a return to prison."

Delia's neatly plucked eyebrows knit together. "It was probably a mistake. Maybe Paul got the time of the meeting wrong."

"I told the federal marshals this when they came here and asked me the same questions as you," Russell adds, shaking his head. "The FBI isn't usually interested in parolees missing a meeting or two. So why are you really here, agents?

"Do you know if Paul is a member of any extremist groups?" Nick asks.

"How do you define an extremist group? People who don't share the same beliefs as you? When did the FBI start investigating a person's thoughts and beliefs?"

"When those individuals make threats against the lives of others."

"The constitution affords us freedom of speech and freedom of assembly."

"The constitution doesn't give anyone the right to threaten the lives of federal agents or anyone else."

"Members of the FBI have received threats?" Russell's brow furrows.

"I can't go into specifics as the investigation is ongoing," Nick replies, kicking himself for revealing information harvested from the message board.

"You know, 9/11 changed the FBI's mission. Before that infamous day, you investigated crimes that had already occurred. After it, you began to try and prevent criminal behavior before it happened. The problem I have is that you can't go very far down that road before you tread on the constitutional rights of individuals. The right to bear arms, freedom of assembly."

"The FBI is tasked with bringing terrorists to justice," Stevie insists.

"That sounds all well and good, but how do you decide who is a terrorist? Freedom fighters like Paul Revere and George Washington? Would they be called terrorists today?"

"If they plan or commit crimes against people or property."

"That's exactly what they did against the British. But my key problem is when you include citizens who you say are planning crimes."

"You'd rather we wait until they've killed or maimed someone before we act?" Stevie looks him in the eye.

"I'm saying people are going to believe what they choose. They might believe in a deep state, a Marxist government takeover, crisis actors, or staged disasters, and there's nothing the federal government can do about it. Instead, the FBI has been forced to invent crimes people *might* commit just so you can call them terrorists and arrest them."

"The FBI should go back to its pre-9/11 purely investigative role," Delia adds. "Only God can see the future."

Russell gives the agents a forced smile. "You junior members of the FBI need to convince your superiors of what Delia just said. You might think you know what these so-called terrorists will do next, but you don't. Trust me."

"I think we're done here today," Nick says. "Thank you both for your time."

"Will you think about what we've said?" Delia asks as she shows the agents to the door.

"Of course," Stevie replies, hoping she sounds convincing. Once the agents are inside the black sedan, she continues, "That was a waste of time."

"Oh, I don't know. They were lying through their teeth. Pretty sure that Paul has been to the ranch recently, and they know exactly who Dirk McCloskey is. Russell Henderson may be a slick talker, but Delia is a terrible liar."

"What about the crap Russell spouted?"

"I don't doubt that he's a member of the Priesthood. He was using his so-called philosophy as an excuse for whatever they're planning to do next. He hinted we have no idea what that is, and I doubt it stops at killing two agents."

"You know we got the information about killing agents from the message board," Stevie reminds him.

"Yeah. It was a mistake to mention that. Don't tell the boss. I'm hoping Russell will think they have a mole in their ranks."

***

"RUSSELL HENDERSON IS definitely up to something," Nick says. "If he isn't a member of the Priesthood, he's a member of some other subversive group."

"He's a guy with an ax to grind," Stevie adds. "Our terrorist is his freedom fighter. But mostly, he complains about how the FBI is arresting people for planning crimes. He sounded like some evil mastermind when he said we don't know what they are up to."

"Who was he referring to?" I ask.

"It sounded like him and his fellow freedom fighters."

"The Priesthood?"

Nick nods. "Could be."

"Hold that thought." I catch sight of Myles coming through the door to our offices.

There's a spring in his step as he breezes up to Nick and me. "I just wanted to let you know that a warrant has been approved to search Pete Barlow's house for the gold bars he may have taken from Leo Kessler. A team should be on-site Saturday to sweep the yard with ground-penetrating radar."

I force a smile. "Thank you for letting me know, sir."

"Is Barlow still in the hospital?"

"Yes, still unconscious. Doctors aren't optimistic."

"If the search team finds anything, he'll be facing charges if he wakes up."

"Yes, sir."

"That's all, Cassie. Carry on." Myles turns and breezes back out of the door.

"That was like a drive-by," Nick says.

"At least he didn't shoot anyone today."

I have just settled into my office chair when my phone chimes. It's the boss again. "Yes, sir?"

Myles says, "As I was leaving the building, I ran into Hazel DeRosa, the reporter from Channel Five. She's looking for you, and you need to hear what she has to say."

Myles has left when I find Hazel in the parking lot. She seems agitated. "I'm sorry to show up like this," she says, "but I don't know who else to turn to."

"We really need a front desk and a receptionist. How can I help?"

"It's Jackie Ricci. I think someone has taken her."

"You'd better come inside."

As we enter the office, I shout, "Nick, Stevie, conference room now." I turn to Hazel. "Can I get you anything? Coffee, tea, water?"

"Water, maybe. I'm feeling a little nauseous." I'd guess she's in her mid-forties. She has a sun-tanned face, and her dark hair is sheared into a stylish pixie-cut. She's wearing a navy jacket over a cream-colored silk blouse and gray slacks.

"Please have a seat. I'll be right back." I crouch at the

fridge under the refreshment table and pull out a bottle of water. When I enter the conference room, Hazel, Stevie, and Nick are seated. "Do you all know one another?"

"We just introduced ourselves," Stevie says.

I set the water bottle in front of Hazel, then take a seat across the table from her. "Why don't you start again from the top?"

Shaky hands finger-comb the sides of her hair. "I fear Jackie Ricci has been abducted. It happened while I was speaking to her on the phone. She was just letting herself into her apartment when a man approached her about a news article. She told me to hold on while she saw what he wanted. There was a scuffling sound, then a clattering noise as if her phone fell to the ground. After that, I heard a stifled scream, then nothing."

"Did you dial 9-1-1?" Nick asks.

"Yeah. A pair of officers showed up, but they didn't seem convinced that anything had happened to Jackie. We drove over to her apartment, but there was nothing to see. I have a key, so we looked inside, but nothing was out of place. I've phoned her a dozen times, but it goes straight to voicemail."

"Why come to us and not your friend, Detective Reed?" I ask, a frown creasing my forehead.

"I'm convinced the group she was investigating has taken her." Hazel opens her purse, finds a handkerchief, and dabs the tears welling up in her eyes.

"The Priesthood?" I ask.

"Yeah. Jackie told me to keep the fact that she was investigating the group a secret. To never mention it to anyone at the police department, including Detective Reed. But I know she's spoken to you on the matter."

I nod. "Sure, so you came to us." I find it interesting that Hazel thinks it possible that Reed could be connected to the Priesthood.

"I told her that messing with those people was playing with fire," Hazel says with a hitch in her voice.

"Did you happen to notice the time when you heard the scuffle?"

She takes a sip of the bottled water before answering. "I did. It was twenty-two minutes past eleven. Here's her address." She slides a slip of paper across the table. I note it on my phone, then text it to the team.

"Nick, have Todd scour surveillance video around the apartment building. After that, you're looking for witnesses while Stevie and I search Jackie's apartment. Tell Todd that if he strikes out with the video, he's to join you."

"Is Todd cleared for fieldwork?" he asks, looking puzzled.

"Only for questioning witnesses. I don't want to involve anyone at the police department." My gaze swings to Hazel. "Did you see any electronic devices in Jackie's apartment?"

"A laptop. I was surprised as Jackie usually takes it into work."

"I may need permission to look at her recent communications. It might give us a hint of who's taken her. If we can still log onto the Priesthood message board, it may tell us if they unmasked her. We don't have time for a warrant."

"Reporter's laptops are all owned by Channel Five. I

expect the station manager will give you permission if you tell him it's a matter of life and death for Jackie."

"Okay, Hazel," I say, rising to my feet. "Let's get going to Jackie's apartment. Stevie and I will follow you in our own car."

Chapter Thirty-Five

"HOW DID THE officers who responded to your 9-1-1 call miss that?" I ask Hazel, pointing to a dark smear on the door to Jackie's apartment.

"When I showed it to them, they said it was old," she replies.

"Would you like to do the honors, Stevie?"

She snaps on rubber gloves, then takes a Q-Tip from the forensic bag and moistens it with drops of water from an ampule. Next, she swipes through the smear on the door. The specimen looks red. That's enough to convince me, but she completes the test by breaking the ampules inside another container and dabbing the Quick Check liquid onto the tip of the swab.

When it turns green, she announces for Hazel's benefit, "It's blood, and it wasn't completely dry, meaning it's recent."

"Strike two for the police," I say.

Hazel uses her key to let us into the apartment while Stevie props the door open with her foot and takes a sample for the lab. There's a slight chance the blood could belong to

Jackie's kidnapper.

The living room feels light and airy. An oversized window offers a marvelous view of the Sierra Nevada Mountains. Hazel follows me as I check out the remaining rooms. The spacious master is decorated in pastels and holds a king bed, while the spare room is filled with packing cases, skis, and luggage.

"Jackie sold her house and downsized after her husband died, but there were items she couldn't bear to part with," Hazel explains.

"Does anything about the apartment look different to you?" I ask. "Anything missing?"

Hazel steps to a desk with a hutch, partially hidden behind a tall ficus plant in the living room. "Everything looks the same as I remember. What are the chances of finding Jackie . . . alive?"

"If the group had wanted her dead, they wouldn't have gone to the trouble of kidnapping her," I say, though I believe the chances are slim. "Was Jackie working on other stories besides the Priesthood?"

"Two days ago, the news director assigned her full time to investigating the group. She was working on a couple of other stories, and they were handed off to me. One was about cancer-causing chemicals in the water, the other about the rise in the cost of lumber driving up house prices. Nothing that would get her killed if that's what you are asking."

Stevie joins us. "Do you know how Jackie first learned about the Priesthood?"

Hazel looks uncomfortable. "We have our own

informants."

"Was her informant a member of the group?" I ask.

"The person in question knew a member."

"Come on, Hazel. This person might have information that could help us locate and rescue Jackie. What is the informant's name?"

Hazel hesitates. "The informant is dead. It was Ricky Kelly."

"Did he ever mention the name of the member he knew?"

Hazel shakes her head. "Sorry, no."

"Damn," Stevie exclaims. "We could look into Ricky's friends."

"Let's not get diverted from looking at the laptop." I step to the desk. "We might be able to use it to monitor the group's message board. Even though Jackie said the members use pseudonyms, I'm hoping Todd can still uncover their identities."

"I'm not trying to get in your way, but don't you need a warrant to use what you find at trial?" Hazel asks.

"We need permission from the owner of the laptop if that's someone other than Jackie or if there's work-product owned by your station."

"The station owns the laptop, so the news director should be able to give you permission on both counts." Hazel retrieves her phone from her bag. "I'll give him a call."

"Please tell him that viewing the laptop will allow us to read the Priesthood's message board. We believe they might be the group that is holding Jackie."

Hazel nods and dials. The conversation lasts all of thirty seconds. When the call ends, she says, "He didn't hesitate. We have permission."

I take a seat at the desk and boot up the laptop. "I want our tech to go through it, but let's see if there's anything obvious that will get us started." Hazel gives me the pin number, and I'm in. "Let's check her emails." I click on the desktop icon. "I'm sorting them by the sender's name, as I don't need to look at ones she received from you. Who is Max Kersey?"

"The news director."

"And Rachel Snyder?"

"Another reporter."

"Zoe Pegney?"

"No idea. Sorry."

"Let's see what they talk about," I say, clicking into a message. "Just girl talk. Let's try another email . . . Nothing interesting."

I'm about to move on to a different sender when I notice something. "Zoe seems concerned about people finding out where she is. She says Jackie is her best friend." I read more of the emails between the two women. "Jackie is suggesting to Zoe that she move farther away and change her first name. She's hiding out from someone." I pull out my phone and call Todd.

"Knock 'em dead computer hacking," he answers.

"Funny guy. Found anything on surveillance video?"

"We have a picture of a guy with a limp body in his arms. I assume it's Jackie. He tosses her in the back of a blue minivan and drives off."

"Good enough for facial recognition?"

"Sorry, no. The camera is mounted on a store across the street, and it's a piece of crap. I'm guessing Jackie is one-fifty. The ease with which he's carrying her says it's our guy who stole the motorcycle and killed Ava. But, I'll keep looking for other cameras."

"Can you run a name for me? Zoe Pegney. P-E-G-N-E-Y."

I hear the rattle of a keyboard, he says. "No one in California by that name." More typing sounds. "Or anywhere in the US. Sounds like a made-up name to me."

"I'm forwarding you a message from Jackie's computer. Can you find where it was sent from?"

"Sure thing."

I forward the message and press send. Soon after, Todd says. "Here it is . . . The IP address isn't hidden. It was sent from . . . A coffee shop in Placerville."

"I was hoping it would lead me to a residence."

"Are there other emails from the same person?" Todd asks. "This Zoe may have sent some from her home."

"More important than those emails is a shortcut on the desktop labeled Priesthood."

"Sweet."

"I'm bringing the laptop in for you to look at. I'm afraid it might go up in a puff of smoke if I click the link."

"We're not dealing with a bunch of Mission Impossible geniuses."

Thirty minutes later, Stevie and I are in Todd's office looking over his shoulder.

"Stand back while I click the icon," he quips.

"Jokes are over," I say.

A login screen appears with the username and password already filled in. Jackie calls herself 'Forrest.' Todd clicks the 'OK' button, and we're into the message board.

He selects several recent messages for us to read. Posters with colorful names like Stonewall and Longstreet grouch about everything from taxes and second amendment rights to free speech, immigration, and crime. But neither the usernames nor the messages give any clues to the identities of the authors. Nor do we see them discuss anything criminal in nature.

I turn to head back to my office when Todd says, "Here's something."

The title of the message is '*Next meeting.*' The body reads, '*Friday, June 26, six p.m. Smoke Tree Barn.*'

"Russell Henderson's ranch, tomorrow," Stevie exclaims.

"They may hold extreme views, but that's not a crime. We can't go rushing in without evidence the group has Jackie, or they've done something criminal," I say.

"Dirk McCloskey and Paul Henderson have skipped parole."

"We have no firm evidence that they are members. The meeting attendees will likely be heavily armed. It could turn into another bloodbath like Ruby Ridge. What stands out to me is the location of the meet. Russell Henderson has to be a member."

"If he is, I can't see him being anything less than the leader of the group," Stevie adds.

"There are a ton of messages," Todd says. "Let me see if

I can put names to some of the authors. Maybe I'll find plans to kill FBI agents."

"Try not to sound so excited about that," Stevie says.

"Before you go, I managed to find Dirk McCloskey's sister," Todd says. "Her name is Norma Hodges. She's local, and I have an address for her."

"Where do I remember that name from?" Stevie asks.

"It's the waitress we met at the Chocolate Bunny Espresso," I tell her. "When we were looking for Maura."

The rest of the afternoon brings no breakthroughs in the search for Jackie. Just more pictures of the kidnapper that weren't good enough to run through facial recognition. It is also galling that the clear shots Todd finds of the stolen minivan's license plate are of no help.

Later in the afternoon, Nick gets back to the office and tells us he found three witnesses to the kidnapping. "They were cooperative, but their descriptions of the suspect varied so wildly as to be useless. He had a beard and mustache, he was clean-shaven, he was Latino, Caucasian, or American Indian, depending on who you choose to believe."

I shake my head. "We can't seem to catch a break with this guy. He has to be the luckiest SOB on the planet."

I'm grateful for Finch's company in the evening. He comes with me to the hospital. Again, there is no change in Jasmin's condition. I'm still not sure whether that's to be expected, but the nurse seems busy and doesn't want to get into details. There isn't a doctor to ask. I remind myself that everything will be answered in a couple of days when doctors attempt to wake my sister.

When we go to leave her bedside, my conscience attacks me. It feels like I should stay with her overnight. But Finch mostly talks me out of the idea that I'm abandoning her.

"We need to eat," he says as we drive away from the hospital.

"Not sure what I feel like," I tell him. "It's been a rotten day. Something comforting, like pizza, fish and chips, or a burrito at the Taco House."

In the end, we go to my place and order in pizza—a Margherita and a Funguy. G*et it, Fungi?*

I feel like we're a domestic couple when he stacks the few plates and forks in the dishwasher. Maybe that's what I'm craving, but is Finch the guy? I tell myself it's silly to think like that at his point. He's the first guy I've dated in a long while.

Afterward, we sit and listen to music and talk about life.

"I'm sorry I had a wobble at the hospital," I say, draining my glass of wine. "I truly appreciate your support."

"Think nothing of it, Cassie. You're a special person."

"I haven't wanted to take a chance on anything or anyone in a really long time. I used to be someone who took chances. But after four years of marriage, Kenny running off with someone who must be more lovable than me was so, so painful. It's made me think risks aren't worth taking. Because something will happen, and I'll be back to feeling horrible again. Does that make sense?"

"It makes perfect sense." Finch smiles. "Come sit closer."

I move to the couch and lean my back into his strong, firm body. My head is on his shoulder, and he gently strokes my hair, sending tingling sensations through my scalp. I feel both soothed and excited.

"But I want to be someone who takes risks again. I really do. You just need to know that I have baggage—Kenny and Jasmin."

"Forget Kenny. He didn't deserve you, and he's gone. Jasmin is out of your hands for the moment."

"I have to face the fact that Jasmin may not wake up. And nothing I do will make the slightest bit of difference," I say.

"That's true of many things in life, but it's not always easy to accept."

"I want to take a chance on you. You just need to know that while I may be a kick-butt FBI agent, I'm insecure when it comes to relationships." I turn to face him, and his lips trail softly across my cheek. "That's why I haven't dated anyone since Kenny left me."

"Hush, Cassie. You're safe," he says. My mouth finds his, and what starts as a slow, gentle caress of our lips falls into a fiery, passionate kiss. Then he tenderly kisses my eyelids, my earlobes, the beating pulse in my neck.

My body squirms against him, and I feel he's as ready as I am.

"Take me to the bedroom," I say softly.

Finch rises and slides his hands under my knees and waist, picking me up as if I weigh nothing. He gazes into my eyes, and I mirror the smile on his lips. Warmth floods my body as he carries me into my bedroom and gently sets me on the bed.

We tug off each other's outer clothing.

His chest looks very pale next to my tawny skin. "Let's take it slow," I whisper in his ear.

He nods, moving his attention to my naked breasts, spending the longest time tracing them with his tongue and lips.

Moving down the bed, he gently slides my panties off and kisses my knees, then gently parts my legs. His nuzzles and kisses slowly move up my inner thighs, sending shock waves through me.

My body and soul are on fire. As much as what he's doing makes me squirm, I beckon him to lie alongside me, and I kiss him on the lips. A full-on kiss that speaks volumes of passion.

My hand moves down his chest and plunges into his shorts, grasping him. "I want to feel you inside me," I whisper in his ear.

"What happened to taking it slow?" he asks with a grin.

"Forget slow. Take me."

Chapter Thirty-Six

"PASS THE BOTTLE," Dirk McCloskey snaps.

"There's just one swig left." Paul Henderson leans across the cab of the Dodge Ram pickup and sets the bottle in Dirk's hand. "You're getting too close to them. They'll spot us in their rearview."

"What if they do? I doubt they've ever seen this truck." McCloskey swings the wheel to follow the black sedan with US government plates as it makes a right onto Manor Drive. Scanning the woodland on both sides of the street, he continues, "We could take them here, no problem. How difficult could it be to kill two women?"

"That's crazy talk. A move like that would bring the feds out in force. That would jeopardize the big operation. It's going down next week."

"How is it going to stop the feebs from finding us?" McCloskey tosses the empty whiskey bottle over his shoulder and wipes a hand across his mouth.

"The fucking FBI won't be worrying about anything but themselves after what dad has in store for them," Paul snickers. "He doesn't want you hanging around the ranch until it's gone down."

"Why the hell not?"

"You keep attracting too much attention. First it was the marshals who came to the ranch, then the feds."

"Like they weren't looking for you as well. Where am I supposed to go?"

"Dad is okay hiding me, but he wants you to stay at the trailer. He's been planning this operation for months."

"That means I'll have to move the reporter. She's a pain in the ass."

"Has she told you anything yet?"

"Nah. But she will. I have my ways," McCloskey snickers.

The two men lapse into silence until the black sedan makes another turn.

"I know exactly where they are going. Norma's place," McCloskey says, swinging the truck into a right-hand turn. "They're getting too close for comfort."

"What could your sister tell them?"

"For starters, she'll let on that you and me know one another. Probably tell them all about my bitch of a wife."

"Big fucking deal." Paul mutters. He falls silent until he sees the black sedan stop in front of a gray and white cottage. "Park here. Don't get too close."

"Told you they were visiting Norma," McCloskey trumpets.

Paul shakes his head and pulls out his phone.

"Who are you calling?"

"Our old buddy. Reed has an interest of his own in the brown agent going away for good. Maybe he can find a way to keep her off our backs for the next week. After that, she'll either be dead or in the hospital."

***

"WHAT A COINCIDENCE THAT Norma Hodges is Dirk McCloskey's sister," Stevie says. "We only spoke to her a week ago."

"We were chasing Maura when we met Norma at the Chocolate Bunny Espresso," I reply, pulling to a stop in front of a cute cottage. It's done out in gray and white with cardinal red shutters. A white picket fence surrounds a neatly mown lawn with a cherry tree at its center.

We climb out of the car and stretch. Stevie unlatches the low gate, and we follow a brick path lined with rose bushes to the porch. The front door opens before I have a chance to knock.

"I couldn't believe it when you called," Norma says, shooing away our IDs and ushering us into a living room smelling of lilac. She's in her mid-forties, with a blonde ponytail and ruby red lips. The vividly-colored tunic top and stretch jeans look comfortable and lived in. "How come I'm so popular with the FBI? Wait, don't answer that just yet. But, do have a seat." She gestures at a comfortable-looking sofa. "Tea or coffee, ladies?"

We usually decline refreshments, but I see the array of pastries laid out on a plate and go for coffee. Stevie follows suit.

"Two coffees coming right up," Norma says, then catches herself with a chuckle. "Oops. I'm thinking I'm working at the Chocolate Bunny."

She returns with a tray, which she balances gracefully on one hand while handing us cups and saucers. "Help yourself to cream and sugar. I didn't know what pastries you'd like, so I brought a selection from the coffee shop." She settles into a well-used recliner.

"This is most kind of you," I say, leaning forward and selecting an old-fashioned donut, setting it on a plate. "What can I get for you, Stevie?"

She takes my hint and chooses an éclair, though I know she watches her weight as much as I do.

"This is really nice of you," she says.

"I think you said on the phone that you wanted to know more about my brother Dirk," Norma says, biting into a strudel.

I nod. "That's right. His name has come up in an investigation, but I want to assure you that we're treating him as a witness."

"Don't worry, dear." She leans forward and places a hand on my arm. "Dirk is a bully who believes the world is against him. He's always been that way, ever since we were kids, but he became much angrier after the incident at the river."

"Incident at the river?"

"Dirk is three years older than me, but we used to have a younger brother named Trey. When Dirk was fourteen, he went to the river with his girlfriend, Katelyn, and Trey, who he was supposed to be babysitting. Trey was six at the time. Dirk went for a smoke, but when he got back, he found our brother missing and Katelyn crying. She said Trey had been wading in the river and got swept away by the strong current."

"How awful," Stevie says. "Was Trey found?"

"His body was recovered downstream. Trey's death was ruled an accident, but our parents blamed Dirk for taking the kid to the river in the first place. Dirk, in turn, blamed Katelyn, but he's since transferred that rage onto all women. Zoe married him, not knowing what she was getting herself into. I'm sure you know he went to prison for killing her."

"Yes, ma'am."

"Zoe was a lovely person. She deserved far better than my brother gave her."

Coming across the uncommon name Zoe twice in a short space of time makes me curious. "Do you recall Zoe's last name?" I chide myself for needing to ask this question of a witness when I could have easily looked it up at the office.

"Zoe Kelly. I was saddened to see on the news that her father was killed just a few days ago in a knife attack."

I nearly cough out the piece of donut in my mouth. I wonder how the hell we missed the connection. "You're saying that Zoe, the wife Dirk murdered ten years ago, was Ricky Kelly's daughter."

"Oh, yes. I thought you would have known."

"We sometimes miss things," I say, shooting a look at Stevie, who appears as shocked as I feel at learning Zoe's connection with one of our murder victims.

"I can't imagine you miss much, my dear."

"So Dirk knew Ricky," I say, thinking aloud.

"Of course. Ricky was Dirk's father-in-law."

"We haven't been able to track Dirk down. Do you know where he might be?"

"I'm afraid I don't. He called me months ago to tell me he'd been released. I think he was in a bar at the time, and he sounded drunk. I haven't heard from him since."

Stevie says, "The only address we have for Dirk is the Smoke Tree Ranch here in Cedar Springs. But when we checked there, they pretended not to know who we were talking about."

"The ranch is owned by Paul Henderson's father," Norma says. "Paul and Dirk have been buddies ever since they were little kids. My parents always believed it was Paul who corrupted Dirk."

"Interesting," I say. "Do you know if they reconnected after getting out of prison?"

"When Dirk called me to say he'd been released, I could hear Paul talking in the background, saying none too nice things about me. To be honest, I was relieved not to hear from Dirk after that. Now be straight with me. Do you suspect my brother of committing another crime?"

"Until we speak to him, there's no way of knowing."

"But he might have done something . . . really bad? The FBI doesn't usually get involved in lesser crimes like robberies."

"We have a policy of not commenting on current investigations. But I can't rule out the possibility that Dirk committed a serious crime. If we can speak to him, we might be able to eliminate him from our inquiries."

"He always maintained his innocence in Zoe's death,

but I never believed him for one moment."

"Is Dirk into conspiracy theories?"

"Oh, yes. He believes elites secretly run everything, and they are trying to establish a global government. He would try to convince anyone who'd listen that events like 9/11 and school shootings were staged. I could go on and on about his stupid ideas."

"Has he ever sought out like-minded individuals?"

"All the Hendersons think the same way as Dirk. Even the daughter, Delia. But why is the FBI interested in my brother's beliefs? As idiotic as they are, they're not a crime."

"It just tells us who he might be associating with," I say, draining my coffee cup.

"Another one?" she asks.

"I'm good, thank you. If it's not too painful, can I ask you about your parents?"

"The attempted murder-suicide?"

"I haven't heard about that. What happened?"

"Trey's death weighed heavily on my father, and it led to endless arguments with mom. Three years after Trey died, he shot her and turned the gun on himself. He died instantly, but mom is in a home, confined to a wheelchair."

"I'm so sorry to hear that."

"Which home is she in?" Stevie asks, nibbling at her éclair.

"It's local. Sunshine Assisted Living Village. Why do you ask?"

"It's just that the place came up in another investigation."

***

TWO HOURS LATER, I'm driving back from lunch when I notice a police cruiser behind me matching my speed and making the same turns. I glance at the dash and see I'm not exceeding the speed limit for once. Though local law enforcement always turns a blind eye when we do. I slow my vehicle to let it by, but it shows no sign of wanting to pass me. To check what it's up to, I make a sharp right at the next lights, sending me back in the direction I've just come.

The cruiser hangs onto my tail, barely a car's length away from my rear bumper. Then red and blue turret lights flash in my rearview. What cop is stupid enough to light up a Bureau car with US government plates?

I drive another couple of blocks, looking for somewhere safe to stop, and the siren behind me starts wailing. I can guess the identity of this joker, but I have to see what he wants.

Finally, I find a place where I can pull over without blocking any traffic lanes. I shut off the engine. Reaching in my pocket, I fish out my phone, set it to record audio, and toss it onto the passenger seat.

I roll my window down as Detective Reed comes to the driver's side of my vehicle and glares at me. As usual, he's in his rumpled suit, but today his tie is missing and his collar open. His face is flushed with barely contained rage.

"You been demoted to traffic patrol now, Reed?" I jest as my fingers find the butt of the weapon holstered at my waist.

"Hands where I can see them," he snaps, his open palm hovering by the side of the pistol strapped to his belt.

"Have you lost your mind, Reed? You just pulled over a car with US government plates, driven by a federal agent. I could bust you for that. What reason could you possibly have for stopping me?"

There are a hundred different ways this could go badly. Maybe he has a scenario in mind that ends up with me being shot. One he can spin and make shooting me seem justified. To be on the safe side, I place both hands on the wheel.

"That's better." His gaze is flicking around the interior of the car, and I wonder if he's on something. "Now, step out of the vehicle."

"Fuck you, Reed. Tell me what this is about."

He pulls a nightstick from his belt and disappears from my view. I hear a sharp rap on the back of my car. He arrives back at my window. "I stopped you for a busted taillight."

It's then that I realize the depths of Reed's paranoia, but I joke, "You've been watching too many bad movies from the sixties, my friend."

"I will never be friends with your kind."

I feel handicapped with Reed having the height advantage, so I say, "I'm getting out of the vehicle." I open the door slowly and climb out carefully to not give him any excuse to go for his pistol. I don't know how he thinks he can spin this, but it won't matter if he puts a bullet in my chest.

Shoving the door closed with my butt, I step to the rear

of the vehicle and inspect the broken taillight. I lean my backside against the trunk, being careful not to stand in the center. "Now explain what the hell you want from me."

"I just stopped you so we can have a chat about the case. I heard you were bothering the Hendersons about Paul and Dirk."

"They friends of yours?"

"What if they are?" he growls.

"Are you trying to warn me off them?"

"They've done nothing wrong, so yeah, leave them alone."

"You stopped me for no reason, and now you're threatening me, Reed?"

"Give me one good reason why I shouldn't threaten an uppity bitch like you." He moves closer and grabs a handful of my shirt, drawing me in, saying, "You're scum, Viera."

I'm moments away from kicking him in the balls and whacking him under the chin as he goes down. "You busted my tail light to warn me off the Hendersons?"

"Nah, you must have backed into something. Even the FBI can't ride around with busted lights." He gives me a sneering grin. "But what if I did warn you off? I could kill you with one quick squeeze of my hand."

"Don't count on it, buddy. ASAC Myles will have your badge and your ass when I get back to the office. You're going to feel the full force of the FBI."

"Oh, I'm scared," he chuckles. "Shaking in my boots. Myles is a pansy like you, and it's going to be a case of he said, she said. He didn't have the balls to arrest me after the SWAT raid, and he won't this time." He lets go of my shirt, shoving me away hard, and I topple onto my ass on the ground.

"Smile, Reed. You're on Candid Camera." I aim my finger at the lens in my vehicle's back window. "Any idiot knows the front and rear cameras are rolling 24/7. There's also a microphone that will have picked up everything you just said. You overplayed your hand."

Reed stiffens, a look of realization crossing his face. "Watch your back, Bollywood," he growls, slinking away like the snake he is.

"Is that another threat?" I shout. Were it not for the camera, I'd have kicked his ass and then some.

He stops and half-turns. "Not from me. Powerful people are coming for you, and I can't stop them. Have a nice day, and get that taillight fixed."

I watch him as he saunters back to his vehicle and gets behind the wheel. He turns the engine over and guns the throttle. His car's front fender barely misses the rear of mine.

"You've fucked yourself, Reed," I holler as he streaks away. And this time, it's not an idle threat.

Chapter Thirty-Seven

"WHAT ARE YOU doing here?" Finch asks, flashing me a smile and pushing his roller chair back from the desk. "You never come to the station."

The detective's bullpen is shabby by anyone's standard. The mismatched office furniture looks decades old, and the drab green walls desperately need a fresh coat of paint.

"Following my boss's orders," I say, placing a hand on top of a file cabinet. "Unfortunately, I'm looking for Detective Reed."

"Haven't seen him all day. I thought you'd sworn off having anything to do with the guy."

"I thought so too. How long have you got?"

"All the time in the world for you." He grins, gesturing at his guest chair. Finch has snagged one of the few dividers in the place. This, along with a couple of strategically positioned file cabinets, gives him a touch of privacy. The only item personalizing his space is a four-by-six framed photo standing beside his desk phone. A much-younger Finch has his arm around a tall, elegant black woman. Brylee, I assume.

I perch on the edge of the seat, and he swivels around to face me. For the next five minutes, I relate Reed's crazy traffic stop. By the end, Finch is staring at me with saucer eyes. "I'm sure it's true, but it's almost difficult to believe."

I bob my head up and scan the office area to make sure it's empty. "Listen to this." I pull out my phone and play him the audio of the first three minutes of Reed's traffic stop. When it ends, I say. "I thought Myles was going to blow his stack when he heard this and saw the video."

"There's a video as well?"

"Yeah. After the bit you just heard, I led Reed to the back of the car, where there's a camera. Myles has written him up on a lengthy list of charges that include wrongful detainment of a federal officer, making terrorist threats, wanton destruction of federal property. He sent me to arrest Reed while he called Holder."

Finch palms his chin thoughtfully. "The SWAT debacle and now this. It's the end of the guy's career."

"He did it to himself, on video, no less. This is the third time Reed has stepped out of line in the last week. Way out of line. I believe he's involved in the Priesthood, but I don't have any proof. Do you have an address for him?"

"I know where he lives. If he's not there, he might be visiting his mother. I'll come with you. You don't want to bring in a guy like Reed on your own."

As we get to our feet, I chuckle, "Because I'm a poor, weak woman?"

"I'd never call you either of those words after last night." His gaze rakes me from head to toe.

"Easy tiger. You can come if only to show me where

Reed lives." I flash my gaze around the room to make sure no one is around, then plant a kiss on his lips.

As we drive across town in my Bureau car, he asks, "What happened to your ride with the busted tail-light?"

"Gone to the shop to be fixed. Reed struck it so hard he dented the bodywork, so there's that too."

"Are you free after work?"

"You want more of the same because I need to catch up on my sleep?"

"Maybe. But mostly, I want to spend time with you."

"Let me see." I stroke my chin as if I'm thinking. After a pause, I say, "Fair enough. But I'll be stopping by the hospital to look in on Jasmin first."

"I'll come with you if that's okay?"

"Sure."

"Holder has put me on the Jackie Ricci kidnapping. Just between you and me, he thinks the Bureau is trying to one-up him."

"There's a minor problem at my end too, but nothing we can't work around."

"Oh, yeah?"

"Reed's actions have further strained Myles' view of the local police. Unfortunately, he tars the entire department with the same brush as Holder and Reed. He's not keen on me collaborating with you guys."

"That's ridiculous." Finch explodes.

"Hear me out first. I don't plan on scaling back on the information you and I share. We'll just have to meet at your office rather than mine. I'm not about to let Myles' proclamations ruin our personal or work relationship. I treasure them both."

I see him chewing over my words, and his dark expression starts to melt. "You trust me, don't you?"

"Of course, I do." I cover his hand with mine. "I don't have sex with people I don't trust. Look, our bosses will never see eye to eye, but we can't become pawns in their battles. We just have to navigate around their mutual hostility and not let it affect what we have together. Agreed?"

"You're right. I saw Myles attacking our relationship, and it felt awful."

"Shake on it," I say, offering my hand as I steer the car with the other.

He grasps my hand. "I will not let Myles or Holder come between us."

"Great."

"Reed lives up here on the left. The house with the green mailbox."

"What a dump," I say, pulling up at the curb. Knee-high weeds surround a run-down house. It's well past the point of needing a fresh coat of paint.

We lean toward each other and kiss.

"Mm, that was nice." I climb out of the car.

We reach the front porch and unholster our weapons. "You think Reed still lives here?" I ask. The place looks deserted.

Finch shrugs. "As far as I know."

"You take the front, and I'll go around back in case he cuts and runs."

The rear of the house looks in worse repair than the

302

front. I can hear Finch hammering on the front door. When no one answers him, I try the handle, and the back door opens.

Unholstering my weapon, I yell, "Police coming in," loudly enough for Finch to hear.

Sighting down the top rail of my pistol, I step into a well-appointed kitchen. Stainless-steel appliances, white-fronted cabinets, and granite countertops. In fact, the whole house turns out to be nicely furnished. Once I've cleared the place, I open the front door for Finch.

"Reed's not here. You said he might be at his mother's. What's the story with her?"

"Stage four cancer. Lung, I think. She lives on her own, but Reed looks in on her every day," Finch says as we shut the house up and head back to the car.

I follow his directions to a two-story adobe house painted beige with a red tile roof.

"Big house for one person," I say, holding the wrought-iron gate open for Finch.

"I believe it used to be the family home. Reed grew up here." Finch steps onto the porch and knocks.

After a long moment, the door opens, revealing an elderly woman with gray hair. She's wearing a light blue robe and leans heavily on an aluminum cane with a wide quad base.

"Joey, how nice to see you," she effuses. The words startle me for a moment. It's so unusual to hear anyone call Finch by his first name. "And who is your pretty friend?"

"Special Agent Viera, ma'am."

The woman throws me a reproachful look and cocks her

head. "We don't stand on ceremony here."

"I'm Cassie, ma'am."

"Calling me ma'am makes me feel even older than I am. I go by Coco. Come through." She shuffles into a living room and eases herself into a recliner.

"We're actually looking for Gary," Finch says.

"He's not here, but he usually stops by in the afternoon. Take a seat while we wait." She waves her walking cane at the couch. "I don't get many visitors." She has a strong jaw and high cheekbones, but cancer and its treatment have left her looking gaunt.

Her gaze fixes on Finch. "Now tell me what you've been up to today. And how you come to be with this lovely young woman."

"We work together."

"Oh, come on, Joey. I can see there's more than that going on between you."

Finch blushes, and I chuckle at her perceptiveness.

"There. What did I say?" She smiles and points a finger at me.

"You're embarrassing her, Coco," he says.

"I can see from here that she doesn't get embarrassed easily."

I find it hard not to snicker at her comment, because I'm more bashful about personal matters than most folks. "You've lived in this house a long time, Coco?"

"Forty-five years come September."

"Do you mind if I ask you some questions about people you might know?"

"Ask whatever you want, my dear. When you have only

a few months left to live, you don't waste time worrying about things that don't matter."

"Do you know Russell Henderson, who owns the horse ranch?"

"Sure. Russell moved into the area a year or two after me." Coco leans forward in her chair. I've piqued her curiosity.

"You get on with the Hendersons?"

"We were good friends when they first arrived. Paul was born two months after my son Gary, and they played together for several years. Later on, Russell grew more rigid in his views. The world was against him. Everything that went wrong with the stables was someone else's fault. Most often, he blamed the government. We stopped socializing when he became tiresome to listen to. Why do you ask?"

"It's just background information for a case," I respond. "Gary and Paul hung around together until they were what age?"

"Seventeen or eighteen, I guess. I forgot to mention Dirk. They were a threesome."

"Dirk McCloskey? I was just talking to his sister this morning."

Coco nods. "The three boys were only a few months apart in age. They didn't want anything to do with Norma."

The connection between Detective Reed and our two prime suspects feels as if someone jabbed me with an ice pick.

"What happened when they were eighteen?" I ask, trying not to sound too much like a bloodhound on a trail.

"Gary entered the police academy and became a

detective." Coco is taking a beat longer to answer my questions. She's getting weary. "Paul and Dirk started getting into trouble with the law. They both killed their wives, you know. I don't know why they were ever let out of prison." Her knuckles turn white as she grips her cane.

"Did Gary stay in touch with them?"

"Gary knew Dirk's wife, Zoe. They dated for a while until she moved on to someone else. You know how it is when you're in your late teens and early twenties. The next thing I heard, she was married to Dirk. I didn't approve, and neither did Gary."

"Why not? Why didn't you approve?" I ask. Out of the corner of my eye, I notice Finch giving me a look. I nod to say I can see Coco is getting exhausted, and I understand his concern.

"Dirk is violent and a nasty piece of work. I never took to him for that reason. After Zoe married him, I saw her once or twice in town, wearing dark glasses."

"You think Dirk was physically abusing her?"

"I know he was. It used to bother Gary. I thought he'd be more upset when Zoe was killed. But he'd been a detective for a good few years by then. I guess you get used to such things."

"We really should be going," Finch says, getting to his feet.

I thank Coco profusely for her patience in answering my questions. She gives us each a boney hug, and we step out into the glaring sunlight.

"Don't be strangers," she shouts after us. "I don't know how much time I have left."

Chapter Thirty-Eight

THERE'S A BUZZ in the air when I get back to the office. I drop my bag on my desk and run into Stevie at the coffee machine. "What's going on?" I ask her.

"You should talk to Todd and Nick. It's all their work."

I find them in Todd's office riveted to his giant screens. Nick defers to Todd, who says, "We've made some headway with the Priesthood's message board. Pull up a chair."

When I'm seated, he continues, "The Priesthood members use the names of Confederate generals as their pseudonyms on the board. It's why Jackie uses the name Forrest. Almost all the messages are posted by Stonewall, Longstreet, Bragg, Pickett, Mosby, Beauregard, and Armistead. The four remaining users only lurk in the background. For the most part, the posts are a litany of gripes and grievances repeated over and over."

He pauses to take a drag of soda. "I found the messages Jackie told you about. Immediately after your incident with the SWAT team, there was a discussion about Beauregard getting shot, so we know that's Brandon Farley's pseudonym. Just yesterday, there was another interesting discussion. Here, look," he says, pointing to the nearest screen. "Bragg berates Pickett, saying that kidnapping a television reporter was foolhardy. So Pickett is likely the guy who took Jackie." He pauses to scroll the messages up the screen.

"A couple of hours later, Stonewall suggests moving up the schedule for something they call the device."

"They could be talking about a bomb," I interject with surprise. "I should get the ATF involved."

"Sure, but there's more. The member named Pickett says that the first order of business is eliminating the two FBI traitors who came to the ranch. His words, not mine. Mosby agrees, saying they have also been poking their noses into our members' families, and the bitch was there when the foreigner shot Beauregard. Armistead says the procurement of materials for the device should continue in parallel with any eliminations."

"Wow, that's chilling on several levels," I say.

"That's an understatement," Stevie adds. "I'm wearing a Kevlar vest twenty-four-seven until we catch these jokers."

"On the upside, we have enough evidence to raid tomorrow's meeting."

"Who are we using for backup?" Nick asks. "We sure don't want to rely on a bunch of police officers who may be sympathizers or even members of the group."

"Myles has already cautioned me about sharing information with the police department. We must tell no one about the raid. Not Officer Mason, not Detective Finch. No one. That said, I'm thinking of taking along a California State Police SWAT team."

Nick turns to me. "This is all well and good, but we don't have definitive evidence tying Dirk or Paul to Ava and Ricky's murders or even a hint at a motive."

"The message about the foolishness of kidnapping a television reporter tells me that a member of the Priesthood has Jackie. And the guy who kidnapped her has the same build as Ava and Ricky's murderer. That links the three crimes."

I can't believe I just said that, and it's Nick who calls me out. "Seriously, boss. That's a connection?"

"At a minimum, we can charge them with conspiracy to kill FBI agents," I reply. "They won't get bail, and we can take our time with the murder and kidnapping charges. Let's not forget that finding Jackie is our highest priority."

"You're going to like what else I found this morning," Todd says. "I came in early to search for more surveillance footage of the kidnapping, and I came across this." His fingers glide over his keyboard, and an image pops up on his screen. It shows the rear view of a man carrying an unconscious woman in his arms.

"You already told me about finding this."

"Check out the back of his neck." He uses his finger on the screen to circle the man's tattoo.

"That tattoo is as unrecognizable as the one on the man who killed Ricky. It wouldn't convince a jury," I say, "but it does appear to be the same guy, and it's a step closer to identifying him."

"So we think he's a member of the Priesthood?" Nick asks.

I nod. "I'm pretty sure this Pickett guy killed Ricky and

Ava and knifed Pete Barlow. We have nothing beyond fuzzy pictures of a tattoo to back that up, so all we can do is follow the evidence and see where it leads."

"We can stick the Priesthood members in interrogation rooms, but I doubt any of them will talk to us," Nick warns.

"Facial recognition will give us their names. I'll make sure we have warrants to search the homes of anyone we pick up. I'm hoping their computers and phones will reveal the pseudonyms they're each using."

"Not sure we can rely on that," Todd says.

"Which is why our number one job is to use other means to identify the people behind those pseudonyms. We have twenty-four hours until we start questioning these idiots. I'm particularly interested in the name of the leader. The one who calls himself Stonewall. Is it in fact Russell Henderson? Let's get to it, people." I blow out a long breath. Sometimes, I think the case is going well; other times, I realize we have nothing concrete on anyone.

"I'm logged into the message board site," Todd advises, "and I'm going through the files one by one looking for actual names. Be aware that they could have signed up as Daffy Duck. Many boards only require an email address."

"Do what you can. Now we know they're building a device, we have no choice but to stage the raid. Can you imagine the headlines if they explode a bomb, and it turns out we knew about it? Can you imagine how we would feel if people were injured or worse?"

"Bomb-making materials may yield evidence against specific members," Nick suggests. "You don't need to prove intent. Possessing the materials carries the same sentence as a finished device."

I get to my feet, feeling a weight on my shoulders. "I'm off upstairs to talk to Myles. We'll be contacting the ATF to see if they can loan us an agent or two for a day."

***

"HERE'S THE PROBLEM I've got, Jackie," Dirk says. This evening his words are slurred, and his balance unsteady from spending hours at the bar with his buddies. "If you don't tell me where to find Zoe, you're of no use to me. You're just eating my food, drinking my water, and filling up my septic tank."

He's wearing his reasonable guy face, but she's seen him switch in an instant to cruel and heartless. She remembers him from before his ten-year stint in prison, and he's aged twenty years at least. He's standing close enough for her to catch the stench of his beer breath. She strains to move away, but she's tethered like a dog to the wall of the trailer.

A cable tie binds her wrists together, and a length of rusty chain secures the leather collar around her neck to a stout eye hook. There's just enough slack for her to reach the toilet at the end of the trailer without choking. The setup looks old and rusty. Jackie suspects she's not the first woman to be restrained in the trailer this way.

"What's the point of telling you anything?" Jackie asks. "I've seen your face. I know who you are. You're going to kill me anyway." She may be unable to save herself, but she can at least save her friend.

From the trailer's rounded corners, she thinks it's an

Airstream. She's seen a dense stand of trees through the windows and a hint of blue sky. But now, it must be evening or nighttime as everything is cloaked in darkness.

The inside of the trailer has cooled down from the sweltering afternoon heat. Jackie shivers in a thin T-shirt and capris, but beads of sweat cling to her forehead.

She cannot recall how she came to be here. The last thing that she can summon is parking her car and entering the apartment building. Then her memory is blank until she woke up shackled. But it's plain to see what befell her. She should have been more careful, but it never occurred to her that Dirk would figure things out this quickly.

"I can make your death quick or painful and slow. It's your choice," he says, as if he's being more than fair.

A drunk Dirk is even more frightening than the sober one.

"Zoe is dead. You killed her," she mutters.

The backhand catches her across the cheek, striking yesterday's bruise, splitting her lip even more.

"Don't lie to me, woman. Paul showed me the photograph of Zoe. My wife is alive and living somewhere near Placerville."

Jackie brings her manacled hands up to her face and smears away the trickle of blood sliding down her chin. "What makes you think I know whether she's alive or dead?"

"You used to be her best friend. Zoe told you everything. I'll bet she made me out to be an ogre."

"I know you used to come home in a drunken rage and beat her because she angered you in some little way." Jackie

312

is no longer watching what she says to Dirk. She's given up hope of ever getting out of there alive. "I bet you kept her on the end of this chain."

The fist strikes her other cheek, and she collapses onto the air mattress. The collar tugs painfully at her neck, forcing her to cough and choke. She opens her eyes and sees stars worming around her vision, splats of bright red blood on the front of her blouse.

Through the haze, she sees her captor experience a moment of realization.

Her pink iPhone appears in his hand.

He's cursing at it as he taps the screen. "How do you open this thing?" He steps to Jackie and grabs her hand. She tries to pull it away from him. Zoe's address is in her contacts. "Hold still, or I'll chop your damn fingers off."

Jackie stops struggling; she knows it's not just a threat, and the thought of having all her fingers cut off is almost more horrific than death.

Finally, Dirk manages to wrench her index finger at the right spot, and Jackie sees the phone open. "Sorry, Zoe," she sobs quietly to herself, "I did everything I could."

"Here it is. Meadow Drive, Placerville. Now, why were you keeping that from me? You could have saved us both a lot of trouble if you'd told me about this in the first place."

Jackie backs as far away from him as the chain will allow. She's expecting a fatal blow or a knife in her gut, but instead, Dirk steps to the trailer door. "Zoe Pegney, it says here. Is that what she's calling herself?"

Jackie can't help but give a slight nod.

"It's time to pay her a visit," he smirks.

With that, Dirk is gone, slamming the trailer door behind him.

Alone, Jackie brings her shaking hands to her face. A mixture of blood and tears trickles down her palms. Her sobs turn into raucous screams. Not for herself, but for what Dirk will do to Zoe when he finds her.

Chapter Thirty-Nine

"IT'S ENCOURAGING TO see Jasmin stirring," Finch says to me as we drive away from the hospital.

"Yeah, but I won't feel relieved until she wakes up completely, and I see she's not gorked."

"Now, who's being pessimistic."

"Just realistic." Putting my feelings about my sister aside, I say, "Listen, there's something I need to tell you. We're raiding the Priesthood meeting at Smoke Tree Ranch tomorrow. We're hoping to get the name of the individual who is holding Jackie. Maybe we'll even pick him up."

"You didn't think to tell me sooner? You know I'm working the kidnapping case."

"I'm telling you now. We've only just decoded posts on their message board that confirm they're involved in criminal activities. If I followed Myles' directives, I wouldn't even be telling you now. We're expecting Detective Reed and some of your officers to be at the meeting."

"What criminal activities?"

I tell him about the threats to my team and the signs that the Priesthood is working on explosive devices.

"Who is assisting you to take down the group?" he asks. I can tell by his tone that he's not happy about being excluded.

"California State Police SWAT is in overall command and will go in first. The ATF is providing agents to search for explosives, and the CHP is sending officers to assist with transport."

"That's quite an operation. Did my name come up when Myles was telling you to keep the raid to yourself?"

I sigh. "Yeah. I guess he's seen us together."

"He doesn't trust me," Finch pouts.

"Look, I trust you, or I wouldn't be telling you now. And I wouldn't be planning on having sex with you tonight."

"I suppose," he concedes.

"We've been through all this. Myles doesn't trust Holder, and we think Reed will be at the meeting. It would be a conflict of interest for you to be there. Don't take it personally. We can't let things like this affect our relationship."

"Don't worry. It won't." He forces a smile as my phone chimes.

"Hey Stevie," I say. "You're on speaker with Finch and me."

"My housemate has had to leave town to visit her sick mother, and I'm feeling vulnerable here at the house. The threats on the board are scary."

"You need to stay with me until we have these jokers locked up."

"Won't Detective Finch be there?"

"Yeah, but it's fine. He'll be in my room, and you can

take the spare. He's nodding okay to that."

"There's strength in numbers," she replies.

"I've ignored what Myles told us and read Finch in on our little operation tomorrow."

"Oh. Right."

"We'll be home in fifteen. Come straight over," I say and end the call.

"You sure you still want me to stay tonight?" Finch asks.

"Of course. As Stevie says, there's strength in numbers. You can play the knight in shining armor to two fair maidens. Who knows what your reward will be, Sir Gallant?"

Finch chuckles. "What about the noise?"

"We'll just have to keep it down. Curb those wild shrieks you make."

"You think I'm the screamer?" he says in mock indignation. "You should hear yourself."

"At least I don't take all day to get there," I say, glancing his way. The longing in his eyes sends a flash of heat through me. "Stop it. You're making me hot."

He shakes his head, grinning.

A little while later, I turn onto my street, and his face becomes more solemn. "I'm sorry, but we need to talk about practicalities. Dangers. A patrol car should be stationed outside your house at night. You're dealing with a bunch of extremists who would like nothing better than to see you and Stevie gone."

"Somehow, Holder heard about the threats on our lives and offered to send a car, but I declined."

"Why?" Finch exclaims.

"That would be a case of the fox guarding the henhouse. We could get an officer who's a member of the group that's threatening to harm us."

"Now, you sound paranoid."

"Just realistic."

Stevie is already waiting on my doorstep when I park in front of my house and cut the engine. I approach the front porch and notice a backpack on the ground by her feet. Her jacket is open, revealing her Kevlar vest and her holstered pistol.

"Hey," I say, stepping past her to slip a key in the lock and open the door. The air is stale, and it's cooled off outside, so I rush around opening windows.

When Finch says hi to Stevie, she asks him if she's intruding.

"Nah," he says, slipping an arm around her waist and shepherding her inside.

"You sure?" she insists. "I imagine you and Cassie were looking forward to an evening alone."

Finch clasps his hands on her shoulders and fixes his gaze on her. "Your and Cassie's safeties are the top priority. She tells me that my role is to be the knight in shining armor." He turns my way. "Of course, I'll be needing to collect the repayment you spoke about."

"Like I'm going to fight you off," I snicker. "Okay, have you two had dinner yet?"

They shake their heads. In fact, Stevie looks kinda pale, which happens when she's hungry.

"I don't feel like cooking, so it's sandwiches, or we order in."

"Can we order in?" Finch asks, looking to Stevie, who nods.

"Sure, but I've had my pizza allotment for this week." I pull a stack of menus from a drawer and toss them onto the kitchen table.

"How about Mexican from *Buenas Comedas*?" he asks.

Stevie nods. "As long as you get a dish of nachos to share. They are to die for."

"You forsaking the Taco House?" I ask him.

"They don't deliver, and I'm not driving halfway across town."

Forty-five minutes later, we're sitting around the table enjoying our meals and bottles of Dos Equis. No one feels especially chatty under the circumstances, but we're enjoying each other's company.

"You were right about the nachos," Finch tells Stevie, dipping a crispy tortilla chip into the remaining sour cream and avocado queso sauce.

"Best in town," she agrees with a smile. "Phew, I'm stuffed already. The fish tacos were great, but I think I've overeaten."

"I'm done too," I say, pushing away the carcass of my burrito. "As tasty as the nachos are, it looks like the rest are yours," I tell Finch. "Anyone want more beer?"

They both decline, and I clear the empty bottles from the table, depositing them in the recycling.

After dinner, I show Stevie the spare room. "I just changed the sheets—one of my least favorite pastimes. Have a feel at the duvet. It's pretty thin, but I can leave you a blanket in case you find it too hot."

"I'm sure it will be fine, Cassie. You don't know how much better I feel staying with you." She unzips her backpack and sets a clean shirt and underwear for tomorrow on the chair.

"Come join us when you're ready. I have ice cream, and we'll see if we can find a movie that works for all of us."

"No romance movies, and no talking animals," Finch yells from the kitchen.

"No war or horror movies either," I shout back.

***

AFTER WATCHING A thriller movie with the others, Stevie bids goodnight and retires to her room, deciding to delay her shower until the morning. She strips off her clothes and slips into a T-shirt and shorts.

Despite the air conditioning being on, the bedroom is stuffy with the window closed, but she dare not leave it open with the threat of an assailant at large. She fluffs the pillow and climbs into bed, turning the duvet down so it just covers her bare legs.

The Priesthood's threatening posts drift through her mind, and scuffling noises come from the other side of the wall. She curses that her foam earplugs are back at home, along with her holistic sleep aid.

But the worst thing she can do at bedtime is to think about her little sister because it assures her of a long sleepless night. Kim was seven and Stevie eleven when Kim's seizures started. An endless series of trips to doctors and hospitals followed, their parents becoming increasingly distraught. Stevie was usually made to sit alone in the waiting room to read or listen to music, but she still heard snippets of conversation through the thin walls. Her sister had a brain tumor. Almost a year to the day after the first seizure episode, Stevie's mother told her that Kim wouldn't be coming home from the hospital this time. Stevie's parents separated a few months later, and her life was never the same again.

After tossing and turning for forty-five minutes, Stevie slips into the darkened kitchen, the hardwood floor icy cold against her bare feet. She pours herself a glass of water from the jug in the fridge, carrying it to a recliner in the living room. Setting her glass on an end table, she flops into the chair and gazes through a window at the almost full moon.

It's quieter and cooler here than in her bedroom, and the haunting memories of her sister fade. Soon she can barely keep her eyes open. When the dreams come, they are dark and ominous. Her sister is with her, alive and well, but rogue police officers intent on killing the pair chase them through underground tunnels.

But she can't save Kim. Stevie tries to save her over and over. But she never will.

Stevie jolts awake and checks her watch. Three-thirty. Damn. It is so like her to have trouble sleeping in a strange bed then doze off for three hours in an easy chair.

As she tries to decide whether to go back to bed, her mind begins to drift again. But a metallic click jars her wide awake.

Getting up from her chair, she tiptoes through the

moon-lit house to investigate the noise. She pauses for a moment at the master bedroom door, but all she can hear is the sound of two people breathing rhythmically. Finch makes the deeper sound and grunts now and then. They aren't the source of the noise.

Unusual sounds are something to be expected in a strange house, she tells herself. However, the feeling that something is wrong won't go away, and she moves into the spare bedroom. By the light of the moon, she reaches into the leather holster atop her neatly folded clothes. As she grabs the pistol, competing voices in her head argue about whether she's being paranoid or acting prudently.

She moves into the living room, her feet silent on the hardwood floor, her senses on alert, scanning the shadows. The drapes at the far end of the room move slightly, and she feels air brush her face. The chirp of the cicadas is too loud.

The patio door is open.

Stevie's skin prickles with fear as she pans her pistol around a room filled with inky shapes. Her eyes strain as she searches the blackness for an intruder. Slowly backing up, she reaches the door to the kitchen. Her hand finds the light switch and flicks it on.

Nothing happens.

It registers that someone has turned off the power to the house.

Not good.

For a long moment, panic seizes her. "FBI. Freeze, or I'll shoot," she calls out.

Listening to the silence of the room, she picks up the sound of slow, calculating breathing. She tries to think who it might be and considers whether to confront the danger herself or wake the others.

In the end, Stevie tells herself she's an FBI agent, trained to confront dangers alone.

Rather than stand still, she moves toward the dining area, her pistol searching for a target. "I know you're there." Her voice sounds high and strained.

As she rounds the couch, a foot flies up, and pain, bright and sharp, shoots through her arm. The pistol flies from her hand, clattering on the floor.

Moonlight glints off the blade of a knife, but the intruder is nothing more than a dark fuzzy shape.

She grabs a lamp off an end table, holding it up, parrying the hand holding the blade.

As the dark shape advances, she retreats to the dining area, taking quick glances at the floor, searching for her pistol.

A shaft of moonlight illuminates the intruder's face, and she gasps at the recognition. She swings the lamp's ceramic base high in the air and brings it down on his head.

The man grunts and staggers sideways.

Her eyes rake the floor.

She sees the pistol glinting in the moonlight and dives for it.

The impact with the floor knocks the wind out of her, but she scoops up the weapon and rolls onto her back, aiming at the black shape.

"Freeze or so help me, God, I'll shoot," she screams, but he jumps on top of her, trying to wrest the weapon from her hands.

Her finger finds the trigger. The sound of the gunshot is deafening in the enclosed space as her pistol spits out a tongue of flame.

A loud shriek escapes the man's lips. "Argh, you bitch." The knife clangs to the floor, and the odor of burned gunpowder hangs in the air.

He clutches his arm and races for the patio door.

Stevie can't shoot him in the back while he's running away. Legally or morally.

The intruder hesitates and turns. "I swear I'll kill you," are the man's final words before he slips through the patio door into the night.

Chapter Forty

THE EXPLOSIVE SOUND of the gunshot jolts me awake. I try clicking on my bedside light, but it doesn't seem to be working.

"What the fuck was that?" Finch exclaims. We're both out of bed in no time, fumbling around our nightstands for our guns.

Grabbing a flashlight, I almost trip over my clothes strewn on the floor. I race across the hallway, then stop short at the door to the living room, my shaft of light raking the darkness. The air is thick with the smell of spent gunpowder.

The beam settles on Stevie standing in the dining area, a pistol still gripped in her hand.

"We had an intruder," she yells, her voice trembling. "It's clear. He's gone."

Finch is right behind me as I move into the room, my weapon still at the ready in case she's missed something. My hand reaches for the light switch, but nothing happens.

"Why don't the lights work?" I say, my mind still fuzzy with sleep.

"He's turned off the main breaker," Stevie replies.

She looks droopy in the semi-darkness, and my protective instincts take over. I rush to where she's standing and throw my arms around her. "You okay?"

"Yeah."

When I step back, she tells us how she couldn't sleep and encountered the intruder in the living room, fought with him. "I think I got him in the arm. I'm sorry I couldn't capture him."

"Are you injured?" I ask, my flashlight raking her slender frame.

"I don't think so."

"There's a bruise on your forehead."

"I'll call 9-1-1," Finch offers, turning to get his phone from the bedroom.

"Wait up," she says. "Let's talk about it first."

"You recognized him?" I exclaim. "Was it someone from the police department?"

"Yeah. Reed. He was slashing the knife from side to side like the person who killed Ava."

"Crap," Finch says and turns to me. "Where's your breaker panel? I can't think straight in the dark."

"At the far end of the patio," I say, slipping an arm around Stevie's waist.

I hand him my flashlight, and he disappears out the patio door, his pistol raised, scanning for danger.

When the lights come on, I survey the scene. The end table is overturned, and the lamp that used to stand on it lies shattered on the floor. A double-edged knife is nearby, and a trail of blood leads out the patio door.

"See anything?" I ask Finch when he comes back into the room.

He shakes his head. "Reed is long gone. We should still call the cops out."

"We'll get someone else who wants to kill us. What's the point of that?" I move into the kitchen. "I'm making coffee. I assume you both want decaf. Then we should all go back to bed and try to get some rest. How about you sleep with me, Stevie, and Finch takes the spare room?"

They nod their approval.

"Looks like someone dialed 9-1-1 for us," Stevie says as we hear the sound of a car stopping outside. Swirling red and blue lights paint the living room walls.

Finch steps to the front window. "Patrol car. Officer Taggart is getting out."

"Damn," I say. "If anyone in the police department is a member of the Priesthood, it's him."

Feet thunder up the front steps, and a fist hammers on the door, "Police. Open up."

I answer the door, and Taggart steps into the room, sniffing the smoke still hanging in the air. "What's going on here?" he asks, pulling out a notebook and eyeing the fallen knife.

"We had an intruder," I say, "But he's long gone."

"Who discharged the weapon?" Taggart stands with his feet apart, his gaze darting from one of us to the other.

"I did," Stevie says. "The intruder came at me with a knife."

"You're Stevie Wells?"

"Agent Wells to you," she snaps.

"Officer Mason's girl," he says with a demeaning grin.

"None of your fucking business."

Taggart writes in his notebook. "You all live here?" His gaze falls on me, and he raises a questioning brow.

"No. I'm the homeowner," I say. "Detective Finch and Agent Wells are staying with me." I need to get rid of Taggart as quickly as possible, so we can all get back to bed.

"What's the purpose of their visit?"

"They're friends."

Taggart's gaze scans each of us in turn. He's not the brightest crayon in the box. I feel sure he wants to know if we're having a threesome, but can't find the words.

"Look, Taggart," Finch says, "You've got your report. Why don't you turn around and leave?"

"I'm going to have to take the weapon that was discharged for fingerprints and ballistics tests."

"Like hell," I exclaim. "It's FBI property, and you have no jurisdiction over it."

"I still need to take it. Give it to me. The knife on the floor as well."

"You have your answer on the pistol. The FBI lab will test the knife for prints."

Taggart strokes his chin for a long while. "What are you not telling me?"

"It's confidential FBI business," Stevie says. "Now, get out of here so we can go back to bed."

"I'm not satisfied with your explanation for discharging the pistol. I could pull you all in for questioning."

"Try that, and I'll call Assistant Special Agent in Charge Myles," I say. "He hates being woken in the middle of the night to deal with officious little pricks like you. He especially hates lowly officers who make threats against his agents. At a minimum, he'll chew your ass out. If you continue making threats, he'll have you arrested. Are we clear, officer?"

Taggart snaps his notebook shut. "We'll deal with this in the morning. I'll be making a report to Chief Holder."

"You do that, sonny," Finch says. "Now turn around and get out of here."

Taggart runs his tongue over his teeth. "You take care, ladies. It's a dangerous world out there."

"You threatening us, Taggart?" I ask, taking a step toward him. "Because threatening a federal agent is a crime, and I'd have no problem with arresting you."

"Merely looking out for your safety, ma'am." He gives us a fake smile. "You never know who's going to come after you. Females in law enforcement are especially vulnerable."

Before I can reply, he turns and lets himself out the front door.

"Misogynistic asshole," Stevie says. "A hundred bucks says he's a member of the Priesthood."

Chapter Forty-One

WHEN I WAKE UP, Stevie has gone. I run my hand over her side of the bed and find it cold. A glance at my watch shows me it's seven-fifteen. I slept later than I intended. The door to the spare room is open, and Finch's bed is empty, making me the last one up.

I pad barefoot into the bathroom. The damp shower stall tells me someone was up bright and early. Finch or Stevie? Why didn't either of them wake me?

The memory of the intruder hits my foggy mind with full force as I sit on the toilet. Gary Reed came into my house, armed with a knife. How many of us did he intend to kill? A shiver passes through me.

How Stevie is holding up after the assault is foremost in my mind as I follow the scent of bacon cooking to the kitchen.

Stevie is bent over the stove, chasing scrambled eggs around a skillet. She turns to me. "Perfect timing, Cassie. We're having one of my famous bacon scrambles. Okay?"

"Sure," I reply. "But damn, girl, that's a shiner."

"Does it look bad?" The purple bruise on the corner of

Stevie's forehead reaches from her hairline to her eyelid. Her blonde hair is tied in a ponytail, but she tries to tug it down to hide her injury.

"A bruise like that is something to be proud of. It says Reed meant business, but you whipped his ass and sent him packing."

"Okay," she says cautiously.

"Where's Finch?"

"He left early to talk to Chief Holder at home. They've already spoken on the phone, and there's an APB out for Reed."

"Oh," I say, trying not to show my disappointment at not seeing Finch. "Let's hope they catch the bastard quickly."

"I made coffee." She pulls a mug from the cupboard, fills it from the carafe, adds creamer, and sets it on the kitchen table. "You want to try some bacon scramble?" She angles the pan for me to see.

"Of course. I'm famished," I fib.

"Sit at the table, and I'll serve. Aren't you freezing in just your night clothes?"

I look down at my T-shirt and shorts, my exposed thighs. "I'll throw on some sweatpants."

"Don't do it for me," she shouts, but I'm halfway to the bedroom.

When we're seated at the table with plates of food, I say, "Mm, this is delicious."

"The grated cheese is the secret. Did you get back to sleep?"

"Didn't think I would, but I was out by the time my head

hit the pillow. I haven't spoken to Finch. Did you sleep?" I ask.

"Actually, yes, which was a surprise, considering I couldn't sleep earlier in the night." Despite her breezy attitude, her tone is carefully controlled. I need to watch her more closely to ensure she's up for active duty.

"It was fortunate that you couldn't sleep, or we might not have heard Reed."

"What do you think he came here to do?"

"Not sure I want to spend any time thinking about that," I say, shoveling in another mouthful of scramble and realizing I'm hungrier than I thought. "Maybe he just intended to frighten us."

Stevie looks at me like she's not buying it. "Reed threatened to kill me as he left."

"I find it hard to believe he was going to kill three people in their sleep." My words sound more convincing than I feel.

"Perhaps he didn't know Finch was here," she suggests. "I think he came for you and me."

"I wouldn't dwell on his motive. Just be happy you got rid of him."

As we clear the table, she says, "I can tell you're watching me, boss. I'm fine. I'm not as delicate a flower as I look."

"Pretty sure Reed would agree with that. But a guy like him isn't going to quit. Until he's caught, we need to stay sharp and focused on our game."

***

"HOW ARE YOU BOTH doing?" Nick asks Stevie and me as we arrive at the office a few minutes late for the eight-thirty team meeting I scheduled. "It sounds like you kicked Reed's butt."

"I didn't do anything. It was all Stevie," I say, setting my purse on my desk. "She tackled a guy twice her size. He was armed with a knife, and she sent him packing with his tail between his legs."

"It was nothing," she says modestly. "I did get a bit banged up." She points her forefinger at the purple bruise above her left eyebrow. "It looks worse than it is."

"Let's talk for a few minutes in the conference room."

As folks take their seats with mugs of coffee, Nick turns to Stevie and me. "Myles stopped by earlier looking for you and Stevie."

"News travels fast," I say.

"Officer Taggart's incident report is doing the rounds. He tried to make out the weapon was fired during some kind of wild party at your house."

"Oh, great. Myles has been reading a totally biased report of the event. Plus, he now knows that Finch was at my house in the middle of the night."

"Myles came around after you'd called me about what really went down," Nick says. "I told him that Reed was the assailant, and that you didn't tell Taggart because you suspect he's involved with the Priesthood. I also told him that Stevie was at your house for her protection."

"How did Myles take it?" Stevie asks, sipping on a mug of black coffee.

"He seemed angrier than ever about Holder's mishandling of the Reed situation. Just before you got here, Myles called and told me he spoke to Holder. There's now a federal arrest warrant out for Reed. The federal all-points bulletin covers airports and the southern border, but we suspect he's gone to ground somewhere."

"That's the best we can do at this point. So what's the charge?" I ask him.

"Attempted murder of a federal agent. Stevie needs to make a statement."

I turn to her. "Let's go see Myles after we're done here. He'll probably get one of the other agents to take your statement."

Stevie nods. "Sure. Has all this activity produced any new information about Reed?"

"No news. He could still be in the area," Nick replies.

I nod in agreement. "Reed might think that the local police department is less likely to pick him up than neighboring forces. I'm hoping he'll be stupid enough to attend this evening's Priesthood meeting."

"That would be sweet," Todd says.

"Back to our own business," I say. "Todd, anything to show and tell about Jackie's computer?" I see he's brought his laptop to the meeting, and that's usually a good sign.

"Plenty." He works the keyboard, sharing his screen with the wall-mounted flat-panel monitor. An address flashes into view. "This is where Zoe Pegney is living in Placerville. Remember, she was the person that Jackie was emailing. The messages gave us reason to believe that she's hiding out from someone."

"Nick, as soon as we're done here, can you get Placerville police to do a wellness check on her?" I ask.

He nods. "Sure thing, boss."

"Jackie visited Zoe Pegney and took pictures of her." Todd works the keyboard. A photograph appears on the flat screen showing two smiling young women leaning over a railing in front of a church. "This is the Eldorado Federated Church. It has an interesting history, but I won't bore you. The picture was taken last year, possibly by a passer-by."

I recognize Jackie and presume the other woman to be Zoe Pegney. She is pretty, her dark curly hair pulled into a loose ponytail. Her high cheekbones and a pale mocha complexion are model-worthy. A smile is tugging at the ends of her full lips. I'm guessing her parents were from different racial backgrounds.

"This next picture is of Zoe Kelly," Todd continues, "and it was used at her memorial service ten years ago."

"The wife Dirk McCloskey was presumed to have killed," Nick adds.

"They sure look very similar," I say, squinting at the screen. "But There's a sadness about the woman in the memorial service image that I don't see in the Placerville photo."

"Not just similar," Todd says. "I ran them through our facial recognition software. It can work with photos that were taken many years apart. It's the same person with a ninety-nine point nine percent probability."

I nod. "That confirms what we've suspected for some time. But only now am I thinking of the implications. For example, who helped Zoe fake the crime scene that made

335

everyone think she was dead? It takes specialized knowledge to fool forensic technicians."

"Unless one of the techs was in on the deception," Nick suggests.

"You can't keep a secret like that if too many people are involved," Stevie says, shaking her head.

"Another of my questions is whether Pete Barlow knew Zoe wasn't dead," I say. "Did he knowingly arrest an innocent man and see that he got convicted?"

Nick leans back in his chair. "Let's say the answer to that question is a yes. What would a man like Dirk McCloskey do if he found out he'd spent ten years in prison for a crime that never even happened."

"It would certainly be a motive for Dirk McCloskey to kill Ava and attempt to kill Pete. He'd also go looking for Zoe to enact retribution."

"Why would he kidnap Jackie Ricci?"

I let out a deep breath, thinking. "I've got it. Jackie was Zoe's best friend, and she would know where to find her. I've been wrong all along in thinking Jackie was taken because she hacked into the Priesthood's message board. We need to find Zoe before Dirk does." I fix my eyes on Nick. "The wellness check won't do it. You need to get Placerville police to take Zoe into protective custody."

"I'll make that call now and hope it's not too late." Nick gets to his feet and leaves the room.

"You think members of the local police department were involved in faking Zoe's death?" Stevie asks.

"It stinks like something Reed would have a hand in. I'd also look at the forensic techs. Jason Clark is the head. Pete

Barlow may be in more of a mood to tell us what he knew if he ever wakes up from the coma."

"Reed would only help Zoe if there was something in it for him."

"When Finch and I interviewed Reed's mother, she said Reed used to date Zoe," I say. "That he didn't seem as cut up as she would have expected when Zoe was presumed dead. That right there says he knew the truth."

"Zoe's faked death blows this investigation wide open," Stevie says. "Where do we start?"

"How about this," I suggest. "Todd, go over the forensic reports from Zoe's supposed murder scene. It might help us learn who was involved in setting it up. Stevie, we need to find out if Dirk McCloskey had a motive to kill Ricky Kelly, his father-in-law. Ricky's girlfriend, Tessa Geddings, might be able to fill in that piece of the puzzle."

As we step out of the conference room, Nick comes toward us, his face grim. "When I spoke to Placerville police, they were already on scene at the house Zoe shared with a woman named Daisy. Apparently, Daisy's body was found in her home this morning. She was the victim of a vicious knife attack. They don't know where Zoe is."

"Damn. We need to find her and pray she's not already dead. Can you liaise with the Placerville police on that aspect?"

"Sure. I already gave them Dirk McCloskey's name as a probable suspect."

Chapter Forty-Two

MY TEAM IS at the Smoke Tree Ranch for the Priesthood's six o'clock meeting, and we're about to kick over a hornet's nest. But I tell myself we're the FBI; it's what we do.

I'm lying on my belly at the edge of a grove of oaks and elms alongside a state SWAT captain named Grady. He's a tall, rawboned man with receding hair and a beige complexion. Early forties, if I had to guess. Before him is a telescope done out in a camouflage design. It's big and impressive and mounted on a low tripod—the type of instrument any amateur astronomer would salivate over. Several cables snake over to a ruggedized laptop.

The rest of my team is on the other side of the SWAT captain. Even Todd is here, though I doubt Myles would approve of the flat-topped military hat that makes him look like a young Fidel Castro. Todd is hefting a professional-looking camera with a telephoto lens and seems excited to be out of the office. I've given him the task of snapping pictures of the Priesthood members as they arrive.

Grady's lanky frame fills the narrow olive-green tarp he brought with him. Thankfully, we're not wearing our suits because the rest of us have to lie on the ground—a mixture of brittle leaves and dry mulch. We're dressed down in jeans, black sweatshirts, and black Kevlar vests with the letters FBI stenciled in white on the front and back.

I'm just hoping none of the twigs digging into my side are poison oak. I'm horribly allergic.

We're on a slight rise overlooking the barn at Smoke Tree Ranch. There's a generous parking lot beside it, and I'm wondering what they use the structure for because it sure as hell isn't housing horses or hay. We've been instructed not to approach the barn until SWAT has secured the scene, but I doubt I'll have the patience to wait.

I check my watch. It's thirteen minutes before the meeting is due to start, and no one has arrived yet. I'm hoping news of the raid hasn't leaked to the Priesthood members.

"Bogey inbound at three o'clock," Grady says, and I wonder if he's been watching too many war movies. We observe a pair of familiar figures climb out of a silver Toyota.

"Well, well," I say. "Officer Taggart. Who would have guessed?"

"Piece of crap," Stevie mutters. "Coming to the house and threatening us. He probably knew Reed was the intruder. There was no 9-1-1 call from a neighbor. After I shot Reed, he probably called Taggart out to harass us."

"You're not wrong," I add.

"And that's Officer Wilson with him," Nick adds.

"You know them?" Grady asks in a clipped voice.

"Not personally, but they're local officers who roll out to

the same crime scenes as we do."

"You expecting to see many law-enforcement personnel at the meeting?"

"Maybe a detective. I don't know exactly how many members are in the group or what the turnout will be."

A frown clouds Grady's face, and irritation flashes across his eyes. "That so?"

The guy is kind of a dick.

A dark blue truck rolls up, and a man I can't recognize at this distance jumps out.

"Facial recognition says that's Paul Henderson." Grady snaps. "That sound right to you?"

I look at him, impressed. "He's expected. I didn't know the fancy telescope could do that."

"We don't all screw around like you feebs," he snaps.

I'm not sure whether I'm supposed to laugh at his joke or if he got out of the wrong side of the bed this morning. From the intense expression etched into his features, I'm thinking it's the way he is.

In the next few minutes, Jason Clark, the head forensic tech, arrives just as a ragtop jeep snakes its way from the main house. Jason waits for the olive-painted vehicle, and he greets Russell and Delia Henderson as they jump out.

"We need to take another look at our recent crime scenes," Nick shouts. "Jason could easily have fixed the evidence to cover for someone."

"Fair point," I respond. Then I ask Grady, "How many strong are you?" My gaze rakes the countryside, but I see no sign of his SWAT team officers.

"Ten plus me. Here's another meeting attendee."

Two people get out of the white four-by-four. "Wow," I say. "Detective Reed. We have a Royal Flush. His upper arm is bandaged, but it's not in a sling, so the injury can't be that bad."

"I wish I'd shot him in the balls," Stevie mutters. "Given him something to remember me by when he's in jail."

"There's an arrest warrant for Reed. Attempted murder of a federal agent." Grady gazes at me with an arched eyebrow.

"That's our warrant," I say. "Just make sure you capture him."

"We'll do what we can. The other one is a Dirk McCloskey," Grady continues. "There's a warrant out for him for skipping parole."

"We get first dibs at him. He's our prime suspect in Jackie Ricci's disappearance." I don't know what kind of system Grady has, but I want one for the team.

McCloskey pauses on the blacktop to scan the surrounding countryside before disappearing inside the barn.

"He's cagey for some reason," Nick mutters, staring through his binoculars.

"Expecting anyone else?" Grady asks.

I want to ask him what he didn't understand about my earlier statement that we don't know the size of the group, but instead, I say, "Let's give them another five minutes."

Grady lets out an impatient breath and goes back to the telescope.

The minutes tick by, and no one else shows. The message board showed there were more Priesthood members than this. Still, nabbing these folks is a good start at rounding up the group.

Finally, Grady snaps, "Time's up." He picks up a hand-held radio with a long antenna. "Sound off, team."

Ten voices reply in sequence with their names and the word, "here."

"Stand by. Go, go, go."

Black-uniformed SWAT officers appear from nowhere and start racing across the open grass toward the barn from all sides.

Then something peculiar happens. Something I wasn't expecting. The Priesthood members flood out of the barn, sprinting in the direction of the main house.

"What the—" Grady explodes.

It's not difficult to connect the dots and see what is about to happen. There's no way for ten officers to capture eight individuals who are fleeing on foot. And there's no way for my team or Grady to help out. We're on the opposite side of the barn to the main house and a hundred and fifty feet away from the action. Nonetheless, I get to my feet and start jogging with my pistol in my hand. Out of the corner of my eye, I see Nick and Stevie follow suit while Grady screams for us to go back.

I know I'll hear from him when this is over, but I keep heading for the barn.

"Let's see if anyone is still inside," I shout between breaths as we approach the entrance. The big double doors are closed, but the regular-sized door is wide open. I peek around the jamb before slipping inside.

The interior of the barn is laid out like a meeting room.

Two lines of folding chairs face a flood-lit stage that's raised a foot or so off the ground. In the center stands Russell Henderson. His sleeves are rolled up to his forearms, and his confident stance suggests he's not too concerned to see us.

"Good evening, Russell," I say, stepping toward him. "Or should I call you Stonewall?"

"Touché, Agent," he replies, flashing me a grimace that shows off his capped teeth. "You may disagree with our beliefs, but we've done nothing wrong."

"That's not at all true, not by any stretch of the imagination." I climb onto the stage, and Stevie follows. "Plotting the death of federal agents is a serious crime. One that can land you in prison for a good while."

"God has a plan for my people. Your sort has no part in it."

"Our sort?" I step behind him, holster my pistol, and pat him down. Russell presents his arms behind him for me to snap on the cuffs. He's way too confident for a man facing years in jail.

"The impure—women, blacks, foreigners."

"You've got me on two counts there, Stonewall."

"You're wasting your time and mine," he insists. "My attorney will make you release us all."

"I sincerely doubt that." I turn him to face me, and he offers no resistance.

"I'm going to join the search team at the house," Nick says, and I nod my approval.

"Where is your daughter Delia?" I ask Russell. "I thought I'd find her here with you."

"I think she's gone to the house. She's very protective of her stuff."

"That's one place she won't be. A separate team sealed off the house before anyone ran out of the barn."

Stevie grabs one of Russell's arms. I take the other, and we walk him to the edge of the stage. "Big step down, cowboy," I say. "I don't want you tripping and suing us."

He gives me a smug smile as we head for the exit.

"By the way, what was that all about? Why did everyone bolt in one direction?"

Russell shrugs. "People do odd things when they're panicked."

"Where is the device you're building?"

"It's not what you think."

"Oh, my. That's a relief," I say with an extra dose of sarcasm. "After reading the posts on your message board, we thought you were building a bomb." I catch Stevie's attention, and we chuckle to one another in mock amusement.

"If we had such devices, we'd only use them to protest our interests here at the ranch. We take precautions against intruders of any type."

Russell's words chill me to the core. I stop and turn to him. "Are you saying the ranch house is protected by explosive devices? That would be totally illegal. Worse than that, ATF agents are working there now."

"We don't want explosions near the ranch itself, but the outbuildings are another matter. I do hope no one is injured by not taking the proper precautions." There's a malevolent sneer on his lips.

I call Grady on the radio while Stevie hangs onto Russell's arm.

"You disobeyed me—" Grady starts.

"Shut up and listen," I snap. "The outbuildings are rigged with explosives."

Chapter Forty-Three

AFTER LEAVING CASSIE and Stevie at the barn, Nick crosses the lawn in front of the Smoke Tree Ranch just as two SWAT officers come through the front door.

The prisoner that the officers are escorting raises his head. Nick gasps, "Taggart? What are you doing here?"

It's one thing to talk about the possibility of Cedar Springs police officers being members of the Priesthood. But Nick thinks it is something else entirely to find Taggart is a member of the group calling for the deaths of Nick and his fellow agents.

Taggart stays silent, his face blank.

"This is the last one. ATF agents are inside." the lead officer says, glancing at Nick's FBI Kevlar vest and the badge suspended around his neck.

Nick shakes his head and steps through the open door. The ranch has a different feel about it from when he and Stevie were here to interview Russell and Delia Henderson. Damn, they talked a good line for a pair of terrorists. Do they even keep any horses at the ranch? He makes a mental note to check—after first ensuring that no Priesthood members are hiding out in the house. Who knows if the SWAT officers missed someone?

Hearing voices, he follows the hallway to a breakfast nook off the kitchen. From there, he steps into another room done out as a kind of workshop. Two men wearing ATF windbreakers are bent over a workbench.

When the nearest agent glances his way, Nick says, "Agent Stone, FBI. What have we here?" He can see they are working on an aluminum pressure cooker with wires leading to a clock.

"Agent Perkins, ATF. We found a sophisticated bomb-making factory. Two completed IEDs and one under construction," the man replies, referring to improvised explosive devices.

"What the hell were these people into?"

"Dunno what targets they had in mind. Our first job is to render them safe."

The second agent turns to Nick. "They used good old-fashioned dynamite as the explosive charge in this one, and it looks unstable. You shouldn't be in here."

"Seen any stragglers from the meeting?"

"Nah, sorry."

"There was just an office girl a few minutes ago," Agent Perkins says.

"Office girl?" Nick asks. "Was she tall, blonde, classy-looking?"

"Big tits? Yeah, we saw her alright."

Delia Henderson. "That was no office girl. Which way did she go?"

"Into the kitchen."

"Out the back door?" Nick asks, feeling the butt of the pistol at his hip.

"Nah. We'd have heard that. The girl is in the house somewhere."

"Detain her if she comes back this way," Nick orders.

Agent Perkins shakes his head. "We've got no time for that."

Nick hurries back into the kitchen, unholstering his weapon. Delia attended the meeting. That makes her as much a part of this as anyone. And just as dangerous, Sighting down his pistol, he moves into the hall.

Opening the first door reveals an audio-visual room with flat-screen monitors and speakers. The equipment is similar to that used at the police station to record interviews, only more upmarket. One of the screens displays a picture of the couch where he waited with Stevie only a couple of days ago.

Damn. The Hendersons overheard everything they said.

The next door he comes to, opens into a conference room with an oversized table and chairs. Nick looks around, but there's no one here and nothing of interest.

The next room holds a king-sized bed. Two white-suited ATF technicians are bending over a chest of drawers.

"Seen a woman, tall, blonde, thirties?" Nick asks.

"Office girl? Down the hall." One of the techs points a hand. "We can't have her here while we collect evidence."

"On it," Nick says, backing out of the room. Everyone is underestimating the woman. The next door is closed, and he hears rustling sounds coming from inside. Raising his pistol, he flings the door open.

Delia Henderson is on her knees beside a bed rooting through the contents of a shoebox. She's dressed in a cream button-up blouse and blue jeans.

"Freeze. FBI." Nick sights her along the top rail of his pistol.

Her blonde hair is done up in a French twist that would look elegant on any other occasion. She gets to her feet. But instead of obeying Nick's order, she dashes to a French door and lets herself out onto a deck.

Nick doesn't have cause to shoot the woman and gives chase, his feet pounding along the wooden boards, which run the entire length of the back of the ranch. He feels like a hurdler in a track event as Delia pulls over chairs and pushes a small table onto its side, trying to slow him down.

She's fast on her feet, but Nick is faster. He's only a few feet behind as she flies down the steps at the end of the deck and into the woodland. He can hear her panting over the sound of his own raspy breath. Nick can't remember running this hard since playing football in high school.

As Delia looks desperately over her shoulder, he powers his legs like pistons. His hand snags the belt at the back of her pants, dragging them both to the ground. But she still has some fight left in her and swings a right hook at Nick's jaw. He is more powerfully built and slugs her in the belly, making her gasp and double into a fetal position.

Hearing a cracking sound, he looks around but sees nothing. Delia is still struggling, but he has both of her arms pinned behind her.

Another much louder sound sends the hairs on the back of his neck to attention. It's not the report of a rifle, but more like the sound a tree makes when it's being sawn down, and the fibers rend apart one by one.

Delia screams as the ground beneath them subsides, and they fall head over heels together. Earth, leaves, and twigs collapse into the hole with them as they tumble down.

Nick's face is inches from Delia's when his shoulder strikes a hard, flat surface, painfully halting their plunge.

"What the fuck just happened?" he asks, pushing himself away from the floor they've landed on. He tries to shake off the debris that half buries them. They are in some kind of cave. Overhead, lights blink on, seemingly aware of their presence.

Delia is stirring, too, groaning about her leg as her hand fumbles through the fallen soil.

"Where are we?" he asks, feeling stunned by the fall. He takes a deep breath and gets to his feet, his head and arm painfully sore. Despite the scorching summer, the air smells earthy and damp.

"The bunker," she gasps. Her hair is awry, her face and clothing smudged with dirt. After a few moments, she pulls herself into a sitting position. "Get over there," she commands.

Nick looks down and sees his pistol in her hand pointed at his chest. He shakes his head in disbelief. "Don't be stupid. Just tell me how we get out of here."

"We can't. Not from the inside. Now get over there," Delia insists, clambering to her feet and brushing the loose dirt from her clothes with her free hand.

Nick ignores her and gazes around the cavern. The floors and walls are made of concrete. Wooden planks form bench seats which run along the sides of the underground space. Raising his gaze, he sees they fell through a spot where several of the stout railroad ties forming the ceiling have been removed. Even supposing they had a ladder to reach the gaping rift, there is no way to climb the loose soil to the surface.

"What was the hole we fell through? Why was it boarded over?"

"They are doing some work on the bunker to improve the ventilation. Putting in a new duct or something. But they couldn't agree about how to hide the vent pipe on the surface."

"What do you use this place for?" he asks, stepping into a separate room with camping cots and sleeping bags dotting the floor.

"We always knew it was only a matter of time before federal agents came here. The bunker is for us to protect ourselves from people like you overstepping their mandate."

"And that's why the members at the meeting ran this way when we raided the barn?" Nick moves over to a steel door with a glowing keypad.

"My job was to act as a lookout at the meeting. I watched the feed from video cameras mounted on the outside of the barn. As soon as I saw cops running toward us, I alerted folk. My father gave the order for everyone to hurry to the bunker."

"That didn't work out too well. You're the only member of the group who made it here, and that was an accident."

Delia hobbles over to where he's standing and jabs the

pistol into his ribs.

"You think this is funny? Go sit over there while I negotiate our release." She fishes a phone from her back pocket and taps the screen. "Damn. No service. I thought they'd fixed that."

"You know you're not going anywhere when we get out? You're making pressure-cooker bombs at the ranch. And don't tell me you didn't know about that."

"I wouldn't worry about what happens when I get out of here because you will be dead," she says, slipping her phone away.

"You're going to shoot me? You'll die in prison for killing a federal agent."

"You talk mighty tough for someone I'm holding at gunpoint." The blast from the pistol is almost deafening in the small space. The odor of spent gunpowder is acrid in the air.

"What the hell did you do that for?" Nick gazes up at the spot she aimed at. A trickle of soil is falling to the concrete floor from the gap between the beams.

"To show you I'm not afraid to use a weapon on you if needs be."

"Okay, you're a tough guy. I get it. Now tell me why we can't get through that door with the right combination?" When Delia doesn't answer, he says, "Come on. Indulge me."

"The door is rigged with explosives. It goes off if a proper protocol isn't used on the keypads."

"And kills everyone in the bunker? Why would you want to do that?"

"No, it's only supposed to kill the people trying to get in. In theory. Obviously, it's never been tested, and I'm unsure what it will do since we didn't enter the bunker through the door."

"Brilliant. Who's the genius who knows how it works?"

"All the members know how to unlock the door, but I'd feel safest if we got my father—he designed it."

Nick moves toward Delia until he feels her breath on his cheeks and looks directly into her eyes.

"What? You're going to try and seduce me?" She jabs the pistol hard into his chest.

"You don't want to shoot me," he says in a soft voice.

She averts her gaze and lets out a long breath. "You're telling me what I want, now? You're part of the great Satan that is the federal government," she says, her voice wavering.

"Have you ever shot anyone before?"

"No, never."

"It's not like you see in the movies. There's blood and gore. The other person often runs around screaming like a wounded animal."

She screws up her face.

"Right now, you might get parole. Shoot me, and you'll go to prison for the rest of your life. For what? The agents outside will arrest you as soon as we get out of here."

Her eyes soften, and she lowers the pistol.

Nick seizes the moment. He grabs her wrist and twists it behind her back.

"You're hurting me," she screams as the pistol clatters to the floor. "Get off me. I was never going to shoot you."

Keeping the pressure on her arm, he picks up the pistol. "That's what happens when you pull a gun on a federal agent. Give me the phone."

"No. Get. Off. Me.

He holds her wrist behind her shoulders and pats her down single-handed until she screams:

"The phone's in my back pocket."

As he pulls it out, she tries to take a swing at him with her free hand, but he pushes her to the floor.

Holding the phone high in the air, he finally gets a signal immediately below the hole they fell through. "You just have to find the right spot." He enters Cassie's cell number and presses the green button. Will she answer a call from an unknown number?

Chapter Forty-Four

"THE OUTBUILDINGS are rigged with explosives, you say?" Grady snaps, his voice so loud I have to move the phone farther from my ear.

"Yeah," I say. "At least that's what Russell implied, and he's looking rather smug."

"Standby, Agent Viera."

I hear him make another call, and there's a muffled conversation before he gets back to me:

"Agent Viera. The ATF agents spotted the tripwires at the two outbuildings. They've rendered them safe."

"How about the stables?"

"No explosives were found there."

"I suppose they didn't want to risk hurting the horses," I suggest.

"No horses there either. Haven't been in a long while."

"Interesting." I end the call and turn to Russell. "Damn. That has to be a blow. So killing federal agents was your backup plan?"

"I'd like to talk to my attorney now," he says.

The western sky is ablaze with reds and yellows from

the setting sun when we step out of the barn. "What a magnificent sky. Let's hope you can see that out of your prison cell, eh?"

My phone rings. I see it's from an unknown number, but answer anyway. Most of the agents and police working here today aren't in my contacts. The message is garbled. The only word I can make out is 'underground.'

"Who was that?" Stevie asks.

I shrug. "No idea. They'll call back if they really need me."

We find Grady at the temporary staging area near the main house. He's talking to a blonde woman in a navy jacket with ATF stenciled on the back.

He turns our way, then focuses on Russell. His gaze becomes cold and calculating, as if he's staring down a venomous snake. "We nearly lost three ATF agents with those tripwires. Agent Wentz here spotted them."

Grady looks about to punch Russell, so I hurry our captive to where two burly CHP officers stand beside the open rear doors of a van.

"Agents Viera and Wells," I say. "You have room for one more?"

They gaze inside the back of the van. "Sorry, no," the tall officer says. "But we can mind him until the van comes back."

"You're taking all the prisoners to the FBI office on Larkspur Lane?"

"Affirmative, ma'am."

After Stevie and I leave Russell with the officers, she asks, "Why do you think he didn't make a run for it with the rest of the Priesthood members?"

"Because he's an arrogant prick who thinks he can smooth-talk his way out of any situation."

We walk back to where Captain Grady is still chatting with Agent Wentz. I can see the attraction between them. She's a looker, and he'd be cute if he wasn't so tightly wound.

"How many did we nab?" I ask.

Grady pulls a scrap of paper from his pocket and angles it toward the temporary floodlight. "Hendersons—Russell and Paul. Officers Williams and Taggart and a forensic tech named Jason Clark."

"How about a Detective Reed or a Dirk McCloskey?

He glances at the list one more time. "That's a negative. They must have gotten away."

"We were also expecting to take Delia Henderson into custody.

"You saw what we were dealing with."

I nod slowly. It's a disappointment, but I can't be too hard on the guy. "About earlier, I'm sorry I disobeyed your command. Put it in the report if you must."

Grady lets out a deep breath, and I see his features relax slightly. "That won't be necessary, Agent Viera."

"Who is leading the team searching the house?"

"That would be me," Agent Wentz says, smiling.

We shake hands, and I introduce Stevie. "We're especially interested in any electronic equipment and want to ensure it comes to us rather than Sacramento."

"Any evidence relating to explosives will have to go to the ATF office in Sac," Wentz tells me.

"What have you found?"

"Three pressure cookers, timers, fertilizer—the usual stuff."

"We can share transcripts of their message boards with you, but we're particularly interested in finding a TV reporter named Jackie Ricci. We believe a member of the group using the moniker Pickett has her. We think we know who that is, and we're hoping Russell Henderson's computer will provide confirmation."

Agent Wentz gives me a long, silent stare. I don't want to name-drop ASAC Myles or his boss, but I'll go to them if I have to.

"We can send the laptops, phones, and tablets to your office, but you must ship them to my office in Sacramento within twenty-four hours. Deal?"

"Deal," I say. "Thank you."

I step away, pull out my phone, and call Todd, telling him he's going to be burning the midnight oil.

He sounds amenable. As soon as I end the call, another one comes in. This one is as equally garbled as the one earlier. I pull the phone from my ear. "The same unknown number as before."

Stevie says, "What did they say this time?"

"I made out the word, 'Nick.' But nothing more. Why would he be calling me on someone else's phone?"

"It's strange we haven't heard from him in a while. I'll call him." Stevie takes out her phone. After a few moments, she continues, "Just went to voicemail."

"Let me try the unknown number, and it sure as hell better not be someone trying to sell me a warranty." When voicemail comes on the line, I say to Stevie. "It's Delia Henderson's number. Why is she calling me about Nick?"

Stevie's phone chirps. Her eyes scan it, and her mouth drops open. "You better look at this, boss."

She shows me two text messages:

Nick is trapped underground in the bunker with Delia.

Do NOT approach. The door is rigged to explode. Get Russell Henderson to open it.

***

REED STUMBLES DOWN the meandering deer trail, each stride marginally shorter and requiring more effort than the last one. It's been twenty minutes since he escaped the raid on the barn. He's been running ever since, afraid of what will happen if the state police capture him. McCloskey also got away from the barn and is somewhere up ahead of him, making for the trailer.

Reed ruminates that the meetings he attends, the groups he belongs to, and his beliefs are his business alone. Not a matter for law enforcement. But for Agent Viera to raid their meeting, she has to have more on the Priesthood than their world views and philosophy.

She's also sure to have a search warrant for the ranch and the outbuildings. Maybe even the bunker. He could deny all knowledge of what was going on there. Russell won't rat him out, but Delia might. Still, it's her word against his, and she was living at the ranch, not him.

It gives him plausible deniability.

Suddenly, his foot catches on a tree root, sending him

sprawling into the ferns and fallen twigs beside the trail. As he lands, he feels a sharp jab in his arm where Agent Wells shot him.

He takes several deep breaths before rolling onto his back to inspect himself for injuries. His friend at the veterinary clinic cleaned and stitched his bullet wound, but the bandage now sports a bright crimson patch. He pulls a silver flask of Irish whiskey from his pocket and takes several long swigs for the pain.

Rage bubbles up inside him for letting a slip of a girl like Stevie Wells get the jump on him.

His next encounter with the woman will be very different from the last one.

He listens for any sign the state police are on his trail, but all he hears is the humming of insects and the wind in the trees. He clambers to his feet and uses his hands to brush down his clothing.

Viera and her team have ruined his life. If they hadn't poked their noses into Ava and Ricky's deaths, he could have swung the investigations any way he wanted.

Someone has to pay. He'll start with the two women. They are the weakest, and they'll never see him coming this time. Agent Stone will be harder to subdue, but it will still be doable if he keeps the element of surprise on his side.

But first, there is the situation at the trailer to deal with.

Damn Zoe. When Reed saw her a few months ago, McCloskey had just gotten out of jail. Reed tried to persuade her to change her first name so McCloskey wouldn't find her.

Now, she's his prisoner.

Reed still cares too much about Zoe to stand by while McCloskey kills her.

Perhaps this time, the guy will listen to common sense.

Chapter Forty-Five

ALMOST AN HOUR after receiving Nick's message, I'm camped out on the ranch's back deck, fifty feet from the entrance to the bunker. The branches and leaves covering the door have been removed, and Captain Grady is studying the control panel through his prized telescope. Stevie and Andrea Wentz are nearby. Some distance off to my right, two members of the state SWAT team are minding Russell Henderson while we decide what to do.

ATF agents just tried an abortive attempt to remove the explosives near the door. It was thought to be the best approach until they found the dynamite was buried too deep to extract. Nobody wanted to try digging near dynamite with a spade or a backhoe.

Despite the depth of the explosives, the agents insist that the charge could quite easily blast a crater twenty feet across and possibly damage the ranch structurally. No one can even hazard a guess at the damage the explosion could do to the bunker itself. Evidently, Russell seriously overestimated the number of sticks of dynamite required to dispatch anyone trying to force their way into the bunker.

We have only a short time to make a decision, as we're fast losing the daylight. To improve communication with Nick and Delia, we've lowered a portable radio through the hole in the top of the bunker, and we're trying to involve them in the decision-making process.

"Tell us more about the cache of firearms you've discovered," Andrea says into the radio.

"The weapons are in an area much larger than the bunker itself," Nick replies. "Most of them are illegal to own privately in the US. I'm looking at bazookas, grenade launchers, and anti-tank weapons, in addition to rifles and handguns. Many of the semi-automatic weapons have been modified for continuous fire."

"That's also illegal," she insists.

"Copy that."

"Do we trust Russell to open a door rigged with dynamite?" Stevie asks. "Lives are at stake."

"His daughter is inside. Is he going to do anything to jeopardize her safety?" I ask.

Stevie shrugs off my comment. "Who knows what their relationship is like? Would she be a martyr to the cause if she dies taking an FBI agent with her?"

Nick pipes up, "I'm going to remind you that Delia can hear what you're all saying. She seems to disagree strongly with Stevie's last statement.

"Oops, sorry," the young agent says. "I don't see what's wrong with my idea of winching them up through the hole in the roof of the bunker."

"We'd need a mobile crane to pull them out," I tell her. "Agent Wentz has a concern that a heavy vehicle might detonate the buried explosives."

"In viral videos, I've seen people and small animals pulled out of wells by a few strong guys with a rope," Nick says, sounding not a little frustrated.

"Understand that none of us are soil engineers," Andrea tells him. "But the ground around the hole you fell through looks too unstable for the rope to bear against. Chances are high that it would cave in, and we'd only get one of you out."

I look up and see one of the SWAT team members guarding Russell has wandered over. "Yes, sergeant?"

"With respect, ma'am. Mr. Henderson can hear your conversation, and he'd like to speak with you."

I look from Andrea to Stevie, giving them a hand shrug. "Let's hear what he has to say, sergeant."

While he's fetching the prisoner, I say, "What about you, Captain Grady? You're uncharacteristically quiet."

"Not my decision, ma'am. If the operation goes south, it won't be my head on the block."

"But you must have an opinion."

"You know the expression opinions are like assholes, ma'am."

"Yeah. Everyone has one, and they all stink," I reply. "So, what's your opinion?"

We look up and see the officers have arrived with Russell Henderson.

"You're not going to intentionally blow your daughter up, are you, sir?" Grady asks him.

"Of course not," Russell replies.

"It's accidentally blowing her up that worries me,"

Andrea snipes.

"Wrongly entering the code to open the door five times in a row is the only way to activate the explosives from outside the bunker. It wouldn't make sense to have a special code to blow ourselves up. We've been in and out of there dozens of times and not had an issue."

"Says the guy who planted six sticks of dynamite in the ground to take out intruders," Andrea says.

Ignoring her, I say to Russell, "Tell me the code to open the door."

"It's three, nine, eight, two, one followed by a pound sign," Russell says. "You're all making a mountain out of a molehill."

"Nick, ask Delia if that's correct."

"She says it is," he replies.

"I've heard enough," I say. "Here's what's going to happen. Captain Grady will use his fancy telescope to monitor your fingers on the keypad, Russell. I will have a pistol pointing at you. If the captain sees you entering too many digits, I will shoot you dead, so help me, God. I'm an excellent shot. Understood?"

"Got it."

"You heard that, Nick?" I ask.

"Yes, ma'am. Okay, by me, and Delia is nodding."

"Shelter as far away from the door as possible in case anything goes wrong." I turn and see ATF Agent Perkins has joined us.

"Give me a moment to get into my bomb disposal suit, and I'll take Mr. Henderson over to the bunker," he offers.

Twenty minutes later, I'm holding my breath as Perkins

trudges up to the door in his heavily armored outfit. He's gripping Russell's upper arm tightly as they stop in front of the keypad.

Grady squints through his telescope. "He's entering three . . . nine . . . eight . . . two . . . one . . . and the pound key. Now, he's opening the door."

I lower my pistol. A tired-looking Nick holds onto Delia as they step out of the bunker. Two state SWAT officers jump off the deck and advance to meet the young woman and her father.

Then all hell breaks loose.

Russell trips Perkins, easily toppling the agent in his heavy bomb disposal suit, and takes off running.

Delia tries to break away from Nick, but he pushes her down onto the ground.

The two SWAT officers race after Russell as he disappears into the woodland. Two more officers jump off the deck to join the pursuit.

"Like no one could see that might happen," Stevie says.

I flash her a side-eye. "Russell won't get far, and Nick is safe. That's what's important. Go help Nick bring in Delia."

***

IT'S DROPPED DARK by the time Stevie and I drive to the hospital, leaving Andrea and her fellow ATF agents to catalog the firearms. Five Priesthood members are in custody at the FBI offices, but Russell is still on the run, a fact that seems to bother Stevie more than it does me.

"It's just a matter of time before he's picked up," I tell

her.

"I guess," she replies.

We lapse into silence for a while, both exhausted after the day's events.

"I hope you don't mind me coming with you," she says. "With Reed still on the loose, I just feel safer sticking together outside of work. And I'd like to see your sister."

"Sure." I flash her a smile. I don't buy that she wants to see Jasmin, but considering what Stevie went through with the intruder just last night, she's doing great.

"Why is Finch not spending the night?"

"Good question. He feels that sleeping in my bed distracted me from protecting you."

"And you agree with him?" she asks.

"Not really, but I have to respect what he believes. The physical side of our relationship is new, so taking a break for an evening or two isn't so bad."

We both have our hands on the butt of our weapons as we cross the dimly lit parking lot to the main entrance.

"I have to confess that I'm not great with hospitals," she says as we ride the elevator to the third level. "I think they remind me of my own sister."

"I don't think anyone is thrilled with them. What happened to your sister?"

"She was four years younger than me. She died when she was eight. Brain tumor," she says as the elevator doors whoosh open.

"I'm sorry."

"Don't be. It was a long time ago."

At the doors to the ICU, I enter the code.

When we pass Pete Barlow's bed, Stevie pauses and says, "I'm sure I saw him move."

"I'm told that happens when they're starting to wake up."

She shivers. "I hope I never end up in a coma. My other fear is being sent to the mortuary while I'm still alive."

When we reach Jasmin's cubicle, we see she's twitching and flexing her fingers. Her head turns from side to side like she's having a bad dream.

"I'm here, Jaz," I tell her, stroking her hair. "I want you back, even if you are your usual annoying self."

The charge nurse shows up, and the news isn't great. "We've been tapering the medicine that's been keeping Jasmin in a coma, but the doctor is concerned that she isn't showing the progress we've hoped for."

My eyes well with tears, but I blink them back. Stevie slips her hand into mine.

I'm grateful she's here. If I were on my own, I'd be sobbing by now. "But it's still possible that my sister might come out of the coma?" I ask the nurse.

"Everyone is different," she says, hurrying off to tend to another patient.

As we make our way across the parking lot to the car, I say, "Let's dine out for a change. It's probably no less safe than eating at home."

"I would go one step further and suggest we check into a hotel for the night. We can share a room, so it doesn't have to cost a lot. I'm afraid of Reed coming into the house in the night again," Stevie admits.

"Do you need to pick up toiletries and a fresh set of

clothes on the way?"

"It's safest to go straight to a hotel in case Reed or one of his friends is watching our homes. I have clean clothes in my locker at work, and I can change when I get in tomorrow."

"Me too. Let's do it. I could use a good night's sleep. How about the Travelodge?"

"Let's stay at the Best Western. No one has been attacked there recently."

"That we know of."

Chapter Forty-Six

THE NEXT MORNING, my phone rings as Stevie and I are changing into fresh work attire in the women's room at the office.

"It's ATF Agent Wentz," the female voice says. "We're still working at the Smoke Tree Ranch."

"You've been there all night?" I ask in surprise.

"I've managed to catch a couple of hours sleep. We thought we were done cataloging the firearms in the bunker. Then one of my agents spotted a trapdoor to yet another underground vault with a cache of weapons. Mostly pistols and assault rifles, but a few rocket launchers."

"What were the Priesthood members doing? Planning on starting a civil war?" I ask, pulling up my gray pants and tucking in my white blouse.

"We have a few ideas, but we need access to Russell Henderson's electronic devices to be sure."

"Come on over to the office. My tech guy has been working on Russell's phone and laptop all night. He may have already found what you're looking for. I'm just about to get a report. The FBI office is on Larkspur."

"I know it well."

"Call me when you get here."

"I was already driving to you on the off-chance. See you in five minutes."

By the time Stevie and I finish dressing and step outside, a black SUV with a Bureau of Alcohol, Tobacco, Firearms, and Explosives insignia is pulling into a parking spot.

Agent Wentz steps out of the vehicle. It would be an understatement to say she looks disheveled. Her pale blue shirt and navy pants are scuffed with red dirt, and her blonde hair hangs loose.

"Excuse my appearance," she says, tucking more of her hair behind one ear. "It's been a hell of a night cataloging the hundreds of weapons."

"What were the Priesthood members doing with them?" Stevie asks, leading the agent through the inner door to our offices.

"Let's see what your tech guy has to say."

I show her into the conference room.

"Tea or coffee, Agent Wentz?" Stevie asks.

"Coffee, black, no sugar, and please call me Andrea."

"Coming right up."

I find Todd in his office, talking to Nick. Both men look droopy and bleary-eyed.

"Did you pull an all-nighter too?" I ask Nick. "After getting trapped in the bunker?"

"Nah. I helped Todd decipher the contents of Russell's laptop and got home late."

"We're meeting now with ATF Agent Andrea Wentz to

review your findings."

When we're all seated at the table with mugs of coffee, I make the introductions and ask who wants to present to the group.

Todd volunteers. "We matched the online names with the members. Russell Henderson is Stonewall, the leader of the group. No surprise there. He's the one who suggested moving up the schedule for the devices we now know are bombs. Officer Taggart is Bragg. He berated Pickett, aka Dirk McCloskey, for kidnapping Jackie."

"Confirming all that is an excellent result," I add.

"McCloskey said that the first order of business is eliminating the two FBI traitors who came to the ranch, pardon my French. Detective Reed is the member who agreed with that statement, and I guess recent events bear that out." Todd throws Stevie a look of sympathy.

I frown. "I think we can dispense with the member's job titles. It's not like they're ever going to serve on the force again."

"Okay. It's Reed who said you've been poking your noses into the Priesthood members' families, his words not mine. Paul Henderson advocated for killing you and Stevie, but here's a surprise. It was Delia Henderson who said the procurement of materials for the devices should continue in parallel with any eliminations."

"It's frightening that you can be so wrong about people," Stevie says. "She seemed nice and acted graciously when we met her at the ranch."

"It wasn't the warm and fuzzy Delia who pulled a gun on me in the bunker," Nick adds, clenching his jaw. "There was a moment when I was sure she was going to shoot me."

"I'm looking forward to interviewing her, right boss?" Stevie asks.

"I get her first," Nick insists.

"You'll both get a crack at her," I reply. "But we have to try and keep emotion out of the interviews."

"Mind if I sit in on them?" Andrea asks, taking another slug of coffee. "I'm mostly interested in Russell Henderson. But with him on the run, I'd like to hear what the other Priesthood members have to say about the arms and explosives."

I nod to her. "Of course. This investigation is fifty percent yours."

"I was telling Cassie and Stevie earlier about the overnight discovery of a second huge cache of weapons in the bunker. Is there anything on the electronic devices explaining that?"

"Getting to it," Todd says brusquely, and I flash him a frown. His eyelids are drooping, and he's obviously fatigued, so I turn to Nick.

"The Priesthood is just one of many like-minded groups all over the country," he says, leaping in to take over the commentary. "We found messages discussing some kind of uprising when the Marxist government seizes power."

"We're pretty safe there," Todd says, "because that's never going to happen."

"The fear is that they'll find another cause to act militant about," Andrea says. "God knows there are plenty to choose from these days." She drains her mug.

"More coffee?" I ask, but she shakes her head.

"Back to the weapons," Nick continues. "The Priesthood was doing a brisk trade, selling arms to other groups across the country. They were using the profits to finance the election of state and local officials who support their views about federal agencies. If you recall, Russell told us that the Bureau is overstepping its original charter. He hates the ATF for regulating firearms and has a beef with every other federal agency."

"That's pretty much what we thought," Andrea says. "Were you able to make a list of the people they were selling to?"

"I can give you about thirty-nine groups. Many of the addresses are post office boxes. Just leave us your contact information, and we'll forward what we know."

"The priority for my team is finding Dirk McCloskey and freeing his captives, Zoe and Jackie," I say.

"I might be able to help with that," Andrea says, pulling her briefcase onto her lap and leafing through the contents. "Here's an aerial view of the Smoke Tree Ranch property." She slides a glossy eight by ten photo across the table. "I can send you an electronic copy of the original, but if you look in this far corner of the photo, you can see a clearing in the woodland." She pulls a pen from her purse and uses it to indicate the location.

We all crane our necks to gaze at the photo.

"There's a cabin and an Airstream trailer nearby it, " Andrea continues. "You'll be able to zoom in and see more detail on the electronic version. As I was driving over here, I got a call from an ATF agent who's been monitoring the entire operation at the ranch by satellite. He's seen vehicles visit the trailer. One of them appears to be the dark blue minivan you're looking for."

"Holy crap. Let's saddle the horses and check it out," I say, getting to my feet.

"What about interviewing the Priesthood members?" Nick asks, rising to his feet.

"We're waiting on an Assistant US Attorney to arrive from Sacramento before we can start. Let's go. Two women need rescuing."

"Who do you have to raid the cabin and the trailer?" Andrea asks.

"Just my two agents and me. If I can get hold of Detective Finch, he should be able to join us. We've had really bad experiences with the local police SWAT. They were infiltrated by Priesthood members, and I don't know that we captured them all at the ranch. So I can't trust them. State Police SWAT and FBI hostage rescue will take too long to get here."

"Count me in," Andrea says, getting to her feet. "I've worked as a field agent for ten years ."

"You're hired," I say, thankful for the help.

***

ZOE LISTENS IN disbelief to the two men standing ten feet from her in the Airstream trailer. Their strident argument about what to do with her and Jackie is giving Zoe the shakes.

Whether the women live or die depends on who wins the debate.

Zoe glances at Jackie, unconscious on the floor, thankful she doesn't get to hear the men talk about them like they are less than human.

Both women are bound hand and foot. Dog collars buckled around their necks are connected by a chain looped through an eye hook on the trailer wall. Neither woman can move very far without tugging on the other.

Reed is standing closest to the door, his face grim. He's wearing brown suit trousers and a stained white T-shirt. His unshaven face and piercing blue eyes are menacing. But to Zoe's astonishment, he's arguing for their release.

"You saw the state cops when they raided the barn. They're mean bastards. Not at all like the pansy FBI agents. It's only a matter of time before they make their way through the woods and find us here."

A crazy smile spreads across McCloskey's lips. He's broad-shouldered and wears bib fronted jeans over a red plaid flannel shirt. He looks like a yokel, but Zoe knows he's cunning and spiteful. And powerfully built. He used to work construction and never had a problem finding employment. She's seen him raise wooden beams single-handed that would require the strengths of two other men.

"Detective Gary Reed suddenly doesn't want me to kill a couple of worthless bitches?" McCloskey scoffs. "What's happened to you, Reed?"

"I'm telling you, the state cops will hunt you down. I know the women seem like loose ends, but you need to disappear into the hills for a stretch, change your name, grow a beard."

"Loose ends? We're talking about my wife Zoe, who

faked her own death, sending me to prison for ten years, and Jackie, the friend who helped her. Hell, they both deserve to die a painful death a dozen times over."

"It's your choice, but I want no part of it," Reed says. "And I'm telling you to get out of here, fast."

"What do you care about me or these women?"

"I care about the cops capturing you because you know too much about what happened at the Barlow residence."

"I only went there to beat up Pete Barlow and maim him," McCloskey insists.

"Like that matters now." Reed shakes his head.

For a few moments, a silence hangs in the air between the two men.

Zoe figures she has nothing to lose by speaking up. "You talk like you're innocent, Dirk, but you're not. I lost track of the number of times you sent me to the hospital."

"Well, no one asked you, did they?" he steps to where Zoe is sitting on the floor and pinches her cheeks between his thumb and forefinger, until she squeals in pain.

"Gary Reed isn't your buddy," she says through gritted teeth.

"Shut up, Zoe," Reed snaps, inching closer to the door and fingering the butt of the revolver in his shoulder holster.

"He's going to kill me anyway, so why should I take all the blame?" she asks.

McCloskey releases the pressure on her face. "What are you saying, Zoe?"

She sees Reed has opened the door and is standing on the threshold. "Go on, run, you cowardly prick. I thought you wanted to help me, but it turned out you only wanted me for yourself."

"Talk. It's your last chance to tell the truth, Zoe," McCloskey growls, roughly lifting the woman's chin so he can gaze into her eyes.

She's fearful of what might happen if she tells the truth, but she continues, "Reed faked my death. All I had to do was give him some of my blood." The words hitch and catch in her throat. "After Detective Barlow arrested you, Reed wouldn't leave me alone. He said I owed him all the sex he wanted. All the weird creepy things he wanted me to do for him." Zoe's sobs come faster.

McCloskey whirls around, his pistol aimed at Reed. "Is this true? You helped Zoe fake her own death?"

"I'm sorry, man," Reed says. He dives sideways out of the trailer as McCloskey's weapon spits.

Zoe hears the sound of Reed crashing through the undergrowth.

McCloskey runs to the door and fires blindly into the dense stand of trees surrounding the trailer. "Scram like the fucking coward you are, Reed. I trusted you when you visited me in prison and told me Pete Barlow had killed Zoe." When the pistol clicks empty, McCloskey lets his arm fall slack by his side.

He steps back inside the trailer and closes the door, tossing the empty pistol onto his bunk.

"While we're all speaking the truth, it's time we had a little chat." He moves to where Jackie is lying and prods her chest with the tip of his boot.

She lets out a grunt.

"Come on, sit up. I didn't hit you that hard, and you need to hear this. If you don't, I'll rip your head from your body and hold it up for Zoe to see."

Jackie flattens her hands on the floor and slowly pushes herself into a sitting position. Her eyes stare vacantly around the trailer.

"Did you hear what Zoe just told me about Reed?" he demands.

Jackie nods slowly.

"Tell me. Was it true?"

"Yeah," she slurs, the words coming haltingly. "Reed faked her death. Then he kept pestering her for sex."

"Damn," McCloskey says, stepping away. After a few moment's thought, he turns back to the women. "None of that changes your punishment. I've been thinking about the manner of your death ever since I found out you were still alive, Zoe. You need to die for real this time. I'll get off scot-free because everyone thinks you're already dead." He chuckles to himself at his cleverness. "Do you want to hear what I'm going to do with you both?"

"Don't keep us in suspense," Jackie spits, her voice thick with sarcasm.

"After lying to the cops, Jackie, and framing me, Zoe, you both need cleansing of your sins. And nothing cleanses like fire. Don't you think that's clever?" He jabs the toe of his boot into Zoe's belly, and she doubles over, coughing. "I know the perfect place to set the fire, so you both die slowly, and the cops can't get here in time to rescue you."

Chapter Forty-Seven

FINCH IS STANDING at the curb outside the police station when I stop to pick him up. He opens the back door and climbs inside. "How are you going to get around the fire?" he asks, leaning between Nick and me in the front seats.

"What fire?" Nick turns and asks.

"The one that started about an hour ago in the woodland between the Smoke Tree Ranch and the Airstream trailer where we're headed. Two air tankers, a copter, and hand crews are working the fire. The area is inaccessible to engines, but a dozer is en route."

"How far is the fire from the trailer?" I ask, pulling away from the curb.

"It's a good distance from it, but the fire is blocking the route you were planning on taking."

"Call me a cynic," Nick says. "But a fire springs up in a spot that's uninhabited, at the exact time we try to rescue the two women? Heck, it's not even a recreation area."

"You're right. It must have been set to slow us down," I say. "Nick, try and contact the incident commander. See if anyone can tell you the direction the fire is moving. Finch, do you have the aerial map Andrea sent you?"

"Right here," he says, pulling out his phone.

"Search for another access road to the trailer. There has to be one. I'll keep driving in the general direction of the ranch, so we don't lose time."

I radio Stevie and Andrea, following behind in the ATF SUV. When I tell them about the fire, Stevie says:

"Wouldn't you know it? Damn Dirk McCloskey to hell."

"I'm going to stay on Skyway Drive and hope Finch comes up with an alternative route soon."

"Got one," he says, and I leave the radio open for Stevie to hear. "The area is crisscrossed by fire roads. In eight-tenths of a mile, make a left onto Powerline Road. A mile later, on the right, there'll be an entrance to a fire road."

"You get all that?" I ask Stevie over the radio.

"Affirmative."

A little later, I hear Nick speaking on the phone to someone about fire lines and wind direction. When he ends the call, he says, "After getting the run-around, I managed to get through to the incident commander. Good news and bad news. They've stopped the forward motion of the fire I was calling about, but another one has sprung up a half-mile away. They were mystified until I advised them that McCloskey might be actively setting the blazes."

We ride in silence until I turn onto the fire road. It's unpaved, like they mostly are, a ruler-straight gash of packed dirt through the heart of the forest.

A glance in the rearview shows me the billowing cloud of dust kicked into the air behind our two vehicles. "McCloskey's going to see us coming." Off to our right, another cloud is visible above the treetops, this one a pall of gray-black smoke. It's partly obscuring the sun, tinting the landscape orange.

"There's a crossroads ahead. Make a right." A hundred yards after I turn, Finch says, "Slow, slow. Stop here. There's a short trail leading to the clearing and the cabin on the left."

I park off to one side so as not to block the road for emergency vehicles. Hurrying around to the back, I pull out Kevlar vests for myself and my two passengers. Removing the trunk's false bottom reveals an array of weapons. I reach in and take out three AR-15's handing them to Nick and Finch. We help ourselves to spare magazines, stowing them in our pockets.

As soon as the five of us are kitted out with vests and weapons, I tell everyone to stay close and keep their heads down as I lead them along the trail. The back of the silver Airstream is just visible through the trees and becomes more distinct the closer we get.

Just before we burst into the open, I stop and raise my hand. We stand motionless, listening. The forest is silent but for the rush of a small breeze through the tops of the pines and cedars high overhead.

Communicating through hand signals, I send Finch and Andrea to the right while Nick, Stevie, and I go left. We hug the tree line circling the edge of the clearing. I've only gone twenty feet when I see the barrel of an AK-47 pointing out of a window.

"Get down," I scream loudly enough for both of our parties to hear.

We dive for cover and land hard in the deer brush as shots ring out.

The breath is knocked out of my lungs, but the bullets whistle over our heads, smashing into trees deep in the forest.

Peering through the twigs and shrubs, I see Finch and Andrea are giving me a thumbs up.

"Looks like we've come to the right place." Stevie is lying on her front near me.

"I was hoping to avoid a hostage situation." I tap Nick's ankle to get his attention. "For fuck's sake, keep your heads down. Both of you."

"Yes, boss," Stevie says, and Nick echoes her words.

"Let's move farther into the trees and work our way around to the front of the trailer."

"Damn," Nick says as we move through the undergrowth, with our heads ducked down. "There's poison oak everywhere."

"Mosquitos too," Stevie adds. "And they're biting."

The front of the trailer comes into view as we circle the clearing. The dark blue minivan is parked close to the front door, and we can now see the ruined remains of the cabin we saw in the aerial photo.

The air has become thick with black smoke from the fire. Fumes curl through pine branches and along the tops of the deer brush.

I draw closer to Nick, who looks as concerned as I feel. "Better call the incident commander for an update."

He pulls out his phone. "No service."

"Can you tune your radio to the fire channel and call

him that way?"

"Trying it," he says. The first voices shout at Nick to get off the air. He identifies himself, and finally a female voice tells him to stand by.

"Commander Rivera here. Who is this?"

"Special Agent Stone," Nick says. "We're outside a trailer about a mile and a half north-west of the original fire."

"What the hell are you people still doing in the fire zone?"

"A suspect who we believe set the fire is holding two women hostages inside. We could use an update."

"Get out of there. That's my update. The perp you're chasing set a half-dozen spot fires. They've joined together into one blaze, and it's moving north toward your location. The fire is only a quarter-mile away from a natural gas pipeline. Once that is impacted, all bets are off. So get out now while you can."

Nick and Stevie's faces look grim as I relay the fire information to Finch and Andrea. "I'm going to try and breach the front door," I tell them. "But everyone else needs to get out of here now."

"I'm not leaving without you," Finch insists, and Stevie agrees.

"If you haven't heard from me in ten minutes, you need to run to the vehicles and get as far away as you can. But right now, Nick, I need you to retrace your steps and start firing toward the back of the trailer to distract McCloskey. Be careful not to hit it." I tell him I'm not sure whether our rounds are capable of piercing the aluminum skin and endangering the hostages.

Pausing at the edge of the clearing, I wait for Nick to start shooting. As expected, McCloskey pokes a rifle through a back window and returns fire. With him suitably distracted, I tell Stevie to stay put while I race across the open ground to the narrow gap between the trailer and the minivan. My adrenaline is pumping and my heart racing as I flatten myself against the Airstream's aluminum skin. But when I turn, I see Stevie's face only inches from mine.

"Can't let you do this on your own, boss."

Now is not the time to discuss her disobeying an order, so I give her a nod.

With our backs to the trailer, we edge closer to the door.

***

INSIDE THE AIRSTREAM, McCloskey pushes away from the window and shoulders the hot AK-47. "The cops are trying to surround us," he mutters under his breath. "We need to leave."

He turns to the two women who are holding one another. Both are petrified by the shooting. "My plan of cleansing you with fire isn't going to work," he snarls. "But it doesn't change the fact that you're both going to die. I have another idea. I'll use water to cleanse you. If you drown, all your sins will be washed away. Nice, huh?"

Zoe's screams are cut short when he slaps her across the face. Not hard enough to knock her to the ground—he needs her to be able to walk.

He fishes a ring of keys from his pocket and yanks on the chain that binds the women's necks together. A yelp comes from Jackie, but he ignores it. The lock securing the chain to the trailer wall clicks open.

"We're going for a little drive," he announces. "If either of you misbehaves, I will shoot the other girl in the hand. While it won't kill her, it will be extremely painful. Got it? "

Both women nod.

***

I SUDDENLY REALIZE that McCloskey is no longer returning fire at Nick's position. I'm counting on the perp having his back to me when I go through the door. It's against regulations to shoot a person in the back, but at this point, I have few qualms about doing that if it's necessary to rescue the women.

I'm inhaling thicker, more caustic-tasting smoke. The fire can't be too far away.

Stevie and I have nearly reached the door when it bursts open, and McCloskey shoves Jackie out of the trailer ahead of him, dragging Zoe behind. A length of chain connects dog collars worn by the two women. The AK-47 is slung over his shoulder.

I get on the ground, pulling Stevie with me. She lands on my chest, knocking the wind out of me for a moment.

It's a flurry of arms and legs as the gunman forces Zoe onto the back seat of the minivan. I don't think he knows we're there, or he would have shot us.

But I can't get a bead on McCloskey—he's being careful to shelter himself behind Jackie, who's standing outside the vehicle as he eases himself into the front seat.

Finally, he yanks on the chain connecting Jackie's neck to Zoe's, pulling the choking reporter into the back of the minivan next to her friend.

There's an opportunity as he leans from the front to pull the rear door closed, and I take it.

But the round from my pistol only grazes the top of his shoulder. He shouts "Bitch," loudly, clearly his go-to word.

I grab a handful of Stevie's shirt and pull her as low as I can, rolling us both part-way under the trailer. I'm expecting the AK-47 to rake the area with fire.

Instead, the minivan's engine revs up, and it takes off around the side of the ruined cabin.

Stevie and I scramble to our feet, and I catch glimpses of Finch and Andrea.

We chase the minivan on foot. The back door is still open and hits a tree with a resounding crash, shattering the glass and slamming the door shut.

Behind the ruined cabin, we come to another fire road.

All we can do is stand and watch the minivan, as it picks up speed and disappears in a cloud of dust and smoke.

Chapter Forty-Eight

"HOW THE HELL did that happen?" I holler as we race through the trees toward the parked cars. The smoke from the fires is getting thicker, the air harder to inhale without coughing and spluttering.

"I swear that dirt road wasn't marked on the map," Finch insists, jogging and wheezing beside me. "I knew there had to be a way in and out of the clearing, but tree branches must have hidden it on the satellite map. There wasn't any time to look in more depth."

"It's not your fault. I'm annoyed at myself for letting McCloskey slip through our fingers with both women."

We reach the vehicles and turn to Finch for direction. I gaze over his shoulder as he works his phone.

"If we retrace our steps to the last intersection and turn right, we should meet the hidden road here." He uses two fingers to expand the view of the area he's talking about.

Above the roar of the fire, we hear helicopters and tanker planes. A red and white whirlybird comes within a couple of hundred yards of our position before unleashing a torrent of water onto the fire.

"It's the best we've got. Let's run with it," I say, my voice cracking into a fit of coughing. Finally, I clear my throat and continue in a hoarse voice. "Andrea and Stevie, you guys follow us like before. Let's get out of this awful smoke."

We pile into the vehicles and turn them around. Once we're past the intersection, I step on the gas, jolting us every which way as we bounce through the ruts.

We pass the junction Finch referred to, and a fire road indeed comes in from the right, as he thought. The smoke situation is considerably better by the time we reach the junction with the highway ten minutes later.

"McCloskey's got quite a lead on us," I say. "Now, which way?"

Finch leans forward between the front seats, showing me the map. "Turning left takes you back into the city. Right takes you to Susanville."

"I can't imagine he'll head back to the city." I wait for a semi to roar past the junction, then swing the car onto the main road, flicking on the lights and siren.

The blacktop runs as straight as an arrow for as far as I can see. With no traffic coming the other way, I overtake the truck and accelerate down the highway. It's a vast improvement after the shake, rattle, and roll we experienced on the fire road.

I'm trying to make up lost time until Nick draws my attention to a vehicle in the distance, stopped at the roadside on the downhill slope into a canyon. "Isn't that them?"

"Yeah," Finch says.

"What's he doing?" I slow to pull in behind the suspect

minivan, but it takes off again. "What do you suppose is his endgame?"

Nick shakes his head. "Nothing good."

The minivan slows as we approach a concrete bridge. A sign warns of road repairs, but there are no Caltrans workers, just orange safety cones and tape sectioning off the roadside at the far end of the bridge. A vehicle must have struck the guardrail. The damaged protective barrier has been removed, and a replacement piece lays uninstalled on the shoulder.

The minivan slows more, and I have to brake hard to avoid running into the back of it.

With tires squealing, it careens into the traffic cones. They fly off the vehicle's roof and sides, a couple of them hitting our hood.

Then, inexplicably, the minivan abruptly swerves to the right and hurtles toward the side of the bridge where the safety barrier is missing.

"NOOOO!" I scream as we watch the minivan seem to hang in the air for a moment. Its front wheels are still turning as it slowly tilts and disappears nose-first over the side of the bridge.

The crash is deafening as it hits the river below, and water shoots into the air, spraying our windshield.

I stop the car askew on the road, blocking both lanes. As we leap out, the ATF vehicle screeches to a halt behind us.

Leaning over the side of the bridge, we see the minivan in the water near the riverbank. The front end is sinking while the back has reared up.

This was McCloskey's endgame all along.

Andrea hurries down the road with flares in her hands as the rest of us jog to the end of the bridge. I dial 9-1-1 and press my phone to my ear as I summon ambulances and the fire department.

We climb over the guardrail onto an area of parched grass. I skid down an earthen slope on my butt to a massive concrete support pillar carrying the bridge forty feet above my head. Working my way around the structure, I gaze at the wrecked minivan.

In the few moments it's taken us to get down here, it's drifted farther into the river and is lower in the water.

Rescue vehicles and ambulances are en route, but both women could be dead by the time they get here—either by drowning or at McCloskey's hand.

I kick off my shoes and drop my pants at the water's edge. Now is not the time for modesty.

Heedless of my own safety, I wade through the water until it comes up to my thighs, then dive in.

At his time of the year, the river isn't high or the current fast-flowing. Still, the water is icy after the baking June sunshine. I'm an excellent swimmer, but the cold jolts my senses as I strike out for the minivan.

Looking over my shoulder, I see Finch and Stevie right behind me. We need to climb inside the van before it drifts into the middle of the river and sinks with the women and our suspect inside.

I guess I shouldn't have worried about the latter score. The driver's door opens, allowing more water to flood into the vehicle and causing the front to sink. Dirk McCloskey appears in the opening, his face bloody. He jumps into the swirling river, and Finch strikes out through the water toward him.

"Let him go," I scream, clutching onto a piece of the van's rear suspension. "Get the women out. We'll pick him up later." I glance at the river bank, which seems farther away, and see Andrea and Nick waiting for McCloskey there. Nick is not a strong swimmer, and I'm glad he is staying put. I don't want to add to the number of people we need to rescue.

Taking a gulp of air, I dive under the water and grab the van's running board, then work my way hand over hand until I'm level with the driver's door.

My limbs are starting to feel numb from the cold, and my breathing is labored. I kick my legs, powering myself inside the front of the flooded vehicle. It takes me several tries to gain my footing on the floor.

Stevie is bobbing nearby in the water.

"No one is going to die here today, not the hostages, not the rescuers," I say half to myself.

I grab the steering wheel for support and reach for Stevie's arm. Our hands lock together, and I pull her onto the passenger seat. She feels even colder than me.

Jackie and Zoe are huddled together in the far back. Both their faces are bloody from the crash, and I hope they don't have significant injuries because I'm going to need their cooperation.

Both women's wrists are cuffed together with plastic ties. There's no way either of them can swim without using their arms. Tread water, maybe, but that's about it. I curse myself for not having a knife to cut them free.

"It's going to be a trick getting them out of there, with their hands bound and a chain connecting their necks," I whisper to Stevie, who is shivering beside me.

My shirt is only slowing me down and making me colder, so I strip down to my bra and underwear.

Through the open door, I see Finch bobbing nearby in the water. "You want me to go in through the back doors?" he shouts.

"Negative," I answer. "The bubble of air in the back may be all that's keeping this thing afloat. I'm going to try to extract the women through the front."

Shooting a leg over the center console, I climb onto the partially submerged back seat.

"Jackie, you come first. Let's see how long the chain is."

"About six feet," she says through chattering teeth. She uses her manacled hands like a single limb to clamber over the seatback to me. Zoe follows suit.

We have them climb onto the front seats. It's cramped with all four of us in such a small space.

Zoe lets out a strident scream, and we grab one another as the minivan suddenly lurches downward. It levels out, leaving about three feet between the water's surface and the roof. Five heads are bobbing in the narrow air space.

It feels to me as if the wheels have settled onto something firm. I look out the shattered windshield and see we're close to another bridge support rising forty feet into the air.

"We need to get onto the roof. From there, we should be able to jump onto the concrete base of that support pillar. If we hang around in the water much longer, we'll all get hypothermia. Stevie and I will boost Jackie up first. Zoe, you will need to move to the door to accommodate the chain and help shove her up. We'll boost you up second."

The chain is barely long enough for the operation.

A commotion nearby in the water captures my attention. Leaning my head outside, I see Finch fighting with McCloskey in the water.

Damn. We don't need this.

Stevie and I grab Jackie's legs and heave. "Move closer to the door, Zoe, or the chain will strangle you both," I scream.

Once Jackie is clear of the water, we lean out of the open door and shove her butt up higher. Even with Zoe right there helping, it takes all of Stevie and my combined strength to heave Jackie's butt onto the roof.

"Shit, that was hard, " Stevie says, gasping for breath.

"One more," I say. Zoe is lighter, a hundred and five tops, and lifting her goes a lot more smoothly.

"Oh, man. I need to spend more time at the gym," Stevie gasps. "My arms are aching."

"We're both cold. You did good," I splutter through chattering teeth. "I'll boost you up next."

But I don't get a chance. Gazing out of the vehicle, I feel a shock flash through me.

Finch is floating face down in the water.

Nick is swimming from the shore, but he has a way to go.

"Wait here," I tell Stevie and dive in. My limbs are weary from the cold, but sheer willpower drives me toward Finch.

Unless I do something, he's a dead man.

I reach him in five powerful strokes and flip him over. My head is right next to his. I can't hear breath sounds, nor can I see his chest rise and fall.

My slim frame doesn't have much natural buoyancy, so I'm treading water furiously as my fingers search his neck for a pulse.

But I can't feel anything.

If the throb of his heart is there, it's very faint. I pinch his nose and give his mouth several strong breaths, trying to clear his airway. When he continues to float motionless, I repeat the breaths.

I don't know how to perform chest compressions in the water, but I figure he will die if I don't do something. The thought almost overwhelms me.

Panic flashes through me as my fist repeatedly thumps his chest.

I'm about to quit from the hopelessness of my actions when Finch starts coughing and spluttering. It's impossible to roll him onto his side without his mouth and nose going below the surface of the water.

"I only just got Finch breathing again," I say as Nick arrives. "He was fighting with McCloskey. Can you float him back to the riverbank and see he gets medical attention?"

"I've got him, boss."

A cacophony of approaching sirens is music to my ears.

Then Stevie lets out an ear-splitting scream.

Turning my head, I see McCloskey has grabbed her leg and is pulling her off the minivan.

She splashes into the water.

Nick looks to me for direction, and I tell him, "Go. I've got this joker. Finch is barely breathing." I pump my arms through the water, powering myself toward her.

Stevie signals she's all right, so I press on to the wrecked minivan.

McCloskey is standing on the running board on the far side of the vehicle. His arms are on the roof, trying to grab one of the chained women.

He's not looking my way, and I don't think he hears me as I climb through the passenger door.

I duck under the surface and open the glove box, searching for anything I can use as a weapon.

Nothing.

Peering through the murky water, I see McCloskey's knife lying on the driver's floor mat. I dive down and retrieve it, but when I surface, he's glaring my way.

His meaty hand makes a grab for my throat. The water slows him down, and I dodge.

Bracing a foot against the passenger seat, I catapult myself toward the open driver's door. I'm half under the water, but the knife is in my outstretched hand. It plunges to the hilt in McCloskey's upper belly.

A look of surprise crosses his face as he looks down and sees the growing crimson plume spreading through the water.

I pull the knife out, so he can't use it on me.

He falls backward with a resounding splash.

His head sinks below the surface.

I should dive in and rescue him, but I first need to get Jackie and Zoe to safety.

The thump of blades beating the air draws my attention. I lean out of the wrecked minivan and look up to see a coastguard helicopter hovering overhead. A helmeted crew member in an orange jumpsuit is sitting with his legs over the side, working a winch that deploys a rescue basket.

He waves, and I wave back.

Chapter Forty-Nine

ONE DAY LATER

IT'S MID-MORNING on Sunday, and I'm sitting next to Assistant US Attorney Pat Scully. Across the interview room table are Delia Henderson and Jim Dixon, her attorney. In return for dropping the explosive and gun-running charges against her, she's spent the last hour giving us details of the Priesthood's involvement in selling weapons to like-minded groups.

Names, dates, the lot.

As a result of her testimony, Paul, her brother, and ex-officers Taggart and Wilson will be going to prison for a long stretch. As will Russell, her father, and ex-detective Reed when we catch them.

What shocks me the most is Delia's calm admission that the group intended to blow up local federal buildings, starting with the FBI Resident Agency Office, where we are now sitting.

"I'd like to remind you that should you decline to testify at the trials of any defendants in the matter, the charges against you will be reinstated," AUSA Scully says. "They carry a maximum penalty of life imprisonment, and you'll be charged to the full extent of the law. Understood?"

"I understand," Delia says meekly. She's wearing an orange jumpsuit, and her blonde hair hangs limply on either side of her pale face. Without makeup, she looks defeated, no longer the confident businesswoman we met at the ranch.

"Let's turn to the other charges," Scully continues, glancing at the folder open on the table before him. "They are plotting to kill federal officers and harboring a fugitive, one Dirk McCloskey."

"How was I to know he'd kidnapped two women?" Delia whines, taking a sip from a bottle of water.

"For the tape, I'm showing Ms. Henderson a transcript of the messages on the Priesthood's board. Do you deny your username is *Armistead*?"

"No, I don't." Her voice is thin and reedy, and she's fiddling with her fingernails.

"Do you deny that you wrote *the procurement of materials for the device should continue in parallel with any eliminations*?"

"If that's what it says, then yeah," she concedes.

"In fact, you're replying to a message from Dirk McCloskey calling for the deaths of Federal Agents Cassie Viera, Nick Stone, and Stevie Wells. As you know, Agent Viera is sitting right there." Scully casts his eyes in my direction.

Delia's eyes well up with tears and flash briefly at me, unable to hold my gaze.

"I'm so sorry. I got caught up in the injustice of a Marxist US government tearing up the constitution and taking away people's guns. You were just a name. I never thought of you or the other girl as real people."

"These are the people you were talking about killing, aren't they?" Scully says.

Delia nods and bursts out sobbing.

"Are you pleading guilty to the charge of plotting to kill federal officers?"

"My client has been nothing but cooperative," Dixon says. "She's exhausted, and I doubt any confession of guilt will be recognized by a court. What exactly do you want from her?"

"Her testimony at McCloskey's trial."

"The television news is saying he's not expected to survive the injuries he sustained at the river yesterday when Agent Viera stabbed him."

"Doctors have upgraded his condition," I say. "He's being discharged into our custody tomorrow."

"The kidnapping charges against him should be a slam-dunk without my client's testimony."

"We believe McCloskey killed Ava Barlow and Ricky Kelly and attempted to murder Pete Barlow. We heard he confessed as much to your client. We don't expect it to go to trial, but we'd like her to testify if it does."

"I need to confer with my client," Dixon says.

Scully and I troop into the corridor. He turns to me. "What's the latest on Detective Finch?"

"Still in the hospital. I'm hopeful that he'll make a full recovery."

"How about Jackie and Zoe?"

"Doctors don't think they'll have any lasting physical effects, but long-term mental issues are another story. The doctor I spoke to said the women could be dealing with those for the rest of their lives."

ASAC Myles joins us. I figure he was watching the interview from the observation room.

"Ah, Cassie, I just got word from the agent in charge of the team that's been digging up Pete Barlow's yard," he says. "They've recovered three gold bars buried under the lawn in plastic bags."

"So Leo Kessler was telling us the truth," I say.

"It seems so." He turns to Scully. "You think Delia Henderson's testimony will be enough to convict McCloskey of the murders?"

"Probably not. The kidnapping charges will send him to prison for life, and we may have to be satisfied with that. But Delia's testimony today will help us close those cases."

"And we're letting her off the charge of plotting to kill federal agents just so you can close the cases?" I suggest, shaking my head. "Despite what she says, she knew full well that McCloskey had kidnapped the two women. She also threatened Agent Nick Stone with a pistol in the underground bunker."

"We'll have her plead to a lesser charge," Scully says. "She'll do a year inside. Delia's a gullible woman who was pressured by her father and brother into joining their cult. That's what the Priesthood was."

"It's not right that she's getting off with so light a sentence," I say.

Before Scully can reply, the door to the interview room opens, and Dixon says, "My client is ready to talk, but only if we can come to an amenable arrangement."

Myles heads back to the observation room while Scully and I take our seats back at the table.

"Okay. What's the proffer?" Dixon asks.

"Two years in state prison and four years' probation," Scully replies. "And she pleads guilty to harboring a fugitive."

"Nine months in the county jail and a year's probation."

"I'm alright on the jail term, but I can't go with so little probation." Scully turns to Delia and says, "Final offer. Nine months in the county jail and three years' probation."

"What if Dirk told me the truth, and he didn't do all those things you're accusing him of?" she asks.

"The offer stands as long as you'll testify about it in court if we ask," Scully says.

She nods slowly. "Yes."

"My client says McCloskey—" Dixon starts.

Scully raises a hand. "She needs to tell us in her own words. And remember, Delia, the offer vanishes if you lie."

She takes in a deep breath. "Dirk was at the ranch two nights ago having a drink with Paul and me. He said Detective Reed visited him in prison several times and fed him lies about Zoe, the wife he had supposedly murdered. Reed told Dirk that Pete Barlow had killed her and then framed him."

"Reed set Barlow up for Zoe's murder?" I say under my breath. "Why?"

Delia pauses to take a sip from her water bottle before

continuing:

"As you can imagine, Dirk's rage against Pete Barlow fermented the whole ten years he was in prison. Dirk went to the Barlow house that morning, intending to beat up Pete. Cripple him for life, Dirk said. Instead, he found Ava dead on the floor. I think Paul had already heard that before, but it was news to me."

"Okay . . ." Scully says in a skeptical tone. "Ava was already dead when he got to the Barlow residence. Is that what he told you?"

Delia nods. "Yeah. I swear it's true."

"You think he was lying because I find it hard to believe he didn't kill Ava?"

"My client can only testify about what McCloskey said," Dixon snaps. "It's impossible for her to know whether he was lying. That is the deal."

"What about killing Ricky Kelly and stabbing Pete Barlow at the hotel?" Scully asks.

"Dirk admitted he was responsible for both of those. He heard from someone at the tire place that Ricky was meeting federal agents behind the Target store. Dirk thought Ricky was about to rat him out for stealing the minivan and going to the Barlow house the morning Ava died. He would have been sent back to prison to serve the rest of his sentence. Probably been charged with Ava's murder."

"So Ricky was killed to silence him?" I ask.

"Yeah."

"He was Dirk's father-in-law."

"I guess so."

"Just to be clear, are you also saying McCloskey admitted attacking Pete Barlow at the Travelodge?"

"Yeah. Like I said earlier, Dirk thought Pete had killed his wife Zoe and framed him. Of course, at that juncture, he didn't know Zoe was still alive."

"Why do you think McCloskey admitted all this so freely to you?"

"He knew his secret was safe with me. After all, we're both members of the Priesthood."

"Yet here you are telling us everything to save your own skin."

Delia straightens and folds her arms across her chest but stays silent.

"The truth is that you know who killed Ava Barlow, don't you?"

She hesitates for a long while. "Maybe."

"Who was it? Who killed Ava?" I snap.

"My client has fulfilled her obligations for the deal we discussed," Dixon says, slapping his notebook shut. "We're done here."

Chapter Fifty

"DO YOU BELIEVE Delia?" Stevie asks. The tussle at the river has left her with a purple bruise on her cheek to go with the one above her eyebrow.

"Yeah. She seemed credible," I reply. "Whether McCloskey was lying to her is another question."

"But he admitted to her that he assaulted Pete and killed Ricky," she insists. "What would he have to gain by lying to Delia about Ava's murder?"

"That's what bothers me," I say, drumming my fingers on the conference room table.

"What a turnaround," Todd says, a smirk tugging at the corners of his lips. "We were convinced that McCloskey killed Ava in revenge for Pete locking him up for a crime he didn't commit."

"We need to stay flexible," I tell him. "Investigate all avenues. Adapt when fresh evidence shows up."

Nick shakes his head. "We have video of McCloskey driving up to the Barlow residence right around the time she died."

"The jury is still out on the question of him killing Ava,"

I reply. "Jason Clark ran the forensic unit when evidence from her murder scene was processed. We now know he's a member of the Priesthood, and we should view his report skeptically. Evidence could easily have been tampered with."

"I hadn't thought of that," Nick replies. "But it still seems a mighty big coincidence that McCloskey showed up at the Barlow house intent on maiming Pete and found Ava recently killed."

I have an idea it might not have been a coincidence, but I'm not ready to share that yet. I say, "It won't hurt to dig a little deeper. Especially now that Delia's statement is on the record. McCloskey's lawyer could bring it up at trial. Nick and Todd, I want you to go to the forensic unit. Have the techs walk you through every scrap of evidence collected at Ava's death scene. See if anything looks hinky. Stevie, you're with me. We're going to visit Ava's next-door neighbor who dialed 9-1-1. What was her name?"

"Mrs. Smythe," Stevie prompts.

"Yeah, the nosy Mrs. Smythe. Let's see if she's hiding something. I rather think she must be."

Twenty minutes later, we pull up in front of the two-story Craftsman house next door to the Barlow residence

We're barely out of the car when the gauzy curtains at a front window quiver.

A stone path leads us across a lawn peppered with rose beds to a narrow porch.

Perla Smythe answers the door, looking exactly as Nick described her. She is in her sixties with gray hair and an aquiline nose. She's wearing a floral housecoat that she pulls tightly around herself. Her coke-bottle glasses give her a bug-eyed look as she peers at Stevie and me inquisitively.

"Mrs. Perla Smythe, we're agents with the Federal Bureau of Investigation. I'm Special Agent Viera, and this is Special Agent Wells." I spell the words out slowly and badge her, wanting her to feel the full force of the FBI.

"Oh, my goodness," she says.

"May we come inside?"

She nods and stands aside, looking up and down the street to see who might have noticed our arrival. Closing the front door, she shows us into the living room. The house looks neatly kept, but everything from the furniture to the rugs and the decorations is from decades ago. Even the television is one of those old box-style affairs like my parents used to watch.

"Do you mind if we sit?" I ask.

"Sure," she says, indicating the couch. "Can I get you anything? Coffee, perhaps."

We both decline, and I have her take a seat in the recliner facing us. It's the most worn chair in the room, and I imagine it's her customary one.

She perches on the edge of the seat cushion, looking uncomfortable. Perla Smythe is exactly where I want her.

"Do you live here alone?" My gaze falls on the photos on the mantel. The one in the center shows a man in his fifties. From his stoop and his pale, drawn face, he's seriously ill.

"That's Edgar," she says, a bit defensively. "He passed eight years ago. I'm all alone now."

"Mrs. Smythe, may I call you Perla?"

"Okay."

"Perla, can you cast your mind back to the morning when Ava Barlow was killed?"

"Okay," she says warily.

"You told Agent Stone you heard Mrs. Barlow scream that morning."

"I certainly did. It was earsplitting, like a wounded animal's cry."

"And you're sure it was Ava you heard."

"I'd swear it was."

"Good, good. How long after you heard her scream did you make the 9-1-1 call?"

"A bit after."

"About how long?"

"I don't know for sure," she says, hedging her response.

"Were you upstairs or down here when you heard the scream?" I ask, trying a different tack.

"I was sitting on the couch where you are, reading the morning paper."

"After hearing the scream, did you go upstairs or stay down here?"

"I stayed down here."

"But you can't see the Barlow residence from here. Those bushes are in the way," I say, pointing out the window.

"They didn't stop me hearing the scream."

"But you didn't call 9-1-1 right away, did you?"

"No."

"What happened at eight fifty-six to prompt you to make the call?"

Perla traces her finger around a flower on her

housecoat, where it falls over her thigh. "I . . . er, heard two men arguing loudly at Ava's house," she admits sheepishly.

"Were they outside the house or inside?"

"They were inside. I know because I ran upstairs to take a look."

"Did you recognize their voices?"

"I never heard them before. I knew it wasn't Pete or Ava's boyfriend. What was his name? I read it in the paper."

"Leo Kessler," Stevie prompts.

"That's what worried me and made me call the police. Ava's scream and then the two strange men's voices coming from her house. I figured they were up to no good."

"Did you see either of them leave?" I ask.

"No. I ran down here to make the call. I don't keep a phone upstairs in case it disturbs me in the night."

"This next question is really important. I don't care what you told anyone before. You won't get into trouble if you tell me the truth now. But if you continue to lie, I'll take you to the police station. Do you understand?"

"Yes." Perla's voice is very small, and she looks like she knows what's coming. She peers intently at the hem of her housecoat as if she expects to find the answer written there.

"What time did you hear Ava Barlow scream?"

"I'm so sorry." She glances at the wall clock over the fireplace. "It was just before eight-thirty. See, I thought if I told the young lady on the phone . . ."

"The dispatcher," Stevie prompts.

"Yes, the dispatcher. If I had told her that I heard two men arguing, the police wouldn't have come to the house. But telling them about the scream did the trick."

"One of my agents spoke to you," I say gently. "Why didn't you tell him the truth about when you heard the scream?"

"I was afraid I'd get into trouble if I changed my story."

We thank a remorseful Perla and say goodbye.

Stevie has her notebook out as we walk to the car. "We know for a fact that McCloskey's blue minivan arrived at the Barlow residence at eight forty-seven. If Mrs. Smythe is telling us the truth now, Ava screamed at least seventeen minutes before our prime suspect got there."

"Exactly. McCloskey may have told Delia the truth when he said he didn't kill Ava."

We get inside the black sedan. The hot June sun is beating down on the windshield. I fire up the engine to get the AC working.

"Maybe Ava screamed at something else, and McCloskey still killed her," Stevie suggests.

"Possibly, but unlikely. We believed what Mrs. Smythe told us at the time because her statement fitted our narrative. Look at what we thought was the timeline. On surveillance video, we see a strange man arrive at the Barlow residence. Perla Smythe hears a scream. The strange man leaves. Ava is found dead by responding officers. It was all very neat and tidy and fitted within the medical examiner's time of death."

"Except that wasn't the true sequence of events."

"Right. We know that now."

"If Perla Smythe had told us the truth from the start, we'd be a lot further ahead. What will you do about her?"

"Nothing. The fault lies with me for being so willing to

410

accept her version of what happened."

"If we assume McCloskey was one of the men Perla heard arguing, who was the other man?"

My phone rings. I glance at the caller ID. Finch.

"I'm pretty sure it was Ava Barlow's killer," I tell Stevie, stepping out of the car to answer the call.

Chapter Fifty-One

"WAS THAT LOVER BOY on the phone?" Stevie asks as I climb back into the car outside Perla Smythe's house.

"Yeah. Doctors kept Finch overnight for observation, but he's about to be released."

"That is great news," she says, tugging on her seatbelt.

"Let's see if doctors will allow us to talk to McCloskey," I say as we pull away from the curb. "I told Finch to stay put at the hospital, and we'll meet up with him there. He wants to hear what McCloskey has to say."

Stevie shakes her head. "Whatever he tells us won't prove anything. He could lie through his teeth."

"If his story meshes with what Delia Henderson and Mrs. Smythe told us, it will give us another data point. He may offer up the name of the man he was arguing with. The man who killed Ava."

"I can't think who it could be."

"You okay after everything that happened at the river yesterday?" I ask.

"Pretty much. Another day, another person socking me in the face. Getting winched up to a helicopter in a basket was a first."

"Not something I'm in a hurry to repeat," I admit.

"You mind if we swing by your house and pick up my personal phone. I don't know how I came to leave it there. I've been getting by with my Bureau phone, but I feel lost without it."

"Of course. It's on the way to the hospital."

"What did Myles have to say about the crash at the river?" she asks.

"Obviously, he was pleased about catching McCloskey and freeing Jackie and Zoe, but he seemed more concerned about the team's wellbeing. I'm starting to warm to the guy."

"He didn't sideline you after stabbing McCloskey?"

"There's sometimes an investigation when an agent is involved in a fatal shooting, but that didn't come close."

My phone chimes. I glance at the dash-mounted display but don't recognize the number.

"Agent Viera."

The voice sounds tentative. "This is the charge nurse in the ICU at Cedar Springs Hospital. I'm calling about your sister, Jasmin Viera. Do I have the right person?"

Every muscle in my body tenses, and my blood freezes in my veins. "Yeah."

"Your sister is awake," the nurse continues. "She's asking for you."

I let out a long breath. "Tell her I'll see her in an hour. I have a piece of business to conduct at the hospital beforehand."

I'm feeling lighter as I park at the curb outside my

house. Jasmin's red pickup in the driveway is no longer a reminder that I might lose my sister. We get out, and I say, "I'm coming in with you. I need to use the bathroom. All this stress has thrown my digestive system off."

Something doesn't feel right as we step inside the house. I don't usually run the AC during the day, but the air is warmer and more humid than usual. As if we left a window open.

Stevie pulls up short, and I stumble into her back.

Then I see why she stopped.

Reed is sitting on a stool at the breakfast bar. A plate holds the remains of a sandwich. One arm is in a sling; his other arm rests on his lap. In his hand is a pistol, and it's pointing our way.

"Good of you to join me, ladies. An unexpected treat. I thought I'd have to wait until the evening to have this little chat."

He slides off the stool.

"One at a time, remove the pistols from your holsters and toss them on the floor. You first, Agent Bollywood."

Reluctantly, I follow his instructions.

"And take out the backup pistol you keep in your ankle holster." He gives me a creepy grin.

I bend over and draw up the hem of my pants, tossing the gun onto the rug.

"Now you, Agent Wells."

Stevie gives him a hateful look, then takes the pistol from her shoulder holster, dropping it to the floor.

Reed moves closer to me. He looks sweatier than usual and he's blowing his boozy breath into my face. Switching his pistol to the hand of his injured arm, he pats me down, then moves on to Stevie.

His hand spends extra time at her breasts. "Nice and firm," he snickers, slapping her butt.

She spits at him.

Reed's lips curl as his hand wipes the glob off his shirt. He lets out a snarl. The backhanded slap across Stevie's face sends her tumbling backward onto the floor.

I take a step toward him, but he swivels the gun my way.

"Don't even think about it, Bollywood. I'm trying my best to wait until later to shoot you. You don't want to miss out on the fun. Now get up," he snaps at Stevie, "I didn't hit you that hard."

She looks more livid than shaken as she slowly climbs to her feet. A line of blood trickles down her chin from her split lip. She wipes it away with the back of her hand.

Her poor face is a battered and bruised mess.

"Go sit over there, both of you," Reed snaps, digging the pistol hard into my ribs. "You girls have ruined my life, and now you're going to pay."

"What the hell do you want?" I ask, parking my butt next to Stevie on the couch.

"A chat before I kill you and your friend. I need to know what the FBI has on me."

My phone buzzes, and I pull it out of my pocket. It's Finch, no doubt wondering where we are.

"Don't answer that," Reed snarls.

But I thumb the answer button as I slip the phone back into my pocket. "Just shut the fuck up. Reed," I bark loudly to cover anything Finch might say. "You come into my house and threaten Stevie and me. Hold us at gunpoint . . ." The pistol whip catches me on the temple, and everything goes black.

There's no way for me to know how long I was out.

Pain, bright and sharp, flashes through my head. I open my eyes, but the room is spinning. Stevie is bending over me, shaking me, telling me to wake up.

But it's not working.

I gaze past her. The room is blurry and out of focus. The pictures on the mantle above the gas fire are dancing.

It feels like I'm watching a movie.

Stevie lets out a howl of pain as Reed roughly yanks her off me and tosses her onto the floor. I suck in air through my teeth, trying to ward off my own aches.

I watch, unable to move, barely able to comprehend.

Stevie is screaming obscenities at Reed.

As the picture clears a bit, I see her start to get up from the floor.

Reed swings his foot.

The toe of his shoe strikes her hard in the head.

Suddenly Stevie is silent and motionless. She's lying on her front, her head turned my way, her eyes closed. I imagine she's out cold, but Reed is still hollering at her for fucking up his life. "If you bitches hadn't interfered, the Ava Barlow case would be closed, and Dirk McCloskey would be in jail for killing her."

As Reed draws his foot back for another kick, I get to my feet and scream, "Stop it. Stop it. You'll kill her." Instinctively, my hand flies to the empty holster at my waist. I take a step toward Stevie. I'd rather Reed take his frustrations out on me.

"Freeze right there!" Reed's face twists in rage. The pistol in his hand is aimed down at Stevie's temple. "One more step, and I'll blow her brains all over your rug. She won't look such a pretty little thing then," he leers.

I stop dead in my tracks, unsure of my next move. "Get the hell away from her, Reed. Pick on someone your own size." My words are slurred, and I figure I might have a concussion.

"You need to quieten down, bitch, and get back in your seat." Reed swings his foot into Stevie's side. "Now is as good a time as any to get rid of this one."

"Fuck you, Reed." Pain is slicing through my head as I collapse back onto the couch.

"You get out of that seat again, and I'll shoot you both dead. That's a promise."

Did Finch get the message? He's our last hope. Or did the call drop before he heard my words?

Reed isn't going to let Stevie or me leave here alive.

Chapter Fifty-Two

My gaze flashes between Reed and Stevie. She's lying on the floor and still not moving. I have to distract Reed, so he'll leave her alone. I have to get him thinking about something else.

Anything other than Stevie.

"You arranged the SWAT raid to kill us, didn't you?" I'm trying to articulate my words clearly, but my brain still feels like a dead weight.

"You and your FBI friends forced my hand. Brandon was supposed to maim you both, so you couldn't work in law enforcement."

"You should have picked someone more reliable," I snap. "Someone who wasn't blinded by his own hatred."

"Then you have to get cute and record me at the traffic stop," Reed glares. He's pacing around the room, all the time watching me, like an animal circling its prey. "I was trying to save you both from this." He waves the pistol around. "I wouldn't have to kill you if you hadn't investigated Ava's death and hadn't been stupid enough to raid the meeting at the barn. You've ruined the Priesthood.

For what? Because you have different beliefs?"

"Yeah. Beliefs that include not blowing up innocent people." The pain in my head is subsiding into a dull throb, and my thoughts are becoming a little clearer.

"*Not* innocent people." He stops and shakes his pistol hand to emphasize the words. "We were planning to blow up the FBI office. Twelve dead agents would have been a good start." He snickers like he's made a joke.

"We put paid to that wet dream."

"You think you've eliminated the Priesthood, but you haven't," he scowls. "There are plenty of folks who think the same as us. They'll take up our cause. Hell, I might try to find a group in another state. You've ruined my life here."

"Before you shoot us, at least tell me why you faked Zoe's death and framed McCloskey?"

"I was saving Zoe from him. He was a brute, always beating her. But we never could arrest him because she'd change her statement, saying she'd slipped and fallen or some such crap."

I silently curse at the way the system fails battered women. They think the only way to stay alive is to lie and not press charges. "Did Barlow know Zoe wasn't dead?"

He shrugs. "At the time, I was a junior detective. I needed his help."

"I read the emails Zoe sent to Jackie. You weren't just rescuing Zoe from Dirk. You were saving her for yourself. You had her over a barrel after she moved to Placerville. She became your little bitch. Your sex slave. Then, when she broke up with you, you never got over it."

"That's where you're wrong." He jabs a finger at me.

"She never broke up with me. If that's what she's telling you, she's lying. You whores are all the same."

"Maybe to morons like you."

Stevie groans and starts to move, attracting Reed's attention, disrupting his train of thought. Does she have a concussion or something worse? It will be better for her if she stays down on the floor.

"Why did you kill Ava Barlow?" I've got to keep Reed distracted, so he doesn't kick her again.

"Wasn't it perfect?" he snickers. "McCloskey showing up right after I killed her? I was planning on sticking him with her murder. I bet you still think him being there was a coincidence."

"It wasn't?" I say, suddenly understanding. "You lured him to the house to set him up?"

"Ha. You were totally clueless until now. I knew McCloskey was gunning for Pete. So I told him it was the perfect time to catch Pete on his own. I promised to be there to help and keep the cops at bay if he wanted to take his time rearranging Pete's body."

"Wasn't McCloskey worried Pete would turn him in? After all, Pete would recognize him."

"McCloskey was going to wear a ski mask. He figured crippling Pete for the rest of his life was a worse punishment than death."

"What happened when McCloskey got to the house and found Ava dead?"

"You should have seen his face when I said there'd been a problem and took him into the kitchen."

"He didn't realize you'd tricked him?"

"Nah." Reed purses his lips. "The guy is as dumb as a rock. I just told him Pete left early, and Ava found out about our plan to work the guy over."

I almost have to admire Reed for the way he set up McCloskey. "You very nearly got away with it, thanks to a nosy neighbor not giving us the whole story."

"I was all set to investigate the case myself until you showed up. I could have glossed over details like the neighbor's testimony. If you hadn't butted in, I'd have been in the clear. McCloskey was the ideal patsy. After all, everyone thought he'd already killed once before," Reed snickers at his own cleverness. "But I didn't reckon on you screwing with my plans. So now you're both going to die for the trouble you've caused me."

"When they find us dead, you'll be the first person they suspect," I tell him.

"It's going to look like you, and little Nancy Drew here shot each other with your own pistols. Perhaps it was a lover's tiff? Or maybe you were fighting over Finch? After your deaths, no one will believe any of your far-fetched ideas. All the evidence you're leaving behind implicates McCloskey in Ava's death." He grins like a crazy person. The guy is drunk with anger, but his fidgeting, his eye movements, and his rapid speech are evidence that he's taken something.

"There's an arrest warrant out for you," I remind him.

"I can ride that out. The only witness to me coming into your house that night will be dead." His gaze flashes to Stevie.

"What about the weapons and explosives at the Smoke

Tree Ranch?"

"I was as shocked as you to learn what the Hendersons were up to," he snickers. "There's not a shred of evidence to connect me to any of it."

I take a deep breath. Our only hope is to stall for time. "You still haven't told me why you killed Ava?" I have to stay optimistic that Finch heard my call and is on the way.

"Stupidly, Pete printed up the old emails he and I exchanged back in the day. Ava was clearing out the desk in his old office and found messages proving I faked Zoe's death. Get this—Ava called me to say the file had to be worth something, or it might find its way to Chief Holder. Jeez, the woman was a piece of work, trying to blackmail me of all people."

"So I've heard. The slashes to Ava's chest were deep. Her hands and forearms were covered in defensive wounds. The attack was frenzied, almost sadistic."

"Perfect, wasn't it?" Reed chuckles, looking out of a front window like he's expecting someone.

Stevie locks eyes with me, and I slowly shake my head. "Stay there," I mouth silently to her, hoping Finch will be here soon.

"Did you hate Ava so much that you had to brutalize her in that way?" I ask.

He turns to me. "It was my fallback plan. When I killed her, I couldn't know for sure that McCloskey would show up. So I tried to make it look like the work of a meth addict, to throw you off track. And it nearly worked." Reed is on the move again, pacing like he can't seem to stand still in one spot.

"McCloskey had it in for Pete because you told him Pete had killed Zoe. But you fed him that lie years ago. You couldn't have known back then that you'd need McCloskey to be the fall guy for Ava's murder."

"I knew when McCloskey got out, he would try to find the person who killed Zoe. Setting him on Pete was a way to hide my role in faking her murder. McCloskey taking the fall for Ava just happened to work out."

"You would have been sprayed with blood when you killed her," I say, "yet there was none on your clothing when I saw you. How did you manage that?"

"I wore a forensic suit and face mask."

"The responding officers said you arrived after them. How did you pull off that trick?"

"Ava screamed more than I expected, so I was antsy to get away from there. As soon as McCloskey left, I slipped out of the back door and stashed the bloody suit in the woodland behind the house. All I needed to do was walk around the block to the front, and presto, I arrived after the officers."

"Why did you brand her with the words, 'YOU ARE NEXT?'"

"To make it look as if she was killed by someone who was coming after Pete. Though I nearly died laughing when McCloskey carved 'RAT' on Ricky's body, and you assumed they were killed by the same person."

"You thought of everything."

"Yeah. I retrieved the bloody suit later and burned it. If a detective can't fake a murder, who can?"

I have no more words to delay Stevie and my

executions. My gaze drifts to her. She's trying to roll over. I'm afraid Reed is going to attack her again. I slowly shake my head, but she's not looking at me anymore.

She lets out a gasp as Reed plants his foot in the center of her back and presses her to the floor, his pistol aimed at her head again.

He looks about to say something, but instead, he pricks up his ears, listening intently to the sound of a car stopping on the street. He moves to a front window and peers around the curtain. "Looks like your buddy Finch is finally here. I was hoping he'd arrive and find your dead bodies. Now he's in time to watch me shoot you both. You're going to welcome him in so he can join the fun."

A car door slams shut. Moments later, we hear footsteps on the front porch. Did Finch catch my phone message when I tried to alert him about Reed? Or is he walking into a trap?

If Reed grabs Finch, there's no question the disgraced detective will carry out his plan to kill all three of us.

He shushes me with a finger to his lips and takes up a shooting stance behind the door, his pistol clutched tightly to his chest.

Finch knocks, calling my name.

The phone call must have dropped, and he missed hearing what was going on. Stevie is moving more, trying to push herself up.

Thankfully, Reed seems more intent on capturing Finch.

Adrenaline shoots through me as I drop to the floor and kneel beside Stevie. My hand on her shoulder gently tells her to stay down. Blood has trickled into her hair and onto her collar from the gash on her lip.

She makes eye contact and blinks. My hand finds hers, and I squeeze.

Finch tries the handle. The front door opens, and he steps inside. "Cassie, where are you—?"

Reed takes a single step and presses the pistol into the side of Finch's head. "Easy there, detective. Come in and join your friends."

Finch hesitates. "What the fuck, Reed?" he exclaims, a look of horror registering on his face as he grasps the position we're in. Then I see his mind working. I know what he's thinking. If he can turn, he can wrest the pistol from Reed's grip.

But it's hopeless. Reed will shoot him first.

I fix my eyes on the drama unfolding between the two men and slide my hand along the leg of Stevie's pants.

As my fingers reach her shoe, she senses what I'm doing and slightly raises her leg.

Brushing over her sock, I slowly tug up the hem of her pants leg, trying not to attract Reed's attention.

Fortunately, he still seems focused on Finch, but his gaze could shift at any moment. "Didn't expect to see me, did you?" Reed says to his new captive. "Come sit on the couch with your girlfriend."

I slide my hand along Stevie's now bare calf until my hand grasps the butt of the small .38-caliber revolver holstered there. Reed was too busy feeling her up to find it earlier.

He registers my movement and turns my way. "Bitch,"

he shouts as he swings his pistol toward me, trying to pull Finch in front of him. But the taller, more powerful man resists.

My revolver fires at the same instant as Reed's pistol.

A pain, the likes of which I've never felt before, shoots through my shoulder as Reed drops to the floor.

As I collapse in agony, Finch steps through the gun smoke, kicking Reed's pistol away from him.

After a glance at Stevie, Finch crosses to where I'm lying. "My God, Cassie."

Grabbing my favorite blanket from the couch, he squats beside me and presses the fabric into my shoulder to stem the blood loss.

"Finch . . . " I groan. His expression tells me it doesn't look good. It feels as if Reed stuck a pitchfork into my chest, and he's twisting it. But the pain also means I'm still alive. That's something to be grateful for.

"You're losing blood fast," he says, pulling out his phone with his free hand. He dials with his thumb. "Detective Finch here. We need an ambulance on the double. Two eighty-nine Willow Drive, Cedar Springs. Two officers down."

Chapter Fifty-Three

WE ARE IN THE ICU interviewing Pete for the first time since he came out of his coma. I'm seated as I get tired easily after the surgery on my shoulder. Thankfully, I don't remember any of it, neither getting wounded nor shooting Reed. My first recollection is of Finch telling me how happy he was to see me, how I'd lost so much blood that doctors weren't sure I was going to wake up, how he was terrified of that possibility.

"McCloskey came to the house to maim me?" Pete Barlow asks in dismay, his brows raised. "Is that what you're telling me?" He's propped up in bed, but his face is still pale, his features drawn. Finch wanted to handcuff him to the bedrail as soon as he became conscious, but the nurse refused to allow it.

"That's what McCloskey is saying," I reply. "Reed told him that you killed Zoe."

Pete's brow furrows, like he's trying to make sense of what I just said. "That's absurd. It was Reed who faked

Zoe's death."

Pete shouldn't need me to explain that Reed was a walking nightmare. I have no regrets that my shot went through the center of his forehead. "Reed arranged to meet McCloskey at your house the morning that Ava was killed," I add. "They were going to give you a beating you wouldn't forget."

"Reed was going to attack me too?" Pete looks panic stricken.

"Supposedly," Finch tells him. "But the whole point was to lure McCloskey to your house so Reed could frame him for Ava's murder. According to McCloskey's account, when he got to the house, instead of having it out with you like he expected, he found Ava dead on the kitchen floor. Reed was standing over her body and fed him some nonsense about you leaving early and Ava finding out what they planned. So, she had to be killed. In reality, Reed killed Ava because she threatened to expose the fact that he faked Zoe's death. McCloskey is not the sharpest knife in the drawer, but he never took Reed's bait to pick up the bloody knife and put his fingerprints on it. McCloskey left the house without ever realizing that Reed was trying to frame him for Ava's murder."

"And Reed was very nearly successful," I add.

"Where is McCloskey now? Is he here at the hospital?" Pete's gaze flashes nervously around the ICU.

"You don't need to worry about him," I say, trying to get the retired detective to focus. "Dirk McCloskey is safely locked away at the FBI offices. You were unconscious the night he was brought here to the hospital, but he was under a heavy police guard."

"Has Chief Holder interviewed him?"

"Holder is taking some leave right now," Finch says. However, he doesn't mention that the chief is being investigated by the state police to determine what he knew about Detectives Reed and Barlow's activities. Besides that, FBI Agents from the Sacramento Field Office are looking into Holder's hiring practices. This is in the wake of Brandon Farley's attack and the number of police officers who were fired when they were found to have ties to the Priesthood.

"We want to ask you about another matter," I say. "And I must warn you that you have the right to remain silent. Anything you say can be used against you in court. You have the right to talk to a lawyer for advice before we ask you any questions."

"Really, agent? What on earth do you think I've done?" Pete splutters.

"Do you wish to have an attorney present?" I ask, ignoring his posturing.

"I'm the victim here. I'm the one who is in the hospital. I don't need an attorney."

"And medically, you're feeling up to answering our questions?"

"Sure," he insists. "The doctors say I'm going to be fine. So what is this about?"

"Alright then. You remember that before you were stabbed, we talked to you about a guy named Leo Kessler?" I'm playing along to see what he volunteers.

Pete looks startled for a moment but quickly recovers.

"Drug dealer, wasn't he?"

"Yeah, you arrested him seven years ago. More recently, he was having an affair with Ava, right up until her death. Chief Holder thought you paid him to murder her."

"As I told Holder, it was poppycock. Anyway, I read in the paper that Reed confessed to killing her. So why are we even talking about Kessler?"

"You remember he's alleging you stole three gold bars from him?" I fidget in my seat, trying to get comfortable. There's a position where my injured shoulder doesn't ache as much, but I can't always find it. I glance at my watch. It's past the time for my next dose of pain pills.

"You can't believe scum like Kessler. They will say anything to mess with your heads."

"An FBI search team has taken your house apart—"

"Of course, they didn't find anything." Pete gives a hollow chortle.

"Not until they scanned your yard with ground-penetrating radar. Want to guess what they dug up?"

Pete's shoulders sag, but he shakes his head.

"Three gold bars. A conservative estimate puts the total value at around two hundred and twenty grand. Care to tell us where you got them?"

"I think I want my attorney now."

"You're going to need a good one. Not just for the gold you stole from Kessler. We know you conspired with Reed to frame McCloskey for Zoe Kelly's murder. You knew Reed had staged Zoe's death, and she was alive and living in Placerville."

"Is that what Reed is saying?" Pete asks, trying to adopt

an air of innocence.

There's a press blackout on Reed's death while the shooting at my house is investigated. Reed's partner, Channel Five reporter Hazel DeRosa, has been informed that her partner was mortally wounded, but she's agreed not to publish the fact. Meanwhile, Myles has hooked me up with a local psychiatrist—FBI procedure after a fatal shooting.

"For us to chat, you need to revoke your request for an attorney," I say, fussing with where the sling runs over my good shoulder, hoping I can mitigate the pain.

"Yeah. I revoke my request for counsel. Is that what Reed is saying because he's lying?"

"Reed isn't saying much anymore because he's in the morgue," Finch tells him.

"He's dead? How?" Pete's gaze flashes between Finch and me.

"Reed tried to kill two federal agents." I point to my shoulder. "And his marksmanship was a bit rusty. Thankfully."

"Damn. Reed wasn't all bad, you know. He took a lot of gang members off our streets."

"You need to start worrying about yourself. The case against you is airtight. We've recovered incriminating documents that were found in the desk in your study. They include printouts of emails you exchanged with Reed around ten years ago. Your buddy, ex-head of forensics, Jason Clark, tried to hide them, but he's now in jail on this and other charges."

"We were trying to do the right thing for Zoe.

McCloskey was a brute. If we'd done nothing, Zoe would be dead by now."

"Why on earth did you print up Reed's emails?"

"I kept them to counter incriminating evidence he might have on me. I never trusted the guy."

"Mutually assured destruction, was it?" I ask. "Like the US and Russia with nuclear weapons?"

"Something similar."

"We'd like you to tell us how much Chief Holder knew," Finch says.

"He was a detective in Sacramento at the time of McCloskey's arrest."

"But he later learned about what you'd done, didn't he?"

"I really want to speak to my attorney now," Pete insists.

"That's one of the things Reed had on Holder, wasn't it?" I ask. "The reason why Holder could never fire him."

"Nurse. Nurse," Pete shouts. "I want these people to go."

The ICU charge nurse appears from nowhere and asks us to leave.

Finch gives me a look. We both hoped Pete would come clean on Holder. We step out of the ICU and pause in the corridor.

"I'd better get going. With Reed gone and Holder under investigation, we're stretched thin," Finch says.

I stand on tiptoes and kiss him goodbye.

"See you this evening for dinner," he whispers. "Maybe watch a Netflix movie afterward?"

"Sure. But remember, you're not supposed to do anything energetic until your lungs heal."

"We'll see about that."

"There's my shoulder to think about too." I give him a wry smile.

"We can get creative." He grins like a Cheshire cat.

"There's one more thing." I slip my hand behind his neck and gaze into his warm caramel eyes.

"What's that?"

"Your near-drowning. Don't you ever scare me like that again."

His grin widens into a big smile. "I can't promise, but I'll sure try not to."

After another kiss, I descend the stairs to the second floor, looking for the room Jackie and Zoe are sharing.

Chapter Fifty-Four

I FREEZE WHEN I SEE the woman speaking to a nurse outside Jackie and Zoe's door.

Hazel DeRosa. Reed's significant other.

She glances my way and rushes to embrace me gently so as not to disturb my injured shoulder.

"I'm sorry—" I start, but she shushes me.

"You had no choice. It's me who's sorry for what you had to go through. I always knew Reed was . . . complicated."

I slip my good arm around her, and we hold each other for a long moment.

"I'm almost glad Gary died," she says. "He wouldn't have done well in prison." Her eyes are misty when we separate. "I'm so sorry for what he did to Agent Wells. How is the young woman?"

"Stevie was discharged today. She has a non-displaced fracture of her cheekbone and bruised ribs. The doctors kept her in an extra day because she was unconscious for so long."

"She gonna be okay?"

"Stevie is in surprisingly good spirits considering." I don't tell Hazel that it may take weeks for Stevie's headaches to taper off.

Hazel looks on the verge of bursting out crying, so I change the subject and ask her about Jackie and Zoe.

"They are resting," Hazel says. "Doctors put them in the same room, thinking they will be a support for each other. They both have bruises and sprained limbs, but nothing they won't recover from, physically. Mentally, they face a long road back. It's something they could be dealing with for a long while. But how are you? How is your shoulder?"

"Sore. The painkillers make me woozy, so I try not to take too many."

"But they were able to fix you up?"

"The bullet damaged a muscle attachment, so I'm scheduled for another surgery tomorrow."

"I'm so sorry." Tears well up again in her eyes.

"It's not your fault, Hazel." I place my hand on her arm.

"What will happen to McCloskey?"

"The federal charges he's facing for killing Ricky and Zoe's housemate Daisy potentially carry the death penalty. But the US Attorney prosecuting his case thinks life imprisonment is a likely outcome."

Hazel shakes her head. "That's nowhere near enough for ruining the lives of two wonderful human beings."

I let out a deep sigh. "The heartache Dirk caused is immeasurable."

"You should have killed him at the river."

"Unfortunately, dispensing street justice isn't in my job description." We share a wan smile before I say, "I should get back to my sister."

"I heard Jasmin came out of her coma. How is she?"

"Her numbers are stable, and she's fully alert. Thankfully, she's not back to her usual annoying self. I'm trying to hold off talking to her about her lifestyle."

"You think she'll listen to the wake-up call?"

"She's amenable to transferring to rehab, so we'll see how that goes. Any change has to come from her. I think she understands that."

Hazel nods and purses her lips. "I also heard that Russell Henderson is in custody."

"Sacramento Airport Police picked him up trying to catch a flight to Honduras using a forged passport. He's currently at the ATF office in Sac answering arms and explosives charges."

"I would have thought there were too many people of color in Honduras for a guy like him."

"You never can tell about folk."

A nurse comes out of Zoe and Jackie's room and asks, "Is either of you with the FBI?"

"I'm Special Agent Viera, ma'am."

"Zoe Kelly is asking to speak with the agent who rescued her from the river."

"That would be me."

"Take care and see you around, Cassie," Hazel says.

I follow the nurse into the hospital room.

"We've given her something to sleep," she says, indicating Jackie, who is in the far bed. "Just talk softly, and you won't disturb her." The nurse draws a curtain across, dividing off Jackie's side of the room, then pulls a chair up to Zoe's bed.

Zoe is pretty, her dark curly hair splayed out on the pillow, propping up her head. Her mocha complexion is marred by a swollen and purple cheek. Yet, despite her ordeal, a smile is tugging at the corners of her full lips.

"I'll leave you alone," the nurse says, bustling from the room.

"I'm Agent Cassie Viera," I tell Zoe.

"I remember you from the river. Please have a seat," she says. "I just want to thank you for rescuing me."

"No problem, it's all part of the job." I settle my behind onto the chair, looking into her surprisingly bright eyes.

"Jackie and I would have died at the river without you, agent."

"Please call me Cassie. How are your injuries?"

"I'm a bit banged up from the crash. I had hypothermia. The doctor is keeping me in here, saying I had a concussion, but there's nothing that won't heal."

"How is Jackie?" I ask.

"She's worse off than me. Hypothermia. A bruised liver. Sprained ankles. Doctors thought she might need surgery for internal bleeding, but fortunately, they changed their minds." Her face clouds for a moment. "Is Dirk locked up?"

"He's very securely behind bars," I assure her.

"But will he get out in another ten years? I can't go through this again."

"He's facing life imprisonment."

"The ten years he served for killing me won't be deducted from his sentence?"

I shake my head. "No chance."

"And how about me? Am I going to jail?" Her eyes narrow.

"That's up to the district attorney, not me. But I'll stick my neck out and say it's very unlikely that you'll be prosecuted."

"I explained to Detective Finch earlier that it was all Gary Reed's idea, and he faked the crime scene. Even so, I shouldn't have gone along with it."

"You did what you had to, and you survived. If you've seen the news, the media is calling you a heroine. The DA won't go against public opinion," I tell her, though it's one thing to fake your own death to get away from someone and quite another thing to frame that someone for murder. "Had Reed lived, he would be facing serious charges."

"Detective Finch told me Gary shot you."

"Yeah. I'll be in here myself for a second surgery tomorrow."

"Are you able to work?"

"I'll be on desk duty for two to three months while my shoulder heals, depending on how the surgery goes." I glance at my watch. "I'd better get going."

"I wish you all the best, Cassie."

"You too, Zoe." I take the hand she's offering and give her a gentle kiss on the forehead. "See you around."

After checking on Jackie and seeing she is still asleep, I head back to the stairs. It's time to make sure Jasmin hasn't changed her mind about rehab.

A note to my readers . . .

Thank you for reading Fatal Ties, and I sincerely hope you enjoyed it!

If so, please tell your friends and family. If it isn't too much trouble, I would really appreciate a brief review. As a self-published author, I rely on each and every reader to help spread the word.

Thank you again, Richard Bannister

Books in the Megan Riley Mystery Thriller Series:
DEVIL'S PASTURE – Book 1

When a woman is found brutally murdered outside a run-down apartment building in an apparently motiveless crime, Detective Megan Riley is shocked to find the victim is a friend whom she hasn't seen in sixteen years. When the murdered woman's partner also turns up dead, Megan is stretched to her breaking point as she battles shadowy figures.

THE LAKE CABIN – Book 2

Two murders appear to be the latest in a series of disappearances and assaults stretching back years. Are two psychopaths acting out their sick fantasies? What is the connection to a decades-old murder that has long been thought solved? And why is Megan's service in Afghanistan, more than a decade earlier, rearing its ugly head?

MAGNOLIA LAKE – Book 3

Ingrid Foster was working on a controversial new drug until

she was murdered four months ago. Sheriff's detectives quickly arrested a petty criminal, but Ingrid's widower, Neil, is convinced they have the wrong person. Working as a private investigator, Megan searches for the true killer, plunging her into a world of lies, blackmail, kidnapping, and intimidation, where no one is who they seem.

LAST CHANCE ROAD – Book 4

Ten years ago, Naomi Falco's body was discovered by the side of a rural trail. Her killer was never caught. Naomi's mother has long suspected a police cover-up, surmising that detectives knew the identity of her daughter's killer but chose not to arrest him. Now the lead detective is terminally ill, and private investigator Megan Riley is hired to uncover the truth before the secrets die with him.

MOSQUITO RIDGE – Book 5

Dead bodies in suitcases are not common in Stockbridge. But Julia Bryant's body was found three months ago, and now there is another victim. Both women were scantily dressed and stuffed in suitcases. There are too many similarities to deny that they were killed by the same person. The tension ratchets up when a fourteen-year-old girl disappears. A scribbled note warns Megan that the girl will die if she doesn't back off the investigation. Megan must act fast to uncover the person holding the missing girl before he makes good on his threat.

Printed in Great Britain
by Amazon